To all who die from hate
To all who survive hate
And to all who love them

Defense of an Other

Grace Mead

Clink
Street

London | New York

Published by Clink Street Publishing 2018

ISBNs:
978-1-912262-25-0 paperback
978-1-912262-26-7 ebook

Contents

Part I 1

    Chapter 1 3

    Chapter 2 14

    Chapter 3 24

    Chapter 4 35

    Chapter 5 45

    Chapter 6 52

    Chapter 7 60

Part II 69

    Chapter 8 71

    Chapter 9 88

    Chapter 10 101

    Chapter 11 113

    Chapter 12 122

    Chapter 13 130

    Chapter 14 142

    Chapter 15 153

    Chapter 16 164

Part III 177

    Chapter 17 179

    Chapter 18 186

    Chapter 19 195

    Chapter 20 209

    Chapter 21 216

    Chapter 22 225

Chapter 23 230
Chapter 24 237

Part IV 241
Chapter 25 243
Chapter 26 251
Chapter 27 258
Chapter 28 268
Chapter 29 281
Chapter 30 286

Questions..289
Afterword..294
A Note on Louisiana and the Characters........................298
Select References and Recommended Reading............299
Acknowledgements 301
About the Author 302

It would be far better indeed for these great social and political problems to be resolved in the political arena by other branches of government. But these are social and political problems which seem at times to defy such resolution. In such situations, under our system, the judiciary must bear a hand and accept its responsibility to assist in the solution where constitutional rights hang in the balance.

—J. Skelly Wright (June 19, 1967)

Part I

Chapter 1

On a Friday that began ordinarily enough, Matt Durant's left hook ended two lives.

Before dawn, Matt had awoken preoccupied with a legal brief. By six that morning, he arrived at his law firm just south of the French Quarter, Farrar Levinson, inserted his key into the shiny brass lock and pushed the door open. For the rest of the day, phone calls and emails required only a fraction of his attention as he remained engrossed in the brief. Around seven-thirty that night, he finished, affixed the electronic signature of the lead partner, Thomas—never Tom—Farrar, uploaded it to the court's electronic filing system, and then printed confirmation he'd filed it on September 7, 2007. He turned off his computer, grabbed his ripped Nike gym bag, and threw it over his shoulder. The office was dark.

Walking down the hallway, he spotted a single light and smiled. Lisa Boudreaux, a new associate, was still at her desk, so he stuck his head into her office. She had dark chocolate hair that fell over her shoulders and down her back, setting off pale skin, with spritely features: high cheekbones and a dainty nose. "You're working too late for a Friday," Matt said.

"I'm not the only one."

"Yeah, well, I had to file a brief today."

"I'm actually trying to do some work too, believe it or not," Lisa said, waving towards her own computer and then the open books scattered about her desk. "You headed for the boxing gym?"

"Yeah," Matt said.

"Are you up to anything fun this weekend?" She cocked her head to the side and enunciated: "Going to the gym doesn't count."

"I don't really have any plans." Matt shook his head. "The weekend kind of snuck up on me again."

"Andrea's not in town?"

"We broke up." Matt stared at the gray carpet.

"Oh really? What happened?"

"I don't want to talk about it," Matt said, raising his gaze to meet hers.

"Sorry."

"Yeah."

"I'm going out with some friends for drinks. You're welcome to come along." Her emerald eyes locked with his, her mouth quirked, and she qualified: "But I guess it's your business if you'd rather hang out with a bunch of sweaty, half-naked men."

Matt blinked, but he kept his expression otherwise blank. "Stressful week," he said. "I need to go to the gym and vent."

"There's such a thing as moderation, you know. In work, in exercise, in play—"

"I know, I know." Matt interrupted. "Maybe I'll join you next Friday night. Try not to stay here too late." He turned toward the door.

"I'll try not to work any harder than you," Lisa said.

Matt left the office, took the streetcar, then walked the rest of the way to Tommy O'Rourke's boxing gym on Baronne Street, near Jackson Avenue. He entered the two-story converted house, ascended rickety stairs, and, at the top, opened the gym door to the sting of bleach.

On Matt's left, Tommy sat tucked behind the desk in his cramped office, reading the newspaper, his face covered in the same stubble that outlined a bald spot atop his head. Matt knocked on the doorframe to say hello, and, in return, Tommy looked over the the paper with hazel eyes and raised a gnarled finger.

The week's stress subsided as Matt removed his jacket, loosened his tie, unbuttoned his shirt, uncinched his belt, and removed his patent-leather shoes, trading them for nylon shorts, an LSU t-shirt, and battered cross-trainers. He rolled sweat-stained yellow wraps around each hand, piling the strips over his knuckles, spooling them around his wrists and then securing them. He slid on eighteen-ounce gloves, fastening the Velcro on the second with his teeth.

The buzzer sounded, and Matt started pounding one of the 150-pound bags hanging from the ceiling by a gunmetal link chain. He wanted to throw two to three hundred punches each three-minute round but never counted; instead, he focused on delivering every blow with maximum speed and power; with each, he tried to break the bag.

Jab, jab, cross. Jab, jab, cross. Neither packed enough power, but each made the bag shudder and swing.

The buzzer signaled the end of his rounds on the heavy bag and he moved to the twenty-foot square ring, where Tommy waited with paddle-shaped focus mitts. With Tommy leading and Matt following, they began to dance.

Tommy swiped at Matt's head with his left mitt and he blocked the shot. Tommy repositioned the mitts and Matt registered the new configuration. Left jab to the head, left jab to the head, right cross to the head, left hook to the body; same combination again. At the end of this set, Tommy held up his left mitt, braced the back with his right hand, and said: *"Double up."*

Thwap, thwap. Matt shot two left hooks into the paddle, and, despite the reinforcement, Tommy's left mitt bent inward. At least he knew how to throw one punch—he'd thrown both hooks in less than half a second.

After three rounds, Tommy traded the mitts for gloves. They began to spar; each pulled his punches about an inch short of contact. As always, it surprised Matt that keeping his arms up for defense was harder than hitting the heavy bag; and, even though Tommy was well into his fifties, Matt's youth was no match for his experience. But he came close with a couple of punches. His breathing was only slightly heavier than normal, but sweat dripped from his face, rose in sheets from his body, and saturated his t-shirt.

Tommy stepped out of the ring, stomping onto the lower two

ropes and lifting the highest, and Matt ducked between them. He finished by slapping a double-end bag, tethered to the floor and ceiling with elastic, which sprang back after each blow and forced him to quicken his punches. Bathed in sweat, Matt nodded to Tommy and ran down the steps.

Outside, Matt boarded another streetcar. Halfway home, his brain reactivated: when he'd first taken up boxing, he'd been able to work himself into an endorphin-induced buzz that, for several hours, obliterated thought and feeling. Now he wondered whether it was time to take up something new.

He rehashed the recent breakup with his girlfriend Andrea, who had moved to New York City after law school graduation three years before. Their relationship had since petered out. And he wondered why—instead of sad, he felt empty, detached, and ambivalent.

Matt walked into his house, opened the refrigerator, ignored the pitcher of water, and instead grabbed a Bud Light. He cracked the beer open, took a swig, and then studied the can. He knew he should try to get out to meet people and make friends, but he couldn't summon the energy—with no plans on the horizon, the beer would likely be the first of several.

After a second beer and a shower, Matt turned on the TiVo and reviewed the week's fare. He settled on another terrible spinoff from a mediocre series: its only redeeming feature was a well-muscled actor with hickory eyes, but the producers had hidden him in an ensemble cast. A pity.

As Matt polished off his third and fourth beers, he checked out the actor and felt a hint of arousal—interest and curiosity gnawed at the edges of his ennui.

Matt finished the six-pack and his thoughts wandered to a loud oomp-oomp club on Bourbon Street called Drink. When Andrea had tried to cajole him into going dancing about a year ago, he'd mentioned—in passing—that Lisa had recommended Drink. Lisa, like many women, hated the wandering hands of strangers in most dance clubs and the men there weren't interested in even the most beautiful women. Andrea had "convinced" him to go to Drink that night.

Impelled toward the gay club again, new excuses multiplied: boredom; an opportunity to converse with strangers; and a chance for social contact without the risk of rejection from anyone he knew. He began to get ready, knowing that, if his resolve faltered, he could always retreat to the couch.

Matt threw on a pair of black pants and a silver-patterned button-up shirt, then ran his fingers through wet, pitch-black hair and swept the front into the same part he'd had for decades: his arctic blue eyes were surrounded by bags dark enough to be mistaken for bruises. He hoped his appearance attractive but nondescript enough to avoid any unwanted attention from the fraternity guys south of St Ann Street. He went outside and hailed a cab.

"Where you goin'?" asked the driver.

"Bourbon and St. Ann, or as close as you can get," Matt said. He fretted about what the driver might think or say about his destination. Then he reassured himself: the city was packed with tourists taking cabs; the Quarter had countless coffeeshops, hotels, bars, and clubs; and in their first week on the job, most New Orleans cab drivers probably saw every combination and permutation of humanity. He'd soon be forgotten.

The driver dropped him off on Canal Street, several blocks south of the club. Heading north, Matt stopped at a souvenir shop advertising crude t-shirts and an ATM machine. He grinned to himself and thought that finally, after so many years, he could afford to withdraw a significant sum of money. He took out the largest round number his bank and the machine permitted in two transactions—$800. He was happy to trade the risk of surrendering it to any mugger for the added, momentary sense of security and the options it created; he also didn't want to use a credit card.

Then he melted into the press of college kids and tourists. He passed a blonde girl who looked about fifteen years old sitting on a curb, drinking a beer and smoking a cigarette. No one else in the crowd, including a cop on a white horse, gave a second glance to her or her pregnant belly.

Moments later, he crossed the velvet line that St Ann drew across Bourbon Street. Joints south of the line catered to college kids, were open to the street and, in addition to huge-ass beers, sold hurricanes and hand-grenades. North of St Ann was the French Quarter's gay area.

He approached Drink still buzzing but under control, as nervousness fluttered his stomach. Above the entrance, the balcony railing flew a rainbow flag and Matt worried about who might see him entering beneath it. But he reminded himself that native New Orleaneans seldom went to the Quarter; they largely considered it only fit for tourists. At French doors, thrown open to the street, a bouncer with a close-shaven crewcut, wearing a leather vest and dog collar, pointed a flashlight at Matt's license, examined it front and back, and then nodded.

Matt stepped into the club. Bass pounded through his head and chest and fluorescent lights seared a pattern of brilliant flashes and fading afterimages onto his retinas. Magenta light bathed a crowd of men writhing to the music and candy-colored lasers, straight as arrows, sliced through the throng. Accustomed to controlling the direction of his eyes around attractive men, Matt realized that he couldn't avoid looking at them here and no one would mind. Tension eased.

He made his way to the bar, sconce-lit, mirrored, and sporting a wooden surface latticed with scratches. The bartender wore a net shirt and the word tacky sprang to Matt's mind, but the guy—or his chest—made it work. "Gin and tonic," Matt said, reaching for his wallet. The bartender handed him the drink.

Matt peered beyond the dance floor to the stage as a spotlight hit it. A statuesque and strong-jawed black woman with gold and turquoise eyeshadow and impossible lashes prominent even in the uneven light of the club took the stage: her gold-sequined dress splintered the white spotlight. She began to lip-syc "Vogue," as a steady pulse alternated with snapping fingers.

A petite man to Matt's left interrupted, shouting, "Let me buy you another. I'm Joey."

Matt turned to size him up. Joey had platinum hair that clashed with darker brows, blue eyes, stood a few inches shorter than Matt, and wore a canary-yellow button-down shirt over a pair of

$200 jeans. Matt frowned inwardly at the hair dye and felt skittish about accepting a drink but thought refusing might be rude. And he didn't know anyone else in the bar. "Thanks," he said.

"I don't think I've seen you here before," Joey said.

"Yeah. I've actually been here a couple of times when my girlfriend wanted to dance."

"Really. Where is she now?" Joey asked, glancing around the bar. "Not many girls in here—it'd be hard to lose one." He locked eyes with Matt, head tilted to the side.

"We broke up," Matt responded.

"Well, color me surprised. When? Just now?"

"No." Matt smiled. "A couple of months ago. She lives in New York, and it was a distance thing."

"Yeah, I'm sure that's what created the distance. So is there anything else I could help you could lose tonight?" Joey's brows climbed toward his hair, emphasizing the contrasting color.

Matt narrowed his eyes, then said: "Subtle. No thanks. I'm flattered, but I've never met anyone who could tempt me into sex with one drink."

Joey snickered. "Well, many of us are surprised by our first reaction to a lack of heterosexual supervision. But maybe we should move on to safer topics for now. What do you do?" Joey spoke in singsong.

"I'm a lawyer."

"Well, we didn't need to get that boring." Joey sighed. "What do you like to do for fun, other than tease cute guys for drinks?"

"I read. And when possible, I eat and drink too much. What do you do?"

"I'm sometimes a sculptor and sometimes a waiter. You can guess which I prefer."

"Everyone has to earn a living," Matt said.

"So, how many more drinks do I need to get in you before I can talk you into a dance?" Joey asked.

"A few."

"That can be arranged."

The next hour passed in a frenzy of shouted conversation and emptied glasses. While ordering another round, out of the corner of his eye, Matt saw Joey signaling to the woman on stage. She started lip syncing: Matt laughed, recognizing The Pussycat Dolls' "Don't Cha."

"I knew that would get a laugh. I know you wish your girlfriend was hot like me," he said, pulling Matt out on the dance floor.

Matt realized that most of the other men had their shirts off—and a few had removed even more. His arms and legs felt liquid—he relaxed, let the beat carry him, stopped fighting off fun and reveled in the moment.

At some point, the performer left the stage but the music continued. A sassy brass opening diverted his attention but, only after several lines slipped past did he recognize Ricky Martin's "La Vida Loca."

Following Ricky Martin came a wall of techno music with little break between songs, which propelled Matt through the night until Joey leaned in to shout, "Do you want to get out of here?"

Matt stilled. "Depends on where you want to go."

"Don't worry, sweetheart. I know you're shy. I was thinking we could walk down to a little place I know close by. They've got great oysters."

"No thanks."

"No? You sure? Is this the end of our evening?"

"Let's just find a back table here," Matt said. "I'm tired of shouting."

"Well, okay. But if you aren't even going to have dinner with me, the next round is on you. Can you grab me a Maker's Mark on the rocks? I'm going to run to the little boys' room." Joey gestured toward the back.

Matt pushed through the crowd to the bar and ordered a Maker's Mark and a bottle of Purple Haze. Then he worked his way to the rear of the club. The place reeked of beer and sickly sweet alcohol, and he was glad he couldn't see the floor as he moved toward the back where the music receded to a soft, dull thump. He could finally hear himself think again—but he wasn't sure he liked it.

"So, what made you finally take the plunge and come here alone?" Joey asked.

"I don't know. I suppose I've always been interested in men and curiosity led me here."

"Was dancing enough to satisfy your curiosity?" Joey grinned.

"For now."

"Why are you afraid to go to a restaurant? We could just be two friends grabbing dinner together," Joey beseeched, appearing unwilling to waste the few hours he'd invested that night with an attractive newcomer, no matter how reluctant. "You are permitted to have gay friends, right? Look, don't get me wrong—I know coming out can be hard—but I don't think you have to be that paranoid."

"Yeah, I know you're right. But I've had some early success in a profession that's very conservative—my name and face are already out there. I haven't seen any signs of discrimination at the office, but why should I take the chance?" Matt shrugged his shoulders, unwilling to add that, most of the time, he felt work was his only bulwark against loneliness and safeguard for sanity. "And what about outside the office? I should probably figure out whether I prefer men before I come out."

"Well, honey, I'd be happy to help you make up your mind. I understand you want to take it slow, but it'd be a real shame to discover you're gay after your twenties have passed. You want to join me in the alley?" Joey cocked his head toward the fire exit.

"I thought you understood I wanted to take it slow."

"Settle down. I just need to take a leak and the bathroom line would keep me from you for far too long."

"I thought pissing in the street could actually get you arrested, even in the Quarter," Matt said.

"Live a little. I piss in that alley every weekend."

"Okay. I could stand to take a leak myself."

Matt stood. The table pitched and rolled in a shift of frame just short of the spins—he was drunk. He followed Joey, and, as they approached the exit, Joey rested his hand on the small of Matt's back. He let it rest there for several seconds, then disentangled himself.

Joey's slight shoulder pushed against the steel door and it swung open, clattered against the alley wall, then, behind them, thudded

11

shut. Rain sleeted down, spilling over a three-foot overhang, stories above. Joey scrambled about five feet down the alley, trying to stay dry by hugging the wall, and then began watering it. Matt ventured ten feet beyond.

"Bashful as always. At least you're consistent," Joey said.

"I just don't want to intimidate you," Matt responded.

Joey tittered. Matt shifted the beer bottle to his left hand, unzipped, and whizzed on the garbage at the foot of the wall.

Movement drew Matt's attention beyond Joey, where the street's light painted the alley's mouth in twilight. Three figures lurched toward them, and the largest, funneled closer by the brick walls, cast a shadow even in the alley's depths. Then he loomed over Joey.

"I told you we'd find a couple of faggots back here," said the massive man. "Hard to believe such little faggots would have cocks big enough to do anything to each other so far apart." He shifted to a soft but ungentle drawl. "So, tell me, little man, are you a faggot 'cause you got a tiny cock?"

"Why? You interested?" Joey approached him and alarmed Matt; by closing the distance, Joey had narrowed their options.

"I could say we're gonna beat the shit out of y'all because of that smart-assed comment. But we've been plannin' to beat the shit out of some fag all night."

His two companions grabbed Joey and pinned his arms behind his back. Matt zipped up. He considered going for help, but the men stood between him and the club door and behind him a large U-Haul truck and a dumpster choked off the exit to the street. He probably couldn't weave his way to either without being caught.

Cornered, outnumbered, and outsized, Matt's adrenaline spiked. Fear tinged with panic and fury spurred him to seize every advantage—rather than dropping the bottle, he dropped the hand holding it to his thigh, tilted it down so the dregs gurgled out, and then pushed it against his leg until he gripped the fat, slick barrel. He steadied himself and started toward the men. "You've had your fun," he said. "Why don't you let him go now? He was just taking a leak, like every other drunk in the Quarter tonight."

"We haven't had our fun. Our fun involves more'n just scarin' your girlfriend here."

The largest man turned toward Joey, pulled back a gargantuan fist, and unloaded it. Joey's nose exploded and he sagged against the men restraining him.

"Tell you what," Joey's assailant said to Matt. "Why don't you just hide over there by that dumpster for a while and we'll think about cutting you some slack."

"Sorry. Can't do that," Matt said.

One of the smaller men dropped Joey's arm and he slumped to the ground. The man stepped out to meet Matt; his right hand went into his pocket; and there was a glint of steel—a four-inch blade. Matt had to act.

As the runt approached, he said: "Last warning. Why dont'cha be smart and get outta here? Maybe you'll get lucky and we won't chase you."

Matt closed the distance and delivered a right uppercut to the body. As the man fell back a half-step, Matt pulled back, rotated his hips, and the muscles in his shoulder blade transformed his mediocre jab into a snapping left hook. Matt slipped it behind the smaller man's guard, pointed the neck of the beer bottle toward the him, and concentrated on punching through his head.

The bottle tip crumpled the smaller man's right temple. On instinct, Matt doubled up and swung again with the same left hook, which came harder. The man's left temple collapsed, the neck of the beer bottle buried in his skull. Matt didn't let go fast enough—inky blood coated his hand before the falling body tore the bottle from his grasp.

Matt rushed past the man's two companions, who were standing stunned. He stuttered to a stop, pulled open the back door, and yelled, "Three rednecks are out here beating the shit out of Joey."

The woman in the gold dress rushed out with a Louisville Slugger, a crowd of patrons surging behind her. The assailants bent over their friend on the ground.

The large man screamed, "Call 911! I think he's dead."

Chapter 2

The scream still echoed in Matt's head as the patrol cars arrived. The flashing lights strobed red, white and blue and with each sweep his right eye twitched. He wiped his left hand against his jeans, but viscous blood and perhaps even brain matter remained—in each flash of light it was brick and burgundy; in darkness, charcoal and sludge.

Uniformed officers divided Matt, Joey and their assailants into groups separated by the emergency vehicles and at a distance from the gathering crowd. They frisked Matt and took his driver's license but didn't ask any questions. Matt went to wipe his hand against his jeans again, but a cop caught his hand; he then photographed it and took a sample of the congealed liquid. The cops started hanging yellow tape: *Crime Scene—Do Not Enter.* EMTs ministered to the prone figure before loading his slight body onto a gurney and into an ambulance, which drove away dark and silent.

"Don't talk to the cops without a lawyer," Matt whispered to himself. "Don't talk to the cops without a lawyer." He concentrated on that single thought and tried to avoid thinking about the harm he'd done to another person.

After twenty minutes or so, a tall, paunchy man with tawny skin and closely cropped hair approached. He wore a wrinkled denim shirt and well-worn khakis, and his eyes were bleary. "I'm Detective Scott Jones. Can you tell me what happened?"

"I don't think I should say anything without representation," Matt said.

"Representation, huh. You a lawyer?" Jones asked, sticking his hands into his pockets. He smiled and the whites of his teeth and eyes popped in the dark, but it hid whether the smile reached his eyes. "You know, I don't think they tell you this in law school, but most of these fights are resolved by talking them through."

Matt had talked himself out of trouble when the cops had broken up a few keg parties during high school, but he knew he was out of his depth. And he was in no shape to answer questions. "I'd still rather have a lawyer. I'm not saying anything."

Detective Jones turned away, went over to Joey, and began talking to him. His voice then rose to a shout, he pointed his finger at Joey, and he shook his head in response to Joey's answers. Matt wondered why on earth the detective would be angry with Joey.

Before Matt could decipher this, the detective abandoned Joey and shifted his attention to the giant and his remaining companion. After a fifteen-minute conversation, Detective Jones marched back to Matt. "I've heard enough. You're under arrest. You have the right to remain silent. Anything you say can and will be used against you in a court of law. You have the right to an attorney. If you cannot afford an attorney, one will be provided for you. Do you understand these rights?"

The detective pushed him against an alley wall more revolting than the floor of the bar and pulled his hands behind his back.

Matt not only understood his rights, he knew their pedigree and origin. "Yes, I understand my rights," Matt said. "I'm invoking my right to remain silent and to counsel. When can I call my lawyer?"

"After booking. Turn around."

The detective ushered Matt toward a waiting squad car and thrust his head down to clear the roof. Matt slunk down in the seat, feeling the adrenaline fade and the leading edge of a wave of depression. Nausea threatened as he tried and failed to find a comfortable position. The squad car pulled away with flashing lights and a blaring siren and the French Quarter rushed past the windows.

The car pulled into the Orleans Parish Prison, a sprawling facility that covered several city blocks. The processing area teemed with black and brown detainees—most were washed-out and subdued. But the flapping and twitching, raucous cursing and foul body odor of a few stood out and drew attention. So Matt too—despite his pale skin—was lost among the brimming multitude caught by police officers and released to prison officials.

Officers took Matt's mugshot in front of a white board that logged his height as five foot ten, took another sample of the drying blood on his left hand, cleaned it with alcohol, and then pressed each digit into black ink and then onto a blotter. As instructed, Matt then blew into a breathalyzer. Each stage was punctuated by a wait that gave Matt time to weigh his options.

He considered refusing the breathalyzer, but he couldn't find the strength. He was guilty of public intoxication and the Fourth Amendment right against unreasonable searches and seizures doesn't protect certain physical characteristics held out to the public, like fingerprints. Besides, he wanted to appear cooperative without jeopardizing his right to remain silent. He had to pick his battles.

A guard finally told Matt he could call his lawyer and pointed to a phone inside a tiny steel closet. Matt knew the phone number for exactly one attorney even remotely capable of handling the situation: his boss, Thomas Farrar.

He'd called Thomas at home before to discuss draft briefs and key documents before depositions, hearings and trials. The lawyer relished the practice of law so much he seemed to welcome the interruptions. He himself would call Matt at all hours of the night and early on weekend mornings with legal ideas he'd had while showering, shaving or eating breakfast—all nuisances that could potentially interfere with his practice. Farrar never seemed to worry about disturbing Matt, who'd labored through many phone conversations trying to mirror his boss's enthusiasm and keep pace with his thoughts. The prospect of calling him now made Matt cringe.

He pushed past his trepidation and dialed Farrar's home phone number. A woman's voice answered with a drowsy, "Hello."

"Mrs Farrar, can I please speak to Thomas? This is Matt Durant, from the office. It's an emergency."

"Of course." She scarcely sounded surprised. Matt heard her say, "Honey, it's Matt from the office. He says it's an emergency."

"Matt, what's the problem?" Farrar asked in a crisp voice.

"Thomas, I've been arrested on felony charges and I'm at the Orleans Parish Prison."

"What the hell? No, don't say anything." Farrar paused for a full thirty seconds—an interminable wait for Matt and a record-setting silence for Farrar. "For the benefit of anyone who might be listening to this phone call or a recording of it, Mr Durant and I are both attorneys. I'm communicating with him to provide legal advice, this is a privileged conversation, and you should stop listening right now." Farrar paused again. "We shouldn't discuss the substance of your problem over the phone. I'm sure this has to be some sort of mistake. But no night-court judge is going to let you bond out over the weekend, so there's not much I can do right now. Monday morning, the DA's office will decide whether to go for an indictment. I'll call their office tonight and leave a message that I'm representing you at least for now, which will give me the right to appear at any grand jury proceeding."

By the end of his instructions, Farrar had taken on the matter-of-fact tone of a lawyer who routinely deals with a wide variety of client emergencies. He'd address practical issues first. Later, he'd worry about Matt and any larger questions raised by his felony arrest.

"I really need to tell you something about what happened tonight," Matt said. "I'm worried some evidence may go missing if we don't get on it right away."

"Well, you're going to have to tell me then. What is it?"

"I was attacked by man with a knife in an alley behind a bar on Bourbon Street." He couldn't bring himself to say St Ann. Matt said, "The alley was behind a bar named Drink. I didn't tell the detective about the knife because I didn't want to say anything to the police, but now I'm afraid they won't look for it. One of the other witnesses probably told him, but still—"

"I hear you. Do you remember the name of the detective who interviewed you?"

"Scott Jones."

"I'll handle it."

"Thanks," Matt said. Apologizing for waking Farrar up didn't seem right. The seriousness of his situation eclipsed any inconvenience.

Matt rapped on the webbed window and an officer appeared. He led Matt through a heavy steel door that separated the booking area from the jail itself. Cells flanked a long corridor that led to a cavernous room containing dozens of people. Matt tamped down his panic about the roommate situation. His stomach unclenched as the officer stopped short of the massive room, opened the cell door to his left, and motioned for Matt to enter.

"It's your lucky night; you get your own cell," the officer said. "Breakfast is at eight. That's only a couple hours away. I suggest you get some sleep. It'll be good practice. You're gonna be doing a lot of sleeping now."

Matt tossed and turned throughout much of the night. Every movement prompted a new question, and the potential answers weren't reassuring. Had he really killed a man? Could he have made it out of the alley before they caught him? Did all this really happen just because he'd decided to visit a gay bar? He wasn't sure when his ricocheting thoughts lost enough momentum for him to fall asleep, but they finally did.

He startled out of twilight sleep to the sound of a metal breakfast tray shoved through a slot in the door. It held some facsimile of orange juice, eggs, and toast, which he choked down for energy and just to do something. Then—mired in melancholy and unable to string more than a handful of sensible thoughts together at a time—he waited through the remainder of a very long weekend and a Monday morning that felt even longer.

On Monday afternoon, about an hour after receiving a lunch fabricated from the same cardboard as breakfast, a guard appeared. "Your lawyer's here. Put your hands through the slot." He cuffed Matt's hands and opened the steel bar door. "Thatta way," the guard said, pointing down the corridor to the portal that led to the booking area. After passing through the threshold, he led Matt to a series of conference rooms with sturdy galvanized doors and plexiglass windows. He allowed Matt to enter the conference room alone.

"Matt, it's good to see you safe and sound, even if the circumstances aren't exactly ideal," Farrar said. The gravel in his voice was as reassuring as his full head of silver hair; his even tan suggested calm. A yellow legal pad filled with his familiar scribbles rested on the table, Attorney Client Privileged, Work Product emblazoned on the upper right corner of the first page. Lisa sat next to Farrar with a piteous expression in her eyes. Humiliation colored Matt's face and made him want to crawl under the table.

"Matt, I'm so sorry this happened to you," Lisa said. She reached out and lightly touched his cuffed hands.

"Events are unfolding very rapidly," Farrar said. "The DA's office secured an indictment this morning for first-degree murder."

"So I did kill a man," Matt said. He tried to bury his feelings under a monotone voice. But his stomach opened like a trapdoor above a bottomless pit—disorientation and guilt overwhelmed him and his gut went into free-fall. He lowered his forehead to his cuffed hands on the table, blinked back tears and exhaled.

After a moment, he pushed his head up. He only had limited time with Farrar and could figure out how to deal with those emotions later. He had to think about his situation analytically and methodically. It was his only hope.

"How could they possibly charge me with first-degree murder?" Matt asked. "Even if I'd meant to kill the guy, which I sure as hell didn't, what sort of aggravating factors would support that charge?"

"The prosecution presented three witnesses to the grand jury," Farrar said. "That detective, Scott Jones, was the first witness." He looked down at his notes.

"The detective testified this Joey Buckner had four grams of cocaine on him when the police searched him. The other two witnesses were the companions of the deceased man in the alley. Their names are Donald Rand and John Harlan. Rand and Harlan testified they found you in the alley buying drugs from Buckner and they attempted to restrain both of you before finding a police officer. They said Buckner tried to escape, Rand hit him, and then you attacked the third man, whose name was Brian Cutler. The DA's office is prosecuting you on the theory you killed Cutler while attempting to purchase cocaine."

Indignation punched through Matt's thin layer of detachment. "That's not even close to what happened!"

"Well, Rand and Harlan are obviously potentially biased witnesses. Why don't you tell us what really happened?" Farrar pushed the legal pad away and set down his Montblanc fountain pen.

Matt regained some sense of calm and recounted the events in the alley in as close to an even voice as he could manage. Before Farrar launched into his questions, Matt had one of his own, "Did you search for the knife?"

"Yes," Farrar said. "I had a private investigator who's a former police officer search the alley. He didn't find anything, but several hours had passed since your arrest. It doesn't necessarily mean anything. The DA's office turned over copies of the police report this morning. They want to move very, very fast on this one. What did you say to the police Friday night?"

"I just told them I wanted to invoke my rights to remain silent and to an attorney."

"Nothing else?"

Matt shook his head. "Nothing else."

"Did you know Buckner had cocaine on him?"

"No," Matt said with an edge of concern. If Farrar didn't believe him, who would? "I told you. I only met him that night. He can testify to that, and the bartender may have overheard something, but the club was pretty loud."

"You had almost $800 in cash on you. Why?"

"I was going to a gay club and wanted to be discreet. I didn't want the bar's name showing up on my credit card bill."

"Even though you'd been there before with a girlfriend?"

"I was being paranoid," Matt said. "I certainly wasn't there with a girlfriend on Friday night."

"You said you'd been drinking. Did the police do a breathalyzer test?"

"Yeah, when they booked me. I'd guess about an hour and a half after being arrested. They didn't tell me the results."

"We'll have to get a copy of those results." Farrar jotted a note.

Matt saw where Farrar was going and didn't like it. "I hope you're not thinking about arguing that I was drunk and had a lower level of intent to set up a plea for a lesser murder charge. I was defending myself and Joey. There were three of those guys and the one who hit Joey was enormous."

"Of course, we'll almost certainly argue self-defense and defense of another. But we need to look at this from every angle and consider every potential argument. You know we do that in every case."

Matt forced himself to breathe.

"What do you think of the fact that Buckner didn't testify in front of the grand jury?" Farrar asked. "Do you think he'll corroborate your version of what happened? You saved him from a pretty severe beating."

"I don't know. Maybe Joey gave a statement that contradicted the other two guys' in the alley and that's why the prosecution didn't present it. Maybe he's flipped, but the DA's office figured they didn't need his testimony and wanted to avoid showing their hand so far before trial. The guy apparently had four grams of coke on him, so I don't know what he'll do."

"I have to ask," said Farrar, "especially given your generation's attitude toward drugs. Did you do any cocaine last night?" Farrar locked eyes with Matt.

"No. Thomas, you know me."

"I certainly thought I did, but you've given me some new information to digest. At the very least, you made some serious errors in judgment, if only by drinking too much and urinating in that back alley. I need to consider whether we can continue to represent you beyond tomorrow's bail hearing. We have obligations to other clients and a murder trial will require enormous resources, for which you can't pay."

"I know," Matt said. He pressed his lips together and felt the blood drain from them. "I didn't assume you'd defend me. I just didn't know who else to call. If you could recommend a good criminal defense attorney, I'd appreciate it."

"What about your parents?" Farrar asked. "Could they help financially?"

"You know my Mom's a nurse, and Dad passed away years ago."

"I know. I just wanted to make certain. Let's talk about the arraignment tomorrow. Given your background, I'll ask the judge to recommend you receive bail despite the first-degree murder charge. The prosecutor will probably concede that to appear reasonable and then press for an unreasonable trial date. He'll have to assume we'll be representing you and he won't want to give us any additional time to prepare."

"What kind of trial date do you think he'll be able to get?"

"Hard to tell. You know the criminal docket's been a mess in the last couple of years since Katrina." He tapped his pen against the legal pad once, then suspended it in the air above it. "I'm guessing he'll try to leverage his concession on bail to convince the judge to set trial for as soon as a month from now. If we represent you, the judge is not going to be as likely to give our office the extension he would give the overburdened public defenders' office. We'll continue to represent you through the arraignment," Farrar said. "I think anything less would be unethical. Lisa will contact your mother. Bail will probably be set at around a million dollars. We can recommend a bail bondsman so your mother can line up the necessary financing. I'm going to consult with my partners about whether we can continue to represent you. Any questions?"

"What do you think about my chances?" Matt asked, fearing the answer.

"I don't know. I don't like that explaining the facts underlying any self-defense claim requires going into the details about your visit to a gay bar. Not sure what a Louisiana jury is going to make of that, but I don't think it's going to help. I also don't like the fact that you already have two witnesses lined up against you. But we just don't know enough yet."

"That's what I thought. Thank you for considering taking the case."

Lisa reached her hand across the table and placed it on Matt's.

"I'm just so sorry. Is there anything else I can do for you?"

"No. I'll be fine until tomorrow. Thanks for the offer."

The three rose and Thomas Farrar knocked on the plexiglass window, summoning the guard. Matt thought perhaps Farrar's willingness to consider taking the case for free signaled that others—even straight white men—could find his actions justified, but then he flashed back to the image and feel of the blood the officers hadn't permitted him to wipe off. The guard opened the door and—after Thomas and Lisa exited—he led Matt outside and down the corridor in the opposite direction, toward the depths of the prison.

Chapter 3

At the arraignment, as Farrar had predicted, the presiding judge allowed the prosecution to fast-track the case—the trial would begin in six weeks.

The news numbed Matt. Six weeks was fast. As the accused, he didn't know how he would bear the next minute, hour or day under the pall of his remorse and a potential punishment that threatened to reduce the rest of his life to shame and self-loathing.

The judge ordered Matt to post a million-dollar bond to stay out of jail until the trial and, despite his limited resources, Farrar advised paying a bail bondsman. Matt's life could depend on appearing confident and resolute in front of a jury and short stints in prison had broken other men. Around four o'clock the afternoon before, his mother, Mary, had convinced her long-time bank in Lafayette to mortgage her house to pay the nonrefundable fee of $100,000. And then she'd made the three-hour drive to New Orleans so she wouldn't miss a moment of the hearing. Farrar and Mary had at least bought Matt provisional freedom.

*

Matt and Mary exited the courthouse and hurried to her Toyota Corolla. As soon as they were inside, she turned to him. Her swollen eyes—spiderwebbed with red veins—filled with fresh tears.

"Honey, I'm so sorry," Mary said. "I know you weren't buying drugs and you certainly wouldn't ever hurt another person unless you absolutely had to." She trembled and reached to pull him into a hug. "Your entire life until now has shown that what that prosecutor said in court today was a lie," Mary said. "After the jury finds you're innocent, can you sue him? They shouldn't be able to do this to people." She patted Matt on the shoulder.

"Mom, for now, let's just try to make sure I'm not convicted. The judicial system's not perfect. We both know there's a real chance I could be convicted."

"Mr Farrar wants us to meet him at the office. We'll get started making sure the system works this time."

Mary put the car in gear and they crawled south into the French Quarter at the speed limit. Windows cracked open to assist air-conditioning well past its prime let in the smell of the streets—vomit hastily dispatched with garden hoses. At first glance, the Quarter appeared largely restored from Hurricane Katrina; storefronts gleamed with fresh paint. But, looking upward, Matt could see that most of the apartments above the first story were deserted and lifeless.

They arrived at the brick office and walked into the lobby. A pearl marble floor, with undertones of gray, spanned the foyer. From their left, behind a high mahogany desk, the receptionist, Donna, said, "Matt, I'm so sorry. This whole thing is just ridiculous."

"Thank you, Donna," Matt responded and meant it. She'd used generic words to console, just as many had after his father's death, but her consistent humor and kindness over the past two years gave them meaning.

"Thomas wants to meet you in the conference room," Donna said.

Matt and Mary entered the ornate conference room, where the marble floor gave way to an Oriental rug dominated by diamond patterns of indigo, rust and gold. Atop the rug sat a French-style mahogany conference table with carved pedestal legs, reeded edges and a surface polished to a high sheen. A cream ceiling supported a crystal chandelier with a solid gold canopy, a gold rod running through the tube and cylindrical shades softening the light.

Matt was surprised to see Farrar, usually the last to arrive at any meeting, waiting. Before Matt and Mary were fully seated, Farrar looked up and began speaking.

"Largely as a result of our review of the police report, the firm has decided to take your case pro bono. We're placing you on administrative leave until the trial is over."

"Thank you," Matt and Mary said in unison. Matt felt relief for the first time since those three thugs had confronted him in the alley.

"Let's talk about the police report," Farrar said. "The biggest problem is that, as you noted when I spoke to you in jail, Detective Jones interviewed Rand and Harlan together on Friday night."

Matt's reflexes kicked in and he picked up a pen and legal pad to take notes. Farrar's eyebrows shot up; Matt put the pen and paper down and Farrar continued. "They had an opportunity to listen to each other's stories," he said. "Detective Jones also really screwed up by asking Rand at the beginning whether they'd seen Buckner attempting to sell you cocaine. Apparently, Jones walked in assuming this was a drug deal gone bad. After he asked that question, Rand took off with his story that they saw you buying drugs and went in to break it up. Harlan heard Rand's version firsthand. And the *Times-Picayune* had an article in the Sunday paper based on a leaked copy of the police report. It summarized Rand's story yet again. The two then had all weekend to get their stories straight."

"Most of the initial work will be done by the private investigator," Farrar said. "We need to start by finding out everything possible about Rand and Harlan. We can only hope they've been in trouble before." Farrar looked steadily at Matt.

"What about Buckner?" Matt asked, jumping straight to the only witness that hadn't threated him physically.

"Buckner's been indicted for possession with intent to distribute. The bad news is he has a prior for possession, so that would put him in prison for at least four or five years. The public defender's office represents him, but the assistant PD told me he'd only had a chance to interview him about facts relevant to bail before his release." Farrar glanced at his notes to double-check. "Buckner's been through the system before. He has to know if his story matches theirs, his lawyer's going to have something to take to the DA's office. We need to plan for trial assuming he'll flip."

"We need to be ready to shred Buckner's credibility," Matt said. He hoped it didn't come to that.

"Right, but investigating Buckner will be the last step. He still might be a friendly witness. So I'll have the investigator start by trying to find anything we can on Rand and Harlan. Of course, we also need to work to uncover corroborating evidence. The knife is the key missing piece, but we need to think more broadly than the knife or even that night in the alley. My tentative view is Matt should testify and we should offer character evidence on his behalf. We need to show he's far more respectable and likable than those thugs." Farrar regarded Matt, then Mary.

"Mr Farrar, I just want to thank you again, but I have a couple of questions," Mary said.

"Go ahead. That's what I'm here for." Farrar turned in his seat to face her.

"The detective interviewing these two guys together and then giving them all weekend to get their stories straight just doesn't sound fair." Despite her red eyes, she faced him with squared shoulders and an upturned face that elongated her neck and strengthened her chin. "Isn't there some legal argument you could make to get the whole case thrown out?"

"Unfortunately, no," Farrar said, shaking his head. "The police have pretty broad discretion in interviewing witnesses." He looked her in the eye. "But we can and will argue to the jury that the detective's interview technique gave them an opportunity to fabricate their story."

"Oh," Mary said. "Well, what do you think our chances are like in front of a jury?" She studied the table, but Farrar didn't look away.

"I wish I knew, but it's too early to say. We just need to do the best we can to build a solid case."

Farrar stood to leave, but before he stepped away from the table, Mary asked, still looking at the table and in a barely audible voice, "Could Matt get the death penalty?"

Farrar paused, until Mary looked up and made eye contact with him "It's certainly possible, but I'll do everything in my power to keep that from happening. If the jury does find Matt guilty—and I'm not saying they will—that same jury will decide whether he should receive the death penalty. So every piece of evidence and every argument we make in the phase to determine whether he's guilty will also be geared toward showing there's no way he deserves the death penalty."

Farrar placed his hand on her shoulder. "Just try to hold yourselves together. The judicial system works most of the time, and I certainly know how to give it a shove in the right direction."

Mary's face was ashen. Matt's dread heightened and the room threatened to spin around him. He concentrated on breathing deeply and slowly, trying to tamp down on his emotions and regain his usual steadiness. He imagined stepping out of his body, pretended the client was a stranger, and heard himself reassuring Mary that Farrar was the "best damned lawyer in town."

After they'd collected themselves, both clutched at the opportunity to engage in routine activities. Mary volunteered to go to the grocery store and Matt decided to go to the gym.

He entered Tommy's un-air-conditioned gym, which stewed under the afternoon heat of early September in New Orleans. He forced himself to keep his eyes forward as—even in this usually comfortable space—he felt the real and imagined stares of other people working out raise the fine hairs on his arms and neck. But he seldom worked out in the middle of the day, he didn't recognize anyone, and the gym's swelter enveloped him, giving the small assurance that he'd be less likely to strain or tear a muscle.

Matt worked through his normal fourteen rounds. He then took off his gloves, unwrapped his hands and put the gloves in the gym bag. He kept his head down as he trod the familiar path toward the stairs. On his way out, he passed the office Tommy had carved out of the space with plywood wall dividers.

"Hey kid," Tommy interrupted, startling Matt. "Come here for a minute." Matt entered the office and pulled the flimsy door shut behind him. "I just wanna say you did the right thing," Tommy said.

"What?"

"I'm bettin' nobody's told you that you did the right thing. You did. I read in the paper about the size of one of those guys and you didn't have a choice. You had to hurt one of 'em real bad or they would've put you in the hospital. Maybe even killed you."

"Thanks," Matt said. "You're right. You are the first to tell me that."

"What do you think about your chances in court?" Tommy asked. He pulled a cigar from a desk drawer and waved it in Matt's direction. Matt shook his head.

"My lawyer would kill me for discussing it outside of his office, but those guys are lying," Matt said. "We just have to hope the jury sees that."

"Well, if there's anything I can do, just say so."

"You know, actually, when I was in jail I started to worry about going to prison." Matt felt blood rush to his face. "You must have read that I was, uh, well, outside a gay bar when the attack happened."

"None of my business," Tommy said.

"Maybe not. But if I go to prison, I don't think the other inmates are going to be as understanding. Prisons have gotten better over the last couple of decades, but I'm really worried about being attacked. Anything you can teach me to help keep that from happening?"

"Well, not exactly my specialty. I always worked straight up boxing. You know Dave Anderson?"

"Yeah, the short black guy," Matt said.

"That's him." Tommy lit the cigar and took a deep pull. "He used to be a Navy SEAL. That's what you need to learn. He comes in to work on his Muay Thai kickboxing. I don't think fancy kicks are what you're looking for, but they use elbows and knees too. You need to learn to fight dirty. And that's what the military teaches."

"It's complicated," Matt said, shrugging his shoulders. "Is there any way to do it on the down-low?" He cocked his head to the side. "There's already been some bad press and there might be more if anyone learns what I'm up to."

"Well, I'm not sure how much *might* should count right now. You go to prison and don't know what you're doing, you're gonna get killed. You can come in when no one else is usin' the gym, if Dave's willing."

"Thanks." Tommy's offer relieved some of the tension from Matt's shoulders.

"I've got another regular who spent some time in the state pen. Don't want to give you his name until I talk to him, but I'll see if he'll meet with you."

"That would be great."

"No problem," Tommy said. "I'll be in touch. Keep your head up."

Matt went outside, called his mother, and asked her to pick him up. He jangled the keys in his pocket while he waited, nervous that recent events would forever unmoor him from his mother, who—no matter the distance between them—had always been his anchor. Mary arrived in her weathered Corolla within minutes and Matt levered himself into the car.

"I picked up some food," Mary said. "I thought I'd make some orange chicken tonight, and I got you enough groceries to last for a while. I also bought you that new biography of Franklin. I know it won't last you long, but it's something you can do at home."

"Thanks, Mom."

"Matt, I need to ask you something." Her voice quavered. "Are you gay?"

His nerves already raw and exposed, Matt's anxiety surged. His stomach sickened as he glanced at the car door handle and thought of opening it and tumbling out to relative safety, but he pushed the idea away. He raised his eyes to his window without registering the view.

"I'm not sure. And I wanted to figure it out for myself before I threw everyone around me into turmoil. I knew it would be hard for you. You always wanted grandchildren, and we both wanted to name a boy after Dad."

"Well, you know you can talk to me about anything, but for what it's worth, I don't think you're gay. I think you're just confused after your breakup with Andrea. That was the most serious relationship you've ever had and that has to count for something, right? And you've dated other girls."

His mother's resistance grated on Matt despite her good intentions; she took him at his word on almost everything else. She was so fundamental and omnipresent—so important to who and what he was—that he loved her with every heartbeat. But for the same reasons—despite his enormous self-control and ability to hide so much from so many—he most often slipped up around her, the person he most wanted to protect. He'd never let a sign of his attraction to other men show through—after all, how often did sons talk to their mothers about who was hot or not? But his sadness and loneliness spilled out as anger and frustration more often around her than anyone else. Why wouldn't she accept the possibility that it was because he was gay and closeted?

"I've always been attracted to other men." Matt looked down at his lap.

"And you kept that secret for how many years?" Mary's eyes widened.

"Since middle school," Matt said.

"Well, you certainly should have known you could tell me. I don't think there's anything wrong with being gay; I just think it makes life a lot harder. And I don't want my child to suffer."

Her words reinforced the hurdles and barriers to Matt's being. Of the few whose opinion mattered, hers mattered most. But he'd been outed as going to a gay club; he wouldn't reject being gay in a way that made it seem blameworthy; and he couldn't deny who he might be—so he could only push back. He tried to lock eyes with her. "I know, Mom, but you have to admit that compromises your objectivity. And that's exactly why I wanted to explore these feelings on my own first."

Though she hadn't yet started the car, she stared ahead: "I guess I can understand that. But we got turmoil anyway. I'd do anything for you and I want you to be happy more than anything else in the world. The thought of you going to prison breaks my heart and I think if you died, I'd die."

31

"I know. Mama, I'm scared," Matt said, his voice breaking. By being, had he put them both at risk?

"I know, baby. At least you have the best lawyers in town. And you're telling the truth. That has to count for something, right?" She rested her hand on his forearm, reassuring him that she did want the best for him, even if she couldn't accept the necessary range of possibilities.

"I wish I could be here for you for the next six weeks," she said. "I've got to go back to work. I don't want to, but the bank wouldn't give me that loan unless I promised to keep my job. You know your daddy didn't have much to leave us, and I think it's more important to be there during the trial. But say the word and I'll quit my job and we'll figure everything else out."

Matt didn't doubt it. "Mom, you being here now is enough. I can't complain about you going back to work when your house and job are keeping me out of jail. And you know I'll pay you back if and when I can. I'll be okay. We can talk on the phone." He forced a smile.

"Enough about these depressing topics for now," Mary said. She started the engine. "I asked that nice girl Lisa to come over to your house for dinner tonight. I think we should just have an enjoyable meal and try to take our minds off some of this for a while."

"That sounds good. Still trying to be a matchmaker, huh?"

"Well, I didn't know a nice boy to invite. I just thought she'd make good company." She put the car in gear to crawl back through the Quarter.

The Toyota finally crossed into Matt's uptown neighborhood. It had suffered less damage during the storm and the residents had the money to rebuild. But scaffolding still surrounded many houses and the tools and detritus of construction littered their yards. Still others sat empty, untouched since the waters had receded.

Around six-thirty that night, the doorbell rang. Lisa stood at the threshold carrying a bottle of Pinot Grigio and Mary waved her into the house with the practiced motion of a runway attendant.

"You didn't have to do that, hon. Dinner's not that fancy," Mary said. "Just some orange chicken and Uncle Ben's rice."

"It's my pleasure," Lisa said. "Everyone at the office feels just awful about what's happened to Matt. What can I do to help?"

"Nothing. We're just about ready to eat."

Matt nodded at Lisa. "Thanks for coming."

"Of course I came. I've always been very curious about your mother. She must have the patience of a saint to have tolerated what you consider a sense of humor all of these years." Lisa smiled and her green eyes lit up.

"Any recent examples of Matt's sense of humor I should know about?" Mary asked. She turned down the gas stove, fluffed the rice with a fork, pulled a salad out of the refrigerator, and passed plates to Matt.

"Let me open this bottle of wine and then we can sit down and discuss your son," Lisa said. The three sat down at an unfinished pine table and Matt was glad he'd at least sprung for four chairs. Even though each was less than fifty bucks, he hardly ever used more than one. Mary spun tales of his childhood and Lisa offered stories about his wry sense of humor at the office.

"I guess recent events have derailed Matt's only stated career goal," Lisa said.

"What's that?" Mary asked.

"When they installed a defibrillator in the office a couple of months ago, Matt said his only goal as a lawyer was to have his second wife before his second heart attack."

"Matthew Durant!" Mary said.

"What?" Matt asked. "I could still at least have two heart attacks no matter what happens, right?"

"Don't talk that way," Mary said. "Did he tell his boss about the wives and the heart attacks?"

"I don't think so," Lisa said. She smiled and shook her head. "And they know that his work is far better than his sense of humor."

"Don't be so sure," Mary said. "Matt's always been just smart enough to get people's goats, and it can get him in real trouble."

"You say that," Lisa said, "but you must be very proud. Matt graduated first in his class from LSU law school and clerked for a Louisiana appellate court."

"Dear, please don't recite his resume. It makes him unbearable," Mary said, shaking her head but smiling.

"Unbearable? I don't know what you're talking about. I've brought enormous pride and honor..." Matt faltered, lost midsentence.

His mother turned to him and said, "You've always made me proud. And a few drinks and some bad luck don't change that. They never will. No matter what happens." She placed her hand on his.

"Thomas is the best trial lawyer in New Orleans," Lisa said. "I'm sure he'll show the jury what really happened."

"I can't believe I killed a man, not to mention that I could be executed for it," Matt said. His stomach sank further as he realized he hadn't even separated his remorse from his fear of punishment—he'd failed at contrition too.

"Enough," Lisa responded. "You did what you had to do, and we'll win."

Chapter 4

When Mary left for Lafayette the next morning, Matt felt a pang at her departure he hadn't experienced since childhood, when she'd dropped him off at school for the first time. He already missed her so much it felt as if someone had reached in, emptied out his guts and replaced them with a lead weight.

Minutes after Mary left, Tommy called. "I spoke to Dave Anderson, and he's coming by tonight. You should show up around nine-thirty." Matt thanked Tommy and said he'd meet Dave at the gym then.

He brewed another pot of chicory coffee because they'd exhausted the first. He opened a biography about Alan Turing. He scanned over technical descriptions, focusing on the mathematician's role in breaking Nazi codes, the moral dilemma between saving Allied lives and tipping the Nazis off that the codes had been broken, and, of course, the insights about Turing's attraction to other men. Having picked up the book to learn something about how Turing had managed being gay in conservative England during World War II, Matt realized he hadn't. The biographer concluded that when faced with the choices of conforming, rebelling, or withdrawing into work, Turing had withdrawn. And, after helping Britain win the war, he'd been convicted of criminal sodomy and suicided. Not helpful—Matt put down the book without finishing it.

Thinking a diversion might help, he turned on the television for background noise and started the Franklin biography, leaping from quote to quote from Franklin's considerable writings, but it brought to mind his mother's thinly veiled and overblown expectations of him—trust her, even when he was facing a trial for murder, to buy him the biography of a genius. Distracted, his shame over being outed in the newspaper, worries about the trial, and fears of decades on death row or life in prison—more daunting than death— intruded, and a wave of terror overtook him. He breathed deeply, reminded himself there was little he could do, and tried to resume reading. Conflicted over who he was and what he'd done even in his own home, he couldn't bear to think of going for a carton of milk and facing the clerk at Circle-K. So he burrowed more deeply in between the pages of the book.

Midafternoon the phone rang. His shoulders spasmed and the book jumped in his lap, but he answered after the second ring.

"Matthew Durant?" asked a woman.

"This is he."

"I'm Kathy Nelson from the New Orleans *Observer*. I wanted to talk to you about what happened in the alley that night."

"You should talk to my lawyer."

"Well, I just thought you'd like to have a chance to tell your side of the story. Sounds to me like the *Times-Picayune* has gotten most of its information from the police and prosecutors. We wanted to give you a chance to tell some folks what actually happened that night."

"Well, it didn't happen like the *Times-Picayune* said it did, but I really can't talk about it. My lawyer's given me very specific instructions." Matt pursed his lips.

"Do you really need someone to speak on your behalf? From what I've heard, you're quite a talented young lawyer. Don't you want to defend yourself in your own words?"

"I will. At trial," Matt said, his jaw tight.

"Isn't that somewhat unusual?"

"I really can't say anything else. Good-bye." He punched the disconnect button and hurled the phone as hard as he could. It hit the wall, split into pieces, scotched the paint and dented the sheetrock.

"Damn it!" he shouted.

He'd clamped down a little too late and risked tipping off the prosecution that he'd testify at trial, increasing the odds they'd spend more time focused on his history and any indiscretions. The reporter was right. It was unusual for a criminal defendant to testify on his own behalf, but he'd spent most of his life building a reputation different from most criminal defendants and was determined to use it when he needed it most.

He went over to his computer, googled the *Observer*, and found a trashy tabloid filled with celebrity gossip. The lead story accused Brad and Angelina of importing babies from foreign countries for bizarre religious ceremonies. Matt hoped even it couldn't fabricate a story from his four words. And besides, who'd ever heard of the *Observer*?

Matt spent the remainder of the day housebound talking himself into a panic and then talking himself down again. Cooking dinner didn't require enough of his attention. He started to prepare some tilapia to cook with basil, tomatoes, and white wine, but it gave him too much time to think. So he stuck a frozen pizza in the oven instead and, while it cooked, he read and watched TV.

At nine-thirty that night, Matt went to the gym. Tommy and Dave Anderson came forward to greet him in the otherwise empty room. Dave was shorter than Matt by a few inches, but with impossibly thick biceps and thighs: he looked like an onyx fireplug.

"Tommy filled me in on what happened to you," Dave said, standing with his legs spread and arms at his side. "He said you'd like to work on some practical self-defense, just in case."

"Yeah. I'm a bit worried about the impact it could have on public perception, but I trust Tommy." As he spoke, he focused on a point in space to Dave's right.

"You can also trust me to keep my mouth shut," Dave said. "If Tommy says there's no way you tried to buy coke and kill someone to cover it up, that's good enough for me. And I don't care who you want to fuck." Dave looked Matt squarely in the eyes and Matt felt compelled to meet his gaze. "What kind of shape are you in?"

"He's in pretty good shape," Tommy said. "He can go fourteen rounds in a combination of bag work, mitt work, and no-contact sparring."

"You'll want to get in better shape, but I want to spend our time on moves that would be illegal in a boxing ring. Mike Tyson, ear-biting illegal," Dave said. "I'll leave conditioning to Tommy. This may seem like a strange question, given what's happened in the last week, but do you have any problem attacking someone in the really vulnerable areas? I mean the eyes, the nose, the throat, and the balls."

"Not if I have to," Matt said, pressing his lips together, head tilted downward, and shaking his head. "I just want to be able to protect myself."

"All right. We'll start with a few moves today. The first is known as the Liverpool kiss. You aren't that big, so a larger man's probably going to get close to you and try to grapple. He gets in that close, you may not be able to throw an effective punch. The simplest move is to head butt him. A powerful head butt can break a nose or cheekbone. So, we're going to practice head butts for a while."

Dave walked Matt over to a heavy bag shaped like a dummy and showed him how to lead with the top of his skull. He practiced the head butt by itself first, slamming the hardest part of his skull into the dummy's face. Tommy then set the timer and Matt began working through three-minute rounds, unleashing a flurry of punches and body blows that culminated with smashing his head into the dummy's face.

It felt good to vent, but he probably overdid it. He had a mild headache by the time Dave signaled for him to stop and Matt was relieved—better to break the phone than his head.

"We're only going to practice one other move today," Dave said. "This requires a bit more skill. I usually don't recommend kicks to someone without significant martial arts experience because it's too easy for your opponent to catch your leg and put you on the ground. But I think we can teach you one effective kick.

"Assume your opponent is standing squared off to you and you're in a normal boxing stance." Dave took the position he wanted Matt to imitate. "You'll turn and pivot on your left foot, bring your right knee straight up, then swivel at the hip so that your leg's roughly parallel to the floor, and then stomp down at a forty-five-degree angle. You want to shift your weight the same way you do when throwing a punch, but the kick'll have a lot more power. Aim for above the knee and try to break whatever you hit. If you break it, you can run away."

"So, I'm going to break a guy's knee then run?" Matt raised his brows.

"You're going to put the guy down hard and then run away whenever possible," Dave said. "Let's practice."

Matt repeated the kick slowly at first, but he built up speed until it was a single fluid motion. The dummy's front legs bent back all the way to the floor with each of his last twenty repetitions. Learning the new moves wasn't too taxing and he'd only built up a light sheen of sweat.

"So, can I get good enough, fast enough? Matt asked.

"Depends." Dave shrugged. "You're in good shape and I can teach you how to fight dirty pretty quickly. But prisoners have a hell of a lot of experience fighting. You're supposed to be smart. You're going to have to maneuver yourself into fights you can win."

"Thanks," Matt said.

"No problem. If I'd been in that alley, I would've done the same thing you did. I'm hoping as a lawyer you know how to use the courts to stay out of prison. But lawyers' track records on staying out of prison aren't so hot."

Matt went home, showered, cranked up the air-conditioning, and crawled into bed.

The next morning, the insistent chime of the doorbell woke him. He rubbed sleep from his eyes with both fists. It wasn't even eight. He threw on a pair of shorts and a t-shirt and headed to the door, where Lisa waited with coffee and beignets.

"Hi," Lisa said. "I wanted to stop by and see how you were doing. I called last night, but you didn't answer." She cocked her head to the side, and her inky black hair spilled onto her shoulder.

"I was at the gym until late last night. And my fancy cordless phone broke. I now only have the fifteen-dollar one I keep in my bedroom to use when the power goes out. Mom bought it as part of the hurricane-preparedness kit she sent, which is also why she made me keep a landline." His excuse was thin; Lisa had also called his cell phone; but he wagered she wouldn't call him on it. "What's up?"

"Especially after our conversation last night, I wanted another chance to catch up with the elusive Matt Durant outside the office. At work, you fill every minute of the day. It doesn't leave much time for conversation and I was getting tired of waiting you out each night so I'd get a chance to catch up with you."

"Thanks for stopping by. I could use the company." Matt stood aside and Lisa beelined for the kitchen island.

"What are you doing to keep yourself busy with all this chaos swirling around you?" Lisa pulled the beignets out of the bag, the scent of fried dough mixing with the smell of chicory.

"I've been reading a lot," Matt said. "I need to head to the library. The job at Farrar Levinson was the first time I made enough money to be able to afford all the books I wanted. But now everything's up in the air, I should try to make money stretch further. And I don't want my mother paying anymore than she already has trying to keep me out of jail. Thomas is working pro bono, but we still have to pay the investigator and the bail bondsman."

"Do you need any help financially? I'm happy to give you what I can." Lisa sprinkled powdered sugar on her beignet, cut it with a knife and fork, blew on the piece and took a bite.

"No. I should be fine. The trial isn't that far away. I just want to ratchet down my spending. Any new information on the case?" Matt asked. He sat down on the faux wood stool, wondering, as he always did, if it would hold his weight.

"Nothing worth reporting," Lisa said. She took the stool to his right. "We know Buckner's in plea negotiations, but we don't know what kind of testimony he's proffered. We're just waiting to see what happens on that front. How are you holding up?"

"My days are turning into long stretches of boredom, interrupted by moments of sickening fear when I think about the trial."

"It's hard to believe you could have avoided this whole mess by running away and letting those assholes beat Buckner," Lisa said.

"Yeah, but somehow I don't think Buckner will be grateful enough to tell the truth, if it means years in prison."

"You're probably right," Lisa said. "Thomas puts the odds of him flipping at over ninety percent. But there's nothing we can do about that other than wait and see."

"So, do you have anything exciting going on in your personal life that could help distract me?" Matt looked at her over his LSU coffee mug.

"Not really. I have a blind date tomorrow night. One of my girlfriends from law school is setting me up with one of her coworkers. Given how my last blind date went, I don't have high hopes." She scrunched her nose as if she'd just smelled something foul.

"How'd your last blind date go?"

"Well, you remember the going-away party for that paralegal, Amanda?"

"I have some vague and blurry memories of that night."

"Well, I took the streetcar into work so I wouldn't have to drive after the party. That night, I also had a blind date with the son of one of Daddy's friends. This guy, Max, was a bad caricature of a used-car salesman. He even sold used cars, if you can believe it. But I figured I'd go out with him once to make Daddy happy.

"I called Max the night before to warn him I might be late because of the party. I was hoping he'd cancel, but he insisted on meeting at nine-thirty at a restaurant in the Quarter. At the restaurant, Max's attempts at conversation were so painful I had to brace myself with even more wine. Before the waiter finished serving the appetizers, I was in the bathroom throwing up."

"That doesn't sound like fun."

"The worst part was I felt guilty because I didn't make it through the entire date. So I agreed go out with him a second time."

"How'd the second date go?"

"That time I actually faked getting sick in the bathroom because the conversation was so bad. I decided I'd rather it get back to Daddy I was drinking too much than suffer through the rest of that meal."

Matt laughed. "Well, at least you know the guy you're seeing tomorrow night isn't a used-car salesman." He paused and asked, "Don't you?" raising his brows.

"Yes. But believe it or not, the fact that he's not a used-car salesman isn't enough to make my heart go pitter-patter. I can't think of a single Lifetime original movie or romance novel that describes the leading man as 'not a used-car salesman.' What about you? Any hot dates recently?"

"No. If I'd had any sort of date in sight, I wouldn't have gone to that club by myself." Matt sighed.

"Why'd you do that? It seems so out of character."

"Sometimes it's easier with strangers. I can rely on them to focus on the superficial and I don't have to see any of them again. It takes the pressure off."

"Why didn't you at least talk about these feelings about maybe being gay with a friend? You could have come to me. You know that, right?" Lisa placed her hand on Matt's bicep, and he resisted the urge to pull way.

"It's hard. I have a very narrow focus in life, which can really help me at work, but often creates problems everywhere else. Andrea had been my best friend for so long, and I obviously felt like I couldn't discuss it with her. Believe it or not, you're probably the closest friend I have other than her. And I felt it was too risky to discuss with anyone from the office."

"Why? There are gay professionals in New Orleans who are out of the closet," Lisa said.

"Sure, but they've figured out for sure they're gay. If I went to someone and described my uncertainty, attraction and confusion, and word leaked out, it could be even more damaging than saying I'm gay. Everyone who hates gay people would hate me too. And I don't even have any friends who are gay. For all I know, they might be mad at me for not knowing for sure."

"I think there's more to it than that," Lisa said. "It's as if you feel that people like and respect you despite who you are, instead of because of it. Why are you so afraid to let people know you're different from what you think they see?"

"I don't know. I think it's been far easier to go through life with a shell. A personality based on my intelligence and hard work. Hiding beneath the surface gives me shelter from the rest of the world. The problem is, as the years go on, I've found myself feeling less like a real person and more like a shell."

"And recent events must not have helped your trust issues," Lisa said, with her hand still on his bicep.

"I don't know." Matt rose and started pacing, while Lisa turned in her stool to face him. He continued: "There are a couple of ways to look at what's happening. One way is to see them as a sign that people generally aren't trustworthy. On the other hand, maybe they're a result of my inability to open up to those who I know are trustworthy. Intellectually, I knew I could have confided in you, my mother or even Andrea, but doing so would force me to admit I'm something different from what I'd pretended to be all these years. And I know I'm privileged and that my job and my Mom and my friends should make me happy, and I don't want to give any of that up. But I just never felt happy."

"Well, I'm here now and always happy to listen," Lisa said. "I also have a friend who'd like to meet you. His name is Eric Duval, and he's an associate with the New Orleans office of Jones Baker. Can you meet him tomorrow night for a drink or something?"

"I'm available, but I think a drink is a bad idea. Maybe we can meet for coffee. Why does he want to meet me?"

"He thought your mug shot was hot." She couldn't resist smiling.

"Bullshit," Matt barked, and stopped pacing.

"Eric has heard a lot about you from me. He's also gay. I think you'll like him a lot, and I think he can at least help you with a piece of what you're going through. And you shouldn't be so hard on yourself."

Lisa mussed his hair. "We all fake it sometimes. Most people just do it in a more obvious and social way. I learned that the summer I worked for my father selling furniture. Yeah, you laugh." Lisa rolled her eyes and continued, "I'd just finished a social-psychology class, and I combined some of those tricks with all those I'd learned from being a Southern woman. We often fake emotions in a healthy way. Everything from lying about how someone's new hairstyle looks to our sympathy over a friend's breakup with a lousy boyfriend. That doesn't make us all liars. Protecting yourself by projecting a different image isn't necessarily a bad thing. You just can't go through life only protecting yourself."

"I know," Matt said. "But I have a feeling that over the next few months I'll need the hardest shell I can develop." He looked down toward his dirty plate.

"Well, maybe. Or maybe if you let the jury see the real you, they'll like you. On a different subject, it sounds like you're still going to the gym. That's good, isn't it?"

"Yeah," Matt said. "It helps with the stress. And it helps me feel as if I might be more prepared if things go really bad."

"Don't even say that," Lisa said. "By the way, do you know that the way you revealed you'd taken up boxing was incredibly typical of you?"

"What you mean?" Matt glanced at her, puzzled.

"You didn't casually mention boxing in conversation. After you'd lost about ten pounds and gained a lot of muscle, people in the office began making comments. Then you said you'd been boxing for a year. Why on earth would you hide that from people?"

"I couldn't bear the thought of telling other people I was boxing until I'd gotten decent at it."

"Why on earth not?" she said, her brows furrowing and head tilted. "So what if you take up a new workout and drop it? Everybody does that. No one would have thought less of you."

"Because I would've been embarrassed. I would have thought less of myself."

"And that's the problem. I don't think you like yourself nearly enough."

"When you've been hiding yourself from everyone for a couple of decades because you're afraid they'll hate you, it's kind of hard to like yourself," he said.

"Well, we're going to make sure you have a chance to let other people know you and like you," Lisa said, rising from her stool and grabbing her bag. "And I have to get to work to help make that happen. Try to hold your head up and don't be such a drama queen. You don't have to take everything so seriously. We all like you so much because we caught glimpses of the real you, not in spite of them."

Chapter 5

As Matt walked into Tommy's gym the next morning, the overcast day pushed its way in, undaunted by the few overhead lights.

Dave approached after Matt finished warming up on the spinning bike. "I've been thinking more about your priorities," he said. "You know how to throw at least one decent punch. I think you might've knocked out that guy in the alley with your left hook, even if you hadn't been holding a bottle. Tommy also says you've got a pretty good boxing defense. There's not much more to that other than ducking, weaving and using the right stance and your forearms to block or brush off anything coming your way. But you need more than one good punch. So I thought we'd work on some different strikes without gloves."

Dave led Matt over to the dummy bag. "Let's start with a finger strike. You should have all four fingers pointed out, like the blade of a knife. Bend 'em slightly so that if you hit bone you don't break a finger. And aim straight for the eyes. Don't wimp out on me. Try it at fifty percent speed."

Matt lined up and threw the finger strike at the end of a left-handed jab, and then a right cross. He jammed his fingers on both hands and cursed, adjusting their curve, and threw again. His hand glanced off the side of the dummy's head. He tried once more and discovered the right motion.

Though Matt usually considered his jab a tool for probing distance that lacked stopping power, the combination he'd thrown in the alley might have been improved by adding a few jabs using his fingers as the business end. Those shots would have done more than just probe the distance and might even have incapacitated

Cutler. And he'd probably be in better shape now if he'd only blinded that idiot.

He kept working until he threw the strike almost as reflexively with his fingers open as he had with a closed fist.

"Let's mix it up now," Dave said. He nodded for Tommy to start the timer, and the red digits on the black box began ticking down the seconds from the three-minute mark.

"Throw your usual combinations and insert some finger strikes. Think of the combinations as building toward the finger strike. It'll work better if your opponent's expecting a closed fist." Satisfied with his progress when the buzzer sounded, Dave told Matt to stop.

"Let's talk about another strike you obviously wouldn't use in a boxing match," Dave said. "I want you to throw your jab and cross now using the heel of your palm. It's heavy, dense and more durable than a closed fist. Don't pull your fingers up too sharply, or you could create enough muscle tension in the wrist to sprain it. Just get your fingers out of the way. This strike works best against the nose and throat. Thrown hard enough from your arm and shoulder, it'll break a nose and can even crush someone's throat. I want to see jab and cross combinations with the heel of the palm."

The buzzer sounded again at the end of the thirty-second break to signal the start of another round. Matt gradually increased the tempo and power of the strike. It was less punishing than a bare-knuckled punch—he could unleash it without gloves or injury, at almost full speed and power. He finished by working through a series of combinations, including closed-fist punches, finger strikes and blows from the heels of his palms.

The timer buzzed again.

"Can you see how the speed and dexterity you've developed with the gloves is helping you with these combinations?" Dave asked.

"Yeah," Matt said.

"Remember, your hands are much lighter without the eighteen-ounce gloves you usually wear. You need to get the feel of throwing punches without that weight. Your hands'll travel faster, but since you're used to relying on the weight of the gloves for momentum, you'll lose some power. I want you to go through several rounds with the gloves and then without every time you train."

Matt nodded, inclining his head toward the floor and back up, but kept his gaze below Dave's eyes.

"Let's move to a part of the body you haven't used very often in the ring until now—the elbow," Dave said. "The most powerful elbow strike starts from boxing stance. Starting in the position from which you'd usually throw right cross, pop the elbow straight up and bring the fist back over your shoulder. You can catch someone by surprise if the person's expecting a right cross. But you need to close with your opponent because your reach is a lot shorter. So bring your right foot forward and step into it. You're going to be throwing hard and forcing the other guy back. You should be able to back him up and then fall back into your boxing stance pretty naturally."

Matt practiced the upward elbow strike for a couple rounds. He stepped forward with his back right foot, powered his weight through the blow, and sent the dummy swinging back. Jab, jab, elbow. Plenty of time. Each shot landed with a satisfying thwack.

"Now practice," Dave advised. "You should also try these strikes on the double-end bags to increase your speed and make them more automatic. I'll think about what we should go over next time."

"Thanks," Matt said.

Tommy approached, and a man behind him stepped out of the shadows. Tommy's companion was tall and bony with leathery skin and watery eyes.

"Matt, this is Frank," Tommy said. "I told you about him. He spent some time in the pen."

Frank brushed stringy brown hair out of his face before extending his hand to shake with Matt. His sneer perhaps aspired to a smile and displayed yellow teeth. "Hey. I understand you got yourself in some trouble."

"That about sums it up."

"When Tommy tol' me you'd be willing to pay me fifty bucks to talk about prison, I couldn't hardly believe it."

"I'll pay you," Matt said. "You have any advice?"

"Yeah. I know Dave's teaching you to win a one-on-one fight, but that's not what you really need to worry about. You need to worry about a group coming after you 'cause it can get real bad, real fast. I got cornered by a gang during my first week." Frank's eyes darted away.

"How do I keep that from happening?" Matt asked. He felt a chill, and it wasn't from sweat evaporating.

"Beat the shit out of another fresh fish right after you get there," Frank said, reconnecting with Matt's eyes. "Make sure it's not someone from a street gang 'cause you never know how connected they're gonna be on the inside. Pick somebody big enough to impress. Make it look harder to make you a bitch and easier to make him one. But it better be somebody small enough to beat. You lose that fight, it's all over. I know a guy who made that mistake. He got punked. A week after, he was wearing lipstick and tyin' his shirt up in a real cute knot. For the rest of his time, he—or she—got traded around."

"I'm a pretty good lawyer," Matt said, pressing his lips together and cocking his head to the side. "Can I offer to help inmates with their cases for protection?"

"Well, you're the lawyer, but seems to me most inmates have lousy legal cases. You really want to lose a gang leader's case?" Frank's weathered skin compressed his eyes into slits. "That could get you killed. If you beat up someone real bad the first day, some gang leader's gonna figure you useful for other things. And he may let you join if he thinks you're useful enough."

"And all I have to do is beat the shit out of some poor guy who other prisoners will then view as weak and victimize for years?" Matt asked, shaking his head slightly.

"Pretty much," Frank said evenly. "You need to do whatever you need to do to survive. Nobody else's gonna do it for you."

"Let me ask you a different question. I guess you know that the fight that landed me in this mess happened behind a gay club. That going to hurt me?" Matt gazed at Frank.

"You know the answer to that question," Frank said. "If they hear about it, they're gonna figure you're gay, which means they're gonna assume you like sex with men. And the cons are gonna figure that means any man. Another reason to beat the shit out of another fresh fish."

"Any advice on the specific gang leaders in prison?" Matt asked.

"Nope," Hodges said. "I got out more'n a year ago, so the leaders could of changed by now. Outdated advice could be worse than no advice. I read about you in the paper and I wouldn't want to be you." He shook his head. "Most people in the pen who shouldn't be there got convicted 'cause a witness lied. If you can cut a deal for anything less than life, you should take it."

After leaving Tommy's Gym, Matt started walking down Jackson Avenue toward the streetcar that would take him home. He spotted Joey Buckner across the street and froze. Stomach aching, he tasted bile in the back of his throat, but he tamped down on the panic to focus on the practical problem.

He needed to avoid that moron; he couldn't say anything that could be twisted to look like witness tampering, and—no matter what he said—he could throw Joey much farther than he trusted him. He didn't want Joey to be able to lie about any conversation to anyone else, but Joey caught his eye and started across the street.

Matt had seconds. Maybe Joey would leave him alone if he saw Matt on the phone. He pulled out his cell and called Lisa at the office. Then he had an idea. "Lisa, it's Matt."

"Hi. I really can't talk right now. I'm trying to get a brief out—"

"No, it's important. Joey Buckner's across the street and he looks like he's coming to talk to me."

"What? You can't talk to him. God knows what the prosecutor would do with that."

"I know, but I have to at least tell him I won't talk to him. I'm going to put my phone in my pocket and leave it on. Can you record the conversation with your voicemail?"

"Matt, this is a bad idea."

"Just do it. Please."

49

"Okay, but maybe I should grab Thomas."

"No time. Just do it." Matt eased the phone into his pocket, careful not to break the connection.

Joey weaved between the traffic—it didn't stop—and approached Matt. Daylight revealed a smattering of acne, a swollen nose and a pair of black eyes. His t-shirt strained and failed to reach his waist, where a tarnished silver stud poked out from a nest of brown hairs. The carpet didn't match the drapes. He wore the same jeans he'd worn that Friday night.

"How've you been?" Joey asked. He stood with his hands hanging loosely at his sides.

"I'm okay. Look, we really shouldn't be talking. I think both our lawyers would agree on that."

"Yeah, I figured as much, but I saw you across the street and wanted to see how you're doing. What's wrong with that?" Matt wondered if the nasal tone came from the injury, but perhaps it was nothing new and shouting over the music at Drink had just masked it. Joey looked down at Matt's feet as he shifted weight from one foot to the other.

"Nothing's wrong with that, but you know the prosecution could make it look like we met and talked about what happened in that alley before the trial."

"Yeah, I guess they could." Joey's features drooped further and he stared down at his own feet. At that moment, Matt knew Joey planned to sell him out.

"I also wanted to say thanks," Joey said. "You could have left me in that alley, but you didn't. I would have gotten hurt even worse than I did if you hadn't stopped those guys."

"Not a problem," Matt said. He worked to keep his expression neutral.

"I've been talking to my lawyer and he's been negotiating with the prosecutors. I guess you found out about the coke—"

"We really can't talk about this," Matt said, shaking his head. "You just need to tell the truth to your lawyer and the prosecutors."

"But you know I could go away for a long time," Joey said, his nasal tone rising to a high-pitched whine bordering on a squeal.

"This isn't the first time I've been caught with drugs. And it's not like it's my fault those assholes jumped us in the alley—"

Matt interrupted. "I have to go. We really shouldn't be talking and I have to meet someone."

Matt strode away and traveled a block before looking over his shoulder to make sure Joey was gone. He called Lisa.

"Did you get it?" he asked.

"I got it, oh, did I get it. You're on your cell phone?"

"Yeah."

"Call back to the firm on a pay phone if you can find one."

Matt located a pay phone and called Lisa; her secretary patched him through to Farrar's office.

"Are you on a pay phone?" Farrar asked.

"Yeah."

"Just in case, my name is Thomas Farrar and I represent Matthew Durant. We're having this conversation so that I can provide legal advice to Mr Durant. This call is privileged." Farrar paused.

"What do you think?" Matt asked.

"I think having Lisa tape that conversation was one of the riskiest things I've ever had a client do. But you're no ordinary client, and this tape is going to be huge."

"So you think you can work with it?" Matt asked.

"Work with it? It's fantastic! He admitted you didn't know about the cocaine, that you saved him in the alley, and that he was working to cut a deal that would keep him out of prison. I'll have Lisa do some research to make sure you're okay in terms of what you said to him. But you told him you shouldn't be talking about the case and asked him to tell the truth. Hard to see how that could be considered tampering."

"So this is good news?" Matt asked.

"You know it's great news. I'm in court all day tomorrow, but let's meet the next day at the office around one-thirty. I'm probably going to reach out to the prosecutor's office before then. I think we have a strong argument they should drop the charges based on the tape. Let's try to end this before it really begins."

"Wonderful," Matt said. A wide smile stretched across his face.

Chapter 6

The next afternoon, Matt left his house at four forty-five, allowing more than enough time to travel to his meeting—or date?—with Eric at PJ's Coffeehouse on Annunciation Street. He waited for the St Charles streetcar, which had plowed through New Orleans for over a hundred years powered by electricity, steam, horse and even mule. He marched the few remaining blocks with his usual long, brisk strides, which helped disguise and take the edge off his anxiety at his approaching, uncertain destination.

He tried to compose himself as he arrived, early as always, but as he entered his eyes darted around and betrayed his nervousness at taking another chance on whether someone was trustworthy. The coffee shop bustled with a cross-section of artistic types, students, businessmen and construction workers: a teenage girl with purple hair and a pierced brow was behind the coffee bar.

Matt spotted a young man with ginger hair, pale skin, freckles and a medium build already seated at a two-top tucked in a corner. He hoped it was Eric; if so, he was even earlier. "Are you Eric?" he asked, rushing into, "I'm Matt. Lisa's friend."

Eric rose, said yes, smiled, and put out his hand. He had a firm, self-assured handshake, and Matt responded with equal pressure.

"It's good to finally meet you," Eric said. "Lisa's told me a lot about you over the past year or so. What do you want to drink?" He nodded toward the coffee bar.

"The iced coffee," Matt said to the barista. Eric asked for the same, and they took their seats at the table for two.

"How are you holding up?" Eric asked.

"It hasn't been pleasant. I really can't talk about the case," Matt said. "And now the newspapers have announced to the entire state of Louisiana that I was in a gay bar." He caught himself: "No offense."

"None taken. I went to quite a few gay bars before deciding I was gay, and certainly long before I came out. People need time and space to figure things out, and I had that. And, when I came out, I was lucky. I grew up in New Orleans, but my parents are originally from the Boston area. Having a child come out of the closet is hard for parents, no matter how liberal they are. But mine at least believed they should be tolerant and supportive, even if they didn't always feel like it. Righteous New England liberalism runs deep in their veins. So, how are your parents handling things?"

"My father passed away years ago." Matt said automatically, using his stock answer for strangers, which created some distance from a pain sharpest many years ago and that had since receded to a tolerable ache.

"I'm sorry to hear that." The waitress brought their drinks, and Matt waited until she departed.

"My mother's tried to be supportive and has repeated she loves me unconditionally, which I already knew. I think she's just scared for me. And, of course, the issue of whether I'm gay has taken a back seat to the trial."

"The two issues seem pretty intertwined to me, rightly or wrongly." Eric took a sip, his lips pressing against a frosted glass displaying brown and tan patches overrun by whorls of white.

"True enough. I doubt those rednecks would have jumped us if we'd been taking a leak outside of Pat O'Brien's." Matt felt a pang at calling his victim—was he a victim?—a redneck. He fidgeted, reached for the milk, realized his coffee was as light as Eric's, and withdrew his hand.

"When did you first realize you might be gay?" Eric asked.

"Well, I've found men much more attractive than women ever since I was attracted to anyone. Maybe middle school? But I managed to distance myself from those feelings with work and booze—both acceptable in Louisiana—for most of my life."

Eric interrupted, "In Louisiana, booze may be more acceptable than work."

Matt couldn't repress a grin.

"Sorry," Eric said. "I couldn't resist. Keep going."

Matt continued, "I'd broken up with my girlfriend a few weeks before I went to Drink and I figured now was as good a time as any to explore and figure out whether those feelings were real. And I wasn't sure that I could ignore them much longer." He chewed on a fingernail.

"It's something that should be so simple for the outside world, isn't it?" Eric said. "Sexual orientation depends on which sex you're more attracted to. On its face, that shouldn't be terribly relevant to anyone you're not interested in or who's not interested in you."

"But complications quickly follow if you make what many consider a wrong choice," Matt responded.

"Yeah, and they're wrong about the wrong part and wrong about the choice part," Eric said. "I didn't experience much out-and-out discrimination but I had a few friends who became more distant, less available and faded from my life after I came out. My best friend didn't take it well. Things have never completely returned to normal between the two of us. But it gets easier, and I now have many new friends who accept me for who I am."

"What about discrimination at work?" Matt asked. "Don't you worry about that?"

"Well, the firm has a policy against discrimination based on sexual orientation, but you do worry about people discriminating in ways that are difficult to catch. I work at a huge firm and, if you get a less desirable assignment, you can drive yourself nuts wondering whether a partner avoided you because you're gay. But there's nothing you can do about what you can't find. So I just try to do my job well, and being happy helps me do it well." Eric shrugged, looked down at the table, and then back up at Matt with the corners of his mouth slyly tilted upward. "To change the subject to something more pleasant, how did flirting with another man feel?" Eric asked.

"It felt natural and incredibly exciting." Matt felt comfortable for the first time in a long while. "I felt as if I was crossing an invisible line between friendly banter and something else that's harder to define."

"Did you make out with this guy?"

"No. I enjoyed flirting with him, but I'm only now learning he wasn't quite my type. He has a belly-button piercing." Matt smiled.

"Was that in the report of some investigator you hired?"

Matt laughed. "Not quite."

"I kind of like piercing and tattoos, but I've avoided both myself because I'm not ready for that kind of commitment. But there's something about a belly-button ring on a guy that doesn't do it for me. Actually, for me, it's as a stop sign. It tells me not to go any lower." Eric smiled, showing white and evenly spaced teeth.

"I couldn't agree more," Matt said.

"So you've never even kissed another guy?"

"No."

"You still have a lot to figure out, don't you?"

"Yeah. And that's why I visited that gay bar by myself," Matt said, coloring. "I was attempting to stay under the radar. It obviously didn't work very fucking well," he finished with more vehemence than he'd intended.

"Well, you've got to kiss a lot of frogs to find a prince," Eric said.

Matt smiled despite himself and found his attention fully engaged for the first time since his arrest. He looked up from his coffee, his eyebrows raised and a gleam in his eyes: "Have you kissed a lot of frogs? Can I see you kiss one? This is Louisiana; we can probably find a frog pretty quickly. And it's not the Amazon, so most are probably not poisonous…" The corners of his mouth ticked downward at the last; after all, he'd found a poisonous Louisiana frog.

Eric, who'd been grinning throughout Matt's patter, looked at him steadily: "At least now you don't have to go running to strangers if you want to talk about your sexuality. I'm here to listen and I'll answer any questions I can. Or tell you how I figured out the answers for myself, even if we have different answers."

"I appreciate that. Sorry I'm not more fun, but I'm just frustrated." Matt picked up one of the paper wrappers that had encased their straws and began shredding it.

"And not just sexually, I'd imagine," Eric said. "I'm kidding. You're in an incredibly difficult situation. You know that Lisa thinks the world of you, right? And she has excellent judgment of other people. After all, she likes me." He smiled.

"I think she's pretty special, too."

"How's your case shaping up? Can you talk about it at all?" Eric asked.

"We're just starting to make some headway. I think folks are going to be pretty surprised when some facts come out about Buckner, for example. But I really shouldn't talk about it in any detail, especially here."

"Thomas Farrar's a great lawyer," Eric said. "I'm sure if anyone can show those assholes are lying, he can. I would have gone to Farrar Levinson if I'd received an offer there."

"What kind of law do you practice?" Matt asked.

"Real estate. It's not terribly exciting, but I enjoy being in the middle of the city's rebuilding efforts."

"How's it going?"

"Well, we've seen many businesses choose to stay and repair or rebuild rather than move out of town, which is good."

"It's good to hear that." Matt smiled uncertainly. Eric, seeming to recognize the hesitation and fear, gently took charge with unobtrusive questions. About an hour into the conversation, the pair ordered another round of drinks. They reached for the milk at the same time and their accidental touch set off a frisson that left Matt disoriented. He wasn't sure he could handle his immediate attraction to Eric in the midst of everything else.

"Hey, have you ever been to the Butterfly Garden and Insectarium?" Eric asked.

"No. Isn't that only for tourists and kids?"

"Well, maybe mostly, but I hear it's fun. I don't have any kids, and I don't think you do either. But there's no reason we should miss out. I can drive. Let's go," Eric said, rising from the table before Matt could answer. Only then was Matt startled to realize that Eric was shorter than him by a few inches.

The two departed in Eric's Land Rover, leaving Annunciation Street and going down Calliope Street to the Audubon Butterfly

Garden and Insectarium. They entered under a silver archway with a crosspiece that displayed *Audubon Insectarium* in black letters and supported the bronze outline of a butterfly.

They paid and began walking through the main hall, which had a black-and-yellow something-a-pede—it had hundreds or thousands of legs and Matt didn't stop to count—and an outsized blue crawfish hanging on the wall. Glass cases were embedded in the walls and interspersed along the hallway.

"Hey," Matt said, intrigued by an exhibit, "check this out."

Inside one of the cases, atop a slim branch, was a black bug with horns and a short snout, the insect equivalent of a triceratops.

Eric wandered over and looked in the case. He read aloud: "The male Atlas beetle is larger than the female and has specialized thorns on the head and thorax that males use to fight each other to gain mating rights with females." Eric rolled his eyes.

"Yeah, but look at this," Matt responded: "For its size, the Atlas beetle is one of the strongest animals on earth and can carry hundreds of times its own weight on its back."

"And I was hoping this field trip would lighten things up," Eric responded. "Come over here and I'll show you something actually found around here. That bug only lives in Asia."

Matt followed him over to the wall. Inside the case was a familiar insect that he didn't usually think of as an insect—a butterfly with a black body, orange wings veined and ringed in black, and white spots dotting both the body and wings.

"That's just a monarch butterfly," Matt said. "It's beautiful, but you see them all the time. I hardly notice them anymore."

"Well, I always enjoy seeing them," Eric said. "And have you ever heard any of this other stuff? As caterpillars, they eat milkweed, which is poisonous to most predators, and then their bright coloring as butterflies warns the predators of the poison. Most of the poison's in the wings, not the body, so if a predator goes for the larger, more fragile wings, it probably won't make it through the poison to kill the butterfly. And in the late summer and early fall—who knows, maybe just in the past few weeks—they migrate from the United States and Canada to Mexico—thousands of miles."

"All interesting," Matt agreed. "Sometimes I think kids learn more than most adults remember."

"By the way," Eric said, "you challenged me to kiss a frog, but will you eat an insect?"

"What?" Matt asked.

"They've got a café here called the Tiny Termite Café, where you sit at a table filled with bugs and can actually eat bugs."

"Why would people in New Orleans, one of the cities with the best food in the world, eat bugs?"

"So that's your excuse?" Eric asked.

"Yes," Matt said, "that's my excuse. But I think it's a pretty good one."

"You've got a point there. Even when you go to an LSU game and everyone's cooking in a parking lot, you can still get fantastic jambalaya, étouffée, and even alligator sausage. Are you an LSU fan?" Eric asked.

"I grew up in Louisiana. Do you really need to ask?"

"My parents have season tickets. Lisa and I were thinking about going to the game this weekend. Would you like to go?"

"I think my mother is going to come back down this weekend," Matt said. "She's insisted she's going to spend every weekend with me until the trial, even if it means making the three-hour drive down every Friday night and back again on Sunday."

"Not a problem," Eric said. "My parents have four tickets they aren't using. We had tickets growing up, but they dropped them when I went away to college. So we fell to the bottom of the list when we started buying them again a couple of years ago. We've only worked our way back to Section 409 in the end zone, but it's still a pretty nice view from up there."

"I'll have to check with Thomas about leaving town," Matt said, "but I'd love to go." He blushed at his word choice. "And I know my mother would enjoy it. When LSU won the national championship in 2003, she told me that it was the happiest day of her life. And to make sure I understood, she added that I might think she had forgotten the day she gave birth to me, and she said she wanted to make clear that she was happier when LSU won the national championship."

"If there's anything that binds this state together, it's that football team," Eric said. "I've got to go home and review some boring real-estate contracts. Do you need a ride?"

Matt declined, figuring he could take the streetcar home and not wanting to impose further.

"We have each other's numbers," Eric said. "I'm hoping to see you again this weekend."

"Absolutely," Matt said. "Thanks for the coffee. And it was a great idea to visit this place." Eric hadn't even reached out to shake Matt's hand, and Matt wasn't sure whether he was relieved or disappointed to avoid even the most casual touch.

Matt watched Eric go and his expression resumed its usually grave cast. He wondered if—with more courage—he could have created a life more like Eric's.

Chapter 7

Matt arrived at Farrar Levinson just after one and waited in the conference room for Farrar and Lisa. He gazed into space and drummed his fingertips—the nails were frayed and the cuticle on his ring finger a bloody mess—on a legal pad. He soon caught himself and threw the top page dotted with crimson into a trash can concealed beneath cabinets against a wall. Ten minutes later, Lisa showed up.

Another fifteen minutes passed, Farrar entered, poured himself a cup of coffee, and then sat and surveyed the two associates. "I just got back from lunch with the prosecutor, Andre Thibedeaux. He listened to the tape and thanked me for the information. He said he'd get back to me, but his initial inclination is to press forward."

"What?" Matt asked.

Farrar glanced down at the notes he'd made shortly after the conversation. "He said that the tape is ambiguous and it could show Buckner was just thanking you for trying to save him from arrest. He also said Buckner's statements didn't change Harlan or Rand's testimony."

"That's crazy," Matt said, slumping back in his chair. Much as he'd tried to keep his expectations low, he felt a pang of disappointment.

"I think so too, but Andre's obviously invested in the case and he's reached an opinion about what happened that night in the alley. I didn't press him. Sometimes when you're negotiating with prosecutors to drop a case, if you get into an argument you've lost. Better to let the tape speak for itself. We'll just have to give him some time and hope he comes around. It does give us some great ammunition for cross-examining Buckner, though."

Matt exhaled, triggering a sharp splinter in his side: so unless he wanted to give up, they'd be going to trial.

Farrar seemed to understand his disappointment. "Look," he said. "It does help our chances. Regardless of what Thibedeaux thinks, Harlan and Rand are going to be lousy witnesses. The investigator hasn't had enough time to dig up any real dirt on them, but I can cross-examine them just using the police report and make them look bad. I'm not worried about their testimony. I've been thinking about the opening statement and Matt's testimony. We have to figure out how to handle Matt's being gay."

"I'm not sure I'm—" Matt started to interrupt with his eyes fixed on the conference-room table.

Farrar steamed ahead: he stood, abandoned his coffee and started to pace. "No. No. No. As you know, the most important thing is that you tell the truth. And you could emphasize this was your first time and you were just experimenting, but I don't think that's going to cut it. The jurors would smell we were trying to avoid it and, even worse, might think you have something else to be ashamed of. You need to dig deeper into the reasons you went to that bar because it's more than just curiosity; lots of straight people never feel that curiosity; I'm more open-minded than most folks around here and I haven't." Farrar stopped pacing and gripped the back of the chair at the head of the table as he faced Matt.

"You need to figure out why you had that curiosity and then distill those emotions—yes, Matt, emotions—and present them in a straightforward way. I think jurors would be more uncomfortable with someone who might be gay, who doesn't fall into any category, than they would be with someone who is gay. I'm not saying you have to figure everything out, but you have to be able to explain to a straight jury why you went there alone instead of to a straight dance club."

Farrar pumped a closed fist to punctuate his next statement: "And then we're going to move on and make this trial about them. Their size, their numbers, and their violence."

He returned his grip to the back of the chair. "That's one of the reasons I wanted this meeting, even before Matt ran into Buckner.

Matt, I need you to be able to describe how and why you went to that bar without a trace of embarrassment. Can you do that?"

"Well, I don't know. I still have trouble talking about this stuff." Matt's weak statement didn't derail the freight train.

"Well, there's no reason we can't start talking through it now. You and Lisa are going to meet at least once a week and you're going to walk through why you went there and what happened that night. You know I don't script questions or answers for witnesses, but I need you to think about those things long and hard. You need to get used to talking about it.

"I don't want any hesitation or self-consciousness from you. They are the ones who should be embarrassed and humiliated. They are the ones who did wrong. And, for God's sake, you need to be able to look at the jurors as you describe what happened. You and Lisa can meet with some secretaries in the room if you need to get used to an audience." Farrar stared with Matt with a familiar intensity that had communicated the importance of many issues the firm had handled on behalf of other clients.

"Another thing. Matt, is there anything in your past the prosecution could use to indict your character? You know as well as I do the state normally wouldn't be able to introduce character evidence, but if we're going to say you're a saint, the judge could let them cross-examine you on anything in your past that could reflect poorly on your character."

"No, there's nothing." With effort, Matt kept his eyes locked with Farrar's.

"Come on." Farrar pumped his hand again several times, as if banging a gavel. "You were never in the wrong place at the wrong time during high school? You never bought pot? You were never arrested for public intoxication?"

"No."

"Well, you know I trust you, but our investigator is going to have to check your background anyway," he said. "All right, everyone now has something to do while we wait for results from the investigation. And that was the initial point of this meeting. Matt, walk me back to my office." Farrar turned to exit the conference room without waiting for Matt's answer, but then turned as another thought struck him. "I actually have an unrelated question for you. Do you still have all that legal research you did on insurance companies' positions on previous claims serving as admissions?"

"I do, but you might want to take a look at the insurers' briefs too. They argue that we inflated the special status admissions have under the law."

"Nonsense. You found that advisory committee's note to the Federal Rules of Evidence describing admissions as eligible for more liberal treatment. The note even describes how they are more trustworthy because the speaker is saying something against interest. That stuff was great. And I'd love to get in front of a jury how the insurance companies had taken the opposite position in another case to deny a claim."

"Yeah, but the insurers argue that law is kind of dated. They say that courts often find the prejudicial effect of those sorts of admissions outweigh their probative value."

Farrar pumped his hand again. "Come on. You found all of that great stuff about how it's classified as non-hearsay automatically under the Federal Rules."

Matt just smiled, shook his head and told him where he could find the case law and other authorities. After all, Farrar was the experienced trial lawyer, and Matt wasn't about to tell him how to try a case.

Matt spent the rest of the week trying to focus on the one thing he was looking forward to, the LSU game. Farrar had obtained permission from the prosecutor's office for him to attend. In the once-brief time between climbing into bed and falling asleep, he clung to the thought of the game. It was the one reason he wanted time to keep moving forward.

*

Saturday morning finally arrived. Eric showed up at Matt's house in his metallic-blue Land Rover. Lisa jumped out of the front and insisted that Mary take her place—then the four were off. Lisa's face was already flushed with excitement, and she smiled even more broadly when she saw Mary was carrying a tin of cookies. Matt knew Lisa would never allow herself to keep cookies in her own home, and she treasured the opportunity to eat a few without the guilt of purchasing or stocking them. Mary guided the conversation throughout the forty-five-minute drive along I-10 to Baton Rouge, avoiding mention of the upcoming trial or any accompanying unpleasantness.

Mary had finagled a parking pass from a friend for a space within blocks of the stadium. A rowdy crew of young men drove by in a pickup truck; those in the bed didn't even try to hide their beers. Matt guessed the price of a parking pass eliminated any objection the police might have. He didn't consider himself a talented enough lawyer to know whether drinking in the back of a pickup violated any open-container laws. Surprisingly, his legal education at LSU hadn't covered that topic.

Matt couldn't believe their luck. Eric had tickets to LSU's sixth game of the season; the top-ranked, undefeated Tigers would be playing the defending national champion Florida Gators. LSU's hard-hitting defense would be pitted against Florida's dual-threat quarterback, possibly the most talented offensive player to emerge in a decade.

Around six o'clock, the four walked to the stadium, which rose above every other building on campus and resembled the Roman Coliseum. The windows of the abandoned dormitories built into the stadium peeked out from between columns. Former governor Huey P. Long had used the dormitories as an excuse to raise additional funds to expand the stadium in the 1930s. Given the state's passion for football, Matt had always marveled that Long needed the excuse.

They joined the rush of the crowd heading up the concrete ramps, and "sweat-infused with bourbon" stood out as the most popular fragrance. Tiger Stadium held almost 93,000 people, or about half the pre-Katrina population of Baton Rouge. And 50,000 more fans remained camped outside, settling for mere proximity to the game.

He stepped out into the stadium seating and felt the familiar vertigo as he stared down at the field from ten stories above. The group took their seats, the teams warmed up and the other sections began to fill.

The teams finished their warm-ups and departed the field. Florida exited the visitor's tunnel and the crowd booed so loudly that Matt could feel the vibration in his breastbone. The announcer then bellowed, "It's Saturday night in Death Valley and here come your Fighting Tigers of LSU." The golden band from Tiger Land launched into "Hey Fighting Tiger," LSU rushed out of the tunnel, and the crowd roared.

As the team took the field, Matt picked out players whose brief autobiographical sketches he knew as well as any political or historical figures'. Number 18, Jacob Hester, was from Shreveport and was listed as six feet tall, but he couldn't really have been more than five foot ten. At 228 pounds, he'd willed his way from his position as an undersized high-school nose tackle to a Division I fullback and hadn't fumbled the ball in three years. Number 79, Herman Johnson, an offensive lineman, had been the largest baby born in Louisiana and, at six foot seven and 356 pounds, was now the largest Tiger to ever wear the uniform. Number 8, Trindon Holliday, was listed as wide receiver but mostly played back. Only five foot six and 160 pounds, it hardly seemed conceivable he could play football in the SEC, but he was the fastest player on the field. He'd broken school records for the 100-meter dash four separate times in 2007, had run 100 meters in as little as 10.2 seconds, and had been national runner-up in the NCAA Track and Field Championship.

Matt's eyes finally settled on one of the defensive tackles—number 72, Glen Dorsey—who, while playing one of the least glamorous positions, had convinced many he was the best player in college football. He came out of his stance with an explosiveness that reminded Matt of the enthusiasm Dorsey must have felt as a child when he was finally able to discard his leg braces and run with the other kids. His passion and determination anchored the team.

In the first half, Florida's star quarterback confounded the LSU defense by putting his team in a position to score a field goal, throwing for a touchdown and running for another. LSU made fewer tackles for a loss than usual. Not for a lack of effort—some of the hits were so hard Matt knew that, closer to the field, each sounded like a pistol shot.

LSU scored midway through the second quarter when LSU's second-string running quarterback powered his way into the end zone. Matt had trashed his voice sometime during the first quarter so he forced out a raspy, primal bellow and pounded his fist against Eric's. The touch sparked a longing that had nothing to do with the game.

The teams went into half-time with Florida leading 17–7. They then traded touchdowns in the third quarter: LSU scored first, but minutes later, Florida's quarterback threw a thirty-seven-yard touchdown pass to regain their ten-point lead.

Three minutes into the fourth quarter, Holliday made an improbable run, slipping and sliding among Florida defenders twice his size to gain sixteen yards. LSU's quarterback then connected with a receiver in the end zone, narrowing Florida's lead to three points.

With ten minutes remaining, the LSU defense took the field. Everyone in the stadium was on their feet. Matt, the players, and the fans knew their noise could disrupt the opposing offense's communications before each play. The LSU defense was working hard on the field and their followers responded enthusiastically whenever a player lifted his arms into the air to call for more noise.

Young African-American cornerbacks, some not yet old enough to drink, directed the predominately white crowd into a frenzy. Glen Dorsey was a 300-pound black man, and—though large black men had stricken white Southerners with fear countless times in Louisiana's past—more than 90,000 fans of both races now joined together to cheer for his success. The crowd's passion worked like alchemy, infused the defense with even more determination, and—by the end of the fourth down—the combination had brought Florida's offense to a halt.

The Tigers received the ball on their forty-yard line and Matt's mother reached out to grasp his hand. Her fingernails dug in and almost drew blood, but Matt welcomed the displacement of larger worries.

The offense then began grinding out the yards, relying on Jacob Hester every other play. Twice they faced the choice of whether to go for it on fourth down, and twice Hester barreled through the defensive line, until—with less than two minutes left in the game—he ran the final two yards and scored the game-winning touchdown.

The crowd erupted. But after being tackled in the end zone, Hester lay on the ground, apparently injured and with his helmet so covered in muck it couldn't be unsnapped. The crowd of almost 100,000 fell silent and players from both teams knelt with their helmets off. When Hester rose and trotted off the field, the LSU and Florida fans all applauded.

With a little over a minute left, Florida drove toward the end zone, but its quarterback's last, desperate heave was batted down in the end zone by a Tiger defender. When the clock reached zero, the stadium exploded in wild fits of glee and the crowd's rapturous outburst bent the laws of physics and threatened to shake the Earth.

Part II

Chapter 8

The first day of trial caught Matt off guard. Anxiety and endless strategy meetings had elongated and dilated the wait, slowing the trial's approach, but the suddenness of its arrival still left him gasping and nauseated.

Matt tried to draw comfort from the familiar routine of dressing for court; he slipped on fine wool pants, fastened the top button of his shirt, and knotted and adjusted his tie. But he had to buckle his belt a couple notches tighter than usual. The attempt to compose himself failed to unknot his stomach, but he was breathing normally again and could at least appear calm. Mary drove them down to Farrar Levinson's offices, where the defense team was assembling.

Donna pointed Matt and Mary to the conference room where Farrar sat working on his opening statement. Mary's left foot bounced on the floor, bringing the right knee atop it closer and closer to the table bottom until she jarred it. Farrar looked up, and she had questions. "How does jury selection work?"

"Well," Farrar said, "the prospective jurors fill out background questionnaires with information like their addresses, occupations and whether they're registered with any political party. The lawyers then have a chance to question each potential juror. If a potential juror is biased, a lawyer can ask the judge to excuse him for cause or because he's biased. The judge can theoretically excuse any number of people for cause. But the prosecution and defense also each have twelve preemptory challenges, so if the judge rejects a challenge for cause, each side can veto any twelve potential jurors for almost any reason. You just can't strike a juror based on race or sex."

"What kind of questions can you ask them?" Mary's foot had stilled, her hands clasped together on the table.

"Well, you ask questions to attempt to determine whether they have a bias obviously. But there are limits. They're not like witnesses. You know witnesses' identities weeks in advance and you usually have documents the witness created, or the testimony of others who were present for the same events. With jurors, figuring out whether they're telling the truth comes down to gut instinct. And you also don't want to ask questions that could make your case look unsympathetic or prejudice the jurors against you."

"It seems like a pretty random way of picking the people who are going to decide whether Matt's guilty." Mary frowned and furrowed her brow.

"It is. But it's better than anything else anyone can come up with." Farrar shrugged. "I'd hate to have a single judge who might have developed opinions about a case before trial making every factual finding."

"How important is jury selection?"

"I think it's pretty important, but you never really know whether a jury's good for you until they read the verdict." Farrar looked down and continued working.

Mary seemed satisfied for the moment and the three sat in silence for the next few minutes before packing up. Lost in thought about the trial, Matt snapped back into awareness again only when he found himself seated at counsel's table.

He'd sat at this same table six months before, when litigating a pro bono case on behalf of an indigent criminal defendant. Like countless courtrooms, there were walnut tables and fixtures, chairs with black-leather seats, and oil portraits of mostly white, male judges. But moving over a single seat altered his perspective—it amplified the adrenaline rush by at least a thousand and heightened his awareness of the presumed race, sex, and orientation of the judges on display.

Juxtaposed against the traditional courtroom was the electronic equipment the firm brought to every trial: a specially constructed black podium with room for binders as well as an oversized laptop flipped back into tablet mode; a projector for displaying images of transcripts, photographs and documents; and a massive white screen that sat opposite the jury box. The laptop fed into separate monitors for the judge, witness and lawyers so that documents could be viewed and any foundation for their admissibility established before being introduced into evidence and displayed to the jury. Each document or picture in the attorney's binder had a barcode; zapping the barcode pulled it up on the podium screen; the lawyer could then control whether it was projected on the monitors for the judge, lawyers, witness, jury or any combination; and the lawyer could then use a stylus to magnify and highlight the parts of the document he wanted to focus the viewers' attention on. The traditional Southern courtroom had ceded a quarter of its space to the deck of the Starship *Enterprise*.

Matt noticed that Judge Masterson's laptop was positioned to his left on the bench and realized for the first time that he was probably left-handed. Mary had always suspected Matt had been born left-handed. At some point before either could remember—perhaps to escape notice—he'd switched, but he'd accidentally learned to shoot pool left-handed and the left side of his body was stronger than the right.

The gallery and the jury box were already filled with prospective jurors who could have been chosen from a random section of Tiger Stadium. They were every size, shape and hue, but there were more blacks than whites. Some wore business-casual attire, while others had taken full advantage of the time off work to appear in jeans. Twelve would decide his guilt or innocence; if they found him guilty, they would also decide whether his punishment would be life imprisonment or death.

The judge's clerk intoned, "All rise. Court is now in session. The Honorable Robert Masterson presiding."

Judge Masterson strode toward the bench. He was in his mid-forties with black thick-rimmed glasses, bushy black brows, dark brown eyes and black hair that he either dyed or kept dark through sheer willpower. He towered over the courtroom before taking his seat. "We begin jury selection today," Judge Masterson said. "As is my usual practice, given that I've permitted the parties to submit questionnaires for the jurors, we'll dispense with questions to the larger group of potential jurors and I'll restrict you to questions of individuals. The first potential juror is James Dixson. Mr Dixson, can you please come up to the witness box?"

James Dixson, a heavyset man, wore a white button-down shirt with one flap of the tail peeking out from ill-fitting pants and a tie fastened too tight, framing his chins, red face and graying comb-over. He approached the witness stand and the judge's clerk administered the oath.

Judge Masterson turned to the assistant district attorney and said, "Mr Thibedeaux, do you have any questions for Mr Dixson?"

Thibedeaux rose. He wore a shiny gray suit remarkable only for its dullness, a red power tie, and had salt and pepper hair with the hint of a bald spot on his crown. Matt wondered how much time he'd spend looking at it during the trial.

"Mr Dixson, have you ever had a sexual relationship with another man?"

Dixson's face reddened further and he fidgeted.

"Objection, Your Honor. Request a sidebar." Farrar began to stand as he spoke; Matt started to rise also. As the defendant, he had the right to listen in on the sidebars, where the lawyers and judges discussed legal issues out of the jury's earshot.

"Overruled, no sidebar." Judge Masterson said, glancing at Farrar then turning back to Dixson. "Answer the question, Mr Dixson."

"I haven't."

"Mr Dixson, are you aware the state has charged Mr Durant with first-degree murder for killing Brian Cutler during an attempt to purchase cocaine?"

"I wasn't, but if you tell me that's what you're accusing him of, I believe you." Dixson looked earnest and eager to please.

"I'll represent to you the minimum prison sentence for first-degree murder is life imprisonment. Now if you hear a case that, to your way of thinking, calls for and warrants imposing a life sentence, will you give it?"

"Yes, sir." Dixson nodded.

"One of the defense's theories may be that the defendant committed manslaughter, which means a killing in sudden passion caused by severe provocation. I'll represent to you the minimum prison sentence for manslaughter is ten years. If you hear a case that, to your way of thinking, calls for and warrants imposing a ten-year prison sentence, will you give it?"

"Yes, sir." Dixon nodded again.

"Mr Dixson, are you aware the state of Louisiana is seeking the death penalty in this case?"

"Well, I figured you might when you said murder."

"Would you share with us your personal feelings, if you could in your own words, about the death penalty, and tell us if you could serve on this jury and actually render a decision that would result in the death of the defendant?" Thibedeaux looked at Dixon but then across the other potential jurors sitting in the gallery to gauge their reactions.

"I'm a big believer in the death penalty." Dixson looked away from Thibedeaux toward Matt. "If I find the defendant over there killed somebody while trying to buy drugs, I wouldn't have any problem voting for it."

"Your Honor, the prosecution has no objection to Mr Dixson."

Farrar rose. "Mr Dixson, have you or your relatives ever been a victim of any crime?"

"About ten years ago, me and my wife got mugged." Dixson looked steadily at Farrar, without blinking or breaking eye contact.

"Did the police ever catch who did it?" Farrar asked, then turned to survey the other potential jurors; Lisa had principal responsibility for monitoring their reactions; but their reactions to some questions were too important for only one lawyer to observe.

"No, sir."

"Can you explain how being mugged affected your attitude toward those accused of committing crimes?"

"Well, I'm not sure it did." Dixson glanced toward the judge and then back to Farrar.

"Mr Dixson, you said you've never had a sexual relationship with another man, correct?"

"Yes, sir."

"Mr Dixson, can you describe your feelings about somebody being gay?" Farrar again turned toward the gallery to survey the reaction of other potential jurors.

"Well, I'm a good Christian, and I think it's a sin. But I don't think it should be a crime neither. Lots of sins aren't crimes."

Farrar turned back toward Dixon and remained engaged this time, creating the impression that he cared not about how others in the gallery reacted to his follow-up question and any answer. "If you learned a witness in this case was gay, would it influence your evaluation of his testimony?"

"Well, I'd consider everything. And I guess that would include whether or not he was a homosexual. If someone would sin by havin' sex with another man, it might affect my decision on whether he'd sin by lyin'." Dixon locked stares with Farrar too; at this point the two might as well have been the only people in the room.

"Mr Dixson, is anyone in your family gay?"

Dixson crossed his arms over his chest. "No, sir."

"Mr Dixson, you testified that you would not have a problem imposing the death penalty if the prosecution showed that Mr Durant killed someone while purchasing drugs, correct?"

"That's right." Dixson nodded.

"If the judge instructed you that the involvement of drugs was only one of many factors you should consider in determining whether to vote for the death penalty, could you follow that instruction?"

"Yes, sir." Dixson uncrossed his arms. "I don't think killing someone during a drug deal necessarily means a person should get the death penalty. I'd consider everything—all the evidence."

"No further questions, Your Honor," Farrar concluded.

"The prosecution has a follow-up question, Your Honor," Thibedeaux said.

"Go ahead," Judge Masterson responded.

"Mr Dixson, if the judge instructed you to disregard a witness's homosexuality when considering the truthfulness of his testimony, do you think that you could follow that instruction?"

"Yes, sir." Dixson sat forward in the witness box as he spoke.

"Your Honor, may we have a sidebar?" Farrar asked.

"Sure." Judge Masterson motioned the lawyers and the court reporter toward the corner of the courtroom nearest the bench and farthest from the witness box. Matt hoped the potential juror couldn't hear them.

"Your Honor, the defense requests the court dismiss Mr Dixson for cause," Farrar said. His tone and gestures were emphatic but muted as he tried to conceal the substance of the conversation and the vehemence of his objections from Mr Dixson and the other potential jurors. "We believe he's biased against gay people, and that requires dismissing him in a case where an essential theme of our defense will be that Mr Cutler and his companions attacked Mr Durant and Mr Buckner because they thought they were gay."

"Your Honor, Mr Dixson didn't express a bias against homosexuality," Thibedeaux responded. He kept his voice low enough and his gestures restrained enough to show respect for the principle of hiding their discussion from the prospective jurors, but he spoke more loudly than Farrar. "He even said it shouldn't be illegal. Homosexuality doesn't have some special, protected status under the law that requires this court to strike every juror who believes it's sinful. Mr Dixson could just as easily have said that his religious beliefs are consistent with his opinion that an adulterer is less likely to tell the truth. That's just a juror bringing life experience to the table, not an expression of partiality. And Mr Dixson said he could ignore his religious views on homosexuality if instructed to do so."

"Mr Farrar, homosexuality is certainly not a protected class under the federal or state constitutions," Judge Masterson said. "And I'm going to keep any juror who says he can follow an instruction to disregard a witness's or the defendant's homosexuality. I'm not excusing Mr Dixson for cause."

"Your Honor, I want to exercise my first preemptory challenge to strike Mr Dixson," Farrar responded.

"Well, then, let's go tell Mr Dixson," Judge Masterson said.

Judge Masterson reassumed his place on the bench and turned

to Mr Dixson, "Thank you for coming in today. We won't need you to serve on this jury. Please return to the court officer running the jury pool, who will decide if you need to sit for another jury."

Farrar and Thibedeaux battled over the various potential jurors for the next few hours based on their best guesses of how factors as varied as socioeconomic background, appearance, education and accent might somehow affect the trial's outcome.

Several potential jurors said being gay was a sin. In response to Farrar's pointed questions, most of those testified that they'd be less likely to believe a gay person's testimony. Judge Masterson spent most of the voir dire working on his computer, but consistently perked up to deny Farrar's requests to excuse such individuals for cause.

Farrar exhausted his discretionary preemptory strikes and three jurors who'd expressed the view that being gay was sinful and would influence their evaluation of testimony were seated over his objections. And, all morning, every potential juror had heard little but gay, gay, gay.

Gideon Whitley took the stand midmorning. Whitley, a local painter, had earned moderate fame by painting pictures of his deceased cat in various shades of yellow. Whitley was tall, bespectacled, and unfortunately had the sallow complexion of one of his cats. He sat perched on the edge of his seat in the witness box. Matt also knew that Whitley was openly and outspokenly gay.

Thibedeaux began his questioning with the thought on the mind of every lawyer in the room. "Are you a homosexual?"

"Yes."

"Do you believe homosexuals are frequently the victims of violence because of their sexual orientation?"

"I'm not intimately familiar with the statistics, so I'd hesitate to use the word frequent." He paused. "But I do believe gay individuals are sometimes physically attacked because they're gay." Whitely eased back into his seat.

"Have you ever been physically attacked or threatened because you're a homosexual?"

"I've certainly been threatened, particularly when I was younger, but I've never been attacked."

"Would you be inclined to believe a homosexual's claim that he was physically attacked because of his sexual orientation?"

"I wouldn't be inclined one way or another based solely on his sexual orientation. I'd have to know more details." Whitley looked over at Farrar to measure his reaction. He obviously wouldn't mind sitting on this jury.

"In this trial, the prosecution will be seeking to prove Mr Durant committed first-degree murder by killing Brian Cutler while attempting to purchase cocaine. What do you think the minimum sentence should be for such a crime?"

"If I had to guess, I'd say that the minimum sentence should be twenty years."

"The prosecution in this case is seeking the death penalty. If the jury determines that Mr Durant committed first-degree murder and aggravating factors are present, Mr Durant will be taken to the Louisiana State Penitentiary. He'll be placed on death row and at some point will be taken to the death house where he will be strapped on a gurney, an IV will be put into his arm, and he'll be injected with a substance that will cause his death as a result of a jury verdict. Under these circumstances, could you vote to impose the death penalty?"

"I oppose the death penalty politically, but if the judge instructed me that if we reached certain factual conclusions the defendant should be executed under the law, I'd make the necessary findings without regard to my political opinions."

"No further questions, Your Honor," Thibedeaux concluded.

Farrar rose. "Do you know the minimum penalty for first-degree murder in the state of Louisiana?"

"No."

"And if the judge instructed you that the minimum penalty for first-degree murder is life imprisonment, would that affect your determination of Mr Durant's guilt or innocence?"

"No."

"Thank you. No further questions, Your Honor."

"Your Honor, may we have a sidebar?" Thibedeaux asked.

"Yes."

The attorneys and Matt followed Judge Masterson to the corner of the courtroom, where they huddled.

"Your Honor, I request that Mr Whitley be excused for cause," Thibedeaux said. "I believe Mr Whitley's testimony demonstrates a reluctance to impose the minimum penalty of life imprisonment."

"Nonsense," Judge Masterson said. "You asked Mr Whitley an open-ended question about what he'd consider a reasonable minimum penalty, but when Mr Farrar informed him of the actual minimum penalty, he said he'd be willing to follow the law and impose that penalty."

"Well, Your Honor, we'd therefore like to exercise a preemptory challenge and strike Mr Whitley," Thibedeaux said.

"Your Honor, we object," Farrar said. "Prosecutors can exercise their preemptory challenges for many reasons, but they can't strike potential jurors solely based on their race or gender. The United States Supreme Court has held such strikes violate a criminal defendant's rights under the federal Constitution, including the Sixth Amendment and the Fourteenth Amendment's Equal Protection Clause. As you just explained, the prosecutor hasn't offered a legitimate reason for striking Mr Whitley."

"I said the prosecutor hadn't offered a legitimate reason for excusing Mr Whitley for cause," Judge Masterson said. "You and I both know preemptory challenges are very different. You just acknowledged they can be exercised for a wide variety of reasons. You also know as well as I do the courts have treated potential discrimination based on race and gender very differently from sexual orientation. The United States Supreme Court has ruled race and gender are suspect classifications under the Equal Protection Clause of the Fourteenth Amendment. There's a very strong presumption that using those criteria is illegitimate and unconstitutional. But the Supreme Court has made also very clear that distinctions based on sexual orientation aren't suspect classifications. There need be only a rational relationship between distinctions based on sexual orientation and the government interest being advanced."

"Your Honor, we'd respectfully submit that a preemptory challenge based on sexual orientation is without rational basis and hence unconstitutional," Farrar argued. "In *Romer v. Evans,* Justice Kennedy's majority opinion striking down a Colorado constitutional amendment stripping gay people of employment protections explained the government must identify a rational link between the classification adopted and the goal obtained. We don't think there's any such rational link here."

"Your Honor," Thibedeaux responded, "we want to exercise a preemptory strike to dismiss Mr Whitley for the same reason we requested you excuse him for cause. We don't believe he'll objectively and fairly consider Mr Durant's guilt in light of a minimum sentence that he considers unreasonable. I also have serious misgivings about whether he'll really be able to ignore his political beliefs about the death penalty."

"I don't buy those as reasons for excusing Mr Whitley for cause," Judge Masterson said, "but I do think those reasons can support the prosecution's exercise of a preemptory challenge. I also find that the entire framework for objecting to a preemptory challenge that may have been exercised on the basis of gender or race doesn't apply to sexual orientation. Unless sexual orientation is a suspect classification, we don't get to the point of examining the prosecutor's motives. It's like any other reason for exercising a preemptory challenge and entirely within the prosecution's discretion. Mr Thibedeaux may exercise his preemptory challenge and Mr Whitley will be excused."

"Your Honor, to preserve the record, I'd also like to make the argument that classifications based on sexual orientation should be considered suspect classifications, and the exclusion of Mr Whitley violates my client's federal constitutional rights, as well as his rights under the Louisiana state constitution," Farrar said.

"You can consider the argument preserved, Mr Farrar, but you know as well as I do it doesn't fly," Judge Masterson said. "The Louisiana constitution prohibits gay marriage, and the Louisiana Supreme Court has upheld the constitutionality of that amendment. There's no possibility homosexuality is a protected class under the Louisiana state constitution. And the United States

Supreme Court has certainly never recognized homosexuality as a suspect classification. It's applied rational basis review to state classifications based on sexual orientation, as you recognized a few minutes ago. Mr Whitley can go home."

Jury selection ended shortly before lunch. Only one juror had a gay relative—an estranged lesbian daughter. Farrar ordinarily wouldn't have taken that juror, but he was out of preemptory strikes. Matt hoped at least some connection to a gay family member could help his cause.

Any jury expert or experienced lawyer would have judged Thibedeaux the winner in the battle to fashion the jury. The twelve individuals who would decide Matt's guilt or innocence had been chosen.

Judge Masterson excused the lawyers and jurors for lunch. His clerk had set aside a small conference room at the rear of the courtroom for the defense team to use during the trial. A messenger from Farrar Levinson had delivered sandwiches, chips, fruit and soft drinks. After the courtroom cleared out, Farrar and the defense team entered the conference room. Farrar shut the door behind them but, as Matt sat down, he wondered whether it was thick enough to keep their conversation private.

Mary was furious. She remained standing, put her hands on her hips, and began tapping her right foot. Matt always tried to steer clear when that foot started tapping, but the room was small, and he suspected it wasn't him she was angry at. He was right.

"What just happened in there?" she asked Farrar.

"We picked a jury."

"I thought you told me lawyers can't strike jurors based on sex? Everyone in the state knows Gideon Whitley is gay."

"That's exactly what I argued to the judge, and he said sexual orientation isn't sex."

"That jury also has several people on it who testified they thought being gay was a sin." She pursed her lips together. "They even said they'd be less likely to believe a gay witness. How did you let that happen?"

"I didn't just let it happen. Matt was standing right next to me when I objected to the judge. He ruled they could serve because they said they could follow instructions to disregard a witness's sexual orientation."

Mary's eyes narrowed. "And did you even think to question these jurors about how their religious beliefs would influence their opinion of a witness who testified he'd had too much to drink?"

Farrar blanched. "That didn't occur to me."

"Well, is it too late now?"

"Yeah. I mean, I can make an objection, but the judge isn't going to let me question them again."

"Mom, he did the best he could, and he did a pretty darned good job."

"You don't even start, Matthew Durant. If you hadn't gotten so drunk, we wouldn't even be here." Matt jerked back in his seat as if he'd been slapped.

Mary's foot stopped tapping, her expression softened, and she walked over to Matt. "Honey, I'm so sorry. I don't know what came over me. You know your drinking drives me crazy, but I didn't mean to snap at you like that." She reached out and pulled Matt's head into her side. She turned to Farrar. "I'm sorry about snapping at you, too. I know you're going out of your way to help us. That judge just made me so mad." She began tapping her left foot, which was located farther away from Matt's body. That was a first.

"It's okay," Farrar said. "I can only imagine what you must be going through. We're going to have to discuss preliminary jury instructions with the judge after lunch, and I don't think I'll get to my opening today, but I need to prepare anyway. Let's just focus on what we can do, which is put on a hell of a case."

Mary nodded.

The lawyers finished wrangling over the proposed preliminary instructions around three o'clock and Judge Masterson announced the prosecution could deliver its opening after a fifteen-minute break. After the break, Judge Masterson invited Thibedeaux to begin.

Thibedeaux drew himself up to his full height and fastened

the top button of his jacket. Matt concentrated on regulating his breathing and maintaining a blank expression. Regardless of who addressed the jury at any given moment, they'd always be scrutinizing him for even a hint of a reaction.

"Ladies and gentlemen, I'd like to begin by echoing Judge Masterson's thanks for your service. I appreciate many of you are being forced to take time away from your jobs and families, which may or may not be a hardship." Thibedeaux smiled, and several jurors grinned in response. "But a man has been murdered and your help, participation and sacrifice are necessary to bring this killer to justice. The state of Louisiana needs you. Although an important case, I don't believe that you'll find it particularly difficult. The evidence will show that on Friday night, September 7, 2007, the defendant Matthew Durant decided to go out drinking in the French Quarter. And he drank plenty.

"Mr Durant's blood-alcohol content that night reached at least 0.18, which is over twice the legal limit for driving. But Mr Durant decided not to limit himself to alcohol. Mr Durant met Joey Buckner, an admitted and convicted drug dealer, in a bar named Drink on Bourbon Street. Mr Durant had at least $800 in his pocket when he met Mr Buckner, and Mr Buckner had over four grams of cocaine in his possession. Mr Buckner will testify that Mr Durant was already intoxicated when he arrived at Drink and that Mr Durant and he shared several additional adult beverages after his arrival. Mr Buckner will also testify that he asked Mr Durant if he wanted to purchase any cocaine, and that he and Mr Durant then ducked out the back door so Mr Durant could buy cocaine from Mr Buckner.

"The evidence will also show three men then happened on them in that alley. Those three men were Brian Cutler, John Harlan and Don Rand. When they saw Buckner and Durant huddled together as they left the club, they suspected that it was a drug deal. And they took action. These men refused to sit idly by and allow Mr Durant to commit a crime on the public streets. The evidence will show Brian Cutler and John Harlan grabbed Mr Buckner, the drug dealer, and restrained him. When Mr Buckner attempted to escape, Don Rand, who as you'll see is a fairly large man, punched Buckner in the nose. That ended Mr Buckner's escape attempt. But while the three men detained Mr Buckner, Mr Durant had started to move down the alley toward them. And so Mr Cutler walked out to meet Mr Durant. And when Mr Durant reached Mr Cutler, he swung his beer bottle at Mr Cutler's temple. And he swung that beer bottle a second time, killing Mr Cutler. The evidence will show that Mr Durant killed him in cold blood so he could avoid being arrested for buying drugs."

Several jurors were wide-eyed. Knowing that you'd been selected to serve on the jury for a murder trial was different from hearing the sordid details.

"Now, you may be thinking to yourself: that sounds pretty simple. Well, I think what happened in that alley is pretty simple. There were only five men in that alley and all of them, other than Mr Durant and his victim, will take the witness stand, swear to tell the truth, and explain that's what happened.

"But the defense will try to wriggle out using a few arguments. First, the defense will attempt to show Mr Buckner isn't a reliable witness. Mr Buckner is a convicted drug dealer, and the state of Louisiana agreed to give him a reduced prison sentence in exchange for his cooperation. Mr Buckner will still go to prison, but not for as long as he would've gone for if he hadn't agreed to testify. And I'll be the first to admit Mr Buckner is no angel. After all, my office is sending him to prison for a year for dealing drugs. Unfortunately, it's a fact of life that criminals are the most frequent witnesses to crimes, particularly crimes such as selling drugs, where everyone involved is a criminal. And criminals rarely volunteer to give testimony that will send them to jail out of the goodness of their hearts. But you can look further than those simple facts of life to find indications that Mr Buckner is telling the truth. As you'll see, Mr Buckner didn't provide us with corroboration about the events that Mr Rand and Mr Harlan had described until after he'd retained a lawyer. And that lawyer summarized Mr Buckner's description of what happened that night after Mr Buckner had been released on bail. The

Louisiana public defender's office was representing Mr Buckner when he told us what had happened in that alley. Those fine folks have a lot of integrity. They'd never knowingly pass along a lie to us. And, as you'll see, there's absolutely no reason to believe they did so in this case."

Thibedeaux's endorsement of the public defender's office was objectionable, but Matt agreed with Farrar's decision to remain silent. It wasn't worth drawing the jurors' attention to it.

"You'll see other evidence Mr Buckner is telling the truth. Mr Durant's lawyer, Mr Farrar, will no doubt spend a lot of time questioning Mr Buckner about his prior criminal conviction. But he may gloss over what he wants you to consider an unimportant detail. Mr Buckner has never been convicted of a violent crime. And Mr Buckner will tell you the defendant's brutality shocked him, and that's part of the reason he's testifying in court against him."

Matt saw a couple of jurors shift in their seats and eyes darted toward him then away uncertainly. He supposed they were wondering at the degree of violence required to shock a drug dealer and ex-convict.

"Perhaps most importantly, though, is that you don't just have the testimony of Mr Buckner," Thibedeaux continued. "Mr Harlan and Mr Rand will also testify. And they'll explain that they were trying to break up a drug deal and summon the police when they approached Mr Durant. And Mr Durant, a highly educated lawyer who made really good money working for Mr Farrar's law firm, realized how much he had to lose from a drug conviction. And when faced with the prospect of losing his comfortable job and way of life, Mr Durant brutally attacked Mr Cutler. Mr Durant wasn't satisfied with throwing a simple punch. He instead used his beer bottle as a weapon to crush Mr Cutler's skull. And Mr Durant hit Mr Cutler with that beer bottle not just once, but twice." Thibedeaux swung his own left arm in a slow motion with the confidence of one who has practiced in front of a mirror. "Mr Durant did *not* act in self-defense, as the defense will claim. Mr Durant's testimony will be contradicted by every other witness to the events of that night. Mr Durant killed Mr Cutler in an attempt to flee and cover up the fact he was buying cocaine. Mr Durant failed in his first attempt to escape justice. You should make sure the defendant fails again in his *second* attempt to escape justice."

Thibedeaux gazed steadily at the jurors for several seconds, as if daring them to aid a felon in his escape.

Chapter 9

That night, Matt dreamt he was back in law school.

In the dream, he woke afraid he was late for a class, felt an itch beneath the covers, and drew his left leg up. A searing pain shot up from his foot as it brushed against the sheet and he looked down to see scarlet bumps oozing yellow pus. The flesh was cracked like hard-baked dirt and he gagged on the sour, rotting odor. It was leprosy.

He was in a doctor's office. The doctor confirmed his suspected diagnosis and asked him if he had a girlfriend. When Matt told the doctor about Andrea, the doctor said she'd need to be told immediately because it was highly contagious. He added little could be done to stop the short-term spread of the disease, but they could hope to kill the infection over time.

Matt wandered in a daze through routine law-school activities: attending classes, making phone calls to clients for the legal clinic and studying. But throughout the day he was acutely conscious of his hidden rash. He wondered how long he could hide it.

Matt woke in his actual bed in New Orleans, the dream interrupted before disclosure. His sheets were soaked with sweat and the alarm clock showed it wasn't even five. He certainly wouldn't be late for court. A single cup of strong coffee banished his grogginess, but he remained shaken.

Matt and Mary arrived at court by eight o'clock and found Farrar reviewing his opening statement.

After what seemed like an interminable wait, Judge Masterson took his seat on the bench around nine. "Any new business we need to attend to before we bring in the jury?" he asked.

Farrar stood. "Your honor, I just wanted to renew our objection to the composition of the jury. We believe seating the three jurors who testified they believe being gay is a sin and allowing the prosecution to strike Mr Whitley were independent violations of our client's constitutional rights."

"Your objection's noted and I'm seating this jury over that objection," Judge Masterson said. "Anything else? No? Please bring in the jury."

As the jury entered the room, Matt surveyed the twelve people culled from a larger, more representative and randomly selected group. Eight of the jurors were white and the jury questionnaires revealed that most were from what counted as the more urban areas of Louisiana in and around New Orleans—according to conventional wisdom urban was good, but white was not. And none of the jurors were gay. Matt—as a lawyer—would have been troubled about their predispositions; as a defendant, he was terrified.

Farrar remained at the podium as the jury entered. He'd worn an expensive suit, as usual. As he flipped a page in the legal pad in front of him, his left cuff slipped up to reveal his sole concession to the sensibilities of the average citizen: a plain steel watch had replaced the one he ordinarily wore to the office, which was solid gold.

"Thank you, Your Honor. Ladies and gentlemen, I'd also like to thank you for your service. As you well know, Mr Durant's life is at stake in this trial, so I'd like to express my appreciation in advance not simply for the time it will take, but also for the conscientious way in which you'll consider the evidence. The evidence will show Mr Durant did not go into that alley to purchase drugs." He surveyed the jury before glaring at the prosecutor's table.

"The prosecutor's claim that he did so is completely inconsistent with the character Mr Durant has demonstrated over the twenty-eight years of his life." He looked back at Matt before turning again to address the jury. "Much of the evidence Mr Thibedeaux failed to mention will establish that Mr Durant was forced to kill Mr Cutler to save himself and Mr Buckner. Mr Durant is a fine young man who after the death of his father decided to attend law school in Louisiana rather than going to an out-of-state school because his mother and he couldn't afford the pricier tuition. After law school, Mr Durant worked for an appellate judge who will testify that Mr Durant displayed the highest ethical standards. So how did Mr Durant wind up here?" Farrar asked with upraised palms, widened eyes and raised eyebrows.

"The evidence will show Mr Durant had recently broken up with his girlfriend of many years. He was experiencing confusion about his sexual orientation. Mr Durant thought he might be gay. And so Mr Durant decided to go to a gay bar to explore those feelings a bit more. He was confused and embarrassed and afraid of how his friends would react. I think after hearing the testimony of Mr Durant's mother and his former boss, you'll realize he could have confided in them. But Mr Durant didn't feel that way on the night of September 7, 2007. Now, Mr Durant had been drinking when he arrived at the bar on that Friday night in September. But the evidence will show Mr Durant had never met Mr Buckner before. And when Mr Buckner struck up a conversation with Mr Durant, he responded just as anyone would in a restaurant or bar. Mr Durant didn't know Mr Buckner was a drug dealer, and he never had any intention of buying drugs. And you will see persuasive corroboration of Mr Durant's testimony. An expert performed a drug test on a hair sample from Mr Durant and he'll testify that test showed the odds that Mr Durant has used any illegal drug during last six years are less than one tenth of one percent. The notion that Mr Durant went into that alley to buy drugs from Mr Buckner is preposterous." Farrar's right hand bobbed up and down for emphasis, fingers relaxed to avoid distracting from his words with any finger pointing.

"Mr Durant will testify that Mr Buckner suggested they go out into the alley to relieve themselves because of a long line for the restroom. And Mr Durant will further testify that's when Brian Cutler, John Harlan and Don Rand accosted them in that alley. Mr Rand threatened, and I quote, to 'beat the shit out of a couple of faggots.'" Farrar spat out the last word. "When Mr Rand takes the stand, take a look at the size of the man. He's well over six foot tall and weighs over three-hundred pounds. And Mr Rand didn't just threaten. Mr Rand hit Mr Buckner and you'll see from medical records that Mr Rand pulverized his nose. Mr Buckner required reconstructive surgery to breathe properly." Farrar took a deep breath himself.

Matt hoped the jurors were reconsidering any assumption that he would be the most violent person in the courtroom.

"After Mr Rand bashed Joey Buckner in the face, well, Mr Durant had a choice. He could attempt to flee, or he could attempt to stop Mr Rand. You'll see pictures of that alley. It might have been at least theoretically possible for Mr Durant to turn and run. But Mr Buckner couldn't run. Mr Rand had injured him too severely. So instead of abandoning him, Mr Durant had to intervene to prevent further violence. And, faced with three men in a dark alley, Mr Durant did hold on to his beer bottle as he walked forward to confront them." Farrar held his left hand up as if grasping a bottle, then raised the right and turned both upward. "I don't know why anyone with any sense would let go of the bottle in that situation. Mr Durant will testify that, as he approached the three men, Mr Cutler broke off to confront them. And when Mr Cutler broke off, Mr Durant saw the blade of a knife. Again, you won't have to rely solely on Mr Durant's testimony. You'll see a digitally enhanced photograph taken from an automated teller machine across the street. Now, Mr Cutler's back is to that camera as he approaches Matt, but you'll see the photographs show the bright flash of a knife in Mr Cutler's hand. And only when Mr Cutler approached with that knife, after the three men in an alley had caused Mr Buckner severe injury, did Matt Durant swing that beer bottle. And we all now know that swinging that beer bottle had terrible consequences." Farrar looked back at the prosecution, implying that among those consequences were Matt's arrest and trial.

"Mr Thibedeaux spent a good deal of time talking about the number of witnesses he has, but you should also consider the quality of their testimony. As Mr Thibedeaux admitted in his opening, Mr Buckner has a strong incentive to lie. His prison sentence of potentially five years will be reduced to only one year, depending on his testimony in this courtroom. Mr Thibedeaux emphasized Mr Buckner has never been convicted of a crime of violence." Farrar shook his head and remained focused on the jurors..

"Well, that's not what you need to decide about Mr Buckner. You'll need to consider whether he's lying to save his hide. And you should consider the evidence of Mr Buckner's criminal record when doing so." Farrar looked back over at the prosecution table but kept the jurors within his line of vision. "Mr Thibedeaux also neglected to mention an important piece of evidence that shows Mr Buckner is lying. A couple of weeks ago, Mr Buckner ran into Mr Durant on the street. And you'll hear a tape recording of that conversation. You'll hear Mr Buckner thank Mr Durant for saving him in that alley, admit Mr Durant didn't know he had cocaine and admit he's planning to sell Mr Durant out. And Mr Durant asks only one thing of Mr Buckner. To tell the truth. I think you'll be able to determine pretty easily that Mr Buckner ignored Mr Durant's plea. As for the testimony of Mr Harlan and Mr Rand, the evidence will show that neither is, as Mr Thibedeaux put it, an angel." With that, Farrar looked at Thibedeaux with disdain before re-engaging the jury.

"And you'll see the detective who arrived in the alley immediately after the incident did something unusual when interviewing them. Not only did he interview them at the same time, but he also suggested at the beginning of the interview that Mr Durant had been buying drugs from Mr Buckner. In other words, the detective offered two men potentially guilty of battery, and certainly angry about the death of their friend, an excuse for their criminal conduct and a way to punish Matt Durant. Don't allow these two men to use the judicial system to punish Matt Durant further for defending himself and Mr Buckner. Thank you."

Matt struggled to suppress his smile while the jury remained in the room. As distasteful as it had been to suffer through Thibedeaux's opening, Farrar's gave him hope.

"Thank you, Mr Farrar," Judge Masterson said. "Let's take an hour-long lunch recess before the state calls its first witness. I'd like to remind the jurors not to discuss the case during the break. I'll see you all in an hour."

Farrar busied himself with editing his cross-examination for the prosecution's first witness. The rest of the defense team had lunch in the courthouse cafeteria and labored to follow the judge's standing instruction to avoid discussing the case in public. They returned to the courtroom well before one.

"All rise. Court is now back in session," Judge Masterson's clerk said.

"Who do you call as your first witness?" Judge Masterson asked Thibedeaux.

"The prosecution calls Detective Scott Jones to the stand."

Detective Jones folded himself into the chair in the witness box. He testified on direct examination that he'd been a detective for fifteen years, had interviewed thousands of witnesses, and had followed his usual protocol in handling the crime scene and interviewing the witnesses. On cross-examination, Farrar scored several points: Jones admitted he'd interviewed Harlan and Rand together, he'd informed them at the outset of the interview that he'd found cocaine in Buckner's possession, and that he'd done so despite the New Orleans Police Department Manual's recommendation that officers obtain witnesses' unaltered recollections before disclosing important facts.

Judge Masterson addressed Mr Thibedeaux. "Please call your next witness."

"The state calls Donald Rand to the stand."

Whispers in the gallery faded to silence, as Rand lumbered toward the witness stand, sat and then swore to tell the truth, the whole truth and nothing but the truth. He filled the witness box as he moved his chair back and shoved the microphone stem forward to make room for his bulk.

Thibedeaux rose to begin his examination. "Mr Rand, have you ever seen the defendant, Matthew Durant, before today?"

"Yes, sir. I saw him on the night of September 7 in an alley in the French Quarter." Rand's voice boomed and he pawed to push the microphone farther from his mouth.

"When you first saw Mr Durant, what was he doing?"

"Well, I was cutting through a back alley with two friends, goin' from bar to bar in the Quarter, and we saw Mr Durant and that other guy, Joey Buckner, in the back alley. The two huddled together and then they went and started taking a leak."

"What happened next?"

"Brian Cutler, one of my buddies, said he'd bet they were doing a drug deal. So we went up to them and told them we wanted them to stop and we were gonna hold them until the police came."

"Why did you decide to intervene and report Mr Durant and Mr Buckner to the police?"

"I grew up in a rough neighborhood. There were lots of drugs in my high school. I had friends end up in jail, and a couple even died from overdoses. I hate drugs and I hate the thought people can buy and sell drugs out in the open like that."

"What happened after you told Mr Durant and Mr Buckner you were going to get the police?"

"Well, Brian and John grabbed Joey Buckner and he tried to squirm away. Their hands slipped and I hit Joey Buckner in the face to stop him from runnin'."

"What happened next?"

"This Durant guy, he started toward us. Brian dropped one of Buckner's arms and went out to meet him to make sure he couldn't get away. When Brian walked up to Durant, the guy just went nuts. He threw a bunch of punches real fast. Then he stabbed Brian in the side of the head with a beer bottle."

"Did Mr Durant stab Mr Cutler in the side of the head with the beer bottle more than once?"

"He stabbed him a couple of times."

"What happened after he stabbed him?"

"Brian fell to the ground. I tried to see what I could do for him, but I could tell it was probably too late. There was blood everywhere and his head had a huge dent in the side. It looked like this Durant guy had broken part of his skull. I yelled for an ambulance, people came running and then the police showed up." Rand's expression remained serious but impassive. Matt imagined the jurors must be deciding whether Rand was an honest man hardened by a rough life or just lying, but their expressions too betrayed no emotion.

"Have you since learned Mr Durant hadn't actually purchased the drugs from Mr Buckner?"

"Yeah, but I also read that he had a bunch of money, and this Buckner guy had cocaine on him."

"Objection. Move to strike. Hearsay and speculation," Farrar said.

"Sustained," Judge Masterson ruled. "Jurors, you should disregard the last question and answer."

"Did you see Mr Cutler pull out a knife as he approached Mr Durant?"

"No. Brian didn't have no knife."

"Do you believe that Mr Durant was attempting to defend himself when he swung the beer bottle?"

"No. He was just looking out for himself. He didn't want to go to jail."

"No further questions, Your Honor."

Farrar stood to begin his cross-examination. "Mr Rand, have you ever pleaded guilty to a crime?"

"Yes, sir."

"What crime did you plead guilty to?"

"Beating up a guy in Houma a few years ago."

"And did you spend any time in prison as a result of that conviction?"

"Yeah. I spent ninety days in jail."

"Was that your first offense?"

"Yes, sir."

"Why'd you serve ninety days in prison if that was your first offense?"

"They said it was a hate crime."

"Did you beat up an African-American man?" Farrar gripped the podium and leaned forward.

"He happened to be black, yeah."

"Did you beat him up because you saw him with a white woman?"

"No, sir."

"Mr Rand, could you please turn to tab one in the binder in front of you." Farrar opened his own binder and asked the judge's clerk to show the document to the judge, opposing counsel and witness on their screens, without showing it to the jury. He zapped a barcode at the bottom of his document so that he could magnify and highlight portions of the document to call Rand's attention to them.

"Do you recognize this document?" Farrar's frown signaled disappointment and frustration with the exercise Rand was forcing him to perform. Matt knew Farrar was actually thrilled; presented with the choice between admitting the truth the easy way or the hard way, Rand had chosen the hard way.

"Yeah, this looks like a transcript of the hearing where I entered my guilty plea."

"And were you under oath at this federal hearing in Houma, Louisiana?"

"Yes, sir." Rand nodded.

"At that hearing, did you say that you'd beaten up the victim, a black man, because he was dating a white friend of yours?"

"Yes, sir. I said that."

"So tell me now, Mr Rand, did you beat up a black man because you saw him with a white woman?"

Rand paused. "Yes, sir. I suppose I did."

"And your earlier testimony about why you beat up that black man was false?"

Rand's eyes darted toward the judge, then Thibedeaux, before landing on Farrar's again. "It wasn't false. I just didn't remember."

"Did you use any insults or racial slurs when you beat up the black man in Houma, Louisiana?"

"Yeah. I think I may have called him a name."

"What name did you call the man you beat up in Houma, Louisiana?"

"I think I may have called him a nigger."

"And did you serve ninety days in federal prison because your battery qualified as a hate crime?"

"That's what the judge said, yeah."

Farrar flipped a page in the binder in front of him on the podium. "How tall are you, Mr Rand?"

"About six-six."

"And how much do you weigh?"

"About three hundred and twenty-five pounds."

"How did you batter this man in Houma, Louisiana?"

"I hit him with my fists."

"Was that man hospitalized?"

"Yes."

"How long was he hospitalized for?"

"A couple of days."

"Have you ever tackled a man?"

"Yeah. I played some football in high school."

"Given that you were aware you'd put a man into the hospital the last time you hit him a few times, why didn't you tackle Mr Buckner?" Farrar cocked his head to the side.

"I was just standing there, so I didn't have a running start." Rand appeared to realize the lameness of his excuse, so added: "And it all happened real fast."

"Would you agree that Mr Buckner is much smaller than you?"

"Yes, sir."

"Do you think that you needed a running start to tackle Mr Buckner?"

"No, but it just wasn't natural for me to tackle him when we were both standing there."

"So you hit Mr Buckner rather than tackling him just because it wasn't natural?" Farrar turned toward the jury while waiting for the answer.

"I told you. It happened real fast." Stubbornness settled into Rand's voice.

Farrar would have to rip it out. "Mr Rand, can you turn to tab two in your binder?" Farrar zapped the page in his binder, putting it on the screen in front of Rand. "Do you recognize this as a picture of the alley where you struck Mr Buckner?"

"Yeah. It's a picture of the alley. I don't know when it was taken."

Farrar moved for its admission into evidence without objection, and it was admitted. He displayed it on the large screen. "This is a photograph of the alley on the night of September 7. Can you identify the man walking toward Matthew Durant?"

"That's Brian Cutler."

"And does Brian Cutler have anything in his hand?"

"I don't know. It looks like something shiny, but it's hard to tell." Rand almost whined the last, a surprising pitch from such a large man.

"Could this picture show that Brian Cutler had a knife in his hand?"

His whine deepened to almost a shout. "He didn't have no knife!"

"Answer the question, please. Could the object in this picture be a knife?"

"I did answer the question. He didn't have no knife." Rand's face flushed and beads of sweat stood out on his forehead.

"Looking at this picture, isn't Mr Cutler's back toward you in the alley?"

"Yeah."

"Could you have seen a knife in Mr Cutler's hand from where you were standing?"

"Maybe not, but I didn't see a knife earlier in the night, or after Durant hit him."

"Did you ever search Mr Cutler for a knife, either before or after he was hit with the bottle?"

"Well, yeah." Rand leapt for the attempt to bolster his lie and added: "I patted him down real quick while he was on the ground."

"Are you testifying that as your friend lay on the ground injured or possibly dead, you searched him?" Farrar locked eyes with Rand.

Rand broke contact and looked out to the gallery, toward a wall clock. "Yeah. I mean, I didn't search him like the police would've, but I did a quick search."

"Did you discard Mr Cutler's knife?"

"No." Rand set his jaw.

"After the police arrived, did you speak to a Detective Jones?"

"Yeah."

"And do you now know that Mr Durant didn't have any drugs in his possession when he was arrested?"

"Yeah, but it was a dark alley and they were huddled together. Looked like they were trading something."

"But you now know, in fact, that you were wrong when you assumed they were exchanging drugs, correct?"

"Yeah."

"Did Detective Jones tell you at the beginning of that conversation the police had found cocaine on Joey Buckner?"

"Yeah." At this point, Rand had no way of knowing when Farrar could prove his lies and when he couldn't, but he knew Jones was a cop, had made a report and would likely testify.

"Did Detective Jones interview you alone?"

"No. John Harlan was standing right there next to me." Rand might be seeking someone to corroborate his story.

"Did you tell Detective Jones you thought you'd seen Mr Buckner and Mr Durant engaged in a drug deal before or after Detective Jones told you that Mr Buckner had been found with four grams of cocaine?"

"After."

"And Mr Harlan heard you say that you thought you'd seen Mr Durant engaged in a drug deal before he said anything to Detective Jones, correct?"

"Yeah."

"And did Mr Harlan hear you reciting all of the facts that you described in response to Mr. Thibedaux's questions today before he said anything to Detective Jones?"

"Maybe not all of 'em," Rand hedged. "But most of 'em."

"No further questions, Your Honor," Farrar concluded.

"We'll take a fifteen-minute break now," Judge Masterson said. "I'll see everyone back here at three-thirty."

The prosecution then called John Harlan to the stand. His testimony in response to Thibedeaux's direct examination was consistent with Rand's and Farrar followed a similar line of cross-examination.

Farrar only had one surprise for Harlan. As he neared the end of his cross-examination, he asked, "Did you graduate from high school?"

"No, sir."

"Were you expelled from high school?"

"Yes."

"Why were you expelled from high school?"

"They found some dope in my locker."

"They found marijuana in your high-school locker and you were expelled, is that correct?"

"Yes."

"But on the night of September 7, you thought you saw two strangers engaged in a drug deal and decided to report it to the police?"

"Yeah, well, I don't do drugs no more."

"No further questions, Your Honor."

Chapter 10

The doorbell rang around seven-thirty that night. To Matt's surprise, Eric stood at the threshold holding a pot containing an orchid: it had a brown stem with slender green branches stretching out and sprouting five elliptical violet petals with white specks and tinted yellow edges. A single, circular petal with jagged edges and without any hint of yellow jutted out.

"That's a beautiful orchid," Matt said.

"It's called a Cambria. I thought I'd bring it by to congratulate you for finishing your first full day of trial."

"Thanks. Come in."

Mary had gone to the grocery store to pick up food, so they had at least a few minutes alone. Matt placed the orchid on the kitchen table, while Eric pulled up a chair.

"How did today go?" Eric asked, inclining his head to the side.

"Better than yesterday," Matt said, looking down at the orchid. "Thomas's opening statement was phenomenal and he tore through three witnesses. Detective Jones, Harlan and Rand." He looked back up at Eric. "I hate to say it out loud, but I think we had a good day."

"Excellent," Eric smiled. "How are you holding up?"

"Last night was tough. We had a bit of a disaster with jury selection. And the day ended with Thibedeaux's opening, which was pretty hard to hear."

"Maybe tonight will be better. You had a good day today."

"I hope so. I'm going to load up on Tylenol PM tonight. I don't like how dopey it makes me in the morning, but I need to get some sleep. I had a terrible nightmare last night."

"What was it about?"

"I dreamt I had leprosy."

Eric laughed. "And what do you think the meaning of that dream was?"

Matt couldn't help but smile and shook his head. "I know I don't need to pay a therapist hundreds of dollars an hour to tell me what the dream was really about. Much of the dream was about knowing I had a terrible secret that was about to be revealed."

"Do you actually know anything about leprosy?" Eric asked.

"I don't know anything about it at all, beyond hearing about it in Sunday school. I thought about looking it up on the web, but I was afraid I'd run across pictures that would make the next dream worse."

"Where's your computer?" Eric asked. "I'll look and that way you won't have to worry about the images."

Matt led Eric toward his bedroom and felt embarrassed about the cheap knock-off furniture. The laptop sat on a stained pine desk, the finest piece in the room. A black faux-iron bed, a blond particle-board dresser, and piles of books rounded out what could only charitably be called a bedroom set. If any of the jurors had stereotypes about gay men, perhaps he should insist on a jury view of his bedroom.

Eric rolled out a black office chair made of space-age plastic and sat at the computer. Matt distanced himself and sat on the bed, ostensibly so he couldn't see the screen.

"I'm going to start with WebMD," Eric said. "Well, it's also called Hansen's disease and it causes skin lesions. No surprise there. Apparently it's caused by bacteria and can now be cured. It also says there's no longer any need to isolate the infected." He shot a glance at Matt on the bed, as if to emphasize their physical distance.

"I'll bet you're skipping over all sorts of symptoms." Matt said, rising and approaching the desk, computer, and Eric.

"I am, but it looks like if you catch it early, you don't have to worry about the severe symptoms. Here's a link to the Centers for Disease Control. In 2003, there were less than 120 cases in the

United States, so your odds seem pretty good. I'm going to try Google now."

Matt looked away from the computer, unwilling to look at the random sample of search results and potential images, but asked, "What came up?"

"There's an organization called American Leprosy Missions. Its website says within days antibiotics can kill the bacteria, and in two weeks there's no risk of spreading it. The first signs are spots. You have any spots?"

Matt shook his head. He was tempted to ask Eric to check, but he was too depleted to flirt. "Nope," he said, both relieved and disappointed with passing up the temptation.

"I think you're safe." Eric rolled the chair back from the desk and swiveled to face Matt. "All right, now that we've diagnosed your non-disease, I need to take off."

"Sure you can't stay for dinner?" Matt asked, wanting to spend more time with Eric and thinking the kitchen safer than the bedroom.

"Nope. I've got some work to do. I just wanted to stop by and see how you're doing. Now that I know you're disease-free, my job here is done. Anything else I can do for you?" Eric looked up at him quizzically.

"No," Matt said. Eric rose and walked out of the bedroom and to the front door. Matt followed and stood awkwardly. Should he at least hug Eric? What if his mother came home? Would she care? The moment passed and left him confused, conflicted and disappointed.

Matt slept better that night. Although twenty-four hours closer to a potential prison sentence—or even death—the transformation from a passive object of the legal system to an active participant gave him comfort. Farrar's opening had finally rolled out his defense.

On Wednesday morning, Thibedeaux called the medical examiner, who testified about Brian Cutler's cause of death. To Matt's shame and dismay—both concealed from the jury—an array of photographs of the damage to Cutler's skull accompanied his testimony. Matt had avoided one set of graphic images, only to run into another that could populate his nightmares. Great. But at least the prosecution had declined Farrar's offer to use the defense team's trial presentation software and equipment, so the jury only viewed select poster-boards rather than every picture, choreographed by Thibedeaux in technicolor, on the big screen. Farrar declined to cross-examine the medical examiner.

The prosecution's final witness was Joey Buckner. Matt wondered whether the prosecution had called him last because they genuinely thought the tape inconsequential or because he was the best they could do. He knew that in his direct examination Thibedeaux would try to take the sting out of the tape and defang Farrar's cross-examination.

Someone had obviously given Joey instructions about the appropriate attire. He wore a dark blue pinstriped suit, a powder cornflower shirt and a yellow tie. His complexion had cleared and his black eyes had faded further to a mottled olive green.

"Mr Buckner, when did you first meet the defendant?" Thibedeaux asked.

"I met him on a Friday night in September at a bar in the French Quarter called Drink."

"Why were you at Drink that night, Mr Buckner?"

"I went to the bar to see if I could find anyone who wanted to buy coke."

"And by coke, do you mean cocaine?"

"Yes."

"And can you please describe your first interaction with Mr Durant?"

"Sure. I met him at the bar. He looked nervous, like lots of guys who come there alone. I thought he might have been married. I didn't see a ring, but they don't always wear rings."

"Who do you mean by 'they'?"

"I mean guys who haven't come out of the closet yet. Drink is a gay bar."

"And what did you say to Mr Durant when you saw him at the bar?"

"I asked him if I could buy him a drink."

Matt wondered if the jurors thought Joey had a habit of picking up married men, but as he surveyed them, their expressions, though rapt, were impassive.

"What happened next?" Thibedeaux asked.

"I bought him a drink, and then we talked about basic background stuff. Where are you from, what do you do for a living, those sorts of things. Matt—I mean Mr Durant—said this was the first time he'd ever been in a gay bar alone, but lots of guys say that." Joey smirked, as if few could resist his charms. "We had some drinks, danced a little and then went back to the bar."

"What happened next?"

"Well, he suggested going to the back of the room so we could hear each other better over the music. He was pretty loaded. Once we got there, I told him I knew he was nervous and I had something that might help take the edge off."

"What did he say in response to your statement that you might have something to take the edge off?"

"He asked me what I had, and I showed him a clear plastic baggie of cocaine. It was pretty obvious what was in there, unless he thought it was sugar." Joey smiled with his lips, but his cheeks and eyes didn't move; the smile was artificial sweetener.

"What was Mr Durant's response?"

"He said he'd never done cocaine before, but he'd always been curious. He said it was a night of firsts, so why not."

"What happened next?"

"I suggested we go outside, where there wouldn't be as many people. He followed me out into the back alley. I put my arm around him as we left the bar. He said he needed to take a leak first, so we did. Then those three guys came walking up the alley. They must've seen my arm around him when we left the bar and thought he was buying drugs." Joey paused, then added: "And I was going to sell him drugs in a few minutes."

"What did the three men do in response?"

"Well, the real big guy, I know now that was Don Rand, he said, 'What the fuck do you guys think you're doing?' And one of the smaller guys, I'm not sure which one, said he bet we were dealing drugs. And the two smaller guys went to grab me. I tried to make a break for it, and the big guy hit me in the face." Matt knew there was a potential hearsay objection, but agreed with Farrar's judgment not to draw further attention to the testimony with an objection.

"What happened next?"

"Matt ran up with that beer bottle. He threw a few punches, real quick. Looked like he'd stunned the smaller guy, and then he reached back and pretty much just jammed the beer bottle into the side of the guy's head." Joey shook his head, as if disgusted.

"What part of the beer bottle did Mr Durant jam into Mr Cutler's head?"

"The neck; the pointed part."

"Did Mr Durant jam the neck of the beer bottle into the side of Mr Cutler's head more than once?"

Joey nodded. "Yeah. He did it twice in a row, real fast."

"As you were watching, did you believe Mr Durant needed to attack Mr Cutler with the beer bottle to defend himself?"

"No, sir." Joey shook his head. "This Cutler guy was dazed from all of Matt's punching. Anyway, defend himself from what? Those guys hit me 'cause I tried to run. I'm no lawyer, but I don't think he gets to defend himself just 'cause they were going to call the police."

"Did Mr Durant kill Mr Cutler as he was attempting to purchase cocaine from you?"

"Yes, he did," Joey said. The question was leading, but even Joey's three-word answer and emphasis sounded rehearsed—his future wouldn't include an Academy Award.

"Have you ever been convicted of a crime?"

"Yes, sir. I was convicted of possession with intent to distribute cocaine a few years ago."

"Why should the jury believe you, given your criminal record?"

"Well, I've sold drugs. But I never hurt anyone, and I never would. Matt knew he was going to hurt this Cutler guy real bad when he swung that beer bottle, maybe even kill him. And I don't want any part of that. So I sure wasn't going to lie for this guy." Joey looked at the jury, as if he expected his concession to boost his credibility, but several jurors looked away.

"Now, did you run into Mr Durant after that night in the alley?"

"I did. I saw him on Jackson Avenue a few weeks ago."

"Did you speak to Mr Durant?"

"Yeah, I did. I just wanted him to know I was sorry about how all this turned out. I mean, he shouldn't have been trying to buy drugs, but I was the one selling the coke to him. And I know if I'd killed someone, it would weigh on me something awful." Even his feigned sympathy was accusatory, and, again, several jurors broke eye contact.

"Did you tell him he didn't know you had cocaine on him that night in the alley?"

"No, I didn't. I told him that I guessed he knew the police had found the cocaine and that my lawyer was negotiating with prosecutors."

"Did he say anything to you?"

"He asked that I tell the truth, but I think he just said that because he was recording the call."

"Objection. Move to strike the last part of the answer. Speculation," Farrar said. His one-word objection, using language familiar to lawyers and laypeople both, unlike a hearsay objection, pointed out the flaw to judge and jury.

"Sustained," Judge Masterson ruled. "Jurors, you will disregard everything after the word truth."

"Have you told the truth today?"

"I have."

"Do you think that's really what Mr Durant wanted?"

"Objection. Speculation," Farrar said.

"Sustained. Do not answer the question."

"Thank you, Mr Buckner. No further questions."

Thibedeaux had pushed too hard and ended on a low note. And Matt couldn't believe he hadn't just played the tape. That was a mistake; the prosecutor had to at least think Joey had a lousy memory, and if he'd introduced the tape into evidence and played it immediately before asking questions about it, Joey's answers would have been more consistent with its substance. By avoiding it, he also showed his discomfort with Joey's actual words.

Farrar stood to question Joey, and Matt sat forward in his seat. Farrar need display no sympathy toward this witness, whose life Matt had protected and who was now lying to avoid a few years in prison at the potential cost of Matt's. He expected the cross-examination to be quick, sharp and brutal.

"Mr Buckner, you testified Mr Rand hit you when you attempted to escape from the alley, correct?"

"Yes."

"How hard did Mr Rand hit you?"

"Pretty hard."

"How many surgeries were required in order to fix the damage Mr Rand did?"

"Two surgeries."

"Were those surgeries for cosmetic purposes?"

"No, sir. The doctor said I needed both of them to breathe right."

"So you suffered a severe injury?"

"Yeah, I guess."

"Did you suffer a severe injury?"

"Yes, I did."

"Were you lying on the ground after Mr Rand hit you?" Matt wondered if Farrar's use of the word "lying" was accidental and suspected not.

"Yeah, I sort of collapsed."

"So despite your severe injury and the fact that you were lying on the ground, you claim to have clearly seen everything that happened after Mr Rand hit you?"

"Yeah, I saw enough."

"If you turn to the first tab in the binder in front of you and look on the screen in front of you, can you tell me what that document is?" Farrar zapped the document.

"An article from the New Orleans *Times-Picayune* about what happened in the alley that night."

"What's the date of the article?"

"Sunday, September 9, 2007."

"Does this article summarize Mr Rand's version of what happened in that alley based on the police report?"

"Yeah, it does."

"Did you read this article?"

"Yeah, I read it."

"Did you read this article before telling anyone else your version of what happened in that alley?"

"Yeah."

"You testified on direct examination you've previously been convicted of possession of cocaine with intent to distribute, correct?"

"Yes."

"Did you plead guilty to that possession charge, or were you convicted after a trial in front of a jury?"

"I was convicted after a trial in front of a jury."

"Did you testify on your own behalf in your trial?"

"Yes."

"Did you testify in that trial you had no idea where the cocaine had come from and that it must have been planted by an angry ex-boyfriend?"

"Yes."

"And did the jury reject your story that the cocaine was planted and convict you?"

"Yes."

"Were you lying when you testified an ex-boyfriend must have planted the cocaine?"

"No."

"You testified on direct that you've previously sold cocaine, correct?"

"Yes."

"Are you testifying that you're a cocaine dealer but on that particular occasion you think that your ex-boyfriend planted the cocaine on you?"

"Yes." A few jurors smiled.

"Did you understand at your previous criminal trial that you were not obligated to testify on your own behalf?"

"Yeah. I understood that."

"Did you testify in your previous trial that your ex-boyfriend must have planted the cocaine because you wanted to stay out of prison?"

"I testified I thought he must have planted the coke because I thought he must have planted the coke."

"I see," Farrar said.

"Objection," Thibedeaux said.

"Stricken," Judge Masterson ruled. "Jurors, please disregard Mr Farrar's statement. He's supposed to only be asking questions. You should focus on the witness's answers, rather than the lawyers' questions or comments." The objection and resulting pause punctuated the rapid-fire questions and Joey's absurd denial.

"The jury in your prior trial found you'd been lying when you said that an ex-boyfriend must have planted the cocaine, correct?"

"I guess so."

"You testified on direct you had a conversation with Mr Durant a few weeks ago, correct?"

"Yeah."

"Do you now know that conversation was tape-recorded?"

"Yeah. Mr Thibedeaux told me."

"But Mr Thibedeaux didn't play that tape when questioning you about that conversation on direct, did he?"

"No."

"I'm now going to play that tape." Farrar zapped a barcode and, as the call began to crackle over the speakers, Matt hoped Farrar hadn't oversold it in opening. The jurors were spellbound; many cocked their heads towards the speakers; others stared into space with rapt expressions; and a few scrutinized Matt, Joey and the lawyers for any reaction. But Matt couldn't tell whether they thought it damning.

Farrar, as expected, then asked leading questions about the tape's contents that repeated parts verbatim, departing from the tape itself only when Joey created openings. Matt homed in on

Joey; he knew the cross-examination would be so focused and rapid he had to choose between looking at Joey or the jurors.

"Was that a tape recording of your conversation with Mr Durant from a couple of weeks ago?"

"Yeah."

"On that tape, you said that you would have gotten hurt worse if Mr Durant hadn't come to your aid, correct?"

"Yeah, but that doesn't mean they weren't holding me for the cops."

"Did you think Mr Harlan and Mr Rand might beat you up some more while they waited for the cops to come?"

"Something like that."

"Something like that, or did you think Mr Harlan and Mr Rand might continue to beat you up absent Mr Durant's intervention?"

"I did. I was scared."

"On that tape, you told Mr Durant you guessed he'd found out about the coke, correct?"

"Yeah."

"You didn't say you guessed Mr Durant knew the police had found the cocaine?"

"No. I didn't use those words."

"And on that tape you said 'those assholes jumped us,' correct?"

"Yeah, but I didn't say why they jumped us."

"On that tape, you said you could go away for a long time, correct?"

"Yeah."

"Have you now entered into a plea agreement with the prosecution regarding the cocaine you had in your possession on the night of September 7?"

"Yeah."

"Was it a condition of your plea agreement that your testimony here today be consistent with your previous statement to the district attorney's office?"

"Yes."

"Do you know what prison sentence you would have received if you hadn't agreed to a plea bargain with the prosecution?"

"I could've gotten about five years."

"Will you receive a prison sentence under the current plea agreement?"

"Yeah. I have to go to prison for a year."

"By testifying here today consistent with your previous statement, are you shaving four years off your potential prison sentence?"

"I am. But that's not why I'm saying what I'm saying." Joey squirmed and pulled his tie up into a tighter knot.

Farrar concluded with Joey's protest. "Nothing further, Your Honor."

Chapter 11

The prosecution rested after Joey's testimony and Thursday morning offered Matt his first opportunity to explain what had happened. The night before, Matt had insisted Farrar spend a couple of extra hours listening to his account and peppering him with potential cross-examination questions. He needed to quiet the doubts that sometimes tugged at the edge of his consciousness late at night, like a barely forgotten dream. And he yearned for impartial observers to absolve him.

"Present your first witness, Mr Farrar," Judge Masterson said.

"I call Matthew Durant to the stand."

Matt stood. Twenty-four eyes bored into him and he knew he was now the exclusive focus of their attention. He concentrated on putting one foot in front of the other and controlling his breathing as he walked up to the witness stand. He was the one telling the truth—he just needed to explain what had happened.

"Do you swear to tell the truth, the whole truth, and nothing but the truth?" Judge Masterson's clerk asked.

"I do," Matt said.

"Mr Durant, can you describe a bit about your background?" Matt knew Farrar was hoping open-ended questions about his background would relax him, cause the questions to recede into the background, and allow the answers to stand out.

"I grew up in Lafayette, Louisiana. My father died when I was fourteen, and my mother works as a nurse. I went to high school in Lafayette, where I also worked various jobs. Through a combination of scholarships and loans, I was able to attend LSU Law

School. After graduation in 2004, I moved to Lafayette and spent a year clerking for Judge Michael Thompson of the Louisiana Third Circuit Court of Appeal. After my clerkship, I went to work for the law firm of Farrar Levinson here in New Orleans." Matt sat back in the witness chair and faced the jury that would decide his fate.

"So you used to work for me, right?"

"Yes."

"Did you go to work on Friday, September 7, 2007?"

"Yes."

"What did you do after leaving work on Friday, September 7?"

"I left work around seven-thirty that evening and went to the gym. After the gym, I went home and watched some TV and drank a few beers. I then decided to take a cab to a club named Drink in the French Quarter."

"What kind of club is Drink?"

"It's a gay club." Matt looked directly at the jurors as he said it, though his eyes swept across the jurors as a group, rather than focusing on any single one. He then returned his attention to Farrar's questions.

"Why did you decide to go to a gay bar that night?"

"I'd just broken up with my girlfriend of several years and I was experiencing some confusion about my sexual orientation. I've had several girlfriends over the years." He paused. "But I've always been attracted to men. Even if I shouldn't be ashamed of that attraction, as I sit here today, it's something that I'd change if I could." Matt's voice softened and he blushed despite the hours of practice. He didn't know whether he was embarrassed about his sexual orientation or embarrassed to be embarrassed.

"I think life's probably much harder in certain ways if you're gay," Matt continued. "But I thought that there wouldn't be as much risk to my reputation if I interacted with strangers. I just wanted to see what going to a gay club by myself would be like."

"Were you nervous?"

"I was very, very nervous. I'd been attracted to other men for years, but I'd managed to avoid it, to repress it perhaps, largely by

114

focusing on school and work. I was nervous about being seen, but more than anything else, I was scared that I'd enjoy it." Matt feared he was departing from Farrar's instruction to state his sexual orientation simply, but he couldn't describe his attraction to men and the resulting inner turmoil—even long before the attempted assault—as simple. It wasn't.

"Why were you scared that you would enjoy it?"

"I wasn't sure how my family, friends or coworkers would react. I've been fortunate enough to gain the respect of many people throughout the course of my education and in the early stages of my career. I've come to crave that respect. I didn't want to lose it."

"What happened when you arrived at Drink?"

"I went to the bar, sat down, and ordered a gin and tonic. Joey Buckner began talking to me and we talked about everyday things for a while. We had a few drinks."

"Did you dance with Mr Buckner?"

"I did." Matt nodded.

"What happened after you danced?"

"We moved to a table in the back of the bar and talked for a bit. Mr Buckner said he needed to use the restroom. He returned and said he hadn't actually used it because the line was too long, and he suggested going out into the alley to relieve ourselves. I told him I was worried about getting arrested for public exposure."

"What did Mr Buckner say in response?"

"He said not to worry because he peed in the alley every weekend." Matt hoped the truthful answer consistent with Joey's appearance before the jury as feckless; though perhaps he was at fault for failing to detect it that night.

"Did you go out into that alley for any reason other than to go to the bathroom?"

"No. I heard Joey testify that I went out there to buy cocaine. He's lying. Neither one of us ever mentioned the word cocaine. I certainly didn't go out there to buy any. I've never bought cocaine in my life." His language was emphatic, but he spoke softly.

"I'd like for you to turn to tab one in your binder." Farrar displayed a picture on the screen. "Is this a picture of you and Mr Buckner exiting the club?"

"Yes."

"What, if anything, does this picture show happened as you went into the alley?"

"He put his hand on the small of my back."

"Do you think someone could have mistaken that for an exchange of drugs?"

"Hard to see how, but I guess it's possible."

"And, just to be perfectly clear, were you buying drugs from Mr Buckner?"

"No."

"What happened after you went out into the alley?"

"Well, we relieved ourselves. As we were finishing, three men approached. One of them, I now know it was Mr Rand, was absolutely enormous. The big guy called us faggots and said they'd been looking for a couple of fucking faggots to beat up."

"What happened next?"

"The two smaller guys grabbed Mr Buckner by both arms and Mr Rand hit him in the face, really hard. Blood was everywhere." Matt broke eye contact with the jury and stared into space. It was the only way to maintain his composure.

"Did you think about running for help at the time?"

"Yes." He looked at the jury as he spoke.

"If you'll turn to tab two in your binder, you'll see another picture." Farrar flashed it on the screen. "Is this a picture of the alley that you were in when you encountered Mr Rand and his companions on the night of September 7?"

"Yes."

"Can you explain, with reference to this picture, why you didn't just run for help?"

"Well, I started to back away, but then I changed my mind." Matt took a deep breath and second-guessed the pause. "Rand and his friends were standing near the exit door of the club on one side of the alley. On the other end of the alley, the path was choked off by a dumpster and a U-Haul truck. I was afraid if I tried to run, they'd catch up and beat me to a pulp. And I was afraid to leave Joey alone with those guys. They'd already hurt him really badly and I was worried they could kill him."

"So what did you do instead?"

"I thought I'd try to break past them into the club, which was full of people. I started to walk toward them, but I didn't make it far. Mr Cutler broke off from the group. As he approached me, he pulled out a knife."

"What did you think when you saw the knife?"

"I was afraid he was going to stab either me or Joey, maybe even kill one of us," Matt said. He fought back tears.

"So, what did you do when you saw Mr Cutler's knife?"

"I went toward him, keeping the beer bottle in my left hand. I threw a couple of left jabs at him, with the beer bottle in my closed fist, and I also threw a right uppercut."

"How long did it take you to throw those three punches?"

"It may have taken two or three seconds."

"What was the effect of those punches on Mr Cutler?"

"I could tell they stunned him, but they didn't have enough power behind them to really stop him. He still had a knife in his hand, and he had two other guys at his back."

"What did you do next?"

"I doubled up and threw two left hooks with the beer bottle in my hand, turned so that the neck of the beer bottle would hit Mr Cutler in the side of the head. It was the only way I could think of to stop him."

"Why did you hit Mr Cutler twice?"

"Well, I've been training in boxing for about a year and a half. After practicing a few months, doubling up, or throwing two punches in quick succession, was instinctive."

"How long did it take you to throw the two punches?"

"It only took about a second, maybe less."

"Were you able to evaluate the effects of the first punch before you threw the second punch?"

"No."

"So why did you throw two punches?"

"Instinct and muscle memory, I guess."

"Did you intend to kill Mr Cutler?"

"No. I just wanted to stop him."

"What happened after you hit Mr Cutler?"

"He went down and his friends rushed to his side. Mr Rand yelled for an ambulance."

"Did you try to run away?"

"No." Matt shook his head. "I ran to the bar for help."

"Why didn't you try to run away?"

"The three guys weren't a threat anymore, and I knew the police were on their way."

"Were you afraid the police would arrest you?"

"I certainly knew it was possible, but I knew I'd acted to defend Joey, and I thought that if I was initially arrested it could be straightened out."

"The prosecution has suggested you went into that alley to buy drugs. Have you ever used cocaine?"

"No."

"Did you take a drug test prior to this trial?"

"Yes."

"And what were the results of that drug test?"

"Negative."

"If you could do it again, what would you have done differently in that alley on the night of September 7?"

"I don't think that I'd have done anything differently once I was in the alley. I've gone over it in my mind again and again. If it had just been me, I would've made a run for it. If I got caught and beaten, then I would have gotten caught and beaten. I probably would have been overwhelmed by the three of them anyway. But I wasn't alone in that alley. Joey was there and he was down on the ground, hurt. I had to try to get to the people inside the club as soon as possible. And then Mr Cutler came at me with a knife. I'm sorry he's dead. I never wanted to take another person's life. But I really don't see how I had any choice." Matt said the last quietly, aware that he was asking the jury to legitimize a decision with terrible consequences.

"You say that you'd do the same thing again to save Mr Buckner, even though he's testified against you?"

"Sure. He may not be telling the truth, but he's a human being. He didn't deserve to die."

"No further questions, Your Honor," Farrar concluded. The jurors remained attentive but impassive; unreadable to Matt. Mary sat on the edge of her seat, well aware that even if the direct examination had gone well, now came the true test.

Thibedeaux rose. "Mr Durant, you said you were drinking throughout the night of September 7, correct?"

"Yes."

"Did the police perform a breathalyzer test when you were arrested late that night?"

"Yes."

"How long had it been since your last drink when the police performed that test?"

"About an hour and a half."

"Do you know what the results of that breathalyzer test were?"

"I believe it was 0.18."

"And are you aware that 0.18 is over twice the legal limit for driving?"

"Objection," Farrar said.

"Overruled. Answer the question, Mr Durant."

"Yes."

"Do you think that being intoxicated could have affected your judgment on the night of September 7?"

"It probably could have affected my judgment at the margins, but as I testified, I can't think of anything I could've done differently in that alley." Matt wondered if he sounded too evasive, and knew that Thibedeaux would press with more focused questions.

"Do you think being intoxicated could have affected your ability to determine whether Mr Cutler had a knife?"

"It may have affected that ability at the margins, but I'm certain he had a knife."

"Do you think being intoxicated could have affected your ability to recall details of that night?"

"It may have affected my ability to recall details, but I clearly recall everything that I just testified to. A threat to your life will sober you up pretty quickly." Again, Matt hoped he didn't sound like he was dodging the question.

"Do you know whether the police found a knife on Mr Cutler?"

"I understand they didn't."

"How much did you earn at Farrar Levinson?"

"I earned about $100,000 a year."

"That would be a lot to lose if your attack on Mr Cutler was unprovoked, wouldn't it?"

"I'm far more concerned about the death penalty than losing my salary."

"Are you concerned enough about the death penalty to lie?"

"No. If I'd wanted to avoid responsibility, I would have tried to run from the alley after hitting Mr Cutler. I didn't." Matt looked at Thibedeaux defiantly, daring him to continue the cross-examination.

Thibedeaux looked at his legal pad, considering his remaining potential questions. "No further questions, Your Honor," he concluded.

"We'll now take our break for lunch," Judge Masterson said. "I remind the jurors not to discuss the case during the break." The jurors went out a door near the bench toward the jury room, and Judge Masterson rose to go to his chambers.

Matt stood, exited the witness stand, and exhaled a small measure of the tension locking up every muscle in his body.

Farrar turned to him and said, "You did well. You're much more credible than the three stooges." His mother hugged him.

After the lunch break, Farrar led the jury on a brisk march through corroborating details. He began with Robert Diener, a delicate man with rimless glasses and a carefully trimmed moustache. Diener was an expert on photography in general and security cameras in particular. He'd analyzed photographs from an ATM machine located on St Ann Street that had captured blurry photographs of the events in the alley; he walked the jury through pictures of Matt and Joey leaving Drink as well as enhanced ones and an analysis that showed an eighty-percent chance Cutler had been holding a finished metal object in his hand. The prosecution, unsurprisingly, focused on the twenty-percent chance that the object wasn't finished metal.

Farrar also presented testimony from Jennifer Dobson, the plastic and reconstructive surgeon who'd repaired Joey's nose. Dobson, a slight woman with mousy brown hair, testified about the severity of Joey's injuries.

Farrar concluded the day with the first character witness, Judge Michael Thompson. Matt had clerked for Judge Thompson on the Louisiana Third Circuit Court of Appeal after law school. As he had during Matt's testimony, Judge Masterson ceased typing on his computer and listened closely to Judge Thompson's testimony. The jurors followed his cue. Judge Thompson testified that Matt was honest, moral and had performed important job responsibilities with a full awareness of their importance. He testified he considered it impossible that Matt had committed the crime with which he was charged. All in all, it was an excellent day for the defense.

Judge Masterson excused the jury. After they had filed out of the room, he turned to the attorneys. "Mr Farrar, how many more witnesses do you intend to call?"

"Your Honor, we currently anticipate calling only one more witness, Mary Durant."

"Very well. I'll see you all in the morning."

Chapter 12

Matt and Mary prepared dinner on Thursday night. Long ago, Mary had found a meatloaf recipe fit for Louisiana; it banished ketchup and oatmeal, replacing them with Worcestershire sauce, whole mustard seed, chili powder and cayenne. Matt couldn't stand the traditional, bland dish: the spicier version, since childhood, had been his comfort food. She took it out of the oven, pulled rice off the stove, and the two sat down to dinner.

"So, Matt, before I went to the grocery store, I went to St Louis Cathedral." So much for a casual dinnertime conversation, thought Matt.

"Mom, hate to break it to you, but you're not Catholic. You're Methodist."

"I know, honey, but it's such a beautiful church. It has stunning paintings inside covering the walls and ceiling, and I just needed a quiet place to think and pray. Besides, nobody asked me if I was Catholic." As usual, she matched his wit, defusing it.

"You do know there's a statue of a Confederate general out front, and the Catholic church thinks being gay is a sin, right?"

"Well, as you pointed out, I'm not Catholic. I know you barely tolerate going to church with me on Christmas and Easter and I guess I appreciate you at least doing that, but sometimes going to church helps me to feel like I'm in the palm of God's hand."

"It doesn't help me. Apparently, I don't get to sit there so it does nothing for me. Lots of people around here think gay people are going to hell. They probably think that Mahatma Gandhi went to hell. I guess I've bet my soul that Gandhi's not in hell."

"Well, would you form an opinion on any historical or legal issue without reading the most important text?"

"No. But you know I had to constantly learn Bible verses growing up, for school and Sunday School." Matt recited, at a blistering pace: "For God so loved the world He sent His only begotten son that whosoever believeth in Him shall not perish but shall have eternal life. John 3:16."

"Did you ever think about what you just recited?"

"Yeah, it says you have to believe in Jesus to avoid hell."

"No it doesn't. Memorizing and reciting is not understanding, and you know that. You're not even trying," Mary said. "I think it says if you believe in, and try to follow, Jesus's teachings, you won't go to hell. It doesn't say if you don't believe in Jesus you'll go to hell. It certainly doesn't mean Mahatma Gandhi's in hell. I know you don't read legal cases that sloppily."

"Well, lots of people think it means that."

"Well, at least since Martin Luther nailed that paper on that church in Germany, you get to read it and decide for yourself. Why don't you think about reading the Gospel and actually using that big brain of yours to think about it? You could use some prayer and support."

"No thanks." Matt needed say nothing further: his mother had to know that he wouldn't restrict himself to the New Testament; that he feared if he read the Bible too closely he would discover himself irredeemable; better to live with that possibility than to study until it became a certainty.

"Well, you can't stop me from praying for you. And I do every night. Ever since you were born."

The phone rang, interrupting them, and Matt ducked into the bedroom to answer, thinking it might be Eric and feeling guilty.

But it was Farrar. "Matt, we have an emergency. I just received a call from Thibedeaux telling me he's going to ask the judge's permission to put on a rebuttal witness. Apparently some guy named Frank Hodges was busted on a parole violation earlier this week. And now he's saying he can testify you were training to kill in that gym you work out in. What do I need to know about this?"

"That's not true. Before that night in the alley, I just went there for exercise. I never even did any full-contact sparring."

"Why were you exercising with a guy on parole?"

"Well, I wasn't exactly exercising with him," Matt said. "Tommy brought him in to talk to me about survival strategies in prison."

"Damn it, Matt," Farrar said. "You had to know how that would look. You're lucky a reporter didn't get hold of it."

"We trained there after-hours, when no one was around."

"Oh, that looks much better," Farrar said. "Didn't you think training to go to prison might make it look as if you expected to go to prison? You're no stranger to the importance of admissions."

"What choice did I have?" Matt asked. "I trust you, Thomas, but come on. I almost got the shit kicked out of me in the middle of the French Quarter because I'm gay." His voice had risen to a shout. "What do you think is going to happen to me if I go to prison?" Matt realized too late his mother had overheard him from the other room and deflated.

"Okay," Farrar said. "We can't change what's already been done. Let's figure out what to do now." He questioned Matt methodically about his single meeting with Hodges for the next half-hour and concluded by telling Matt to "get this Tommy O'Rourke guy over to the office tonight so I can interview him."

Tommy readily agreed to meet with Farrar, but when Matt phoned to inform the trial lawyer, he told Matt not to come into the office.

"I want to hear Tommy's version of events without interruption. And we're not going to make the same mistake that idiot Detective Jones did by having you listen to it." So Matt was relegated to crawling into bed.

Andre Thibedeaux had requested a conference with Judge Masterson first thing in the morning, before he called the jury into the courtroom. The defense team was subdued that morning and hardly spoke to one other. Matt hoped the judge couldn't detect their mood and he could mask it later when the jury entered the courtroom.

"Your Honor, I received a message while in trial yesterday from a parole officer," Thibedeaux said. "He indicated they had a parolee named Frank Hodges who'd tested positive for cocaine. When he came in yesterday to meet with the officer, he offered something in exchange for leniency."

"They usually do," Judge Masterson said. "How on earth does that have anything to do with this case?"

"Mr Hodges will testify Mr Durant was training in deadly hand-to-hand combat techniques to prepare for going to prison. We think his testimony will rebut the defendant's self-defense claim."

"Your Honor, we object," Farrar responded. "The prosecution shouldn't be able to introduce such inflammatory testimony about what happened after September 7. Hasn't the prosecution pre-sented enough witnesses with a criminal background in this trial? And it's far too late in the day for them to call a surprise witness." Matt could tell Farrar was working hard to avoid any suggestion of shrillness and sound authoritative—he just barely succeeded.

"Mr Thibedeaux, why didn't you investigate this earlier?" Judge Masterson asked.

"Your Honor, we attempted to interview the owner of the gym as well as a handful of regular customers," Thibedeaux said. "Everyone refused to talk to us."

"Your Honor," Farrar began, "we'd like to object on the addi-tional grounds any such training after the night of September 7 is irrelevant to what Mr Durant did on September 7. Any slight probative value would be substantially outweighed by the risk of enormous, unfair prejudice."

"It's relevant," Thibedeaux insisted. "Training to prepare to go to prison and what he said while training are admissions. They show his consciousness that he is, in fact, guilty."

"Consciousness there's a risk one might go to prison is hardly consciousness of guilt," Farrar said. "And as for whether Mr Durant reasonably held on to that beer bottle, the prosecution should have done a more thorough investigation and explored this line of evidence during their direct case."

"We still have one more witness in the defense case, right?" Judge Masterson asked.

"Yes, Your Honor," Farrar responded.

"Well, why don't I take some more time to consider the issue of whether Mr Hodges can testify? I'll rule after the defense's last witness is done."

"Thank you, Your Honor," Thibedeaux responded. Farrar remained impassive; a poker face was his best bet. Matt exhaled and tried to put the thought of Hodges' potential testimony out of his mind because there was nothing to be done about it at the moment—at times repression could be adaptive.

Judge Masterson arrived back at the bench, instructed his clerk to bring in the jury, and addressed them. "Ladies and gentlemen of the jury, I apologize for the late start. From time to time, legal issues may arise in this case I don't want to waste your time with. One of those issues came up this morning, so I had to discuss it with the attorneys before we could begin. I thank you for your patience. Mr Farrar, your next witness."

"Thank you, Your Honor. The defense calls Mary Durant to the stand."

Mary took her seat in the witness box, pallid and wan against the dark wood and leather. Her lips were tightly drawn and her white knuckles clutched the strap of the black leather tote in her lap.

"Ms Durant, can you please describe your relationship to the defendant?"

"I'm his mother."

"Was Matt ever in any sort of trouble growing up?"

"No. He was a pleasure. I'm sure he got a few detentions, but he was a model student and child." Mary actually managed a smile before her normally anxious expression reasserted itself. "Matt's only flaw was that he's always been very serious. I sometimes worried he just didn't have enough fun."

"Is Matt an honest person?"

"He's honest to a fault. Again, I think that's part of his seriousness. He's been so intense over the years, and he's constantly pushing himself. I think he does it in part because he knows other young lawyers may have had the advantage of going to fancier schools." She shook her head and some of the tension left her shoulders. "The only thing he can be sure of is they haven't lived through the demands he places on himself."

"Is there anything else bearing on Matt's character you'd like to share with the jury?"

"He's always done a lot of volunteer work. In high school, he taught several illiterate adults how to read. Once he was in law school, he began to do volunteer work through the law. He's helped many poor people accused of crimes just because he wants to be sure they have adequate legal representation."

"Knowing Matt's character as you do, do you think he would ever buy drugs?"

"No. Absolutely not." Mary said. She straightened her spine and squared her shoulders as she looked at the jury.

"Have you ever seen any signs that Matt used drugs?"

"No. He drinks, especially on weekends, like most other people in Louisiana, but I don't think he's ever done drugs. Matt's tremendously driven and I don't think he'd impair himself in a way that could compromise his goals."

"Did you know that Matt was confused about his sexual orientation?"

"No. I mean, he's always had girlfriends." Mary looked down at her lap. "I blame myself in a way for him having to get drunk to go to that gay bar. He should've known that he could talk to me about anything. He shouldn't have worried about how I would react. We've gotten through a lot together."

"Do you think that Matt would ever kill anyone to cover up his participation in a drug deal?"

"No. You have to understand that what Matt says happened in that alley is consistent with everything I know and love about him. He wouldn't have seriously considered abandoning someone else who was in trouble. Matt would never leave someone defenseless. I think in some ways he's here today because he was too rigid about his standards. In the face of hate, he tried to do the right thing. But hateful people are least likely to respond to the right thing in the right way."

"No further questions, Your Honor," Farrar concluded. Thibedeaux declined to ask Mary any questions. Mary rose, with her hands trembling, and Matt felt a pang of guilt for putting her through the ordeal of the trial and her testimony; perhaps by failing to acknowledge he was gay he'd simply replaced one trial with a different, far harsher one.

"Ladies and gentlemen," Judge Masterson began, "I think we should break for the weekend now. I know it's early, but the lawyers and I need to discuss some legal issues before you return. Please remember not to discuss the case with anyone. Thank you, and have a good weekend."

The lawyers and spectators rose and watched the jurors file out the rear door behind the jury box.

"As far as I can see, we have two issues to resolve this afternoon," Judge Masterson said. "The first is the status of Mr Hodges, and the second is the proposed jury instructions. As for Mr Hodges, I'm going to let him testify on Monday. I appreciate the defense is upset the prosecution didn't find the witness sooner, but I think it's relevant testimony and I won't exclude it because they weren't able to discover these facts earlier. But as far as I understand it, Mr Hodges will only be testifying Mr Durant received additional training to prepare for the possibility he might go to prison, correct?"

"Yes, Your Honor," Thibedeaux said.

"Very well. You're going to be on a very short leash. As for the jury instructions, my clerk is handing those out as I speak. The instructions supplied by the parties were blatantly partisan and the version I'm handing out has been adapted from my prior charges in other murder cases. You may review them over lunch, and we'll meet again this afternoon to discuss them. Anything else?"

"Your Honor," Mr Farrar said. "We'd like to reiterate our objection to the surprise witness, but if Mr Hodges testifies, we'd like to be able to call another witness in response. We'd like to call Tommy O'Rourke, who owns the gym where Mr Durant supposedly received this specialized training."

"I've heard your objection and already overruled it. As for Mr O'Rourke, you may call him on Monday after the testimony of Mr Hodges."

As Judge Masterson had forewarned, his jury instructions were neutral and largely drawn from standard jury instructions. Farrar and Matt were optimistic the charge would assist this jury in deciding the case correctly. Only one concern lingered in the back of Matt's mind: if the jury decided the case the wrong way, it wouldn't provide any ammunition for an appeal.

Chapter 13

On Monday morning, Matt arrived at counsel table. He dreaded the thought of Hodges testifying—the ex-con could have made a story up out of whole cloth to ingratiate himself to the prosecutors.

Hodges might feel constrained to tell the truth because of Farrar's potential cross-examination or Tommy's testimony. But Matt had lost track of what the truth might be from Hodges's perspective. He didn't know what Hodges might have heard at the gym: How long the parolee waited before the training session he'd attended? How close had he been while he and Dave had been talking? Had Dave said Matt didn't need the bottle in the first or second training session? And what exact words had he used in response to Hodges's suggestion he attack a smaller, weaker inmate? Since Thursday night, he'd wracked his brain for additional details, but he could only pick out fragments. He had no idea what the man would say.

Judge Masterson took the bench. "I've been thinking about Mr Hodges over the weekend and I want a preview of his testimony before the jury hears it." Matt tamped down the upwelling of relief and couldn't bear to look back at Mary; he didn't want to see her hopes rise only to be dashed; and he didn't want to broadcast to the Judge that the considered Hodges' testimony important.

Judge Masterson continued: "I know that means keeping them waiting, but I want to hear exactly what Mr Hodges has to say. Is he here?"

Hodges approached the witness stand, wearing khakis and a button-down shirt. He brushed back his long hair as he sat; and he kept his lips pressed together, likely a habit to conceal his yellowed teeth. Matt wondered if it was drug-use or stress that had Hodges looking pale and shaken. From the jury's perspective, maybe it wouldn't matter.

"Mr Thibedeaux?" Judge Masterson asked.

"Mr Hodges, have you seen Matthew Durant before today?"

"Yeah, I met him at Tommy O'Rourke's boxing gym." Hodges remained close-mouthed and spoke softly.

"What was the purpose of that meeting?"

"He wanted to learn how to stay safe in prison."

"What was Mr Durant doing when you arrived?"

"Dave Anderson, who used to be a Navy SEAL, was showing him some self-defense techniques."

"Do you know why Mr Anderson was showing Mr Durant some self-defense techniques?"

"Well, I assume—"

"Objection, speculation" Farrar said.

"There's no jury here, so I can hear it," Judge Masterson said. "But I do want his testimony to focus on what he knows, what he and Mr Durant said and what he and Mr Durant did. Not what he assumes or speculates."

"I'll move on, Your Honor. Mr Hodges, did Mr Durant say why he wanted to meet with you?"

"I said I'd heard he was in a bit of trouble and he said that about summed it up."

"Did you offer any strategies for Mr Durant to pursue once he was in prison?"

"Yeah, I told him he should beat up someone as soon as he got there. It would show the other inmates he could handle himself."

"How did Mr Durant respond to your suggestion?"

"He said he was a pretty good lawyer and asked why he couldn't offer to help inmates with their cases for protection."

"What did you say in response?"

"I told him most convicts have lousy legal cases." He shrugged. "And if he lost a case, it could get him killed."

"Did Mr Durant say anything in response?"

"Naw." Hodges shook his head. "He just asked whether I thought the other cons would attack him if they heard he was gay."

"Wait a minute," Judge Masterson said. "Maybe I can cut to the chase. Please tell us everything else that Mr Durant said in response to your recommendation he attack another inmate."

"He said he understood me."

"That's it?" Judge Masterson asked, eyebrows shooting above the black frames of his glasses.

"That's it."

"I've heard enough," Judge Masterson said. "Mr Hodges, please leave the room while the lawyers and I discuss some legal issues." He glared at Thibedeaux as Hodges stood and walked out of the room.

"This is garbage," Judge Masterson said. "Those don't sound like admissions to me. Do you still want to present this witness or have I spared you some embarrassment in front of the jury?"

"Your Honor, I believe his testimony is relevant—"

"No. It's not. We're not doing this. Not in a murder trial. Are you prepared to deliver your closing statement?" Judge Masterson crossed his arms.

"Well, Your Honor, I'd expected we'd have two more witnesses today."

"Who you also knew would probably be done by lunch, especially if you had any idea Mr Hodges's testimony was going to be so thin."

"If I could just have a few minutes, Your Honor."

"You have fifteen. The jury's waiting and, while you may be determined to waste their time, I'm not." Judge Masterson rose before his clerk could announce his departure. The lawyers and spectators stood in a ragtag fashion.

Matt couldn't help but smile. Hodges had sounded pretty lame, but he still wasn't sure what the jury would have made of the precautions he'd taken against going to prison. Now they were back where they had ended last week, with the prosecution's case in shambles. And if Thibedeaux and Farrar had to deliver their closing statements on short notice, Matt thought that favored Farrar.

Thibedeaux scribbled furiously throughout the break. As they waited, he joined Mary in the galley, where she grasped his hand

and he looked up to see a wan smile; she was trying to encourage them both. He wanted to avoid distracting Farrar from his preparations so simply squeezed back.

The jury filed back into the room after precisely fifteen minutes and Judge Masterson instructed Thibedeaux to proceed with his argument.

"Ladies and gentlemen," Thibedeaux said. "I'd like to conclude the trial the same way I began, by thanking you for your service. That service will not last much longer." He departed the lectern and walked toward the jury.

"Your service should end quickly because this isn't a complicated or difficult case. There were three eyewitnesses to what happened in that alley on the night of September 7, and every single one testified they saw the same thing: Matt Durant, frantic at the thought of being discovered purchasing drugs, killed Brian Cutler in an attempt to cover up his criminal activities." Thibedeaux looked at Matt as he levied the charge.

"Against the weight of the consistent testimony from three eyewitnesses, you have only the testimony of Matthew Durant. He's potentially facing the death penalty, and it's not surprising that a lawyer could come up with an artful self-defense theory in the face of such a penalty. But Mr Durant's claim of self-defense simply doesn't hold up. Most importantly, the police didn't find a knife in that alley, on Mr Cutler or anywhere else. Mr Durant's attorney points to a fuzzy picture that might show a piece of metal to argue Mr Cutler had a knife that night. But you heard Mr Durant's expert admit that at least one out of five times that computer program will misidentify metal. And a piece of metal isn't necessarily a knife. Mr Durant's attorney also attempted to attack Detective Jones for failing to investigate his claim of self-defense more thoroughly. Of course, Detective Jones wasn't even aware of Mr Durant's claim of self-defense at the time. None of the witnesses he interviewed raised the possibility. And Mr Durant's attorney hasn't explained how Detective Jones was supposed to guess Matthew Durant's version of events." Thibedeaux cast a scornful look at Farrar. "Mr Durant also called a variety of character witnesses, including his mother. The prosecution doesn't dispute Mr Durant is intelligent and a technically capable attorney or that his mother loves him, but very little of that testimony spoke to his character for honesty or morality. It boiled down to testimony that Mr Durant is a very smart and capable young man, which no one disputes. That supposed character evidence also shows Mr Durant had a great deal to lose if he were convicted of attempting to purchase cocaine. Mr Durant, for the first time in his life, was making a considerable amount of money. Mr Durant also craves the respect of his bosses and he testified that he went out of his way to conceal his sexual orientation to keep it. What lengths do you think he would go to in order to cover up the fact he'd tried to buy cocaine?" Thibedeaux raised and lowered his hands to punctuate the question, and finished with his left finger pointed toward Matt.

"Mr Durant admittedly had a strong motive to lie about attempting to purchase drugs before his arrest. He has an even stronger motive to lie now. How did Mr Farrar respond? With a hodge-podge of attacks on the character of the three eyewitnesses who saw Mr Durant commit this murder. Mr Rand is lying because he was arrested for battery. Mr Buckner is lying because of an ambiguous tape and because criminals most frequently witness criminal acts. And then we come to the best of his excuses, that Mr Harlan is lying because he got into trouble with his high-school principal. Mr Durant's mother testified that he'd received detentions, but I didn't cross-examine her about those. None of the various reasons Mr Farrar has offered throughout the trial justify ignoring the testimony of three eyewitnesses. And don't forget, Mr Durant has the strongest motive to lie." Thiebedeaux raised an arm and open palm toward the defense table, in a sweeping gesture.

"Mr Durant has the most to lose. He could potentially be facing the death penalty. We may not have scoured Mr Durant's elementary-school years for detentions to prove he's lied before. But that's because we didn't need to. If Mr Durant ever had a reason to lie in his life, it was in this courtroom to you. The overwhelming evidence shows Mr Durant deliberately chose to use deadly force to prevent Mr Cutler from stopping his crime. You should find him guilty of first-degree murder."

Matt thought that Thibedeaux had done a good job with what he had, but he also knew that as a lawyer, if this was his case, he wouldn't have been satisfied with it.

"We'll take our lunch break now. Be back here at one-thirty. Please remember not to discuss the case," Judge Masterson said.

Matt was relieved Farrar would have the additional hour to prepare. Thibedeaux hadn't just wasted the jury's time this morning; he'd also given Farrar an advantage.

Matt, Lisa and Mary retreated to the small conference room. Farrar joined them so he could ask questions of Lisa as he continued to work on his closing statement. Matt didn't mind keeping quiet. Mary held his hand and he waited for Farrar to put an end to this mess.

*

At one-thirty sharp, the jury filed in and Judge Masterson asked, "Mr Farrar, your closing?"

Farrar drew himself up to his full height and carried his legal pad to the podium. He pushed back the microphone. He didn't need it. "Ladies and gentlemen, I, too, would like to begin by thanking you for your service. I, too, think your deliberations should be brief, although it won't surprise you to hear I disagree with Mr Thibedeaux about the correct outcome." Farrar smiled at the jurors. "I believe if you apply common sense to this case, you'll quickly reach a verdict of not guilty. Mr Thibedeaux who, unlike me, will have the opportunity to speak to you once more, addressed Mr Durant's credibility and motives, but he gave short shrift to the credibility of his witnesses. He doesn't want you to dwell on those problems." Farrar turned toward the prosecution table before reengaging the jury.

"Let's spend a little bit of time on them, though. I wouldn't want you to think I wasted your time during the trial." Farrar smiled again. "Let's start with Mr Rand. Mr Rand has a history of committing hate crimes, has previously beaten a black man for dating a white woman, and severely injured Joey Buckner when he easily could have restrained him. Mr Rand also initially lied to you about why he'd attacked the black man dating his white friend. Even after pleading guilty to a hate crime, he still tried to lie to you about his motive for that crime. I think we can all safely say after his testimony that we wouldn't want to run into him in a dark alley. But there's more. Mr Rand, like Mr Harlan, had the oldest motive known to man for lying in this courtroom: vengeance. Mr Durant killed their friend. I believe the evidence shows he did it in defense of Joey Buckner. But it does give those two men an incredibly powerful reason to lie to you.

"Now let's talk about Mr Harlan. Mr Thibedeaux belittled Mr Harlan's testimony about being expelled from high school. He failed to mention Mr Harlan was also a close friend of Brian Cutler's. And Mr Harlan's testimony about his previous marijuana possession might not have been very important in the abstract. It might be a teenage indiscretion, as Mr Thibedeaux—a prosecutor—would have you believe. But Mr Harlan swore to tell the truth, the whole truth and nothing but the truth, and then claimed he attacked Mr Buckner because he hates all forms of drug use. And that just doesn't add up. As the Judge will instruct you, you don't leave your common sense at the door when you enter this courtroom." He turned back to Thibedeaux to place the blame where it lay: "And that testimony makes no sense."

He walked toward the jury and engaged them directly. "Finally, we come to Mr Buckner. Any fair evaluation of his testimony in this courtroom leads to the inescapable conclusion that he lied in his last criminal trial. And by testifying in this courtroom, Mr Buckner saved himself from four additional years in prison. But, as if we needed more, Mr Buckner admitted on tape that Mr Durant hadn't known about the cocaine, admitted that he feared more severe injury if Mr Durant hadn't intervened, and admitted he was negotiating with prosecutors because he was afraid of going to prison for a long time. Mr Thibedeaux shouldn't get points for gathering together such a motley collection of criminals.

"Mr Thibedeaux also failed to address the unique opportunities in this case that permitted his witnesses to coordinate and fabricate their stories. Detective Jones interviewed Mr Rand and Mr Harlan together and Detective Jones suggested to them that Mr Durant was buying drugs from Mr Buckner. And only after the New Orleans *Times-Picayune* had summarized Mr Harlan's and Mr Rand's version of events did Mr Buckner come to the prosecution. And, lo and behold, Mr Buckner's story matches the descriptions in the *Times-Picayune* article word for word. These individuals not only had a track record of dishonesty and criminal activity. They also had the motive and opportunity to be dishonest." Any hint of playfulness disappeared and Farrar looked directly at Thibedeaux. "And these men have the gall to call Matthew Durant a liar?"

He continued: "Matt has no criminal record, has been involved in charitable work throughout his life, and has tried to do everything in his power to spare his mother the cost of his education. Every single witness who's known Matt for more than one night testified that he would never buy drugs, let alone kill someone to cover up the fact he was buying drugs. Every single witness. And I shudder to think, based on the testimony and evidence we've heard, of the sorts of witnesses who would volunteer to vouch for the character of Mr Buckner, Mr Harlan or Mr Rand. The evidence of what happened on September 7 also corroborates Matt's testimony. You heard Dr. Dobson testify that Mr Rand had completely destroyed Mr Buckner's nose. This wasn't the type of broken nose your son gets in a peewee football game. Mr Rand pulverized Mr Buckner's nose with severe violence. Mr Rand's claim he was acting to prevent Mr Buckner from escaping would be laughable if the consequences weren't so deadly serious. And Mr Buckner's statements on that tape also corroborated Matt Durant's testimony about what happened in that alley.

"Finally, what happened in that alley is perfectly consistent with Matthew Durant's character. He could have turned and run away after hitting Mr Cutler with the beer bottle. He didn't because he wanted to get Mr Buckner help as quickly as possible. So he ran into the bar and alerted everyone in the bar immediately after he hit Mr Cutler. Does that sound like the act of a guilty man? Mr Thibedeaux throws up a series of diversions in response. He pointed out the picture showing Mr Cutler holding a knife is fuzzy. But you also heard Mr Diener testify there's an eighty-percent chance Mr Cutler was holding an object that could be a knife in his hand when the picture was taken. And, as Judge Masterson will instruct you, it's not the defendant's burden to show Mr Cutler had a knife. The prosecution must prove beyond a reasonable doubt that Mr Durant did not act in self-defense or in the defense of Mr Buckner. And I think an eighty-percent chance Mr Cutler was carrying a knife goes much further than creating reasonable doubt. Mr Thibedeaux argues that no knife was found in that alley. He also attempts to explain why Detective Jones didn't look harder for a knife. Actually, it's irrelevant why Detective Jones chose not to search too hard for that knife. But the sloppiness of that search does explain why the police didn't find it. And it's also irrelevant whether or not Mr Cutler even had a knife. When three large men jump two smaller men in an alley and employ enough force to injure one of them so badly he requires two operations, I don't think they also need to be armed to the teeth for Mr Durant to reasonably fear he and Mr Buckner would suffer grave bodily injury. The law failed Mr Durant once in the past few months. The law failed to protect him from the hate of Mr Cutler, Mr Harlan and Mr Rand in that alley. Police officers can't be everywhere at all times to protect us from criminals. And that's why Matt Durant was forced to defend himself. But you shouldn't let Mr Thibedeaux transform the law into an instrument that allows these criminals to further harm Mr Durant."

"Thank you, Mr Farrar," Judge Masterson said. "Mr Thibedeaux, would you like to deliver a rebuttal?"

Thibedeaux jumped to his feet and boomed out, "Actually, Your Honor, uh," he trailed off. "I don't think that's necessary." Thibedeaux was attempting to hide a weak argument behind bravado and Matt suspected he'd failed.

"Very well. I'll now instruct you on the law that governs this case," Judge Masterson said. Judge Masterson proceeded to deliver the instructions he'd previously presented to the parties. "Given the lateness of the hour," Judge Masterson continued, "you'll begin your deliberations first thing in the morning."

After the jury had left the room, Judge Masterson turned to the lawyers.

"I don't think there's anything else that we need to deal with. Each side should have at least one lawyer in the courtroom at all times empowered to aid in crafting responses to any jury requests for testimony, evidence, or further instructions. Thank you."

Matt and Mary returned to his house. Mary cooked a Greek chicken recipe with capers, tomatoes and black olives over egg noodles. The pair opened a bottle of Yellow Tail Pinot Grigio. The sun had long since set and three fluorescent torch lamps dimly lit the room.

Mary turned to Matt and said, "So you're the expert on this stuff. What can we expect?" She sipped honey-colored wine, almost luminescent in the dim light, then cut the chicken before switching to fork and spoon to twirl the pasta.

"I don't know. The jury's deliberation process is pretty opaque. They might send out some notes asking for testimony, evidence or a clarification of the instructions, but they also could just return with a verdict in a few hours." Matt cut through the chicken and pasta and mixed it all together; he'd never learned the trick of twirling pasta; and he didn't bother to switch his fork to his right hand before raising the food to his mouth.

"I find it hard to believe they could find you guilty. All of those witnesses basically admitted they were criminals," Mary said.

"I know, Mom, but they don't know me as well as you do. And we have no idea how my being gay will play in the jury room," Matt said, shaking his head.

"When did it go from being confused about your sexual orientation to being gay?" She looked up sharply, and Matt didn't need to know where he'd really learned to be a lawyer.

"I don't know, Mom. Probably when that distinction stopped mattering to anyone else."

"That Eric seems like a nice guy. And he's cute," Mary said, her fear of her son remaining alone forever peeking through her humor.

"Mom, let me explain something to you about being gay." Matt sipped his own wine. "No matter how successful the match, you can't have grandchildren," Matt said.

"I know that," Mary said, gesturing toward him with her spoon. "But you could always adopt."

"I can't even imagine how much having children must change your life," Matt said, bracing himself with more wine. "Especially seeing what you've gone through in the course of this trial."

"It changes your life in enormous and unexpected ways," Mary said. "But the overwhelming love you feel for your children makes those changes seem natural. The problem is that chance then affects not only your own life, but also the independent and separate lives of your children. You know if I could trade places with you, I'd do it in a second." She reached out and grasped his hand.

"I know, Mom. No matter what happens, neither of us will ever have any doubt about how much we love each other," Matt said, softly, realizing the fear of losing that love is what had kept him in the closet but that the trial, at least, had revealed its durability.

"Agreed." She let go of his hand and returned her attention to the meal she had cooked, her love's practical product. "But you avoided my question about Eric."

"I don't know. He seems like a great guy. I think he would have been there throughout the trial if he hadn't been afraid of hurting my case. I know he's insisted on receiving nightly updates from Lisa. I also think he's very attractive." Matt blushed.

"I told you he was cute."

"I told you so? Really, Mom. And who's the child here?" Matt teased. "But I can't imagine really getting involved with him right now. He doesn't need a boyfriend who's in jail."

"But why don't you think about what you need?" Mary asked hotly. "If you'd considered your needs honestly and tried to meet them, maybe you wouldn't have been cruising a gay bar in the first place." Matt knew she believed he deserved others' love, but it didn't mean he did.

"Lots of straight people cruise bars, too."

"And I'd have the same criticism of them. It's okay to need other people in this world. We all do. You aren't going to protect yourself from the same loss you experienced with your father by keeping everyone at a distance. You're just going to be lonely. And even though this trial is an extreme example of the danger of loneliness, it's dangerous." She paused, unable to voice the gravest dangers. "At the very least, you end up drinking too much."

"I know, but what would you have me do now?" Matt asked.

"I feel as if you're protecting me by refusing to discuss your fears about going to prison or even, God forbid, receiving the death penalty," Mary said. "I know that conversation would tear me apart, but I'm willing to have it. And I want to have it, if you need to." She returned her hand to his, but his palm supported hers, as it usually did.

"I know, Mama. I'm just trying to deal with one issue at a time. I'm trying to compartmentalize in order to survive."

"Life's about more than just survival." She shook her head.

"I know."

"And talking to Eric in some ways doesn't carry the same risks," Mary said. "I'm sure he cares about you, but that affection hasn't deepened. Discussing your fears and anxieties, at least with him, might help you a lot. I think he'd be glad to do it."

"I know, Mama."

"If you know I'm always right, why don't you just do what I tell you? It would make everything a lot simpler."

"Thanks, Mama. I'll think about it," Matt said.

"Your welcome," she said curtly, sparking a smile from Matt. But then she continued, "This conversation means the world to me. I'll always treasure the time we've been able to spend together. To be honest, it's actually better than watching LSU win the national championship."

"I know, Mom. I love you, too."

Chapter 14

After waiting all day at the office to hear from the jury—and hearing nothing—Mary volunteered to take Farrar and Lisa out to dinner, but Farrar declined. The strained expression on his face showed Matt it pained the trial attorney to know what such generosity might cost Mary. Matt also knew, from prior trials, that after working so many late nights Farrar wanted to have dinner with his family.

Matt, Mary and Lisa decided that the three of them, at least, could go to dinner. Lisa suggested Jacques-Imo's Café in uptown New Orleans, a casual restaurant where they could buy good food at a fraction of the price of some of the more expensive restaurants. Matt thought the food, drink and jovial atmosphere could serve as a fragile prop for an enjoyable evening. Lisa also invited Eric.

A pickup truck was parked in front of the restaurant, displaying to the street hubcaps painted in a swirl of orange, yellow and teal, molding with a smattering of impressionistic orange and yellow flowers and a panel with a teal alligator. White lettering on the side read: Jacques-Imo's: Real Nawlins Food. In its bed, under a wrought-iron canopy, was a table for two. Another sign in front of the peach, two-story restaurant warned: Warm Beer, Lousy Food, Poor Service.

The main dining room was a riot of color: cherry-red and fire-yellow patterned tablecloths; paintings squeezed onto every square foot of the walls, crammed into every crevice and even nailed flat to the ceiling; closer to the bar, the ceiling was painted lavender with dark, twisting tree trunks and curling branches evocative of bayou trees. Behind the bar, another sign read: Shut Up and Drink. Atop the bar sat a two-foot frog, upright on its hind legs with one webbed front foot atop the other—as if it were dancing.

Matt laughed to himself. Surely Lisa couldn't have known?

Matt and Mary ducked through the narrow doorway and pushed their way through the crowd. Lisa and Eric already sat at a table drinking among the chatter of the other restaurant patrons.

"Hi, Mary, Matt," Lisa said. "We ordered some champagne to celebrate the end of the first week of trial and your testimony."

Matt grinned and took the glass offered to him. "Let's just hope it's enough," he said.

"The testimony or the champagne?" Lisa retorted, then pivoted. "And let's not hope that tonight. Tonight, let's just enjoy each other's company."

As the group progressed through each course, their collective anxiety was blunted by the fact that nothing more could be done for the moment. Faces flushed, the group eased into the ebb and flow of the conversation.

"Well, Eric, what do you do?" Mary asked.

"I'm a real-estate lawyer, which basically means I draft documents for large real-estate projects that almost no one reads cover to cover, but that contain remarkably few typos."

"It can't be that dull." Mary laughed.

"Well, it's interesting because I get to see the various commercial real-estate projects being launched in the wake of Katrina. And I figure many lawyers are paid a premium to do work most people find extremely boring," Eric said.

"What do you think of the rebuilding effort?" Mary asked.

"It's going in fits and starts. The private companies involved are doing a better job than the government. So the areas you'd expect them to rebuild first are being rebuilt first," Eric said.

"What do you mean?" Mary asked.

The surreal risks posed by the trial, the suspension of any influence over the outcome, and the single glass of champagne combined to make Matt feel a reckless sense of abandon. If he was going to face trial on murder charges before a jury that believed him to be gay, why shouldn't he enjoy some of the benefits? He moved his hand under the table and rested it slyly on the inside of Eric's knee. A part of him was shocked at his own audacity, but for once in his life he felt he lacked a measure of self-control. Damn, it was liberating.

Eric blushed.

"Is something about that question embarrassing?" Mary asked.

"No, it's just—"

"Well, your face just turned as red as your hair."

"No, I was just thinking that the statement was somewhat disloyal because most of our clients have the money to choose to rebuild in the Quarter or Uptown."

"Well, shouldn't we rebuild the whole city?" Mary asked.

"Yeah, the length of the project shouldn't discourage you," Matt said. He slid his hand further up Eric's leg so that it was now resting mid-thigh.

"No, length has never discouraged me," Eric said. "It's just that I think perhaps we need to rebuild a few more homes in the Ninth Ward before we rebuild all of the bars in the Quarter."

"But the city needs to bring tourism back, right?" Mary asked.

"I suppose it's simply there's so much to do that we need to be working on all fronts simultaneously," Eric said. "Excuse me. I need to use the restroom." Matt grinned and Eric shot him a superficially stern look. Matt glanced toward the bathroom and saw yet another sign, thinking the place perhaps came with instructions for those it overserved. It said: Be nice or leave!

Mary was in the midst of an animated discussion with Lisa when Eric returned to the table. She refocused her attention on Eric. "Do you think there's a lot of corruption going on in the rebuilding effort?" Mary asked, in a state and city where corruption was—like in many other places—perennial but seemed more flamboyant. "I'm just scared the federal government is going to find out there were a couple of crooks and the money will dry up for everyone."

"Well, I don't think any of our clients are involved in any

corruption, but they can afford us," Eric said. "They're generally not the people with their hands in the till."

Conversation then turned to a Louisiana politician who had been discovered with hundreds of thousands of dollars in his freezer. They discussed the history of dishonesty and fraud in Louisiana and they considered whether various levels of government office gave you license to a certain number of felonies. After all, Edwin Edwards had been a four-term governor, despite five indictments.

Matt volunteered that the discussion reminded him of his favorite line from Governor Edwards. "Apparently, when he was running for reelection as governor while under indictment, a reporter asked him whether the indictment would hurt his chances. Governor Edwards responded the only way he could lose the election would be if he were caught in bed with a dead girl or a live boy. And he went on to win." Immediately after delivering the punch line, Matt realized his mistake.

Mary's eyes watered, she verged on tears, and Eric turned white.

"I'm so sorry, Matt," Mary said. "I can understand why you wouldn't want to admit you might be gay in a state where that's a punchline."

"It's okay," Matt said. "It's an old joke. And times are changing."

"Well, what do you think?" Mary asked Eric. "How much have attitudes changed?"

"As the official expert on all things gay, I hate to say it, but I don't think they've changed that much," Eric said. "I think it's telling Edwards used the word boy instead of man and implied sex with a boy was worse than sex with a girl. Associating gay sex with bestiality and pedophilia is one of the nastiest and most persistent stereotypes. Many people still associate being sex between two adults of the same gender with bestiality and child molestation and ignore whether, like being gay, it harms no one or whether, like bestiality, it harms an animal, or whether, far worse, like child molestation, it destroys lives. And they make those leaps ignoring that many people in straight relationships or who are abstinent commit those crimes.

Eric continued: "That said, I still find it hard to believe the jury will convict Matt. This just isn't a close case. He's tried as hard as he can to live an ethical and moral life and it's his word against a bunch of thugs. These three guys rank well below the crookedest Louisiana politicians."

"I hope you're right," Mary said. "I suppose there's nothing we can do about it now."

"What's everyone having for dessert?" Mary asked. "I think Matt needs some chocolate now."

"Mom," he smiled, "you only say that because you want to share it. Did you really just exploit your son's murder trial to avoid drawing attention to your love for chocolate?"

"I did no such thing. I just know you like chocolate." The group laughed and the gallows humor allowed them to finish the meal on a lighter note.

The bill arrived and Eric had to intervene loudly to convince Mary to allow him to pay his share. Lisa also insisted on paying for herself and Matt knew that Mary was relieved despite her loud protests.

After the bill had been paid, Eric asked, "Mary, do you mind if I borrow Matt for a while?"

"Of course I don't mind. I need to go to bed anyway," she said. Lisa excused herself as well.

Eric asked if Matt wanted to go to Maison Bourbon Jazz Club in the Quarter, where one of his favorite bands was playing, and Matt agreed.

In front, another sign announced that it was dedicated to the preservation of jazz. Passing through the front doors, Matt noticed an oak bar to the right, a flagstone wall behind them, antique brick walls, and a plank ceiling that matched the bar. Eric ordered them both old-fashioneds and they sat opposite each other in cushioned chairs.

"I just wanted to let you know why I haven't come to see any of the trial," Eric said. Matt was surprised: he hadn't expected Eric to attend; he wasn't sure he'd ever expect anyone other than his mother or friends forged through work to stand by him; he certainly wouldn't expect anyone he'd just met to do so.

"What? Don't be silly," Matt said. "You brought me that orchid and you've been supportive in so many other ways. You debunked my leprosy fears, after all." He smiled.

"Well, I would have liked to go to court and show my support, but I was afraid if a reporter or someone else saw me there, I could make things worse. I've been out of the closet for a while." Eric looked at him steadily.

"That makes sense," Matt said. "Let's not talk about the trial."

"All right, Atlas," Eric said. "I'd like to make a toast then. Part of that exhibit about the monarch butterfly that said after spending much of its life as a caterpillar eating poison, the butterfly must learn to fly, fly some thousand miles to Mexico and reproduce, all in only a few weeks. I think that makes it more beautiful, not less. So here's to living life—and tonight—like that butterfly."

The two clinked glasses and each took a sip.

"So, have you had any hot dates lately?" Matt's nervousness at the obviousness of the question displaced any fears about the trial for a moment.

"No," Eric smiled broadly, flashing white teeth in the dimness of the bar. People had complimented Matt on his smile, and he wondered if Eric's orthodontist and his had used the same blueprints.

Eric continued: "I got out of my first long-term relationship a few months ago and I suppose I haven't gotten back into the swing of things yet."

"What about vacations?" Matt asked, hoping to slide past the topic of dating now that he'd gotten the answer he'd been hoping for.

"I don't plan on taking a vacation anytime soon," Eric said.

"Know any good stories?" Matt asked. This was Louisiana after all.

"Okay, okay," Eric said. "Did I ever tell you about how my younger brother was such a screw-up that before leaving town the only thing my parents asked was that he not hot-box the house?"

"What's hot-boxing?"

"It's when you try to create an airtight seal on every door and window of the house and fill it with pot smoke."

"No," Matt said, "but that sounds more like it. Did I ever tell you about the time I was sent to the principal's office as a kid?"

"No," Eric said, "but I find it hard to imagine you in the principal's office."

"I was pretty depressed then, but no one would have called it that when and where I grew up. There was some bullying. A kid put thumbtacks on my chair, I sat on them and yelled. Okay, well, it may have been a squeal."

"And you wonder why you were bullied," Eric responded.

"When the substitute teacher didn't do anything about it, I got mad and put the tacks on her chair. She sent me to the principal's office."

"That sounds reasonable."

"And while waiting outside his office, I realized it was silly to worry because I was just adding another layer of unpleasantness on top of what would be an unpleasant meeting and extending the period of unpleasantness. So I forced myself to stop worrying."

"Is that really possible?" Eric asked. "You know, there are limits to your white-knuckle approach to life."

"Anyway, the principal asked if there was anyone I needed to apologize to. I answered the substitute pretty quickly, but then he asked me whether there was anyone else. I said: 'You, for taking up your time?'" Matt's pitch rose toward the end of the question, and he said, "and I said it just like that, as if it were kind of a guess, because it was."

"The principal said: 'No, that's what I'm here for. But don't you think you need to apologize to Jesus?' He then led us in prayer so that I could apologize."

Eric laughed and said: "I'm pretty sure Jesus has better things to worry about."

"But when I came home sobbing—partly because of the tacks and partly because the principal scared me—Mom was furious. She dragged me back down to that school. I'm not sure what she said to that principal—she left me waiting outside his office—but I definitely know I wouldn't have wanted to be him."

"Your Mom's great." Eric said. "At least you know she's always in your corner, right?"

"There is that," Matt said.

He wanted to take Eric's hand and restore the elixir of humor and flirtatiousness that had overcome him during dinner, but they were in public, in a straight bar. The two then swapped lighter stories of growing up, with a Southerner's sense of where to take poetic license and an implicit understanding of when the other had.

At some point, a jazz quintet took the stage, playing Thelonious Monk, and the occasional disapproving looks from more serious jazz listeners reduced them to whispers. But they kept trading one-liners and giggles that gave way to laughs, tromping over the line between respect for the musicians and merriment.

Matt realized their drinks were empty. But he didn't need or want another. A gaunt, hollow-checked trumpet player approached the microphone and began to sing a jazz classic with an unknown songwriter, performed by most notable artists for almost a hundred years: My Funny Valentine.

"Well," Eric said, "I'm betting that's the best song we're going to hear all night. Do you want to get out of here and go somewhere we can talk without getting in trouble?"

"Sure," Matt said, his heart in his throat.

"I wouldn't want to wake your Mom up," Eric said. "We could go to my place."

"Sure," Matt responded. On the ride there, Matt's tactic for defusing nervous tension in one-on-one interactions—banter—failed him. Flirtation might precipitate an outcome he didn't like; after all, he'd talked himself into every relationship with a woman that had ended poorly; so silence reined. After arriving at the apartment, Eric poured water for each.

"So, now that we have some more privacy, how are you really holding up?" Eric asked.

"I'm pretty much a wreck. You can tell when I'm really nervous or in trouble because I go silent and expressionless. As events around me worsen, I withdraw into myself. I suppose that ability to withdraw is what allowed me to kill someone else." Matt realized he had potentially revealed his level of anxiety during the car ride over, but he was too worn down to care. For once, he wanted someone who really knew him and seemed to like him to shoulder a fraction of his loneliness and its burden, no matter that imposing on them might be selfish. Perhaps trying to prevent his pain from spilling over to those he cared about was impossible unless he found a measure of happiness.

"You did what you had to do." Eric said. "You should focus on the remainder of your life tonight, not the life of that asshole."

"Focusing on the remainder of my life is precisely what makes me want to vomit. There is, quite literally, nothing else that I can do to prevent myself from going to prison…or the death chamber." Matt reached for his glass, shaving a few inches off the distance between himself and Eric.

"We could run away to Mexico," Eric said. "I might have to stop by an ATM, but then we could drive across the border."

"And my mother would lose everything," Matt said.

"Which she would gladly do. I can't believe I'm the one telling you to lighten up. What happened to waiting outside the principal's office?"

"I was just trying to put up a front for both of us," Matt said. "No one could face the death penalty and really think of it as comparable to the seeing the principal."

"I know. By the way, I also think you did the right thing by taking those training sessions at Tommy's gym."

"It's so hard," Matt said. He replaced his glass on the coffee table and studied it. "It's not as if I didn't see how that could be used against me, but if I failed to do anything to prepare, I'd be even more afraid of what could happen in prison. Odds are I'd still get beaten and raped. But at least the training allows me to feel like I did something. Even if I can't protect myself, I'm hoping it could help me preserve some shred of dignity. When I think of how hard prison could be, it makes me wonder whether I'd prefer the death penalty."

"Don't talk like that." Eric gently turned Matt's face toward him. "There's no reason to think you'll be convicted. I still think the jury will see the difference between your character and that of the witnesses testifying against you. And, prison or no prison, we all have to find small things that give us pleasure in life. You're still allowed to read books in prison, you're still permitted to write, and you can even continue legal work for yourself and others. And there's always the hope of clemency from the governor. You should be a prime candidate."

"I know. It's just hard."

"You're an exceptional person who found himself in an impossible situation. That's not your fault, no matter the jury's verdict," Eric said.

Matt suddenly felt lightheaded. Maybe the two drinks had gone to his head because he'd been drinking so little recently. But he'd only had two, and he'd been drinking water since.

"Thanks. And now I think we should shift gears. What do you have to say that can help distract me?" Matt asked.

"Well, have I ever told you about the garage door?" Eric asked.

"No."

"I'm a first child, and this story pretty much reveals the differences between a first child and a third child. My father was very strict when I was growing up. Fair but strict. But by the time my little brother came along, as my mother put it, they were tired. One morning, my parents are sitting at breakfast when they hear a huge crash from the garage. My youngest brother comes storming in the house in a rage and shouts, 'Who the hell left the garage door down?' My father just started laughing so hard he couldn't get angry." Matt had trouble keeping a straight face himself.

"But there's a lesson there for first children. Sometimes life really is what you make of it. That my little brother was able to see the garage door's intervention as someone else's fault saved him some grief. It certainly injected some humor into the situation. And don't think for a second he was unaware of the humorous value in storming into the house and blaming someone else for leaving the garage door down."

"I hear you," Matt said.

Matt reveled in Eric's bonhomie. Eric took his hand and looked directly into his eyes. To Matt's surprise, he leaned in and kissed Eric, tentatively at first, but without any thought of keeping his lips together. The whiskers on their faces scratched each other and what began softly quickly became consuming. He no longer noticed the bristles. Eric's strong arms and broad chest made Matt lose track of where he was as they ran their hands over each other's firm bodies.

Eric broke off. Matt couldn't have guessed how long they'd been making out if someone had held a gun to his head.

"I know this may be too soon for you, especially with everything else that's going on," Eric said.

"Let's consider this an example of making the most of life," Matt said. "I probably wouldn't have the guts to do this if I wasn't facing possible life imprisonment tomorrow. But there's nowhere I'd rather spend what could be my last free night than with you."

Eric led Matt into his bedroom. He didn't get much sleep that night, but for very different reasons than he'd anticipated that morning.

Chapter 15

Matt woke in Eric's arms but felt awkward: his discomfort at becoming more entangled with Eric while the jury was still out made a repeat performance impossible, but he knew he would forever remember the experience fondly. So he gave Eric a light kiss on the cheek, taking care not to wake him, left a one-word note of thanks in his kitchen and returned to his own house.

Matt walked into his kitchen that morning to see Mary brewing a pot of coffee and knew from past experience he'd hear nothing other than a mumbled "Good morning" until after her first cup. He allowed her to pour herself the first, but soon after poured his own, and both sat at the kitchen table.

After she'd processed her thoughts, and poured a second cup to activate her brain, she said, "You know, I normally wouldn't approve of anything you might have been doing staying out so late with a boy—or girl—this soon. But I like Eric and I think the circumstances are unusual. I hope it gave you some happiness."

Matt wondered whether that felt like a concession or sacrifice to her. But he said: "It did, Mom. As cheesy as it sounds and despite everything else that's going on, I feel a glow that even the prospect of the verdict can't tarnish."

"Good, then let's get to court," Mary responded.

Matt arrived at his usual seat at the counsel's table, thrumming from a combination of elation, fatigue and anxiety.

Farrar turned to Matt and said, "You look exhausted. At least you don't have to worry about the jury studying you all day."

Judge Masterson's clerk interrupted and said, "All rise. Court is in session. The Honorable Robert Masterson presiding."

Judge Masterson and the lawyers took their seats.

"The jury is present and complete," Judge Masterson said. "The jurors are continuing their deliberations in the jury room. I don't think there's any other business before us, so I'll see you all if we hear anything."

There was nothing left for the defense team to do. Lisa volunteered to remain in the courtroom while everyone else went to the cafeteria for coffee. They gathered around a table and Farrar regaled them with war stories from previous trials in the prosecutor's office and private practice. His anecdotes were periodically interrupted by emails and phone calls while the morning passed with the agonizing slowness usually reserved for religious ceremonies.

At about eleven o'clock, Lisa came down to the cafeteria and reported that the clerk had announced the jury was back. Matt resisted the urge to run in two directions at once and returned to the courtroom with everyone else.

Judge Masterson took his place. "The jury has reached a verdict. I know this has been a hard-fought case, but I'd appreciate it if everyone could attempt to maintain their composure when the verdict's read. This jury may also have to decide whether to impose the death penalty and I don't want that decision colored by anyone's reaction to the verdict. If anyone feels like they can't control themselves, they should leave the courtroom. My clerk will now bring the jury in."

As the jurors came into the room, not one looked in Matt's direction. The pit forming in his stomach sucked in a deep breath that he hoped was imperceptible. Judge Masterson asked, "Mr Foreperson, have you reached a unanimous verdict?"

"We have, Your Honor."

"What is your verdict?"

"We find the defendant, Matthew Durant, guilty of first-degree murder."

Matt's chest collapsed on itself. Mary's face turned bright red and she began crying hysterically; tears streamed down her face, mucus ran from her nose and whimpers rose from her throat.

"Thank you," Judge Masterson said. "Ladies and gentlemen, I want to thank you for your service. You'll also need to decide whether Mr Durant should receive life in prison or the death penalty. But there are various things that the lawyers and I need to do to prepare for that proceeding. As much as I hate to inconvenience you, I'm going to have to ask you to wait until next Monday before beginning again because the lawyers and I need to prepare for the penalty phase of the trial. I thank you again for your service, remind you not to discuss the case, and you are excused until Monday."

After the jury had exited the courtroom, Judge Masterson turned to address Matt. "The jury has found you guilty, and the minimum sentence is life imprisonment—I hereby revoke your bail. You will be remanded into the custody of the Orleans Parish Prison pending the outcome of the sentencing hearing. Officer, take Mr Durant into custody."

Mary's intermittent low and broken sounds built to a shriek of "nooooo" as she rushed forward to throw her entire weight between the court officer and Matt. The large man easily brushed her aside and Lisa and Farrar pulled her back before Judge Masterson could threaten her with contempt. Matt once again felt cold metal handcuffs encircle his wrists and pin his arms behind his back.

*

Matt next snapped to when shuffling up the stairs of a modified school bus with five other prisoners. He'd spent his previous stint in Orleans Parish Prison in his own cell, but he suspected his only opportunity for another solitary berth now would be on death row.

Under the weight of despair, his whole face and body sagged— his mouth, chin, shoulders and back slackened and his knees bent though the shock of the conviction reverberated through his bones. His stomach sickened at the thought of his mother's uncontrollable grief in the courtroom. For so long she'd entrusted her hopes and happiness to Matt's drive toward success and that drive had now ended.

The prisoners each occupied an individual bench, so by turning toward the window he was able to find some small measure of privacy. As he peered out the window at the passing French Quarter, he couldn't hold back his tears. He worried about the impression crying might make on the other prisoners, but he lacked the strength to gather himself. He hoped they couldn't see his face. The jury's finding that he'd lied made him feel dirty and threatened to obliterate that he'd told the truth.

The bus came to a stop long before he was prepared. The guard at the front gestured the prisoners toward the door and Matt, with the aid of another officer, descended the steps in cuffs and shackles.

The processing that followed left no doubt about Matt's separation from the rest of humanity. He was searched and relinquished his few personal possessions to an indifferent guard behind a mesh metal screen. Another officer ushered him to a small shower, instructed him to strip naked, and doused him with a thick powder. Instructions to "wash it off real good so it don't burn" were impossible to follow in the fifteen seconds he was given to shower. The water changed the powder to paste; he stepped out and a chemical burn began at his armpits and reached critical mass in his crotch; tears welled up again, the physical pain serving as both cause and excuse.

The guard then led Matt down a hallway edged with cells and brought him to number 415.

"This is it. Your new home. Don't get too used to it, 'cause you're only here until the jury decides your sentence. Your cellmate is Dwayne Turner," the guard said.

Matt looked into the cell as his shackles and cuffs were unlocked. Dwayne was a small black man with fuzz covering his head. "Matt Durant," he said, extending his hand. Dwayne looked at it disdainfully, but he was no larger than himself. He immediately second-guessed the thought—he wasn't sure he could handle a seasoned criminal of any size.

"Hey man, you leave me alone and I'll leave you alone." Dwayne flashed gold teeth that implied neither wealth nor happiness. "You must have done something wrong to be one of the only white dudes in here, but I don't really care. Got me?"

"Yeah, I've got you, but mind if I ask a couple of questions?" Matt asked.

"Naw. Go ahead."

"What's the schedule like in here?"

"We spend mos' of our time in this cell. Prison's overcrowded, so they'se shut down the cafeteria. Each wing only gets to go outside one hour a week. Everyone s'posed to be here temporary-like, so I guess they don't figure they need to make it too nice."

"What about contact with the other prisoners?" Matt asked.

"There ain't much, which is good for your lily-white ass."

"Is there anything to read?" Matt asked.

"They got a liberry cart comes around every day. But mos' folks just watch that," Dwayne said. He pointed to a fuzzy black-and-white television set blaring out in the hallway. "Guards like it when we watch TV 'cause it makes their job easier. You get used to the noise."

"What about writing materials?"

"Comes around with the liberry cart. You got credit for paper, pens, envelopes, stamps, and stuff based on how much cash you had in your pockets when you got here," Dwayne said. "And you can add money if you got someone on the outside to help you do it."

"Thanks."

"Got a couple of hours tonight 'til dinner. Then it's lights out. Not much to do other'n watch TV until dinner."

Matt clambered into the available, top bunk and lay down on a thin pad that did nothing to soften the metal underneath: he had a feeling sleep would become his principal pastime over the next few weeks. He woke a few hours later to a meal he tried not to think about as he shoved it into his mouth.

The lights went out a couple of hours after dinner. Before that, the television set had been the only way to tell time. Broadcast time and temperature updates appeared less frequently than he remembered on the outside, but four or five sitcoms were shown between dinner and lights out.

In the darkness, Matt could hear the noises of men confined in the nearby cells. Sobs and grunts rose above the sounds of heavy breathing and snores. Despite Dwayne's suggestion that they not bother each other, his cellmate didn't have any compunction about masturbating himself to sleep. As Matt lay awake, trying to ignore the shaking of the bunk bed, he no longer felt the urge to cry. Dull, wooden thoughts about what could possibly happen next had replaced tears.

The next morning, breakfast was remarkable only for how disgusting it was. After *The Tyra Show*, Matt was relieved to see that a trusty came around with a cart of books and writing materials. He borrowed copies of a couple of books he'd already read, along with some pens, paper, envelopes and stamps. He was happy to have something to divert him from the insipid programming, which seemed a form of punishment in and of itself.

Matt returned to his bunk and attempted to compose a letter to his mother, who he worried was more upset and hurt than him by the jury's verdict. He found it odd to print by hand again, which he did slowly and deliberately, bearing down too hard on his limited supply of paper:

Dear Mom:

I wanted to write and let you know everything is going as well as it could. The verdict yesterday was a terrible blow, but there are small things in here for me to enjoy. The sensation of writing a letter by hand, without rushing in the way that we all type nowadays, is something to relish. And I managed to get copies of a couple of good books: *To Kill a Mockingbird* and *Huck Finn*. I've read both before, but they're certainly worth rereading. I'll now have the time to focus on the placement of every word, as the authors did.

I'm physically safe. I have a cellmate, but he and I have agreed to leave each other alone. I'll only have about two hours' worth of exposure to the other inmates each week in the exercise yard and the showers, and I understand both facilities are under video surveillance and closely supervised by the guards.

Other than letting you know I'm safe and as well as can be, I just wanted to thank you. You've shown me more love than would have been possible from any other human being. I've enjoyed our conversations and the time that we've spent together at every age, and you've shown me enough love in the last twenty-eight years to last a lifetime.

I also want to let you know your primary obligation now is to enjoy life for me. Minister to a patient who recovers against the odds and describe the recovery to me; go on dates and tell me about them; go to LSU games and describe them to me. I'm depending on you to live a happy and full life so I can enjoy it vicariously.

Love,
Matt

Matt folded the letter, sealed the envelope, wrote his mother's address on the front and, after consultation with Dwayne, finally added the return address of his new home before affixing a stamp. His letter—even if a bit formal—at least was designed to give his mother some hope, but now he felt drained as he considered living up to the promises he'd made. He wanted to write letters to Eric, Lisa, Farrar and all the others who had lent him so much support over the past few weeks and months, but he lacked the energy.

Matt spent the remainder of the day with his attention listlessly drifting between the drafting letters in his head, the books, the television set, and sleep. He and Dwayne barely spoke.

The next morning was indistinguishable from the first. Matt worked up the courage to write to Eric:

Dear Eric,

I wanted to write to thank you for your support and friendship throughout the trial. I wish we could have had more time together, but that doesn't lessen my appreciation for the time that we did spend together. The night before they took me to prison was perhaps the best night of my life.

Thank you for continuing to push me to reveal something of myself to you rather than simply hiding behind banter. I couldn't have made it through the trial without your support and your example. And it makes my time in here easier to bear.

I'm physically safe and as well as can be. I just wanted to drop you a short note to express my appreciation for everything you did for me.

Take Care,
Matt

His hand trembled as he finished the letter. He wasn't sure whether he was exhausted from depression or because his metabolism had already slowed dramatically in only a few days of imprisonment—he wondered if other simple tasks would soon be overwhelming.

Around one o'clock that afternoon, a guard came to the cell door and said, "Time for exercise and showers."

The officers opened the entire row of cell doors lining the corridor and escorted the prisoners outside to a yard ringed with concertina wire and cameras. The inmates trudged around the yard with blank expressions: no one seemed particularly interested in him for the first ten minutes and the relief lightened his step. The video surveillance and the fact that the other detainees had yet to be sentenced reassured him that the rest of the exercise period would be uneventful. It was.

The prisoners were then led to a communal shower with no

walls or partitions. Here too surveillance cameras abounded: it appeared prison administrators had decided to focus it on the common areas where violence or assault would be more likely.

The late afternoon and evening faded into an indistinguishable blur and before Matt realized it, he woke up the next morning to the same bland meal that he'd eaten yesterday.

After he finished, the guard approached the cell door. "Durant, your lawyer wants to see you. Put your hands through the slot so I can cuff you."

Matt stuck his hands through the bars and received the handcuffs with outstretched palms. Foregoing shackles, the guard led him to an interview room. Matt walked in to find his mother and Farrar waiting for him.

"We can't supervise this interview because your lawyer's here," the guard said, "but don't abuse the privilege or we'll turn on the cameras without the sound. And we can restrict access to your lawyers if we have to."

The door clanged shut and Mary rushed forward to hug him in the awkward way that a diminutive mother embraces her son's larger frame.

"Matt, I'm so sorry. I love you so much."

"It's all right, Mama. It's just good to see you."

The pair parted and Farrar reached forward to shake his hand. Matt responded by using both hands to clasp Farrar's, not in an imitation of some politician's idea of warmth, but because his were cuffed together.

"I'm sorry, Matt. I've failed you. A jury should never have believed those criminals over you."

"You didn't fail me. You tried a great case and I'll forever be grateful. The system failed, not you."

"Well, we can consider how the system failed when we reach the point of crafting an appeal. For now, we need to focus on your sentencing," Farrar said. "You're a first-time offender without any history of violence, so we should be able to convince the jury not to sentence you to death. Saving your life is our sole focus now."

Depression deadened Matt's ability to process the news; he wasn't at all certain he wanted to live longer in prison.

"Our case should be pretty simple. We'll rely on testimony from your mother and Judge Thompson, of course, but we need to identify the other character witnesses we should call on your behalf."

The group discussed Matt's various charitable activities over the years and composed a short list of people to contact. Each one had dedicated his or her life to helping others, and Matt had always felt that his few hours of charitable work a week paled in comparison to their commitment.

"Finally, I'd like to testify in the penalty phase," Farrar said. "That's a bit tricky because, as you know, there are ethical restrictions against the lead trial attorney testifying as a witness. We need to decide who will represent you as your lawyer during this phase. I have several ideas…"

Matt interrupted: "I'd be happy to have Lisa handle the sentencing phase." He thought highly of the skills of few lawyers, and he trusted no one who he hadn't known closely. "I know she's less experienced than some other possible lawyers, but she knows the case backwards and forwards and this phase should be straightforward—an opening, the examinations of the character witnesses and a closing."

Matt continued: "And thank you for volunteering to testify, but if testifying is going to negatively impact the firm or its business—"

"Stop," Farrar responded. "Any impact on the firm or me is negligible compared to what you're going through. We're not giving up on the rest of your life and we're not going to let you give up either. I don't have much more to say, but if I remain here for a half-hour or so with you and your mother, it will give you some privacy. Let me work at the end of this table and the two of you can catch up."

Matt and his mother went to the corner of the conference room.

"Matt, I'm going to have to go back to Lafayette. Mr Farrar and I tried to visit earlier, but the jail had some official policy about giving you a few days to adjust before they'd allow visitors. I'd like to take more time off of work, but the hospital's pretty conservative and I think they've had about enough."

"I know, Mom," Matt said. "I figured the hospital probably wouldn't react well to your taking so much personal time to attend the trial. I wrote you a letter, but I also want to let you know I'm safe."

"I don't want you to worry too much about the next phase of the trial or the state penitentiary," Mary said. "Remember, half the things you worry about never happen." The words were betrayed by her quavering voice.

"You know, I've always considered that expression odd, coming from you. You worry more than anyone else I know, Mom. I sometimes think that was my best feature as a lawyer. My anxiety created a fine eye for detail." Matt tried to smile.

"I know," Mary said. "And I'm worried. But there's nothing we can do about the jury verdict now. I just want you to know that I love you, I believe in you and I'll never stop fighting for you. You're in my prayers every night."

"I know, Mom." As always, Matt felt conflicted when he heard that: he knew that the God some prayed too didn't protect those like him.

Farrar looked up and said, "I'm sorry, but I think we've exhausted our time. We don't want to push our luck and jeopardize any further visits."

His mother gave him a hug, pressing his arms against his clammy pits, and—when she finally released him—he had to force himself to release her in turn so she wouldn't feel his desperation. Matt felt like it would be the last time he'd see her, even if he knew better.

Chapter 16

The following Monday, Matt was led back to the courthouse through the prisoners' entrance, took his seat, and then looked up—the sight of the empty jury box caused his emotions to surge. The memory of the recent verdict merged with his fear in a torrent that threatened to sweep him away; the same jury that had concluded he'd lied about the events in the alley would now determine whether he lived or died. He shuddered for a fraction of a second and the shakes settled in his right eye, where the muscles continued to twitch. He thought he'd just managed to rein in his emotions, get the eye under control, assumed an impassive expression, and hoped no one had noticed.

Lisa, rather than Thomas, sat to Matt's immediate left, studying her outline for the direct examination of her first witness and mouthing the words silently. Her trembling hand as she wrote wasn't reassuring, but her intelligence had always been obvious, and—despite his hatred of himself and disbelief that anyone could have such feelings toward him—he'd learned to trust her loyalty and passion even if he chalked it up to an unusually kind soul. Besides, the examinations would be straightforward, right?

Judge Masterson entered and took his place on the bench. "Are there any legal issues that we need to address before we bring in the jury?" he asked the lawyers. Both Thibedeaux and Lisa said there were none. Judge Masterson instructed his clerk to bring in the jury.

"Ladies and gentlemen, we now enter the penalty phase of the trial," Judge Masterson said. "The only question before you will be whether Mr Durant should receive life imprisonment or the death penalty for the murder of Brian Cutler. The prosecutor and defense will not present opening arguments as they did in the guilt phase. We'll proceed directly to the prosecution's presentation of evidence, followed by the defense's presentation of evidence, and then concluding statements. Mr Thibedeaux, your first witness?"

"The state calls Betsey Trudeau," Thibedeaux said.

Betsey made her way to the stand, dressed in a simple black pencil skirt and a plain white blouse, which set off a weary face and bleached blonde hair.

"What was your relationship to Brian Cutler?"

"I was his fiancée."

"How long had you been dating Mr Cutler?"

"We started dating my senior year in high school, four years ago. When we met at a party, he'd already graduated and was working on the offshore rigs."

"Can you describe your relationship with Mr Cutler to the jury?"

"Brian was a good man. We never had much, but he shared everything he had. He spent more money on my Christmas presents than he spent on himself in a month. He liked watching football and drinking beer. Most other folks probably wouldn't think he was any different from a lot of other men in Houma, but he was my man."

"Can you describe how you felt when you heard about Brian Cutler's death?"

"Donnie Rand called me on the phone. I knew Brian, Donnie and John had gone down to New Orleans to celebrate getting off of the rig. Donnie said they'd run into a problem in an alley and a guy had hit Brian with a beer bottle. He said Brian was dead." Her tired and pink eyes turned such a violent shade of crimson that her clear tears came as a surprise.

"How did you feel when you heard that?"

"I felt like somebody ripped my heart out of my chest. It hurt so bad I thought I'd never be able to catch my breath again."

"How do you feel now?"

"It still hurts real bad, like a constant ache, but I can breathe better."

"How did Brian Cutler's death change your life?"

"I had to stop planning the wedding, that's for sure. We'd also been talkin' about having kids and now that's never gonna happen. His last name is gonna disappear, 'cause his only living family are his momma and sisters."

"Did Brian Cutler's death change your future financially?"

"Sure, I mean, I don't know when I'll actually be able to afford a house now. But that don't matter. I just want him back, 'specially when the nights get cooler. It's awful quiet at night and that's when I miss him the most. I wish I could just laugh with him again or share a story from work. What I miss most is just havin' him near me. Knowin' he was near me gave me so much comfort."

"Do you think Matthew Durant deserves the jury's mercy?"

"No, I don't," Betsey said. She straightened her spine, squared her shoulders, and pressed her lips tightly together before continuing: "Mr Durant prob'ly didn't think much of Brian, bein' a fancy lawyer and all, but I loved Brian, and he was all I had in this world. I think this Durant guy should get the same as he gave to Brian. The state should kill him. I wish they could crush his skull with a beer bottle."

Matt's shame flared up. He liked to think hitting Cutler with the beer bottle had been necessary, but putting a face on the victim made him somehow doubt it. Maybe the jury had been right.

"No further questions, Your Honor."

"No questions, Your Honor," Lisa said.

"Mr Thibedeaux, your next witness," Judge Masterson said.

"The state calls Anna Lee Cutler to the stand," Thibedeaux responded.

Anna Lee Cutler, an older version of Betsey who'd obviously given up on dyeing her hair, took the stand. The extra two decades had carved deep lines into her face—if poverty had an expression, Anna Lee Cutler bore it.

"Ms Cutler, what was your relationship to Brian?"

"I'm his mother."

"How did you learn that Brian had been killed?"

"Donnie Rand called me and said that a guy down in New Orleans had attacked Brian with a beer bottle and bashed in his head. Donnie said Brian was dead."

"How did you feel when you learned Brian was dead?"

"No mother should ever have to hear that her son has died. I ain't made much of my life, but I was always proud of my boy and the way he treated Betsey. I'd always hoped that when I passed, a piece of me would live on through Brian, Betsey and, God willing, their kids. But mostly it just hurt." Anna Lee began sobbing, barely able to continue speaking. She reached into her purse. Even her tissues had seen better days and, as she attempted to unravel one, it disintegrated in her hands. Thibedeaux offered her a handkerchief and she wiped her eyes with it.

"How do you feel now?" Thibedeaux asked.

"I miss him, and it hurts just as much as it did when Donnie told me. I'm not sure how I'm gonna get through this."

"Do you think that the jury should show mercy to Mr Durant?"

"No, I don't. I think that he should suffer the same as he gave my boy. I think they should vote to put him to death."

"No further questions, Your Honor," Thibedeaux concluded.

"Ms Boudreaux, do you have any questions for the witness?" Judge Masterson asked.

"Yes, Your Honor," Lisa said. Matt knew he wouldn't have been able to cross-examine Brian's mother to save himself.

"Ms Cutler, let me first say that I'm sorry for your loss. You testified that no mother should know the pain of losing a child, correct?"

"I said that."

"Does that include Matthew Durant's mother?"

"Well, I reckon her son should have thought about that before he killed mine. At least his momma'll get to say good-bye to her son. My boy died in a dirty back alley and I couldn't even tell him I loved him before he went."

"If Matthew Durant is executed, do you think it will cause his mother significant pain?"

"Yeah, I reckon it'll hurt her pretty bad. Maybe she should have raised him better." Guilt coursed through Matt for exposing his mother to such accusations and in that moment he wanted nothing more than to stop hurting those around him.

"No further questions, Your Honor," Lisa concluded. Cross-examining Anna Lee Cutler had been a mistake and Lisa hadn't gotten anything useful, but it had been a harmless mistake. The jury knew Anna Lee Cutler was angry and bitter about the death of her son after the direct examination, and her testimony on cross was just confirmatory.

"Your Honor, the state has no further witnesses," Thibedeaux said.

"Ms Boudreaux, would the defense like to present any witnesses?" Judge Masterson asked.

"We'd like to begin by asking that the court permit the jury to consider the testimony of Judge Michael Thompson, who testified earlier in the trial, on the question of whether Mr Durant should receive the death penalty."

"The jury may consider that evidence. Do you have any additional witnesses?"

"Yes, Your Honor. The defense calls Jason Shapiro." Shapiro, the director of the LSU legal-aid clinic, was in his early forties and had a bald patch. He testified that Matt had provided much-needed legal assistance and emotional support to indigent criminal defendants throughout law school. He also testified that the prosecution's allegations were completely inconsistent with Matt's character. Thibedeaux declined to ask any questions.

Lisa then called Heather Cox to the stand. A thin and frail woman slowly made her way up to the front of the courtroom with the aid of a cane.

"Ms Cox, can you please explain how you know Matthew Durant?"

"Starting in about 1990 when he was in junior high, Matt started tutoring illiterate adults at a community center I run."

"How many people did Matthew Durant teach how to read?"

"He taught four adults how to read before he left for college. I understand that he also spent some time tutoring down in Baton Rouge and New Orleans."

"How many years did Mr Durant tutor illiterate adults at your community center?"

"He was a tutor for five years."

"What did you learn of his character during that period of time?"

"I learned Matt is an extremely intelligent young man who is deeply sympathetic to those who don't have his natural abilities. I also learned he is capable of extremely complex reasoning and I enjoyed several conversations we had about literature. More importantly, though, he put his intellect to work to try to figure out simple and original ways to explain concepts to those with less ability or simply less education."

"Were you surprised when you learned Mr Durant had been convicted of murder?"

"I was more than surprised. It was perhaps the most unexpected and stunning thing I've ever heard in my life."

"No further questions, Your Honor," Lisa concluded.

"Your Honor, the state doesn't have any questions for this witness," Mr Thibedeaux said.

"Would you like to call your next witness, Ms Boudreaux?" Judge Masterson said.

"Your Honor, we'd like to call Thomas Farrar to the stand."

"Your Honor, we object because of Mr Farrar's role as trial counsel," Thibedeaux said.

"Overruled," Judge Masterson said. "Presumably Ms Boudreaux is handling this phase of the trial because Mr Farrar is testifying. He's also been Mr Durant's employer for years. Mr Durant is entitled to present his testimony."

"Thank you, Your Honor," Lisa said.

Farrar approached the stand, bowed and subdued. He swore to tell the truth with his eyes slightly downcast.

"Mr Farrar, how do you know Matthew Durant?"

"Matt Durant has worked for my law firm for the last two years."

"Over the past two years, what opinion, if any, have you formed about his character?"

"Matt's an upstanding young man. He's conscientious of our ethical duties to our clients and he performs his work with an eye toward those duties, rather than impressing his superiors. Matt's excellent when working with clients, witnesses and coworkers, in part because he's such an obviously caring person. He listens to others carefully which, as you might expect, is relatively rare for a lawyer. He's one of the best young men I have ever met. I'd be proud to call him my son."

"Were you surprised by the jury's verdict?"

"I was very surprised. I suppose I didn't communicate Matt's honesty and integrity effectively enough, even though I know it in my heart." Turning to the jury and raising his eyes, Farrar continued in a steady voice that did little to conceal his desperation, saying, "I know you've already made the decision Matt's guilty, but I beg you to spare his life. Even if you're right about what happened in that alley, nothing else in Matt's life suggests the death penalty would be an appropriate punishment. Please spare him."

"No further questions, Your Honor," Lisa said.

"No questions, Your Honor," Mr Thibedeaux said.

"The defense calls Mary Durant to the stand," Lisa said.

Mary approached the stand yet again and swore once more to tell the truth, invoking the specter of God's wrath for his sake. Guilt plagued him.

"Ms Durant, did the jury's verdict make you reconsider any testimony you gave during the first phase of your son's trial?"

"No, it did not."

"Do you have anything else to add on the subject of whether Matt should receive the death penalty?"

"Please don't kill my son." Mary turned and looked at the twelve individuals seated in the jury box. Many averted their eyes. "Matt can do a great deal of good, if you'll let him. At the very least, he can teach prisoners to read and write. Matt could have become a law-school professor and, if you give him a chance, he can still help some prisoners develop the skills to earn an honest living outside of prison. Every witness at this trial has testified that Matt has done much good in his life. No matter what you think happened in that alley, Matt's not some sort of depraved killer. He at least deserves the opportunity to try and find meaning to his life in prison."

"No further questions, Your Honor."

"No questions, Your Honor," Mr Thibedeaux said.

"Do you have any other witnesses, Ms Boudreaux?" Judge Masterson asked.

"No, Your Honor. The defense rests."

"Ladies and gentlemen, let's take a break for lunch and then we'll hear closing arguments," Judge Masterson said. The jurors left the room and Judge Masterson turned to the attorneys. "My clerk is handing out a copy of my proposed instructions, which shouldn't be controversial. They're in a standard form approved by the Louisiana Supreme Court. We'll reconvene at one and I'll entertain any objections before closing arguments."

Farrar had convinced the guards to allow the defense team to meet in the conference room during the recess. A messenger from Farrar Levinson had delivered lunch. The defense team reviewed the instructions but, as Judge Masterson had warned, there was nothing objectionable. The group in the room, which included Mary, alternated between silence and strained talk of everyday things. The small talk focused Matt's attention on how quickly and dramatically his life had changed. He tried to shove down those thoughts for fear they'd taint the precious, limited time he had remaining with those he loved.

He had to return to his regular seat in the courtroom too soon. Judge Masterson entered and confirmed that the lawyers didn't have any objections to his proposed instructions.

After the jury had filed in, taken their seats and settled in, Judge Masterson addressed them, saying, "We'll now hear closing arguments from the prosecution and defense on the issue of whether Mr Durant should receive the death penalty. Mr Thibedeaux?"

"Ladies and gentlemen, I'd like to begin by thanking you for your patience and hard work," Thibedeaux said. "In this penalty phase of the trial, you're considering a broad array of evidence about Matthew Durant and the impact of the murder of Brian Cutler. Judge Masterson will instruct you on how to weigh that evidence." Thibedeaux employed none of the theatrical gestures common in his closing during the guilt phase. "I'd ask merely that you remember why we're here. We're not here because Matthew Durant is a brilliant young man who has treated some people well in his life."

Thibedeaux's eyes hardened as he said, "We're here because you determined Matthew Durant intentionally bashed in the skull of Brian Cutler with a beer bottle to cover up his attempt to buy drugs. And you should ask why a young man who would demonstrate such callous disregard for the life of another person would engage in charitable acts. I'd suggest Mr Durant engaged in charity to bolster and enhance his reputation rather than to improve the lives of others. Mr Durant revealed his true character on the night he crushed Brian Cutler's skull. And you heard testimony about the effect of Brian Cutler's death. Brian Cutler is not some fancy, highly educated lawyer. Brian Cutler was a plainspoken oil-rig worker. But Brian Cutler's fiancée and his mother testified his death will change their lives forever. You have the chance to show that Brian Cutler's life was worth at least as much as Matthew Durant's life. I'd suggest that Mr Cutler's life was worth far more than Mr Durant's because Mr Durant punctured Brian Cutler's skull with a beer bottle. And you should punish Matthew Durant accordingly. Thank you."

"Ms Boudreaux?" Judge Masterson asked.

"Ladies and gentlemen, I'd also like to thank you for your long and difficult service. Mr Thibedeaux spent a great deal of time discussing facts that you've already determined because, under the law as Judge Masterson will describe it to you, Mr Durant does not deserve the death penalty. Judge Masterson will provide you with a long list of aggravating factors that may warrant the death penalty, and those aggravating factors are pretty horrific. They involve crimes such as forcible rape, killing a police officer, killing a witness, killing someone under the age of twelve and killing someone over the age of sixty-five. The only aggravating factor that even arguably applies in this case is that Mr Durant is alleged to have been purchasing cocaine. That's it. And that single factor is not enough to justify a death sentence," Lisa said.

"You've heard testimony from a wide variety of people who've known Mr Durant throughout his life. Those individuals all testified Mr Durant is a moral person who treated others in his life with kindness. He taught several illiterate adults how to read; he represented impoverished people accused of crimes for free; and he treated his coworkers with respect. As Judge Masterson will instruct you, if you find Mr Durant shouldn't receive the death penalty, he will go to prison for life. Ms Cutler and Ms Trudeau will have the death they desire so strongly. Matt will grow old and die alone in prison. And I think that's sufficient punishment for the crime that you found this exemplary young man has committed."

Matt swallowed as he considered the best-case scenario.

Lisa continued, saying, "And I submit the evidence of Mr Durant's character shows more than that Mr Durant doesn't deserve the death penalty. The evidence shows Mr Durant can and will continue to benefit others in prison. Mr Durant has the academic qualifications and background necessary to teach law school. Can you imagine the good he'll do for other prisoners with his ability to teach? I simply ask that you give him the opportunity. Thank you."

Matt mouthed, "Thank you," to Lisa as she rejoined him at counsel's table. He'd been right about her intelligence and passion; in the end, he didn't think her inexperience had mattered.

"Thank you, Ms Boudreaux," Judge Masterson said. "Ladies and gentlemen, I'll now instruct you on the law that governs your decision about whether Mr Durant should receive the death penalty or life imprisonment. You should focus on the circumstances of the offense, the character and propensities of the offender and the impact that the death has had on the family members. Louisiana law sets forth several aggravating circumstances you may consider in deciding whether to impose the death penalty."

Judge Masterson then recited a list of twelve potential aggravating factors with the only pertinent factor being that "the offender was engaged in the distribution, exchange, sale or purchase, or any attempt thereof, of a controlled substance." Judge Masterson instructed the jury that it must consider eight different mitigating factors. "Under Louisiana law, I'm also obligated to instruct you the alternatives are life imprisonment without parole or execution. Although a parole board cannot shorten a life sentence in this case, the governor of the state is empowered to grant reprieves, pardons and commutations of either a life sentence or the death penalty. You must find a sentence of death is warranted unanimously. If you cannot decide unanimously, then Mr Durant will receive a sentence of life imprisonment. You may now retire to consider your verdict."

After Judge Masterson delivered the instructions, the defense team returned to the conference room. Though everyone in the room knew it was one of their final chances to be together, no one spoke: the weight of what was to come overwhelmed their ability to be present in the moment, let alone make the most of it. And the clerk announced that the jury had reached a verdict in fifteen minutes. The jurors took their seats and Judge Masterson asked, "Have you reached a decision on the appropriate sentence?"

The jury foreperson responded, "We have, Your Honor."

"What is your decision?"

"We've decided Matthew Durant should be imprisoned for life, without the possibility of parole."

Matt felt a rush of happiness before realizing how little he had to be happy about. Even Thibedeaux didn't look disappointed and the defense team collectively slumped in relief. Matt wondered whose testimony had affected the jurors the most and guessed it was his mother's. After bringing him into this world, Mary hadn't been willing to watch him depart it, shifting to him the enormous, looming burden of living.

"These proceedings are concluded," Judge Masterson said. "Jurors, thank you for your service. Officers, remand Mr Durant into the custody of the Wheaton State Penitentiary."

Farrar had convinced the court officer to allow him and Mary to meet with Matt one last time in the conference room in the back area of the courthouse. Farrar said, "Matt, I'm going to have Lisa start reviewing the record immediately, so we can begin work on the motion for a new trial as the first step toward appeal. We'll do everything in our power to get this verdict overturned."

"Thank you again. If not for all of your hard work, I might very well be facing execution," Matt said.

"Matt, I love you so much," Mary said. "You know I'll write and visit as often as I can. I'm still proud of you. I don't care what those twelve idiots think."

Part III

Chapter 17

Matt boarded another converted school bus with men unaccustomed to wearing suits: all on their last trip of over a few miles. They stared out the windows as the city of New Orleans retreated from the side windows to the rear, the bus traveled west on I-10 near Baton Rouge and Matt caught sight of Tiger Stadium—he couldn't bear to blink; he didn't want to shorten his last look by a millisecond.

The traces of Baton Rouge fell away, and, as they entered rural Louisiana, they traveled through a procession of one-stoplight towns. Wheaton State Penitentiary was a small prison compared to its more famous neighbor, Angola, and had been opened as a maximum-security alternative. Matt hoped it hadn't avoided the intense court supervision of Angola following decades of institutionalized brutality.

As with his initial trip to the Orleans Parish Prison, each prisoner had an individual bench. The humiliation of being chained soon faded into the background, reduced to a quiet burn. But he could hardly contain his panic as they approached their destination. His right eye began to twitch, and, when he lifted his cuffed hands in front of him they were unsteady, so he lowered them again to his knees, hoping no one had noticed.

The bus stopped at the Angola prison entrance. A red-brick sign, surrounded by well-tended bushes, some bursting with flowers like cotton poufs and others with slender red stalks, announced: *Louisiana State Penitentiary*. Behind that sign, a second quoted a former inmate and then the Bible: *You are entering the land of new beginnings; I've learned to forgive and forget about the things that are behind me. I am pressing forth and reaching for the things that are before me...*

On the driver's side was a tan booth with glass windows—the guard within controlled the black bars that bisected the roadway; a witness to the toll on those who arrived and the few who left. Sand-colored guard towers dominated the horizon.

As the bus continued through the prison, Matt noticed that at least two-thirds of the prisoners were black and only a third white—the opposite of Louisiana's population outside. It drove past two blue water tanks with swirls of white and paintings of a fisherman in a Louisiana bayou, a Native American chief and the eye of Mike the Tiger. It then traversed a small part of Angola, formed from 18,000 acres of a former slave plantation and holding some 5000 prisoners, almost all convicted of violent crimes and sentenced to life without the possibility of parole.

A file of convicts marched past, all black, carrying hoes and wearing jeans and white shirts. Most wore head coverings—fashioned from t-shirts or bandanas or rags—to shelter them from the sun but all still sweated heavily. Above them loomed a horse supporting a squat, ogre-like guard. In the distance, Matt also spied, through razor and concertina wire, a silent church steeple with a belfry but no lantern.

The driver finally pulled through another gate with a large sign that said *Wheaton State Penitentiary*, located within Angola's boundaries, at the edge of Lake Killarney. The bus came to a stop.

"Get up. Get off," a guard said.

The new prisoners staggered out of the bus and uniformed officers used nightsticks to prod them into some semblance of a formation. They assembled in front of a low, sprawling complex of buildings.

A priggish man with a belly overhanging a large belt buckle strode out of the building and into the yard. "I'm Warden Paxson and I'd say welcome to Wheaton, but I don't expect you're too glad to be here. Lots of you spent some time in jail before coming here. I know they call Orleans Parish Prison a prison, but it's mostly a jail. I want to make sure you know the difference between jail and a real prison. Jail's where they hold you before you get tried and sentenced. Jail's temporary and there ain't much to do there other'n wait. This is prison, where you'll serve a very long sentence, and I'm gonna tell you the most important rule we have. Nobody just waits. Everybody works."

Paxson continued: "We grow some cotton and some sugarcane and we try and make a profit. You're gonna work hard so the good people of Louisiana don't spend more money than they have to housing and feeding a bunch of criminals. The guards and other prisoners will tell you the other rules. You should follow 'em if you want to stick around. You mess around, we'll send you over to Camp J at Angola, and I figure some of you've already heard about that." Matt shuddered, thinking of the factual findings by courts he'd read that had compelled a federal court in New Orleans to run the prison for decades and hoping the judicial supervision had improved conditions. The warden turned and walked away.

The prisoners entered a processing area, their handcuffs were removed, and they turned in their clothing and personal belongings. They were then escorted into group showers complete with soap dispensers that claimed to exterminate lice.

Matt was nervous, but everyone in the group looked anxious. Though none of the guards accompanied them into the showers, cameras were sprinkled throughout. Their LED lights glowed red and reassured Matt that the cameras, at least, were watching.

After showers they received state-issued blue jeans, white t-shirts, boxer shorts, socks and sneakers. They were then marched into a barber shop, where wizened, elderly inmates shaved their heads. The guards were present for the shearing, so the new arrivals had little opportunity to interact with the veterans.

The men were then released into a broad yard surrounded by a seven-foot chain-link fence.

After the last of them had made their way into the yard, a large-boned uniformed guard with a sunburnt face and sandy hair addressed the group. "My name is Lieutenant Dietrich. You're gonna go directly to your cells for the rest of the day. You're each bunking with an inmate who's been here at least five years. Enjoy your afternoon rest because y'all are gonna work tomorrow." Lieutenant Dietrich motioned to a group of waiting low-level officers who escorted the prisoners to a building with a sign on the front that described it as Building 6.

As they stood in front of Building 6, Matt sized up the small black inmate in front of him and considered Frank Hodges's advice. He visualized pushing the man's shoulder and spinning him around to launch a finger strike at his eyes. It would only take seconds and he might even blind him. Word of that could get around quickly and establish a reputation that could protect him. He shook his head—he couldn't do it; he'd already killed a man and he couldn't cripple a stranger just to improve his odds of staying safe.

He didn't have the chance to move beyond these thoughts before he found himself alone in a cell with the door slammed shut, where he eventually drifted off to sleep.

Late the next afternoon, as the window bars fragmented and attenuated light from a low sun, about forty prisoners filed down the corridor of Building 6 and lined up in front of the cell doors. A black man with a rangy frame—a walking skeleton with little flesh, let alone fat—and a bushy afro stood several inches taller than Matt in front of the cell door. After half a minute, a guard tripped the electric switch that opened the doors and the man ducked his head as he entered.

"Matt Durant," Matt said. He stood and offered his right hand.

"Tyrone Jansen. I guess you're a fresh fish." Tyrone ignored Matt's hand, sat on the bottom bunk, folded his frame into the confined space and crossed his arms over his chest.

Matt stayed standing next to the locked cell door, reluctant to approach the bunks and close the space with Tyrone. "Why are we in individual cells? I thought Angola had a dormitory layout," Matt asked.

"Well, this here's a medium-security wing. They started puttin' the newbies in here to give 'em a chance to get used to prison before sticking 'em in with everyone else. S'posed to protect you, I guess."

"Why are you in the medium-security wing?"

"They put some of the so-called model prisoners in this wing. I guess they figured we could show you the ropes." Tyrone settled back in the lower bunk and closed his eyes.

"What's it take to be a model prisoner?"

"Mostly just stayin' out of trouble."

"What happens next?"

"In 'bout thirty minutes we go eat with everybody else. The old cons and the fresh fish eat together."

"Should I be worried about dinner?" Matt asked. He felt like a six-year-old harassing an adult with questions.

"Naw," Tyrone shook his head, eyes still shut. "There's lots of guards at dinner. Guards and cameras, those're your friends if you wanna stay safe. I know you." Tyrone sat up and rested his elbows on knees higher than his bunk. "You that faggot lawyer from New Orleans."

Matt's stomach sank. "I was convicted of killing a guy outside a gay club, yeah."

"Well, I ain't into that shit. Just keep your hands to yourself. I'm not looking for a sweetheart."

"Do I need to worry the other prisoners will think I'm gay?"

"Yeah, you need to worry," Tyrone said. He raised his eyebrows and gave Matt an incredulous look. "Those guys out there'll think you want it, and that's a problem if you don't wanna give it."

"When's that going to be a problem?"

"Well, maybe as soon as tomorrow, when you gotta go out and work. But you gonna work as part of a crew from this block for now, and that ain't so bad. The gang leaders got their spies in here, but they don't want to lose 'em by having 'em do anything too nasty. You gotta worry when you get tossed in the general population. So 'less you really piss somebody off, that means you gotta worry after you've been thrown in the buildings with the older cons."

"Who are the gang leaders?" Matt pressed, willing to run the risk of irritating his new cellmate for inside information that could potentially keep him safe.

"There's only one white leader here, name's Bill Sands, and he's head of the White Brotherhood. There's a brother too, Parnell Jefferson. Makes sense 'cause it ain't like Angola. It's about half whites an' half brothers here."

"How do I protect myself?"

"You should prob'ly become some big, mean guy's bitch. You like that shit anyway, right?" Tyrone smiled. "I figure you get some big motherfucker to protect you, you don't need to worry so much about takin' a beating or getting the HIV."

"And if I don't want to be some big guy's bitch?"

Tyrone laughed.

"If you got the answer to that one, you really must be as smart as you s'posed to be."

"Any of these leaders recently convicted?" Matt had begun to irritate even himself with his questioning, but learning more helped keep his fear under control.

"Yeah, Parnell just got convicted about six weeks ago. He was in Angola before and his gang has peeps inside and outside so he became a leader real quick. Why you ask?"

"It's easier to get a criminal conviction reversed the first time the appellate courts hear the case. Do you know Parnell? Can you introduce me?"

"Yeah, I know him. But I'm on this block 'cause I stay out of that shit. What in it for me?"

"What do you want?"

"If I could get a hundred bucks in the store, it'd make my life a whole lot nicer."

"Done. I can deposit a hundred bucks on your behalf. I'll write my mother." Matt wanted to take back the reference to his mother immediately, but Tyrone didn't react. He thought it sounded juvenile—and his instinct toward a prissy word like behalf didn't help either—he needed to pay closer attention to how he structured his thoughts and make certain they didn't infect his speech. He also knew from Hodges that most inmates quickly lost all contact with the outside world and he didn't want to add to any jealousy.

"When the money's there, I take you to meet Parnell."

A guard shouted down the hallway, "Suppertime."

Tyrone joined Matt in front of the cell door. A buzzer sounded, the door opened, and the prisoners went to dinner, but there was no trouble there. Matt suffered interested stares, but the presence of the guards and cameras persuaded the other inmates to look rather than touch.

He choked down the bland meal and followed Tyrone's lead by avoiding conversation with others at the table. Then they returned to their cell. After lights out, he could hear the wracking sobs of other new prisoners. Matt, at least, had learned to cry silently.

Chapter 18

The guards' shouts woke everyone in Building 6 and, out of habit, Matt glanced at the top of his wrist—where his watch used to be—but instead found a patch of white skin. Soon even the patch of white skin would fade and there were few clocks in the prison. Why bother? Most prisoners would be told when and where they needed to be for life.

After breakfast, the inmates were led out into the yard.

Lieutenant Dietrich walked out to meet the group in front of the bunker-like cafeteria. "Today ya'll will start working to earn your keep. The great state of Louisiana will give you four cents an hour toward your commissary accounts for your work. As new prisoners, we're assuming you lack any skills. But we hope you can dig ditches. You're being issued shovels. Don't abuse them. If you do, you'll get a ticket straight to Camp J next door, and I promise you don't want to spend time there. It makes this place look like Sunday school."

The guards corralled the prisoners into a line, issued a shovel to each inmate, and marched them out along a black tar roadway. After a mile or so, the group took a right onto a dirt road that cut through a cotton field, which they followed until it intersected another black surface sweating noxious petrochemical fumes.

Matt plodded toward the ditch and thought about how hard he'd worked to get an education to fulfill his parents' dream that he earn his living with his head, not his hands. At an early age, before his father's death, he'd seen the effects of constant physical toil on the body and mind. His father had been up before the crack of dawn, worked until dusk and came home reeking of sweat, too tired at dinner to talk. That memory lingered.

"All right. This is where you start," Lieutenant Dietrich said. "You'll get out of Building 6 and become eligible for more glamorous employment when you've finished the ditches on the sides of this road."

Matt found himself standing next to Tyrone. He hefted his shovel and then stomped down to drive the blade below the top layer of hard-caked dirt and into the loamy subsoil deposited by the Mississippi. He felt the weight of each shovelful in his shoulders and back. After an hour and a half, beneath work gloves worn thin many years before, blisters formed. By the time a guard ordered a break, the sun had begun to blaze.

As they rested, Matt kept to himself as he gazed across the fields and saw other inmates working with hoes. The job was hot, hard and unpleasant, but the presence of the guards comforted him. He only faced discomfort, not any sort of real threat. After about fifteen minutes, a guard shouted for the prisoners to return to work.

The remainder of the day passed slowly and the burning in Matt's hands and the strain in his back worsened. New blisters developed and the ones from the morning burst. Late in the afternoon, Lieutenant Dietrich returned and marched the men back to Building 6. Matt reconsidered whether the labor had only caused discomfort and thought he might collapse from relief.

He entered the cell, adding his stench to Tyrone's strong body odor.

"Don' worry 'bout the stink. It'll get better. We'll be dry by mornin'. And I'm guessin' you don't want to spend any more time in the showers than you have to," Tyrone said and snorted.

"Do you have paper, an envelope and a stamp I could use?" Matt asked. "I want to get a letter off to my Mom as soon as possible so I can get your hundred dollars."

"Sure. I'll give it to ya for only five bucks. You can add it to the hundred," Tyrone said.

"Thanks."

Matt lay on the scratchy wool blanket covering his bunk and tried to write a letter on a cheap legal pad with a flimsy cardboard back:

Dear Mom,

I'm safe in Wheaton State Penitentiary. My cellmate, Tyrone, loaned me the materials to write this letter.

The new inmates are housed in a medium-security facility called Building 6. We get three meals a day that are large enough to keep us going. On my first full day, they put us to work digging ditches. I think prison may put me in the best shape of my life. I haven't had the chance to visit the library yet.

I was hoping you could do me a favor. You know I gave you power of attorney over the bit of money I had managed to save. Could you please deposit $200 in my commissary account as well as $105 in Tyrone Jansen's account? He's been in prison for over five years and has no one on the outside to help him out. The money at the commissary allows us to buy better toothpaste, toothbrushes and writing materials. If you could also send me a package of letter-sized legal pads with thick cardboard backs, some pens, stamps and envelopes, that would be great.

I hope all is going well for you. I think of you often.

Love,
Matt

Matt folded the letter, addressed the envelope, and added a stamp. He hoped his mother bought his "everything is fine" routine but doubted she would.

The guards shouted out that suppertime had arrived.

"You can send that from the cafeteria," Tyrone said. "They take 'bout one, two days longer 'n the post office. Not quite sure why, but they'se probably reading our mail. And I'll introduce you to Parnell soon as I get the money."

"Thanks," Matt said. He found it difficult to believe his letter to his mother would stand out to a censor among the other inmates' correspondence. He wondered whether he'd ever again have any-thing of interest he could report without causing her a nervous breakdown. Censorship wasn't his most pressing concern.

Over the next week, Matt's aching back and bloody hands adapted to digging ditches for eight hours a day. On Friday, he received notice that $200 had been placed in his commissary account. Tyrone also learned $105 had been placed in his account.

After they returned from the fields on Friday, Tyrone asked, "You ready to meet Parnell at dinner tonight?"

"Yeah," Matt said.

"You know this is goddam dangerous. I still think you'd be better off picking some big bull and giving him some for protec-tion. Hell, you gay, ain't you? People in here like anybody else. They like to think the guy they're doin' is interested. You could set your-self up real nice. You fuck up this thing with Parnell, you gonna be lucky if'n you end up in the infirmary for a long time."

"But if it goes well, I could be safe in here for years."

"Yeah. Right." Tyrone shook his head.

They received their slop in the cafeteria line. Tyrone led Matt to a table of large black men, where a dark-skinned man with a shaved head and broad nose sat at the head of the table: his arms were a mixture of crude prison tattoos forming intricate patterns with more professional, colorful ones, but Matt felt certain he'd heard or read somewhere he shouldn't ask about them; they could be gang tattoos or just personal, and he didn't want to offend by mistake.

"Yo, Parnell," Tyrone said. "My new cellmate wants to talk to ya."

"You shoulda taught him better 'n that, brother." Parnell said. "No fresh fish should ever wanna talk to me. And they definitely don' want me askin' to talk to them. What's he got to say?"

Matt didn't wait for a more direct invitation. He swallowed hard and said, "My name's Matt Durant. I was convicted of murder in New Orleans, where I was a lawyer. And I wasn't just any lawyer. I graduated first in my class from LSU law school. I also worked for an appellate court judge for a year doing criminal work, and then worked for the best litigation firm in Louisiana. I'm not asking you take my word for it. Ask your lawyer."

"So what? I'm sure your momma's proud, but what's that got to do with me?" Tyrone asked.

"You just got here," Matt said. "Your case should still be in front of the trial court or on direct appeal before the Louisiana appellate courts, which is good. It means you have a better shot at winning. I'd like to review the record of your trial and help out with the legal briefs. In exchange, I'd like a job in the library and protection."

"You gonna write down that fancy education and job so I can tell my lawyer?"

"I already have." Matt looked around to make certain the guards weren't watching, then slipped Parnell a sheet of yellow paper that spelled out his qualifications. He'd handwritten the most important resume he'd ever submit on thin, cheap paper, chosen because it was easy to conceal.

"I can get you a job in the liberry, but that means gettin' you out of Building 6," Parnell said. "I can prob'ly get Tyrone out too, if he's willing to go out with the rest of us again. But you gonna do more than review my file. You check out, I'se gonna set up my own little law firm in here."

"That's fine. Can you protect me in the general population?"

"See, thas why it ain't a good idea for the fresh fish to talk to me. Anyone at this table think I can protect the faggot lawyer?"

Every other man at the table laughed and one guffawed—howling and slapping his knee, then wiping tears from his eyes. These men would follow Parnell's slightest suggestion without hesitation, and with feigned or real enthusiasm. Even their mirth menaced.

"Yeah, I can protect ya. Won't be too hard neither. But you gotta remember somethin'. Our deal's gonna piss off Bill somethin' fierce, 'cause you're white. And you ain't gonna be doin' any work for him. I can protect you from him as long as I want, but thas just another reason you gonna work real hard to stay in my good graces."

"That's fine. I will."

"And one more thing. I fucking hate lawyers," Parnell said. "On the outside, you assholes take lots of money and never guarantee nothin'. I spend that money on guns or drugs and some mother-fucka don't give 'em to me, I put a cap in his ass. In here if'n you don't get me results, a new trial, shorter sentence, some shit like that, then they'se gonna be consequences."

"I understand," Matt said. "I think your lawyer will tell you I'm smarter than anyone you've had working for you. And I figured there'd have to be some sort of guarantee." Matt's stomach sunk as he spoke and the exchange reinforced that failing to manage this client's expectations could be fatal.

"And another thing. I think I'm gonna go ahead and have you transferred and if my lawyer don't recommend you, then we'll have another bitch in the buildin'. So you better hope you get a real good recommendation."

"Okay," Matt said. He managed to hold himself together. He and Tyrone walked to their table, where Matt attempted to bypass chewing, swallowing and tasting to skip to digestion. He forced himself to eat the meal; the stress was taking a toll on him and he'd lost at least ten pounds in the last couple of months—he had to keep putting food into his body, even if it sat in his stomach like a hunk of cement.

When Tyrone and Matt returned to their cell, Matt asked, "Are you all right with a transfer to the general population?"

"Yeah, I been here a long time. Nobody gonna blame me for what you do or don't do. I'm gonna tell folks that you paid me for the introduction and Parnell didn't give me no choice. When he hears 'bout the money, tho', Bill's gonna want to get his hands on you even more. You workin' hard to make those folks notice you, so you best get results for Parnell," Tyrone said. "You may be smart, but such a thing as too smart."

*

Matt spent the next day digging ditches, but as he was preparing to leave for dinner a guard came for him and Tyrone. The guard was about five-eight and a 180 pounds. He had dusky hair, pale greasy skin, and bug eyes with a copper nametag that read *Ted Cook*.

"All right," the guard said. "Durant and Jansen, you guys are getting transferred to my building, Building 2. I don't know why, but Parnell asked for you. You guys are gonna have to miss dinner tonight."

Ted cuffed them, which Matt thought excessive given prisoners routinely walked around without any sort of restraint. He then opened the cell door and led them to Building 2, where he unlocked their handcuffs at the front door, opened it, and led them in. Men trickled in from dinner in ones and twos.

"Welcome to Building 2. I own this building and I don't put up with no shit. Strip," Ted said, staring at Matt. Many of the inmates from Parnell's table in the cafeteria were lounging around.

"What?" Matt asked.

"You heard me. Get naked."

Matt began to take his clothes off, as slowly as he dared. He peeled the white t-shirt off, unsnapped his jeans, unzipped his fly, and lowered them to the ground. He stood there in his boxer shorts and socks.

"I said I want you naked. Get rid of the fucking shorts."

Matt shucked his boxer shorts and socks. He reddened, knowing fright and embarrassment had caused his exposed parts to shrink. And his chest, shoulders and arms were spindly compared to the other men in the room.

"Now bend down and show these guys your ass," Ted said.

Matt turned his back toward the room's occupants and touched his toes.

"Spread 'em." Matt reached back and spread his cheeks and his heart leapt into the back of his mouth. He wanted to vomit. Had Parnell's lawyer said he wasn't qualified? This guard wasn't going to have them run a train on him, was he?

"Now," Ted said. "Repeat after me. I'm a faggot lawyer who likes to take cock up my ass."

"I'm a faggot lawyer who likes to take cock up my ass," Matt said. His eyes leaked tears and he gave thanks the other men in the room couldn't see his face.

"Thas enough," Parnell interrupted. "Stand up and get dressed. Ted, this guy's my new lawyer. My lawyer on the outside said he's real fuckin' smart, so you ain't gonna mess with him 'less I tell you to. Understand?"

"Sure, Parnell," Ted said. He trailed off into a whine: "I was just tryin' to have some fun."

"Well, don't have your fun with him. Leave." Ted scampered out of the room and Matt put his clothes back on as Parnell approached.

"Don't mind Ted. He'll do what he's told. He likes to pull that shit with fresh fish ever since he learned about those guards in them Iraqi prisons. He gets his rocks off by doin' shit they weren't even s'posed to be doin' to Iraqis. And don't get him started talkin' about it. He won't stop."

"Thanks," Matt said. He'd managed to wipe his face with his t-shirt on his way up from the ground. He hoped Parnell couldn't tell he'd been crying.

"Make yourself comfortable. I already tole the guys in here you'se off-limits. Talked to my lawyer on the phone and he said you should be as smart as you say. He also say it take more'n bein' smart to be a good lawyer.

"You start workin' in the liberry tomorrow. My file should already be there and you ain't got too much other work to do. I also tole a couple of guys if you fuck up they gots dibs. Some wanna beat the shit out of you and some wanna fuck the shit out of you. You fuck up, I don't much care what they wanna do. I promise it'll hurt real bad."

"I hear you. Thanks," Matt said.

He surveyed the room, which resembled a military barracks more than a prison. Steel cots were covered with thin mattresses, sheets and polyester blankets. An open doorway in the back led to what he assumed was a bathroom, and on his way toward the back of the room and only open bed, he noticed a corner held a camera. He doubted its once-glowing LED light, now dull and lifeless, had failed on its own.

A couple of hours later the lights blinked and a minute later went dark. As Matt lay there, unlike his first night in Building 6, he heard no weeping or sobbing. He saw a series of men retreating in pairs to the bathroom at the back of the dormitory. The sounds left little doubt about what they were doing.

He turned over in his bed and resolved to get at least a few hours of sleep. He thought the spartan room, stripped of security devices, had one thing in common with Orleans Parish Prison and Building 6—all warehoused the bodies of lost souls.

Chapter 19

"Durant," Ted barked from the doorway of Building 2. Matt shambled forward and, as he approached, saw Ted's chin was coated with lotion, sweat and spittle. "You must be pretty special. Parnell tells me to leave you alone and now you get a new job in the library. But you'd best know, I don't do everything Parnell tells me."

"Should I tell Parnell that?" Matt regretted his words instantly.

"Why don't you shut the fuck up? Go." Ted colored. His reaction confirmed Matt's guess based on the guard's swift response to Parnell's instruction the night before—he was controlled by Parnell.

Ted didn't bother with the handcuffs this time. Matt wondered if it was because of Parnell's influence or because the threat of losing his new privileges guaranteed his good behavior, but suspected if he lost his new privileges it would signal a move by Parnell, not the guards.

Ted and Matt climbed into an ancient, dingy truck and they traveled down the road toward the main complex of Angola. Ted led him to a large library.

"Luther, get your ass out here," Ted shouted.

The black man who Matt assumed to be Luther had a short afro flecked with gray and a round face dotted with freckles. Luther's gray hair was the only sign he was over forty.

"I'm gonna leave you two," Ted said. "Durant, you might wanna check out the *Observer* website while you're here. You'll figure out why you're so famous." He sneered, revealing nicotine-stained teeth.

"I'm Luther Johnson." The librarian extended his hand. "Not

quite sure how you got this job, but you're going to help me out around here. They supposedly brought you over from Wheaton so you could fill their book orders. They fill out requests for books at dinner and you'll provide them with their books in the cafeteria."

Matt noted Luther spoke with the measured pace of a man who'd educated himself late in life. He attempted to banish the thought immediately—was he being racist? It seemed to matter in a way with Luther it didn't with Parnell. Maybe Luther was just thoughtful and deliberate. "My name's Matt Durant. I got this job because I used to be a lawyer, and I traded my legal services to Parnell for protection."

"Ah. That would explain why they sent over Parnell's legal file, then. I wondered about that."

"I'm just doing my best to survive," Matt said. "Can you show me what I'm going to be doing?"

"It's not that complicated," Luther responded. "We have a full set of law books with state and federal cases. We also have a West Digest System that sorts cases by legal topic. I think a court may have had something to do with the availability of those law books, but they also keep the inmates happy. The guards would rather have the inmates harassing the courts than them." Luther gestured toward various areas of the library as he described them.

"We also have a pretty extensive collection of fiction. We even have some classics, history, philosophy and biographies. Prison is pretty boring, so even as hard as the warden works folks around here, some people get up to some pretty serious reading after a few years."

The rough-hewn pine bookshelves held old books that exuded the musty undertone common to all libraries, which made Matt realize he might be able to bury himself in books here just as he had in school, libraries, bookstores, coffee shops, offices and any-where else he found himself throughout his whole life.

"We also have computers," Luther said, pointing to a wall in the main room lined with computers, boxy CRT monitors, and a couple of immediate successors to the dot-matrix printer. "About half aren't connected to the internet and are just for word processing. The ones connected to the internet are monitored by an outside company and the guards, so we don't have to mess with that."

"What am I going to be doing?" Matt asked.

"You'll file newly acquired and returned books, help maintain the library catalog and do some light cleaning. But today I think it would be a good idea to review Parnell's file."

"Thanks," Matt said.

"Least I can do. You're the one dealing with the devil. You know, Parnell was here at Angola for about ten years in the nineties for possession of pot—he somehow got his conviction and sentence reduced to that and I don't wanna know how—but everyone in the state knew he deserved to be in Angola, so that's where he ended up.

"He took over huge parts of the prison. When they convicted him the second time, I think they sent him to Wheaton so he couldn't build an army as large as last time. Fewer blacks are housed at Wheaton and even fewer are desperate enough to do the really dirty work. But Parnell's still tough and ruthless. And he'll do anything to keep the reputation he has at both prisons."

"I figured he was a serious player. But that means he can provide me with some protection, right?"

"Hey, I know where I've seen your picture before," Luther said as recognition dawned. "You're that lawyer from New Orleans who killed the guy in an alley in the Quarter."

"Yeah, that's me."

"Well, I don't know you had much choice other than to try to cut a deal with Parnell, then. You have a huge target painted on your back. You're gay so every bull out there is going to assume you're better at sex and might even enjoy it. And you were rich on the outside, which is another reason to hate you."

"I wasn't that rich. My mother's a nurse."

"Yeah, well, you were a lawyer making six figures a year. Men here have killed for a lot less.

"Parnell's file is right here," Luther said, pointing to two boxes that were each two feet long. He had mixed feelings about the size of the file; it improved the odds of finding something useful, but it would also take longer. He was torn between diving into the file and checking the computer for that damned *Observer* article.

After Luther had showed him to the card catalog, Matt pulled a chair up to a table. On second thought, he returned to the card catalog and searched for a treatise on Louisiana criminal law, figuring the book could serve as a useful shortcut. He assumed he'd have to take similar shortcuts to learn the relevant facts from the record of Parnell's trial. He began by reviewing the opening statements, closing statements and jury instructions. He'd just started on the jury instructions when Luther interrupted.

"We should go eat now if we want lunch," Luther said. "You going to keep working?"

"No, I should eat."

They went to the cafeteria at Angola, which fed hundreds of prisoners, and many nodded to Luther as they walked through the cafeteria to a table, where the seated prisoners appeared to have separated themselves from the others by age rather than race. White or black, all appeared to be at least fifty-five or sixty and Matt guessed that Luther might be older than he looked.

"What's happening today, fellas?" Luther asked as he put his tray on the table. He sat next to a grizzled white prisoner with more white hair growing from his large ears than from his liver-spotted scalp.

"Bob and I were just talking about when things in here was the worst," the man next to Luther said. "He says it was in the late seventies when the state cut back so much on money, but I don't think he gets a vote 'cause he wasn't here in the early seventies. That was before the courts got involved."

"How long have you been here?" Matt asked.

"Name's George," the prisoner said.

"Matt Durant. Sorry. I didn't mean to be rude."

"No, not a problem. Not many new guys are interested in us. I been here for fifty years. Killed a man when I was twenty-two and I been here since."

"So what was the worst period in prison?"

"Well, before seventy-five or so, when the courts didn't pay no attention to this place, things were pretty rough. Guards didn't even try to hide the fact the prisoners were running the joint. There weren't as many guards and a lot more trustees. Seems like we had a killing every day back then. I used to sleep on my back with a baking pan strapped to my chest so nobody could stab me at night. And I hadn't even done nothing to make anybody mad."

"Are things that much better now?" Matt asked.

George laughed and said, "You kidding me? You leave other folks alone now and don't get on the wrong side of anybody, you got a real good shot at a peaceful life. Back then, if you hadn't killed to get in here, you sure were gonna have to kill someone once you got here."

Luther had finished his lunch. "That's enough with the history lesson. We've got to get back to the library. We've got work to do."

Matt stood and nodded to George. "It was good to meet you."

"You too, kid," George said. "Good luck."

After returning to the library, Matt convinced himself he should take a break to check out the *Observer* article Ted had mentioned. He ran a search for "Durant" and what passed for an op-ed piece popped up:

Jury Convicts Lawyer Who Claimed Self-Defense While Training to Kill

Matthew Durant, a young New Orleans attorney on trial for murder, continued his training to kill up until the first day of trial. Durant killed Brian Cutler in an alley in the French Quarter. Prosecutors claimed Durant killed him to avoid being arrested for purchasing cocaine. Durant and his defense team argued he was defending himself after being attacked because of his sexual orientation. Despite the presiding judge's exclusion of critical evidence, those jurors reached the right verdict and convicted Matthew Durant.

Both the prosecution and defense largely ignored the training in violence that Durant sought out immediately before the trial. The prosecution tried to present one witness to testify about it at the end of the trial. Andre Thibedeaux, the prosecutor, explained that no one else from the gym had been willing to talk to them, but the trial judge ruled the evidence inadmissible.

The *Observer* has investigated Durant's training and learned further details. Frank Hodges, the witness whose testimony the judge excluded, gave an exclusive interview to the *Observer*. Durant had been training for over a year and a half at Tommy O'Rourke's boxing gym, where he learned traditional boxing techniques.

But Tommy's Boxing Gym taught Matthew Durant much more than he needed to know to stay fit. In the weeks leading up to the trial, Durant expanded his training regimen beyond boxing to prepare for a possible prison sentence.

O'Rourke arranged for individuals with military and prison experience to teach Durant deadly self-defense techniques. And those advisors told the man accused of murder to become even more aggressive. These more recent training sessions focused on techniques that are illegal in the boxing ring, including kicks that could disable and finger strikes that could destroy airways. Hodges, himself a former prisoner, even counseled Durant to kill another prisoner early in his stay to make the other inmates respect him.

What's most surprising, perhaps, is that this training wasn't discussed in front of the jury. The judge's ruling was wrong. A person who engages in a rigorous training program to learn to kill shouldn't be able to claim self-defense with the impunity of an innocent. And what does it say about Durant's belief about his guilt that he began preparing to go to prison even before the trial began?

The good citizens on the jury fortunately decided this case correctly without Hodges's testimony, but the *Observer* hopes the trial judge's legal ruling won't set any sort of precedent.

Matt balled his hands into fists under the table. The article carried an old picture of him taken from Farrar Levinson's website with a caption that read: *Wealthy lawyer Matt Durant had access to better lawyers than most, and he needed them. Unlike OJ, even his fancy lawyers couldn't get him off.*

Matt now knew where the guards and prisoners had learned about the trial. It wasn't a piece of a reputable reporting in a paper like the *Times-Picayune*. They were eating up this garbage, or Ted's version of it. He suspected Ted wasn't charitable or accurate when summarizing the story and hated to think of what an inaccurate version of the article would sound like.

He pushed back his chair and took Parnell's files and the criminal law treatise into a corner, far away from the computers.

For the first couple of hours, he found nothing. But he did a double take when he reached the instruction on attempted murder—it appeared garbled—so he consulted the treatise passage on the relevant jury instruction again. The judge had committed a common mistake and instructed the jurors on the wrong level of intent required to commit attempted murder. He'd discovered the sort of legal mistake that could result in reversal and a new trial. A tentative grin spread across his face.

Matt rose from the table, approached Luther, and offered to help sort books.

"You find something already?" Luther asked.

"I think so. I just want to shove it to the back of my mind and give it some more thought. I can do that while I shelve books." Matt had learned at Farrar Levinson that the trick when under the greatest pressure was to buy time somehow to think the issue through thoroughly. Letters and briefs could be written quickly if Matt had already mapped out the argument in his head. Rewriting a bad draft filled with weak arguments would take much longer than thinking the argument through properly in the first place.

Matt filled the rest of his afternoon in the library, shelving books and mulling over how he'd present the argument to Parnell. Managing Parnell's expectations had become even more important and difficult after locating tentatively positive information. Promise too much and his client would be sure to be disappointed. Rehearsing the presentation in his mind, he scarcely noticed his surroundings in the library or later as Ted drove him back to Wheaton's Building 2.

Matt waited just inside the doorway for about ten minutes before Parnell walked in surrounded by followers. Parnell had an ambiguous day job that he suspected involved little work. He nodded to Parnell as he entered.

"I can discuss your case whenever you'd like," Matt said.

"Let me relax for a bit and then eat," Parnell said. Matt couldn't figure out whether the seasoned convict was faking disinterest or was genuinely disinterested. Desperate people had probably made wild promises to Parnell over the years. He might be projecting indifference to impress the other inmates or to protect himself from the possibility of disappointment. It was impossible to tell.

Parnell didn't approach Matt until after dinner, soon before the lights were scheduled to turn off for the night. He motioned to Matt and rose to go into the bathroom, the only semiprivate structure in the barracks. The two men were soon alone.

"All right. Tell me what you found in one day my other lawyer ain't found yet."

"I think I've found an error in the jury instructions."

"What's that mean?"

"You were convicted of attempted murder. To prove that you committed attempted murder, the prosecution needed to show you took some act to attempt to kill someone intending to kill a person. The judge instead told the jury you needed only to have taken an act that could result in death with the intent to cause great bodily harm."

"What's the difference?"

"I haven't thoroughly reviewed the evidence, but it seems to me like the prosecution had evidence you fired your gun in the middle of a pretty chaotic SWAT raid. Firing a gun always poses the risk of killing someone. Even if you fire a gun into the air, there's the risk that the bullet will kill someone when it falls back to the ground. And firing it during that raid created a significant risk of a firefight. So the prosecution could easily show that you took an act that could result in death. Under the judge's instructions, the prosecution then only had to show you intended to injure, rather than kill, someone. If the prosecution had instead been forced to prove that you intended to kill one of the cops, it would have been harder for the jury to find you guilty."

"Don't sound like a great argument to me. Thos're just words," Parnell said doubtfully.

Matt kept his hands at his sides and resisted the urge to gesture as he talked. He was afraid they'd shake. "What makes it a great argument is that the Louisiana Supreme Court has ruled it's legal error for the judge to give the instruction that he gave. There are some problems with the argument and you just touched on one, but it's solid."

"What are they?"

"Well, let's start with the problem you just pointed out. The appellate court could find the jury would have found you guilty no matter how the judge had instructed them. That's called harmless error. But the appellate court has to conclude that, properly instructed, no reasonable juror would have decided to acquit you. And that's a pretty high standard."

"Okay. I can see how that might work. What are the other problems? I wanna hear 'em all now, not after it's too late."

"Your lawyer objected to the attempted murder charge, but he didn't raise this specific argument. The appellate court could find your lawyer waived the argument, which would make it harder for us to win."

"What do you think of my lawyer?"

"Your lawyer is okay, not great. I suspect your lawyer's well aware of your business activities, right?"

"Yeah. He know a lot. I use him to make shit confidential. Sometimes he sends me packages."

"Lawyers are conservative. A lawyer with a lot of talent is going to avoid the kind of work that could get him in trouble. If he's good enough, he doesn't need to do anything that could get him in trouble to make lots of money. You should really think about hiring different lawyers when you have a lot at stake in a criminal trial. They may not, uh, know your business as well, but that could actually be an advantage." Matt wished he hadn't stammered.

"Never thought of it that way before. What happens if this court says the judge got it wrong?" Parnell asked.

"You aren't going to get out of prison immediately," Matt said. "Your lawyer has already filed papers asking the trial judge for a new trial, but he'll probably refuse. Then we appeal. And if we win the appeal from that decision, you could get a new trial on at least the attempted murder charge and I'm going to try to fashion an argument for an entirely new trial on all charges."

"It's a start," Parnell admitted.

"Yeah, it's a start. I only spent a few hours with the record and I haven't read the entire transcript yet, but I wanted to let you know what I'd found."

"Yeah, you did good. You safe for now."

"Thanks," Matt said.

When Matt returned to his bunk, he noticed three letters sitting on his pallet. Tyrone said, "The guards delivered those this morning after you left. I forgot until now."

"Thanks," Matt said. He wondered why they hadn't been on his bed before dinner, but he decided it didn't matter. He picked up the envelopes. One was from his mother, one with Lisa's name atop an unfamiliar address and one from Farrar Levinson. He decided to save the one from his mother for last and opened the letter from Farrar Levinson. Immediately beneath the letterhead, starting on the left margin, was stamped: Privileged & Confidential, Attorney-Client Communication:

Dear Matt,

I wanted to update you on the status of your post-trial brief and appeal. As you might imagine, we've been combing the record for some sort of reversible error. The post-trial brief is our first task. We'll argue that the verdict was not supported by the evidence and was against the weight of the evidence, but, as you know, that has little chance of convincing the trial judge.

I hate to report that your best legal argument is probably a long shot. We'll argue that Judge Masterson erred in permitting the prosecutor to strike a gay juror and in seating jurors that expressed negative feelings about gays. As you know, if Judge Masterson had permitted the prosecution to strike jurors based on their race or gender, we'd have an excellent argument for a new trial. But the courts have provided safeguards against discrimination based on race and gender that they haven't extended to sexual orientation.

The argument will likely fail in front of every Louisiana court, ranging from Judge Masterson to the Louisiana appellate court to the Louisiana Supreme Court. We would really be angling to have the United States Supreme Court take the case. You know as well as I do that the Supreme Court receives over 6000 requests to hear cases each year and only hears about 60 or 70, so it's a real long shot.

I was hoping that we might be able to convert one of our jury arguments about Detective Jones's interview technique into a legal appellate argument. Lisa has researched the issue, but we haven't come up with anything yet. As you know, appellate courts are loath to interfere with the jury's weighing of the evidence that way. We're looking for other evidentiary and instructional errors, but we haven't found anything promising yet.

My respect for you as a lawyer hasn't changed and I'm going to send you a copy of your file. If you see anything that Lisa and

I've missed, please let me know. I hope you're doing as well as possible, and I want to repeat that the verdict against you was a travesty.

Sincerely,
Thomas Farrar

Matt folded the letter in half and closed his eyes. Farrar's report confirmed his initial feeling that he didn't have any legal arguments likely to succeed on appeal. Their successful track record with legal rulings in front of Judge Masterson meant that they'd be asking a court to second-guess the jury's findings of fact. Appellate courts didn't do that. A brief could describe the facts favorably to create atmosphere and color, but the prosecution witnesses' history of criminal convictions, for example, wouldn't be considered by the appellate court as a legal reason to reverse the verdict.

Matt opened the letter from Lisa, hoping for something to cheer him up:

Atlas—

Lisa offered to mail this letter for me, and I've never had a pen pal before so I thought I'd drop you a line.

I was obviously upset to learn of the verdict, but I hope you'll hang in there. From what I know of you, you will.

Lisa and I are up to no good, as usual. We went out to Superior Mexican restaurant on Friday night dressed to the nines. As I suspect you know, they make their margaritas with grain alcohol. We each had one and that pretty much was the beginning and end of the night. We wound up back at Lisa's watching Bobby Flay on the Food Network, who I think she's a bit obsessed with.

On Saturday, I'd resolved to follow your lead and start working out. And I definitely managed to buy workout clothes. Does that count as working out? I think it does.

Oh well, off to work, but please write back. You can write to Lisa's address.

Take Care,
M

Matt smiled. Eric had written the letter from a return address that wouldn't identify him and elliptically enough that it could be from Lisa's girlfriend rather than her gay friend. He'd have to think of something funny to write back.

Matt finally opened the letter from his mother:

Dear Matt,

Thank you so much for your letter. I'm so happy to hear you're safe. You're right that exercise could help.

The big news around here is that LSU is playing Tennessee in the SEC championship. It's all anyone around here ever talks about. I hope you're going to get a chance to watch it on TV at least.

I was happy to send the money. Mr Farrar says he won't take anything for the trial or the appeal. He says the appeal will only require a fraction of the time the trial did, especially since he and Lisa tried the case and will also be working on the appeal. And it's your money. You earned it and you should be able to spend it.

I also changed jobs and I'm now working at St Paul's. I'm working on nights and weekends, which has put a bit of a damper on my social life, but the people are so much nicer.

I'm thinking about going over to Dallas soon to do some shopping with some of the other nurses. We think we might be able to get the hospital to spring for a trip to a physical-therapy conference. It's worth a shot at least. I'm sure we won't be staying at a five-star hotel, but it's nice to get out of Lafayette every now and again.

I just want to repeat, and I'll never be able to repeat it often enough, that I love you and I'm proud of you. I know you couldn't abandon Joey Buckner in that alley or he would have gotten hurt very badly. I pray for you every morning and every evening. A mother couldn't be prouder of her son.

Love,
Mom

Tears sprang to his eyes. He well knew his mother's hard work and insistence on reading to him at night when he was little—no matter how tired she was—had paved his educational path. It was no more his money than hers.

She also hated working weekends and the other nurses at the hospital had been her closest friends for over a decade. She hadn't left her job because she'd wanted to—she'd lost it because of the time she'd taken off for the trial; because the hospital didn't want to employ a nurse who'd raised a murderer; or both. And who knew what would have happened if she hadn't taken time off to support him and testify at his trial.

Matt felt his frustration build. Farrar and Lisa had worked throughout the trial for him and failed. And now his mother had probably been fired for giving the testimony that might have saved his life.

He'd had enough. He'd been forced to sit on the sidelines as twelve strangers decided whether he'd live or die. The argument about striking a gay juror was a long shot, but Matt knew he was also an exceptional lawyer, as naturally talented as anyone he'd ever known. And he had nothing but time in here.

This wasn't right, and he'd trained for years to persuade appellate courts to right wrongs—he'd work on Parnell's case to survive, but he'd work on his own case to get the hell out of Wheaton.

Chapter 20

Matt woke the next morning with a driving need to establish a routine so he could work on Parnell's case to stay safe while devoting all of his other mental energy to his own. He'd reread the principal cases every day; he'd write and rewrite briefs until he'd committed every possible permutation of every sentence to memory; and he'd spend every free moment thinking about new approaches and novel arguments.

At the library that morning, he pulled all of the Supreme Court cases where the Court had struck down laws discriminating against gays. He read them over and over again. He could make this work. He had to.

That afternoon, Matt sorted and catalogued books. He was filling out the orders for Wheaton when he noticed something odd: all of the men in Building 2 were ordering case reporters and requesting volume numbers that were multiples of seven. Sometimes it was the seventh book in the *Supreme Court Reporter*, sometimes the fourteenth book in the *Federal Reporter*, and sometimes the thirty-fifth book in the *Southern Reporter*. But always a multiple of seven. Matt considered examining the books more closely, but Luther's raised voice distracted him.

"Damn it, Reggie," Luther said. "There's a difference between a short *i* and short *e* sound." Matt looked over to see Luther working with a man in his seventies at one of the wooden tables in the library.

"But you don' hear it when people talk."

"You don't hear it when ignorant brothers and hicks talk, but the whole point of this is so you don't sound like an ignorant brother. There's a difference between pin and pen. Can you hear it?"

"Who you calling ignorant?" Reggie was massive, with a square jaw and thick brow, and—in that moment—that he was a septuagenarian didn't make him seem less a threat. Matt started to worry about Luther's safety and thought about calling the guards.

"I saved your ass more than once in here and you know it," Reggie said. "You could at least be polite. I figured out how to survive in here, so I ain't too dumb."

"Sorry," Luther said. "I get frustrated because I know you're smart and I just don't want anyone to think less of you when they hear you talk. Let's try it again and don't worry about the difference between the short *i* and *e*."

Matt thought the teaching method unorthodox and sensed a long-shared history between the two. He shook his head and decided that he certainly didn't need to call the guards. But he might need to find an emergency substitute teacher.

On a Sunday afternoon, a guard summoned Matt from the barracks, informing him that he had a visitor. As a new inmate, Matt was only eligible to meet them in the more restricted spaces and that was a rule Parnell hadn't bothered to relax.

The officer led Matt to one of the main buildings and into a cavernous room with whitewashed walls, flimsy orange plastic chairs and the sour body odor of a crowd of inmates meeting with family. Matt was surprised to see Eric sitting at a table in the right rear corner.

Despite his shame at his surroundings, a smile cracked Matt's usually glum expression. "Long time no see," Matt said.

"Well, I wasn't sure whether or not I should come." Eric's voice was almost drowned out by the other visitors clamoring to be heard over one another.

Matt leaned forward so he could hear every word. "What made you decide to visit?" he asked.

"I was worried about you and I just wanted to come see you. I spoke to your mom and she said you'd appreciate the company," Eric said.

"Well, I'm glad you decided to come," Matt said.

"Your mother is just worried to death about you, to quote her."

"Yeah, well, she's died of worry many times before, but a bit of worry now seems appropriate."

Eric's face paled. "I hope I'm not making things worse by visiting. I could imagine as hard as it is to be what you are anywhere, it'd be particularly tough in here."

"Yeah," Matt said. "I'm doing some legal work in exchange for protection right now."

"What happens if you disappoint your client?" Eric asked, frowning.

"I'm trying not to think about that. Waiting in the principal's office and all. I'm just trying to enjoy the security for now. I read and write more than I speak to others, which isn't that much different from life on the outside."

"Where do they have you working?" Eric asked.

"My client arranged for me to work in the library. I always kind of had an urge to be a librarian, and the books are very comforting. But enough about me. What's going on with you?"

"Didn't you hear about what happened this weekend?" Eric asked. "Don't they let you watch college football in here?"

"No," Matt said. "No court has yet ruled the constitutional bar against cruel and unusual punishment requires broadcasting college football games."

"It's been a crazy weekend and I was up late last night. Surely you at least know LSU's lost two games since the Florida game."

"Yeah."

"They were ranked seventh in the country going in this weekend and they beat Tennessee in the SEC championship. Late last night, West Virginia and Missouri, which were ranked third and fourth, lost. So now it's between Oklahoma, Georgia and LSU to play Ohio State for the national championship. Most people seem to think LSU's going to be the first two-loss team to play for the national championship. They're announcing who will play in the championship game tonight."

"Wow. My mother must be ecstatic," Matt said. His pride and happiness at LSU's victory was made bittersweet by the fact that, if they played for the national championship for only the second time in over fifty years, he wouldn't be able to watch.

"The best part is that the national championship game will be in New Orleans this year."

"That's amazing. Any chance you'll get to go?"

"I don't know. Let's not jinx it by talking about it. They still have to be selected tonight."

"Okay. Switching gears. Any talk in the legal community about my conviction?" Matt asked, fearing the answer.

"Of course people gossiped at first, but it's starting to die down. The biggest topic of debate is whether Judge Masterson was right to allow the prosecution to strike that juror. All the lawyers recognize he didn't have a choice under existing precedent in Louisiana, but there's at least a debate whether that precedent is correct. So some good has come out of this."

"Joey Buckner's still alive, too. That's another good thing that came of this," Matt said.

"I don't know how you can say that," Eric responded. He gripped the arms of his plastic chair. "You had the same choice, saving your ass or saving his, and you chose to save his. And then he pays you back by testifying against you."

"I'd like to say I cling to saving Buckner's life because I'm forgiving, but I think I probably cling to it because it's one of the few ways for me to find meaning in this whole mess." Matt looked out into space, careful not to make eye contact with any of the other inmates.

"Oh," Eric said. "I brought you a couple of books. The guards already searched them, so I think I can just hand them to you. I know you're working in the library, but I thought you might still like some books of your own."

"Albert Camus's *The Plague*?" Matt asked. "Are things really so bad that reducing life to a nihilistic struggle is the best I can do?"

"Your mother said it was one of your favorite books. I didn't think—"

"Calm down," Matt said. "I'm just joking. At least you didn't bring *The Stranger*. I hope I'm slightly more sympathetic than the murderer there."

"You're no murderer. But you are far more sympathetic," Eric said. "So I thought of a good story for you on the drive here. Did I ever tell you about my college roommate and the couch?"

"No. Please do."

"We had a set of really cheap couches we'd bought in our sopho-more year and stored for the summer. When we moved into a new apartment, the full-sized couch wouldn't fit up the narrow stairs to the second floor of the duplex. We knew we couldn't throw it out easily because it was so large, so my roommate suggested we just tell the people running the storage place that the couch had been in the unit when we rented it. I told him I couldn't do it with a straight face. So my roommate went into the storage facility's office and told them we'd moved out of the unit but that 'By the way, the couch is still in there.' When they asked my roommate what he could possibly mean, he said the couch had been in the unit when we rented it and it was still there. When they got aggres-sive and said they never would have rented a unit with a couch in it, he escalated and told them that it wasn't like he was asking for the discount from the rent for the storage unit that he was entitled to. That cut off any further discussion..."

Matt and Eric continued in that vein, sharing stories about life before they knew each other as if they were meeting in a New Orleans restaurant rather than in the highly restricted visiting area of a state penitentiary. The conversation allowed Matt to briefly escape his immediate environment.

After an hour or so, Eric left and Matt was faced with reality again. So, when he returned to Building 2, he plunged into *The Plague*. In the opening paragraph, Camus described the town fea-tured in the novel as "ugly," but Matt suspected it probably wasn't nearly as ugly as Wheaton.

Matt's first Christmas in prison was as depressing as he'd expected. The warden at least announced that—as his gift to the inmates—in a couple of weeks they would be given the opportunity to watch the live television broadcast of LSU playing in the national cham-pionship game. So the topic that had dominated conversations throughout Louisiana spread to the inside. The men all looked forward to the game despite the fact that a recent LSU star, now in the NFL, had worked as a prison guard before college.

*

On January 7, the Wheaton cafeteria was filled beyond capacity with men seated in the aisles and standing along walls. They chattered, coughed, grunted and laughed quietly while listening to the announcers and waiting for the game to begin.

Ted turned down the volume on the television set, strode to the front of the room, and started tapping his baton against his left palm. "The warden was very generous to allow you to watch this game as a present, but he and Lieutenant Dietrich have left me in charge. If I hear any noise or any commotion other than just clappin', I'll break this up."

The warden and Lieutenant Dietrich had pulled rank to avoid nighttime duty, but a score of other guards were there. They were nervous about so many prisoners gathering, and Ted could use the slightest hint of trouble as an excuse to disperse them all.

Matt had been lucky enough to secure a seat in the second row so he could see the screen clearly. The Ohio State Buckeyes scored ten unanswered points in the first six minutes of the game and it sucked any ambient noise out of the cafeteria.

LSU responded by giving the ball to Jacob Hester, who ran head-on into the teeth of the Ohio State defense five separate times. On four of his five carries, he gained less than four yards, but he finally battered his way into field goal range. The kick was good, LSU was on the scoreboard and Matt felt his stomach relax.

The defense limited Ohio State to fourteen yards on the next series and LSU had the ball again. This time Hester only lowered his head and pounded away twice before his steady determination bolstered the confidence of the rest of the team. Less than a minute later, LSU's quarterback rifled a thirteen-yard pass to a tight end for a touchdown and the tie.

Matt started to rise from his seat and had to reverse direction halfway up and clamp his mouth shut to cut short his shout. Looking around, he saw various men contorted in unnatural positions to avoid making noise. But they largely succeeded in remaining silent.

Ohio State's offense made it easier for the men to keep quiet by marching fifty-five yards down the field in less than two minutes. The Tiger defense dug in and stopped them at the LSU twenty-one-yard line and the Buckeyes' kicker went onto the field. The center snapped the ball, the kicker whipped his right leg up until his foot was level with the top of his helmet, and the ball launched into the air. At the same instant, a 300-pound defensive lineman crashed through and got a hand on the ball—he'd blocked the kick. Matt bit down on his tongue until he tasted blood to stay quiet.

A single black inmate on the front row let out a yelp. Parnell locked eyes with a white man in the second row who had shoulder-length blond hair and pointed. The man responded by flicking the black man's ear and he went silent so the inmates could watch the rest of the game. The remaining prisoners—black and white—celebrated the blocked field goal that ultimately won LSU the national championship with a subdued golf clap.

Chapter 21

A few weeks later, Matt returned to Building 2 from the library to find Tyrone missing; at first he thought he might just be late returning from work, but after a half-hour, he began to worry. When he asked around Building 2 before dinner, another prisoner whispered that Tyrone had somehow run afoul of Parnell, who'd had him beaten out in the fields. Fear clenched Matt's gut throughout the meal as he weighed his options, but he knew he had to approach Parnell.

After returning to Building 2, Matt asked Parnell if he could have a word with him, at his convenience.

Shortly before the lights were scheduled to go out, Parnell gestured for Matt to accompany him to the bathroom. When they were alone, Matt asked: "Do you know where Tyrone is? He didn't return from work and I'm worried about him."

"That asshole was tryin' to sell white lightnin'." Parnell said, crossing his arms beneath his bulky chest and over a rotund stomach.

White lightning was the homemade alcohol inmates brewed through a process and from ingredients that Matt didn't want to know, in part because he couldn't forget the one detail he'd learned—fermenting it somehow involved a toilet. "He damned well knows he can't do that under my nose. He got beat up pretty bad. He gonna be in the infirmary for a good long while now."

"As long as he stops, is he going to be safe?" Matt asked, careful to mimic Parnell and use the passive voice.

"Why? You got somethin' to do with his operation?" Parnell asked.

"No," Matt responded. "But Tyrone was my cellmate and he introduced me to you. I just want to make sure he's going to be okay."

Parnell leaned in toward Matt, inches from his face. "Yeah, well, I didn't think you had the balls to do somethin' like that," Parnell said, his breath sour. "And I ain't sure whether Tyrone's gonna be safe. I ain't decided if I'm through with him." Parnell's breath was sour.

Matt found it difficult to believe selling white lightning warranted more than a beating, even in Parnell's mind. He wondered whether Parnell was trying to manipulate him by exaggerating the threat and likelihood of violence. Wheaton wasn't Angola in the early seventies, after all, and even Parnell had to pay some attention to the risk of detection and punishment: manipulation might be a smarter first step, even for him.

"Is there a way I can help you change your mind, assuming that Tyrone stops selling white lightning?" Matt asked.

"You still haven't figured this shit out, have you?" Parnell asked with genuine wonder. "This is fucking prison, man, not some argument about who college students are gonna pick as their student body president. You don't owe Tyrone shit. I know you paid him good money to meet me, and he ain't done nothin' else for you."

"I just want to know if there's some way I can help you change your mind," Matt said.

"There's one thing you could do." Parnell leaned back, creating some physical distance. "Some of my boys jumped one of the White Brotherhood and beat him up pretty bad. Bill agreed that it would end there, if'n he got a favor from me. You know what favor Bill wants?"

"No," Matt said. His heart sank at the possibility Bill might want a turn with the prison's most educated and outed gay man.

"He wants help with some damned fool lawsuit."

"What kind of lawsuit?"

"One of his guys wants to sue to try to get the cameras outta the main showers." Parnell pointed toward the dead camera in the corner ceiling of their bathroom. "Some argument 'bout how it violates the right to privacy."

217

"That's a loser," Matt said. "Federal courts have rejected the argument that prisoners' privacy rights outweigh the security interest in having cameras in the showers."

"So what? I ain't askin' you to win this one. Just put in some effort and make sure his papers get typed up nice. You can talk to Bill and tell him the lawsuit is shitty if you want."

"How bad was Tyrone beaten up?"

"Pretty bad." Parnell shook his head. "He should be in the infirmary for another coupla nights."

"Can I have until tomorrow night to think about this?"

"Yeah, I'm feelin' generous. But remember, you do this for me and Tyrone starts selling shit again under my nose, he's dead anyway."

"I'll be sure to pass that along."

Matt turned to the trough and relieved himself. There was a time when the thought of peeing in front of Parnell would have made him bladder shy, but such useless fears and anxieties had already fallen away.

*

While working in the library the next morning, Luther noticed Matt was working even more quietly and with greater preoccupation than usual. Luther approached Matt at the cart that held the books he was shelving.

"Something wrong?" Luther asked.

Matt briefly explained.

"You've figured out Tyrone wasn't selling white lightning, right?" Luther asked Matt, cocking his head to the side.

"I suspected that."

"Tyrone's knows better. And if he'd wanted to make a play to be a leader or a dealer, he would have done it years ago."

"So why did Parnell have Tyrone beaten badly enough to put him in the infirmary?"

"Why do you think?"

"He's manipulating me."

"That's right. He's testing to see if he can get at you through Tyrone." Luther looked evenly at Matt.

"So does that mean that he won't really kill Tyrone if I don't take over this case for Bill?"

"No. Just like he had Tyrone beaten to show you he could hurt you, he could have Tyrone killed to show you he could kill someone you really do care about." Matt's stomach sank as he realized the threat behind Parnell's manipulation was very real.

"So what do I do?"

"Depends. If you're just looking out for yourself, which is hard enough in here, you probably tell Parnell you aren't going to handle the lawsuit for Bill."

"Why?"

"If Parnell can get at you by hurting Tyrone, you're going to have a much harder time if things go bad. Are you going to protect both Tyrone and yourself if things go south? You and I both know you can't do that."

"But if I don't protect Tyrone, aren't I going to be even more isolated?" Matt asked. "Why would any other prisoner ever become friends with me if it just made them more vulnerable? I can't protect myself, but I can at least avoid alienating too many people."

"Avoid alienating too many people?" Luther said, relaxing the formality of his usual diction. "You have any idea how much you already pissed everyone off? Some folk hate you 'cause you were rich on the outside; some folk hate you for bein' white; some folk hate you 'cause you're really gay and they want to prove they ain't gay; the White Brotherhood hates you for going to Parnell *and* being gay; and some other folk hate you for lining up a cushy job in the liberry without getting beaten up even once. You didn't have no control over some of those things when you walked into this prison, but ever since you got here you've only given folks more reasons to hate you." Luther shook his head.

"But I'm certainly not going to help my cause by refusing to help Tyrone," Matt said.

"You also have to think about the nature of this favor." Luther had regained his composure and he spoke in a reasonable tone, saying, "Parnell wants to watch you handle a case where the outcome doesn't matter. He wants to be able to tell when you aren't working as hard or as well as you can work, so he can compare it to his case. Parnell's very, very smart and don't let his speech fool you. He speaks like a brother because he needs to in this place, but he's at least as smart as you. If Parnell had grown up in a middle-class family, he'd be CEO of a big company. He might have picked Enron, but it'd be a big company. Drugs were the shortest path to money and he took it. Not all criminals are stupid."

"I don't see how I have a choice," Matt said.

"You have a choice," Luther said. "Let Tyrone take his chances with Parnell. Protecting someone you don't owe anything to got you here in the first place. Now that you're here, you should really just worry about protecting yourself."

"I am worried about protecting myself," Matt said. "I'm worried that I can't do it alone. And if, in the future, no one in Tyrone's position will help me out, then I'm fucked. Maybe not today or tomorrow, but I'm fucked."

"Matt, sorry to say this to you, but you're fucked anyway. We all are."

Matt spent the rest of the afternoon doing legal research for Parnell's appellate brief. The legal error during Parnell's trial was simple and egregious. Matt hoped that if he could win Parnell a new trial, all could be forgiven and some of the pressure would be off.

After dinner that night, he approached Parnell again and the two men met in the bathroom at the rear of the barracks. "Okay, I'll do it," Matt said.

"Bill wants to talk to you first and you can tell him what a lousy idea this lawsuit is. If you wanna volunteer to take on another case for him, that fine with me. I just owe Bill a favor and I don't give a shit what case you work on. You better tell your friend Tyrone when he gets back he needs to stop selling white lightnin' or you ain't gonna be able to protect him no more. 'Cause you ain't."

Matt slept well that night, knowing he'd done the right thing, even it jeopardized his safety. He felt as if he were playing a losing game; a single misstep or piece of bad luck would lead to serious violence. The self-defense sessions with Tommy and Dave hadn't equipped him to fight Parnell's entire gang.

The next evening, Tyrone still hadn't returned to Building 2, and Matt wondered about the severity of his injuries.

Before dinner, Parnell sought Matt out for the first time. "Bill wants to meet with you, so you gonna sit at his table tonight," Parnell ordered. "We can't arrange nothin' more private, so that's gonna have to do."

"All right. I'm safe sitting at his table, right?" Matt asked.

"So long as you still working on my case and you don't fuck up, you safe," Parnell said. Parnell's assurance was laden with enough qualifications to make any lawyer proud.

After filling his tray in the line at the cafeteria, Matt looked across the room for Bill. He spotted a tall man with filthy, shoulder-length blond hair, surprised to recognize him as the man Parnell had signaled during the football game to discipline the black man in the front row. He supposed that, when they needed to, Parnell's gang and the White Brotherhood could cooperate.

The most distinctive feature of the White Brotherhood members was a swastika tattooed across the forehead. The brand must remind members of how much they had to lose by falling out of favor. On the off chance the black half of the population in Wheaton—or, if transferred to Angola, the mostly black prisoners there—hadn't already identified all of the White Brotherhood's members, a glance could identify an unprotected outcast.

The men around Bill had left a space next to him. Matt took the empty seat. He held out his hand, just as he would if meeting with an executive for a corporate client. "Matt Durant."

"I know," Bill said. "I hear you're some kind of superlawyer, and Parnell agreed you could help me out with a case."

"Parnell's explained it to me, but I'd like to hear more about it from the guy who's suing."

"That can wait. I want to know why you went to Parnell for

protection," Bill said, locking eyes with Matt, who had difficulty focusing on the eyes beneath the swastika.

"I went to Parnell because he's been recently convicted. Under the law, appeals immediately after trial have a far greater chance of success. I thought there was a better chance that I could do something for him."

"Sure, but you're white. Notice how many white guys there are in Parnell's crew?"

"None."

"That's right." Bill gestured toward Matt with an open palm. "You could have appealed to my better nature for help, as a white man," Bill said as he pulled his hand in toward his chest.

"I was also slightly worried about the fact I was beaten up outside a gay bar. From what I remember, Hitler set out to kill all of the gays in Europe."

"If you'd told me you weren't gay, it would have been enough. You're not fucking any of those niggers, are you?" His eyes narrowed: apparently, his hate had a hierarchy.

"No," Matt said. Bill had a wild-eyed intensity; he hadn't blinked since Matt sat down.

"You should think about your long-term best interests. You can become a friend and brother to the men in my group. Those niggers are never going to be your friends or brothers. They're just going to use you for one thing or another until you're all used up."

"I hear you," Matt said. "Now, can we talk about this case?" He wanted and hoped to disengage—and perhaps deescalate—by shifting the discussion to an issue more familiar.

"Yeah. The guy who's suing is to your left. John Walker."

Matt stuck out his hand to John, who was a mousy man, with brown hair and brown eyes, and introduced himself. "Why don't you tell me what this lawsuit is about?"

"I wanna sue to get the cameras out of the showers. Don't we have privacy rights or something in there under the Constitution? If there are privacy rights that protect abortions, there's got to be a right for the guards not to see us naked in the shower." John looked up, but down again quickly. The man had a timid twitchiness, and

Matt wondered if it was from years of exposure to the prison's predators.

"Unfortunately, the courts have rejected precisely that argument," Matt said. "The constitutional rights of prisoners are far more limited than the rights of the general population. State governments can limit the privacy rights of prisoners for security reasons. I can draft a brief that reads well and looks professional, but it's not going to have much chance of winning." Matt turned to Bill. "That being said, I'm happy to work on another case for you. I can talk to some of your guys and see who has the best case."

"No," Bill said. "You aren't getting this, are you?"

"What do you mean?" Matt asked.

"If there aren't any cameras in the bathrooms, what happens?"

"I imagine there'd be more beatings and rapes in the showers," Matt said.

"Maybe," Bill said. "What's the best way to protect yourself from getting beat up or and raped when the guards aren't around? You should know the answer to this one."

"You have to get the protection of a gang."

"Or the White Brotherhood," Bill said, shaking his head. "We're not a gang."

"Banning the cameras from the showers, where all of the inmates are required to go, would increase the power of Parnell's gang and White Brotherhood and reduce the power of the guards," Matt said.

"Yep," Bill replied. "That's why even if there's only a one percent chance of this lawsuit working, it's worth a shot." Apparently Bill didn't have the pull to have the cameras turned off in his building; or perhaps he did, but he wanted them turned off throughout the rest of the prison's bathrooms. Maybe to spread his influence further?

"But I'm telling you that you don't even have a one percent chance of winning," Matt said. He was beginning to get frustrated.

"And I'm telling you you're supposed to be some sort of hotshot lawyer. Larry Bird didn't become Larry Bird by doing the same thing as every other basketball player. He became a superstar by doing shit other basketball players couldn't do. And that's what I need you to do."

"I hear you and I'll try my best," Matt said. "It would be helpful if we could argue they don't need to remove the cameras entirely. Can you think of a compromise solution that would remove the cameras only from certain areas in the bathrooms and still allow you to work? That's what I need from you."

"See, there you go. A good idea already. I'll get back to you with something besides removing all of the cameras."

Dinner ended and Matt returned to Building 2. As he fell asleep that night, he considered that he'd already been maneuvered into arguing an untenable legal position. Matt remembered Parnell had originally told him that he would work on cases for others, and then he realized why Parnell hadn't followed through on a larger scale. Parnell didn't want him to develop any friendships or earn any favors, and he'd already maneuvered him into handling a case likely to fail so that he couldn't. Matt needed to find another way to win allies.

Chapter 22

A few days later, Tyrone returned to Building 2 with a broken nose and collarbone. He couldn't work yet, so he whiled away his days in the barracks. When Matt asked him about the reasons for the beating, he refused to say anything—after Matt passed along Parnell's warning, Tyrone just sat there sullenly.

One afternoon, Matt was sorting books in the library while he watched Luther tutor an inmate. He realized that the way to make friends was right in front of him: he could teach someone how to read. Other inmates could offer that skill, but he could do it better than most.

When Luther finished his session, Matt approached him. "Luther, I was thinking about spending an hour or so each afternoon tutoring an inmate. How do I go about doing that?"

"Well, if you could tutor Reggie, it'd be a huge favor to me. I love him like a brother and he protected me for years, but we always end up fightin' whenever I try and teach him."

"I'd be happy to teach Reggie," Matt said. He felt a twinge of disappointment. Reggie had been a force to be reckoned with in a different generation and was an inmate in Angola, not Wheaton.

"Any way I could also tutor some folks from Wheaton?"

"I wouldn't push it now. They aren't allowed to come over here even to use the computers. They have to handwrite all their legal papers. That's why you take books to them."

"I figured as much," Matt said. Tutoring Reggie would at least be a start, and maybe he could offer more advice on how to survive. But he suspected Reggie's strategy for survival had depended on brute force, rather than sophistication or subtlety.

"You're new, so you aren't supposed to have the privileges to tutor," Luther said. "You're gonna have to get permission. And you can't go through Parnell because I'd imagine he guards your time pretty jealously. You're going to have to ask Ted."

Matt wasn't thrilled about asking Ted, who would probably just tell Parnell. But he needed to reach out and develop other friendships and resources.

*

Ted arrived that evening to pick him up from the library.

Matt waited until they were alone in the pickup truck on the road back to Wheaton. "Ted, I have a question for you," he said, hoping to placate the guard by asking permission to even ask a question.

"Yeah."

"I was wondering if I could tutor an illiterate inmate from Angola in the library during the afternoons, like Luther does."

"Well, hell, you aren't even supposed to be in there, but it couldn't hurt," Ted said, keeping his eyes on the dirt road.

Matt felt a small triumph. It sounded like Ted had paid so little attention to his request that he might not even tell Parnell. And surely it wouldn't create problems with Parnell even if he found out. It was only an hour a day, or at least he could tell Parnell that, so he had a plausible reason for not running it by the man to whom he'd at least superficially ceded control.

The next day, in the library, Luther and Matt approached Reggie, who was already seated at one of the conference-room tables.

"So Luther, you gonna be in the rodeo this year?" Reggie asked.

"What are you talking about?" Matt asked.

"You ain't heard about the rodeo?" Reggie asked. "Every year for decades the Warden's been havin' a rodeo for us prisoners to participate in. We ain't allowed to train for it. Those of us who been 'round long enough know it's a sucker's bet. But Luther here decided he was gonna win a belt buckle 'bout twenty-five years ago."

"I wanted to give it to my son," Luther said quietly.

"Now Luther ain't that athletic, so the only thing he could do was play convict's poker."

"What's convict's poker?" Matt asked.

"They sit down a bunch a cons 'round a bright red table, shock a bull, and the last con to get up from the table and run away from the bull wins. They shocked that bull, an' firs' thing you know, I don' know who took off faster, Luther or the bull." Reggie cracked a wide smile, showing missing teeth.

"Well," Luther said, "I decided if I was going to lose, I was going to lose in a way that made sure I didn't get hurt."

"Can inmates at Wheaton participate?" Matt asked.

"Yeah," Reggie said, "but I told you it's a sucker's bet. Why you wanna perform like a monkey for some outside visitors?" Reggie asked, with a quizzical expression. Matt wondered if he thought it below the status of a lawyer, who had services to trade, but, if so, he underestimated Matt's willingness to explore every option to survive.

"Just curious," Matt said. Being underestimated could have its advantages.

"Well, don't be," Luther said, with a pointed look, likely remembering how his single attempt in convict's poker had embarrassed him in front of the other inmates, perhaps leaving him vulnerable.

Matt and Reggie then sat and plodded through phonetics. Reggie showed deliberate determination and never once, over the course of two hours, asked for a break; he lacked aptitude and enthusiasm, but he kept putting one foot in front of the other.

After he'd left, Matt asked Luther: "Why's he learning to read so late? Why bother?"

"Well," Luther said, "his son came to visit for the first time in ten years a year or so ago. Told him he had a grandkid. When Reggie asked if he could see his grandkid, his son asked him why he'd bring him to meet his granddaddy, a convict who can't even read. Asked what kinda example that would set. Reggie figured he couldn't fix the convict part but maybe he could fix the reading part."

Matt's conversation with Luther made him think of those in his life who'd communicated with him in prison and he decided to write to Eric and his mother. He began with the letter to Eric because the relationship was less laden with history, even if it had held a different kind of promise now transmuted to wistfulness.

Dear M—

Thanks so much for the note, which put a smile on my face. Around here workout clothes are the same clothes we always wear, jeans and a t-shirt. Digging ditches is incredible exercise, though—I'll bet I'm in better shape than you'll ever be. Perhaps you could open a gym on the outside that copies the workout here. Then maybe you can start a new line of athleisure and make us both rich. But I think if people on the outside were restricted to one outfit choice, they probably wouldn't dress in the equivalent of sweats all the time.

I firmly believe the deliberately casual look is spreading from California. I was eating dinner in a nice restaurant in the Quarter last winter and a guy in what looked like a sweat suit he'd stolen from a homeless person walked in. I thought to myself, "He's either a billionaire or a genius." Got to talking to him, though, and he was neither—just a visiting professor from Dartmouth.

He also told me it was an Ivy League school. Who knows that? I just thought it was where Michael Corleone went to college in *The Godfather.* And that he felt he had to tell me didn't speak too highly of it or him.

Anyway, hope you recovered from your hangover and actually managed to work out.

Take care,

A

Matt turned to the letter to his mother:

Dear Mom,

I know you must be happy about LSU winning the national championship! You certainly deserve some good news.

I have some good news to report, too. I got a job in the library organizing and shelving books and tutoring other inmates. It's wonderful to be surrounded by books again. And I'm being paid—like I was as a lawyer—to sit alone in a room with books and read and think. I guess it's only four cents an hour, but I did it for free for decades in school so I think I'm still coming out ahead.

Also, there's no librarian's paradox here like I told you about in the university libraries. There, first thing, they give you a long lecture about the billion and one different ways you can damage a book and how a misplaced book among millions can be lost for a hundred years. It's as if the librarians don't want anyone ever reading or using the books. Here, the librarians are prisoners who love books and that form of escape. The inmates who visit do too. Hard to imagine more appreciative patrons than prisoners who come to the library willingly.

Well, I'm off to dinner.

Love,
Matt

Matt thought his mother too naïve to think it unusual he'd already been assigned to the library and hoped the letter came off as reassuring and genuine—he worried it was transparent.

But, after his last conversation with Luther, Matt realized he'd never heard any other prisoner talk about family visits, probably because, after a few years, they ceased. His mother, at least, would be in contact until the day one of them died, and he would do his best not to punish her for that.

Chapter 23

As winter gave way to spring and then a summer heat that imitated hell, Matt fell into a routine working in the library and on his three cases. Relentless stress turned to monotony and even as fanatical as he was about his responsibilities on the outside, in prison, with nothing else to do, his focus on the details of the cases bordered on obsession.

When not dwelling on the cases, he wrote letters; he also read and reread those he'd received from his Mom, Lisa and Eric.

Eric responded to the suggestion he open a gym:

A—

Hope all is well and you're staying safe. I've been considering your recommendation to invest in a gym. I think I'd have to go to a gym—at least once—before I invested in one. I did recently think about going to the gym for at least thirty seconds.

If I went to the gym, I would be paying money to do work and I usually prefer it the other way around. You're getting paid to work, even if it's only four cents an hour. Right now I just eat less—which means I spend less money and have more free time to have more fun. Seems like a win–win. And I don't do athleisure.

I'm imaging you pronouncing that word *athleyzure* because someone once told you that was the refined way to pronounce leisure. But I don't hang out with the *Roozvelts* discussing such things, and I wouldn't be caught dead in athleyzure or pronouncing it that way. I don't avoid athleisure because I'm a snob, but because I'm vain and I don't wear pajamas in public. Remember the 1980s: our poor sartorial choices live on forever in pictures. As for not pronouncing leisure the preferred way, I don't care if people initially think me dumb as a result. They'll figure it out eventually.

Try to stay cool in the heat.

Take care,
M

That summer, he also received a pensive letter from his mother:

Dear Matt,

You know I've enjoyed our casual letters back and forth for months now, but I wanted to write a separate one about some things that have been bothering me ever since your trial.

I'm worried that because some of those jurors said they were influenced by you being gay, you'll somehow hold that against God. I don't usually talk about religion with you, but I really don't want you to reject any possible comfort right now.

For those jurors to say you being gay would affect their decision about whether you'd lie or commit murder was sinful. Throughout the Gospel, Jesus ministers to tax collectors, prostitutes and lepers, healing despite what many said were their sins. He does so with compassion, not judgment.

When Jesus does show anger in the Gospels, it's almost always toward the scribes and Pharisees—religious leaders who berated others for not following their view of religion and judged others for breaking rules like not working on the Sabbath. He also speaks of the importance of humility, including humility in prayer, and chastises the scribes and Pharisees for condemning others based on their rigid interpretations of the Torah. He is far more critical of those who use religion as an excuse to collect money for themselves than those who collect money for the government.

When Jesus talks about the importance of measuring people by their deeds over the course of a lifetime, rather than just their words, he says to those religious leaders who had rejected John the Baptist, "[T]ruly I tell you the tax collectors and the prostitutes are going into the kingdom of God ahead of you."

Even if being gay were a sin—and I'm not saying it is—I can't believe God, Jesus or the Holy Spirit would ever believe it a reason for one human being to judge another. On the cross, Jesus told one of the criminals he would be with him in Paradise that day, and if Paradise remained open to that criminal, then surely those who may commit a sin that harms no one don't deserve punishment for it in this life or the next.

I'm still struggling with lots of issues—including, thanks to you, why Mahatma Gandhi isn't in hell and what the Bible says about being gay. I don't worry so much about those because they're not as important—we all sin. I think the Gospels say those not raised as Christians will likely be measured by their deeds. Those of us raised as Christians can and should always repent.

I struggle more with what the Gospel is clear about. I have to forgive those men who attacked you, forgive Joey Buckner and forgive those jurors. And I'm angry with all of them every day you spend in there, which I need to work on. And that's hard, but I do get some peace when I pray every night.

I hope you don't mind a letter like this every now and again. I just want to keep your mind and your heart open to the comfort that God can give you in as much privacy as you need, even if you pray with your heart and don't make a sound or even move your lips. It can still quiet your mind and soul.

Love,
Mom

Matt blinked away tears in his bunk. Didn't she understand he had to focus on survival? How could he have time for a God who—according to many—had no space for him? And if he studied the Bible he might decide that it definitively said being gay was sinful. What would he do with that? How could that possibly help? How was he supposed to have the confidence and the trust—and yes, the faith—to believe in a God that so many said judged him as sinful for being? It threatened to undermine him further, not offer support. He just couldn't do it.

On a Friday after dinner, two of the larger inmates grabbed Matt from his bunk and frog-marched him into the bathroom at the back of the barracks.

Parnell waited there, his brow furrowed in anger and his lips drawn back in a feral expression. "You need to tell me what the fuck this is right now," he said, thrusting papers at Matt, who scanned a letter from Parnell's lawyer.

"We discussed this." Matt's hands shook, as he scanned the page; thanks to his training, it required little thought. "The trial judge denied your motion for a new trial, but we expected that."

"This means you lost, you son of a bitch!" Parnell bellowed. His dark face turned purple.

"This means we lost the first round, which we expected to lose," Matt said.

"You're my fucking lawyer and you're within my control. That means you never fucking expect to lose," Parnell shouted.

"Of course we fucking expect to lose!" Matt shouted back, fear spawning anger. "As your lawyer, I have to accurately assess your prospects for success at each stage of the case. Your outside lawyer had to argue to the judge he'd committed a legal error to preserve the arguments for appeal so we can present them to a different court. That appellate court functions as his boss. The trial judge isn't going to just come out and admit he's wrong. Is your outside lawyer telling you anything different?"

"No," Parnell said, shaking his head but with wide eyes and dilated pupils still hot with fury. "But he's only working for money. He ain't working to save his ass the way you are. I'm going to fucking let some of these guys run a train on you all night long."

Matt felt the blood drain from his face, but his anger short-circuited good sense. "That's not going to change a goddamned thing and you know it. Why the fuck wouldn't I be working as hard as I could for you?" Matt asked.

"I dunno. I jus' know we lost." Parnell forced the words out of a clenched jaw.

"We didn't lose. We lost the opening motion."

"What happens next?"

"We file a brief with the appellate court, the judge's bosses. The appellate court doesn't have the same vested interest in finding that the judge ruled correctly during the trial. They won't be trying to cover their own asses. The appellate court's also bound by Louisiana State Supreme Court precedent ruling that the instruction was in error. Now, the argument isn't certain, but that's always been our best shot. And this opinion doesn't change that."

"It don't?" Parnell asked as his face relaxed slightly, his anger blunted.

"No, it doesn't. Courts almost never grant re-hearings because the trial judge would have to admit he did something wrong. Judges are people, too, and most don't like to admit they're wrong."

"Jus' like you don't want to admit you were wrong when you wrote that damn brief to the judge?" Parnell asked.

"No," Matt said. "Not like me. I told you we had to make this motion as a procedural formality and there was almost no chance the judge would grant a new hearing. You know that."

"Yeah, you did," Parnell said. "I ain't gonna have anything done to you tonight, but we gonna talk again tomorrow night after I get my outside lawyer on the phone. You not safe yet. And you ain't gonna work on any other cases 'cept my appeal. You got that? Forget that law-firm idea you had."

"What about the case for Bill?"

"You can work on that case, too. You gonna work on my case and Bill's case. Nothin' else. And I'm still thinking about havin' a train run on your ass tomorrow night." He raised a colossal right fist and shook it with menace. "You got that, you fucker?"

Matt resisted the urge to flinch with all his might, hoping that strength respected strength. "Yes, I got that," he said.

Matt lay awake all night. As soon as he arrived at the library in the morning, he sent Parnell's attorney an email asking for the written opinion. He received a copy by midmorning and spent the rest of the day scrutinizing it; the judge hadn't protected himself completely and he considered ways to undermine the opinion on appeal, even going so far as to draft the introduction for Parnell's appellate brief.

Matt neglected his library work that day, but Luther didn't ask any questions about his failure to attend to his usual chores. Matt assumed the veteran prisoner had learned of the opinion, and of Parnell's reaction.

When Matt returned to Building 2 that afternoon, Parnell had him marched back to the bathroom. "I talked to my lawyer and he said you was right; this was just a formality," Parnell said.

"I looked at the opinion more closely this afternoon, if you want to talk about it," Matt said.

"Go ahead."

"You remember I told you our best argument was that the attempted murder instruction was legally erroneous, right?" Matt said, cocking his head to the side.

"Yeah, that's the argument this judge already rejected. Twice, if I'm countin' right."

"And do you remember there were also two problems with that argument that I explained to you?"

"Go over 'em again."

"The first problem is that your trial lawyer objected to the instruction but didn't state the objection as precisely as possible. I

235

was concerned that might be interpreted as a waiver, which would make it much harder to raise on appeal. The second problem is the trial judge could find that the instruction didn't matter because the proof of your guilt was overwhelming. The good thing about this opinion is that the prosecution made both of those arguments to the judge, but the judge didn't adopt either of them. The judge just said the instruction was legally correct, which is wrong. That helps because the trial judge is in the best position to make factual findings about what happened in the trial, such as whether the argument was waived and whether the evidence against you was overwhelming. That means this opinion really is a formality and we can argue to the appellate court the trial judge didn't find either waiver or harmless error."

"I'm gonna check that with my outside lawyer."

"You should." Having his interpretation of the opinion double-checked was the least of his fears.

"You okay for now, bitch. But you best produce results soon."

After Parnell blew out of the bathroom, Matt suddenly felt nauseated. He spent the next half-hour vomiting, well aware doing so left him bent over the toilet.

Chapter 24

As fall approached, Matt's powerlessness and anger overwhelmed him; he'd filed Parnell's brief with the appellate court and could do no more. He stewed over the letter from his mother about religion which lingered and generated accusations more damning than those expressed by her or the jurors: Why hadn't he just turned the other cheek? Did it matter that Joey was in danger? Would turning the other cheek have earned forgiveness for being unable to police his attraction to other men?

Mired in such thoughts, he had signed up for what Reggie had described as a "sucker's bet"—the rodeo held in October in the prison stadium that seated 7500 members of the general public.

The first Sunday in October arrived, and, on the grounds outside, the convicts sold food to the public that none of the sellers could have afforded on their paltry wage. It ranged from crawfish, which you could find outside of Tiger Stadium, to fried Coke, made of frozen Coca-Cola-flavored batter deep-fried and topped with syrup, cinnamon sugar and a cherry, a caloric poison for members of the same public that had populated the convicts' juries.

The warden, for rodeo days, insisted the prisoners wear black-and-white striped shirts that evoked stereotypes, which he thought made for better marketing and showmanship. Prisoners also sold crafts, from carved chess sets to oil paintings of the flowers cultivated on the prison's grounds. One prisoner sold canary-yellow balloons, and his doleful face lit up whenever he sold one to a child.

Some prisoners took the opportunity to see family and friends outside the more restricted visiting areas. An inmate carried his son—who must have still been in kindergarten—in his arms, and each of the child's giggles prompted a broad smile. Matt hadn't told his mom or anyone else he was participating; he was ashamed of risking his life and health; and he suspected the scene inside the arena wouldn't be as cheerful.

As the start time approached, the public trickled into the seats. Warden Paxon opened the ceremony by entering behind two sable 2000-pound Percheron draft horses pulling a rickety wooden cart. He was followed by a white inmate riding a bay toting an American flag, an African-American inmate on liver-spotted pinto bearing a Confederate battle flag, and a monkey on a collie. The crowd laughed at the tail-end of the procession.

The rodeo entrants then, also under the Warden's instructions and in front of the crowd's watchful eyes, walked into the square dirt arena, formed a circle and held hands as a prayer was said, including an invocation to watch over their spiritual well-being as well as their health and safety.

Following the prayer and the clearing of the dirt arena, electric shocks launched six angry bulls out of shoots, each with a convict atop, in an event unique to the Angola rodeo called the Bust Out. The convicts' only opportunity to prepare was at the school of hard knocks; those who'd participated in the event in earlier years had learned a few things about staying on. A convict was thrown immediately in front of a shoot and the angry bull leapt toward him, grasping him in his horns and shaking him furiously.

The crowd cheered. Convict clowns distracted the bull and lured it away and the event continued for another few seconds, until all convicts save one had been thrown from their bulls. The crowd cheered again.

The prisoners then watched silently as paramedics tended to the gored prisoner at the side of the arena, while the crowd noise subsided to disinterested chatter. He was carried off on a stretcher without delaying the festivities and without the crowd noticing.

The afternoon progressed through a series of events, some of which could only be found at the prison rodeo. In wild cow milking, teams of convicts chased cows around the arena trying to milk them and the first team to secure enough milk won. Even in the more traditional events, like bull riding, untrained convicts wearing what the guards called "nigger-rigged" safety equipment reduced them to grotesque spectacles.

Matt had signed up for only one event—convict poker. He joined three other inmates sitting around a poker table made of cheap plastic, surrounded by chairs of the same material. Over their striped shirts Matt and the other players wore bulletproof vests, and on their heads they wore hockey helmets.

A bull was released—incented by cattle prod—and convict clowns in white with red suspenders and neon-orange trimmings lured it toward the table. The 2000-pound animal bucked around the table for tens of seconds and the first player peeled away, running toward the side of the arena and to relative safety. Matt found he didn't care if he lived, died or was injured. Tired, he stayed seated.

The bull sprinted back toward the table and lunged at a clown on the opposite side, upending the table and tossing one of the two other remaining players to the ground. The third bolted and the bull chased him toward the side of the arena. Matt—already the winner by default—remained seated. The player reached safety some fifteen seconds later, and—only then—did the bull, the clowns and the crowd notice that Matt had remained seated instead of escaping to safety to claim his prize.

The bull turned back but the clowns were so surprised that they didn't goad it toward or away from him. For a full sixty seconds, Matt stared at the bull from his lone seat in the middle of the arena—daring, asking and even begging it to hurt or kill him. But the bull ignored him and wandered around the sides of the arena. The crowd—boisterous half a minute ago at the sight of the convict fleeing—fell silent.

Part IV

Chapter 25

Over the next year and a half, Matt ground out days at the pace of a glacier—he repressed any hint of rising expectations about his appeal and his life sentence froze his melancholy.

Only communications with the outside world marked time and leavened life. Unlike other prisoners, he sent and received weekly letters from Eric—using a pseudonym and Lisa's home address—and daily letters from his mother.

A letter from Eric stood out:

A—

Hope all is well and you're staying safe. So my parents took me to *Rent* on Broadway years ago, but Lisa wanted to see it and just made me watch the movie on DVD.

I read some nonsense that the play hasn't aged well because it's about spoiled kids trying to get out of paying their rent and using a protest to save the homeless from being evicted from a park as an excuse. It does revolve around three couples, and two now seem somewhat superficial and melodramatic.

But the real hero is part of the third couple. They've apparently missed the not-so-subtle hint of her name—Angel. Even though she's poor, when she first meets the man who would become her boyfriend, he's just been mugged, is coatless and she insists on buying him a new one. She volunteers immediately that she's HIV-positive, and he—a professor—volunteers the same.

When the two later run into a woman selling the stolen coat, she insists on buying it back.

She loves readily, without any of the "angst" of the kids from wealthier families. When her boyfriend first asks if they're a "thing," she responds, "we're everything." In the second act, while the other couples bicker, she dies.

At Angel's funeral, we learn that she taught all of them the meaning of love and every major character invokes her as an inspiration for pursuing love. She intervenes near the end by appearing in the white light during a death scene and encourages the person close to death to return to the one she loves.

I watched it twice, and I got it. You'd think if people were going to bother to write a review, they'd at least bother to analyze all the characters!

Oh well, I'm not going to complain about being forced to watch a movie to you. Except I just did.

Hang in there,
M

Matt remembered the movie version, which he'd "allowed" Lisa to drag him to the movie theater to see, and she must have told Eric. Eric was right. Angel was the hero, but his letter omitted what no prison censor or nosy inmate would likely know, let alone remember. She—or perhaps he—had been a drag queen, and her relationship with her boyfriend queer.

His mother's letters mostly recounted her routine, but she couldn't help but try to help. She wrote a second letter about religion:

Dear Matt,

I figure I get credit for sending so many letters now prattling about my job and other boring things that I get to bother you again with a serious letter, even though I didn't hear a peep from you about the last one.

I've been thinking more about religion and being gay. I remember when you were little and learning to ride a bike and you fell and insisted you'd broken something and needed to go to the hospital. When I said you were fine, you said you couldn't walk and dragged yourself around the house using your hands for three days. It's hard enough to tell you to do something, much less to stop being something. So, I still don't know much about being gay, but I'm not going to tell you to stop. If only because my life's too short.

I guess I'll start with Mahatma Gandhi, even though that kind of feels like a lawyer's trick and I'm not an expert on recent Indian history. But Gandhi was a lawyer too, so I guess I'll indulge you. Jesus, in most places, seems to limit the require-ment of belief in Him to—as He puts it in Matthew—"everyone who hears these words," so that might save Gandhi.

And when the Pharisees said that Jesus could only cast out demons because he was allied with Satan, Jesus introduced the concept of a house divided: "Every kingdom divided against itself is laid waste and no city or house divided against itself will stand." He goes on to say: "Whoever is not with me is against me, and whoever does not gather with me scatters. Therefore I tell you, people will be forgiven for every sin and blasphemy, but blasphemy against the Spirit will not be forgiven. Whoever speaks a word against the Son of Man will be forgiven, but who-ever speaks against the Holy Spirit will not be forgiven, either in this age or the age to come." Even if Gandhi didn't believe in Jesus, his life's work certainly reflected the Spirit and he spoke for peaceful protest and good works.

And as I mentioned in my last letter about religion, Jesus said that some of the prohibitions in the Old Testament—like the bans against eating unclean foods, failing to wash your hands before eating or working on the Sabbath—give way to the need to eat or to work to heal. They gave way to the necessities of life and deeds for others that reflect the Spirit. If so, then surely they also give way to the need to love and love for others, no matter what sex or gender. After all, Jesus identifies loving God and loving others as the highest commandment.

And, by the way, I'm not encouraging you to eat without washing your hands. Please wash them before eating whenever possible.

Love,
Mom

Matt snorted at the last line, typical of his mother. But he realized that she, from her own anxiety-tinged perspective, hadn't given up hope. For so long, he'd concentrated on working, surviving and putting one foot in front of the other that he hadn't thought about why. He'd always known that his depression and its collateral consequences—if unchecked and uncontrolled—could devastate. Perhaps that explained the *why*; he needed to minimize the burden his pain imposed on those he loved. And, perhaps in combination with a sliver of belief in the possibility of release, the same mixture of books and work could also keep him going here. He knew his mother feared his death more than anything else in the world; after all, she'd once told him that she couldn't imagine ever not loving her child, unless he became a serial murderer or committed some other atrocity. So maybe he need only, for her sake, try to keep putting one foot in front of the other here too.

*

Matt also spent many days in the library. On one, he entered, nodded to Luther, and sat down with his legal file. His case had proceeded rapidly by legal standards perhaps because of its high profile, Farrar's stature with the bar, or the legal arguments were novel. The Louisiana Supreme Court had affirmed his conviction, provoking mild disappointment, but his reaction annoyed him as much as the decision itself. He'd known the cases upholding the state's ban against gay marriage made the result foreordained. He spent the morning testing the analysis in the opinion against his own research and readings of the cases.

About half an hour before lunch, Matt checked his email to confirm Parnell's lawyer hadn't sent him any new information. He pulled out Parnell's file, glanced at the transcript of the appellate argument, and considered rereading it yet again. The judges had been disturbed by the erroneous instruction but, as Matt had predicted, they'd expressed reluctance to disturb the jury's verdict because of the ambiguous objections made by Parnell's trial counsel and the other overwhelming evidence of his guilt.

Matt didn't know what to make of the delay and he worried the judges were working to find evidence in the record showing waiver and harmless error. He shoved Parnell's file aside. There wasn't anything he could do about it now.

After lunch with Luther's friends, Reggie arrived at the library. Reggie pulled out a seat and placed his tattered reader on the table. Matt asked him to open to page forty-six and he began deliberately sounding out words. It had taken Matt weeks to teach him the alphabet. He couldn't even begin to guess at the scope of Reggie's learning disabilities, but he made up for his lack of natural aptitude with a slow and steady determination. That made sense. After all, a life sentence could cultivate patience in even the most impatient men.

After they finished, Reggie asked: "You mind some advice?" He pushed the book across the table toward Matt.

"No," Matt responded.

"You need to work with who you are and what you got to make friends and stay outta trouble," Reggie said, with his hands resting on the table's edge.

"What do you mean?" Matt asked.

"We'se all different, or mos' people who matter are. I figger if'n you're different enough, you got two choices—you can let folks trample on you or you can lead 'em. Take that rodeo. You know I called it a sucker's bet. That used to be real different. Mos' folks round here were happy for the chance to win fifty or a hundred bucks by riding in it—that's a lot of money to mos' of 'em. I called it out as the bullshit it was, showin' I didn't need the money and warn't gonna be their monkey. But you did somethin' different."

"Yeah, something stupid," Matt said. Reggie shook his head.

"Maybe, but you shouldn't tell that to nobody else. You showed you could control your fear. You didn't jes' beat those other cons roun' that table. You stared down that big crazy bull and made the crowd go quiet. People ain't gonna forget that."

"Yeah, well, we'll see," Matt said. "I heard you tell Luther you'd saved him from a few beatings," Matt said.

"Yep, that was back in the bad ole days."

"Any tips for if I get cornered?"

"When it's time, you gotta move fast," Reggie said.

"What do you mean?"

"Most folks talk too much. A guy's tryin' to scare ya and he usually ends up givin' a lecture. I think mebbe he's tryin' to talk himself into it too. Soon as you figure out a guy's gonna hurt you, you gotta hurt him first. If they'se busy runnin' their mouth, they'se gonna be slow."

"Sort of like in a James Bond movie where the villain explains the evil plot?" Matt asked.

"Dunno 'bout that," Reggie said. "I jes' knows you best move fast."

About a week later, Matt learned, while working in the library, that the United States Court of Appeals for the Fifth Circuit had affirmed the dismissal of the lawsuit challenging the use of video cameras in the bathrooms. Matt had cabined the inmates' request for relief so that they sought to conceal only the toilets and doorless stalls. But, as he'd predicted, the court had hewed to existing federal precedent and ruled against the prisoners. Bill should have let him pick the case.

Matt returned from work that day and Parnell told him he should sit next to Bill at dinner that night. Matt didn't know how Parnell already knew, but he did. Matt arrived at the cafeteria, loaded his tray and carried it over to the open seat next to Bill. He felt his heart in his throat, terrified by Bill and his own anxiety. If he was this worried about Bill, he wondered how he could possibly stay under control if Parnell turned on him. Matt sat.

"So, you heard about the decision?" Bill asked.

"Yeah," Matt said. "It's too bad, but we expected to lose."

"God, I fucking hate lawyers," Bill said. "What good did you do me?"

"You had a better chance of winning your case," Matt said.

"Yeah, but I lost and I had to use up my favor for nothing." Bill shook his head. "Just like on the outside where we have to pay you assholes even when we lose. But in here, I pay the jailhouse lawyers what I think they deserve. And that payment ain't always positive. I wanted to pay you real good, 'cause I don't think I got very much for the favor Parnell owed me. I almost convinced him he should let me have a shot at you just to put the fear of God in you about losing his case. But he hasn't gone for it yet."

Matt exhaled suddenly, incapable of concealing his relief at Parnell's continued protection. He looked at the plate of food he hadn't touched and tried to keep his expression blank.

"But if you lose Parnell's case, his boys gonna take the first shot at you, and then we get a shot," Bill said. "Winning his case just became that much more important to protecting that virgin ass of yours. Or maybe it ain't virgin, but you sure are worried about it if it ain't."

"Okay," Matt said. "But the brief I wrote was far more professional than anything written in this prison—and better than most briefs written by private lawyers. You also didn't listen to me about the merits of the camera case, and I can't help you if you don't listen to me. You have lots of cases among all the members of the Brotherhood, and if you'd let me screen them for the strongest case, we would have had a better chance of winning."

"I thought you'd have some excuse," Bill said. "Tell you what, you lose Parnell's case, we're gonna be waitin' in line to pound your ass. After we pound your ass, we might be able to reach some sort of deal about you working for protection. But hear me now. Your special status in this prison will fucking end and you will happily be some bull's bitch. You understand me?"

"I hear you," Matt said. The last time he'd been as careful to connote comprehension without agreement was in a negotiation with an opposing lawyer in a multimillion-dollar litigation. Times had changed.

Chapter 26

On an early Saturday morning, one of the guards unexpectedly escorted Matt toward the main building at Angola. Matt wondered why, as the guard led him through a maze of walls made of cinderblocks, the once-white paint covering them dulled to bone, and opened a steel door to a conference room. Farrar and Lisa sat in black folding chairs at an egg-white table. Matt worried that Farrar Levinson had decided to drop his case, but warm and open greetings from the two allayed that concern.

"Matt, it's good to see you. You look healthy," Farrar said, rising, flashing a smile revealing white teeth and shaking Matt's hand firmly.

"Matt, I'm so glad to see you in one piece," Lisa added, hugging him. "We've all been so worried." She ended her sentence without the tentative pitch habitual before his trial. She seemed more poised and confident.

"Thanks for coming out to see me," Matt said. "You didn't need to. We can talk about the case over the phone." The three settled in their chairs.

"We wanted to check up on you," Farrar said. "But we also need to discuss your case. As I told you a year and a half ago, our best shot is probably still a cert petition to the United States Supreme Court."

"And that's not much of a shot because they choose to hear less than one percent of those appeals," Matt said.

"I know. I'm sorry," Farrar said, with a more serious cast.

"It's hardly your fault you tried such a good case that grounds for reversal are scarce."

"We showed up here today because we only have forty-five days from the order of the Louisiana Supreme Court to file the petition. We wanted to discuss it with you."

"I've been thinking about that. I'd like to write the first draft," Matt said, asserting himself. "No one has spent more time examining the relevant case law. And I have the time. I've been doing some jailhouse legal work for other inmates, but I have a very limited number of cases. And we've finished briefing and argument in my most important client's case."

"Is that how you've kept yourself safe?" Farrar asked, tilting his head to the side with raised eyebrows.

"Yeah. I've been doing some work for a couple of inmates and I've been dancing very quickly to make sure my clients stay satisfied. I thought I'd write the first draft of the cert petition and then y'all could edit, check and file it under the firm's name," Matt said.

"Well, I'm not going to object to you taking a shot at the first draft," Farrar said. "In fact, you might think about signing and filing the brief under your own name. The firm could sign as co-counsel."

"Couldn't that backfire?" Matt asked. "Federal judges pride themselves on their neutrality and independence. I don't want to do anything that looks like a cheap ploy for sympathy."

"I'd agree with that generally," Farrar said. "But you can address that with the tone of the brief, which, knowing you, will read very professionally."

"I also hate the idea of being affiliated with all of the other briefs written by prisoners. I think the judges and clerks at least subconsciously associate pro se briefs with weaker arguments."

"I know you want to distance yourself from other pro se petitioners," Farrar responded, "but your case is different. There have been several articles about your case in the *American Lawyer*. And one of your former professors from LSU has published a law review article arguing that the law should be changed based on your case. I think the justices and clerks will be familiar with the facts and your legal qualifications before the petition hits their desks. And, again, I think the tone of the brief can eliminate those dangers. I also think the Supreme Court's decision in *Lawrence v. Texas* bodes well. In *Lawrence*, the court struck down a law that made sodomy a misdemeanor and resulted in a fine of less than a hundred dollars. You're looking at spending the rest of your life in here."

"Thanks for the reminder," Matt said, gesturing toward the cinderblock wall to his right.

"No problem," Farrar said. He smiled again.

"Okay," Matt said. "I'll take a shot at the first draft." Matt wondered if Farrar's persuasiveness actually suggested the opposite, but he wasn't going to give up any chance to regain some control over his life.

The next weekend brought an even better surprise because Eric had informed him in a guarded letter that he would be visiting him, in person, on Sunday in Butler Park—an outdoor park where prisoners with longer tenure had the privilege of receiving visitors. Matt arrived early that morning and sat at a park bench connected to a table for four, anxious about potentially taking up two extra seats but hoping that no one would join them.

Across from the park, the prison cemetery contained the bodies of those who died in prison and penury with no one left to care about or for their remains. In between the two, the Louisiana sun had bleached the St. Augustine grass a salty hue to match pines with desiccated trunks and branches with few needles. White crosses dotted the cemetery and Matt thought it eerie and blasphemous how much they resembled the crosses at Arlington Cemetery; he supposed we all die, our bodies ultimately forgotten, continuing on this earth only in others' impressions and memories.

Through the barren branches, Matt located a bright blue sky and the hint of a lingering moon. On the edge of the park, over the peak of a rolling hill, Matt knew that convicts led some visitors to have sex, almost fully clothed, while the other prisoners and even the guards pretended not to notice.

He wasn't too lost in his reverie to miss Eric's approach; against the landscape, his copper hair stood out as one of the few bright colors. While others hugged ferociously, he and Eric exchanged smiles and shook hands. Eric placed his left hand over their hands and Matt noticed a wedding band. Matt hoped that it was camouflage and not some symbol of commitment; after all, in Louisina, gay marriage was illegal.

"Well," Eric said, "this is a fairly unique weekend road trip for me," as the two settled on the benches.

"Not exactly driving to Baton Rouge to see a game, is it?" Matt asked.

"Nope. It took about an hour longer," Eric responded with a grin.

Matt laughed. "Have you made it to the gym yet, or just bought the clothes?"

"Well, I have spent a lot of time thinking about going to the gym. And I've read that all of the best athletes visualize their top performances before they have them."

"Well, yes," Matt said, "but I suspect elite athletes know what to visualize. A quarterback knows what a perfect pass looks and feels like; a tennis player knows the same about the perfect serve. Have you ever seen the inside of a gym?" Matt raised a single eyebrow.

"I'm offended. I've definitely walked by several and looked in, and I picked up Lisa from the gym once." Matt smiled. The mention of a woman, who any listener could assume was Eric's girlfriend or wife, made him feel safer. Eric continued: "Really, I think I should probably buy myself a large trophy so I can better visualize what winning looks like."

Matt laughed again. "You do know that people our age who take up new gym sports have generally passed the age when they give out medals and trophies. I think half-marathons and marathons are the exception. You don't want to run a marathon, do you?"

"God no." Eric gasped. "It was named after a battle a guy ran 20-plus miles to report—but even though the battle didn't kill him the run did. Why on earth would I want to do that?"

"So, changing the subject, have you been back to the jazz club or the Insectarium?" Matt asked.

"The jazz club, no, the Insectarium, yes," Eric responded. "I didn't bring it, but they sell certificates to adopt bugs as a gimmick to raise money to support the place. I bought you one for the Atlas beetle, but I didn't bring it in case they wouldn't let you keep it. I can mail it."

"They'll let you," Matt said. As they spoke, couples had already begun stealing away to the area over the hill for greater intimacy. Matt forced himself to ignore them, wondered whether Eric noticed and realized the couples were pretty obvious. Matt felt blood rush to his face.

"I also bought a certificate for that other bug," Eric said, "but I'm going to hold onto that one until you get out of here." He reached toward Matt with his right hand across the table, only to withdraw it. "It may only live for weeks, but I suspect your years in here will make you appreciate life even more than that insect when you get out."

Matt nodded, swallowing the knot in his throat and blinking back tears as he felt overwhelmed by Eric's subtle support, veiled from listeners and watchers. He yearned to reach out and hold Eric's hand but knew it was too dangerous. Perhaps sensing the tension, Eric quickly diverted the conversation to lighter topics, frequently mentioning Lisa and trying to avoid anything that would suggest wealth. He succeeded on all fronts and Matt was dazzled by novel layers and depths of communication. After an hour or so, Eric departed, leaving Matt hollow.

The next day, while in the library, Matt sensed Luther standing over his right shoulder. "Do you need me to do anything?" he asked, turning around.

"No," Luther responded. "I actually have a favor to ask you."

"What?" Matt asked.

"Well, you know I've been here for over thirty years, so I don't have much money." Luther wrung his hands. "The thing is my brother got sick and now he can't put food on the table. My brother's kids are the closest thing I'm going to have to children in my life. I know you have some money on the outside, probably not a lot, but you have some." Luther looked down at his feet and muttered, "I was hoping maybe you could lend my brother a thousand dollars or so."

"Of course," Matt said, glad to be able to do something for his friend. "Just don't tell anyone else. I don't want people to know."

"Thank you so much. I feel terrible asking, but some things are more important than pride," Luther said.

"You must think I'm a spoiled brat." Matt shook his head. "I had a great job and a loving family and I threw it all away with a stupid, drunken mistake."

"The way I figure, being spoiled is less about what you have and more about what you think you should have," Luther said. "In the old neighborhood, I knew families making $50–60,000 a year whose kids were spoiled rotten. They felt entitled to everything that money could buy. I don't think you ever believed you deserved anything you had. And that's the opposite of being spoiled. Hell, I don't think you even believe you deserve to be free."

"It's hard," Matt said. "There's a part of me I learned a long time ago, rightly or wrongly, to hate."

"Let me ask you something," Luther said. "You must have some gay friends. Do you hate them?"

"How could you even ask that?"

"I've always wanted to say this to a lawyer. Just answer the question. Do you hate them?"

"No."

"Do you think less of them because they're gay?"

"No."

"Then why would you think less of—much less hate—yourself?"

"Well, I've always expected a lot more of myself than everyone else," Matt said, studying the floor.

"If it doesn't make you think less of them, then why does it make you think less of yourself?"

"I don't know. Maybe it shouldn't." At the last, Matt managed to raise his head.

"Maybe it's just that simple. I know you don't think it is, and you like to think yourself in circles, but you've got to be careful with that. Don't let your feelings about who or what you are compromise any legal work you do to get out of here. You want to punish yourself by getting drunk, fine. But the stakes are too high to let your ghosts and doubts damn you to life in here."

"I know."

"Knowing and doing are two different things," Luther said. "Is Parnell letting you work on your own case?"

"Yeah," Matt said, looking at Luther directly now that the subject had shifted away from himself. "I even have the time to work on other inmates' cases, but he won't let me do it."

"I noticed his lawyer's started sending you packages," Luther said. "You want to be careful with that."

"I haven't seen anything in them that shouldn't be there," Matt said.

"Good. You know you're playing a real dangerous game with Parnell, don't you? I'm hearing rumors that we were right when we guessed Tyrone wasn't selling white lightnin'. Parnell pressured Tyrone to take a beating so he could find out whether you were vulnerable to threats against him."

"I haven't heard those rumors," Matt said. "I guess it makes me less trusting of Tyrone but, to be honest, we were never that close. I just didn't want word to get out that I didn't protect my friends."

"Have any of the other inmates tried to convince you to work on their cases behind Parnell's back?"

"No. They're too afraid of Parnell."

"You know those guys aren't going to protect you if Parnell's appeal fails, right? If these guys won't even ask you to work on their cases behind his back, they certainly aren't going to help you if Parnell makes a move."

"I know, but they may be able to give me some warning or something," Matt said.

"That's probably the best you can hope for, but what are you going to do with a warning?" Luther asked.

"I don't know," Matt said. He could only deal with one problem at a time.

Chapter 27

Months passed with the constant threat of the Louisiana appellate court rejecting Parnell's arguments, but Matt carved out a life that brought him some happiness in the limited space available at Wheaton.

He sublimated his loneliness and frustration into work on his own cert petition to the United States Supreme Court. In the final draft, the first sentence read: *Letting prosecutors pick jurors who malign gays and exclude all who might be sympathetic violates a gay criminal defendant's constitutional rights.*

He read, wrote letters to Eric and his mother and received guests in Butler Park. Parnell's ban on legal work for other inmates gave Matt the time and space to lose himself in a series of books, and the regular written and episodic personal contacts with the outside world helped him stay sane.

On a Thursday in September 2009, just as the heat had begun to abate, a guard asked Matt to go to Butler Park, where he was shocked to see his mother, Lisa, Eric and Farrar all seated, alone in the park, at a single picnic table. Genuinely puzzled at first, he tried and failed to clamp down on upwelling hope.

"Matt, I have some very big news," Farrar said, rising to shake his hand. "The Supreme Court agreed to hear your case."

Tears welled up in Matt's eyes and he thought, as he shook Farrar's hand weakly, that today, at least, he'd allow himself to dream.

"You know as well as I do that the chance of reversal is still very slim, but there's now at least a chance," Farrar said. "And you should enjoy it today." Farrar smiled broadly.

"I couldn't agree more," Mary said, rising to hug him, glancing around at the other inmates and guards, and then settling back onto the bench. "I'm so happy." She shook her head. "The only way that jury could have convicted you is because you're gay. Surely judges smart enough to be on the Supreme Court will see that."

"Matt, we brought you something; sort of a congratulatory gift." Farrar held out a wrapped package.

Matt opened the package to find a book: *The Count of Montecristo.* "Thank you. But is this a sign that you think I need to stage a prison break?"

"Not at all," Farrar said. "Read the inscription."

"'To a man who has stood tall in the face of grave injustice. We're all honored to love you and labor on your behalf.'"

Matt felt fresh tears coming to his eyes. "Thank you, everyone, for everything. In the spirit of enjoying the moment, let's not handicap this appeal. Now, nothing terribly exciting is happening in here, so what's going on in your lives?"

The conversation turned to more mundane matters and Lisa and Farrar excused themselves after about an hour or so, leaving Matt alone with his mother and Eric.

"Matt, I want you to know how proud I am," Mary said. "I'm sure you wrote a wonderful brief and that's one of the reasons that the Supreme Court agreed to hear the case."

"I don't know, Mom."

"Well, I would think there aren't very many lawyers out there who've been able to convince the United States Supreme Court to hear their case."

"There aren't very many; you're right, Mary," Eric said, shaking his head. "I read the brief and I wish that I could be half the lawyer your son is."

"I'm not exactly an outstanding member of the bar at the moment," Matt said.

"You're twice the lawyer most of those members of the bar are, and you damn well know it," Eric said, eyes flashing with an anger Matt hoped was directed at others.

After lunch and more casual conversation, Mary excused

herself to begin the drive back to Lafayette. Eric lingered, saying, "You should check the back cover of the book."

Matt opened the book and a newspaper clipping fell out. It was an editorial published in the *Times-Picayune* and written by a prominent libertarian law professor:

Local Lawyer's Case Before Supreme Court Reveals Need for Reform

The United States Supreme Court has agreed to consider whether the prosecution's dismissal of a gay juror in the murder trial of Matthew Durant justifies granting him a new trial. I'm confident that the Supreme Court will adequately address the narrow question of constitutional law before it.

I write instead to address voters and local government officials. Regardless of whether Mr Durant was constitutionally entitled to have available and eligible gay jurors hear his case, this newspaper believes that the prosecutor's office, local courts and state legislature should ban prosecutors from using preemptory challenges to strike gay jurors because they don't want them to participate in deciding whether a gay defendant is guilty or innocent.

New Orleans is an old city with a long history of diversity and the legal system should embrace that diversity. Just as state prosecutors are not allowed to strike jurors based on their race or gender, state prosecutors should not be permitted to strike jurors based on sexual orientation. Gay men and women have made many valuable contributions to this city and they should be entitled to a jury of their peers just like every other citizen in Louisiana.

"I insisted we include that article," Eric said. "I know the *Times-Picayune* may have hurt your case during the trial. After all, who really knows if jurors follow instructions not to read the paper, but this is unbelievable. You may save someone from suffering the same fate—or worse."

"A single editorial is hardly significant reform," Matt said.

"It's a start," Eric said. "And you worked to convince others of the legal and moral need to protect gay people from behind bars with very few resources and despite the fact you've been convicted of murder. It's pretty impressive."

"The editorial doesn't make me unhappy." Matt smiled.

"How are things going in there?" Eric asked, nodding toward the main complex of buildings.

"The situation is stable." Matt shrugged. "We're still waiting to hear from the Louisiana appellate court about my most important client's case. If Parnell loses, things are going to go south real fast."

"Do you have a plan if he loses?"

"I think I've convinced his outside attorney to send me the decision first, which is likely to be issued while I'm at work in the library. If Parnell loses, the best I can hope for is to throw myself on the mercy of the guards and ask for protective custody."

"If you ask for protective custody, will you lose your job in the library?" Eric asked, implying the questions behind the question about Matt's long-term safety and whether, if isolated in protective custody, solitary confinement could compromise his sanity.

"I hope not, but Parnell is very powerful. If the guards think he's really going to come after me, they probably won't believe I'm going to be safe working in the library," Matt said, answering only the question asked and ignoring those unasked.

"You know you're constantly in my thoughts, right?" Eric asked, looking directly into Matt's eyes.

"I know, and it helps."

Matt stood. Eric looked at him, obviously wanting to hug him, but uneasy about the potential consequences. And Matt feared that if he held Eric again they might become inseparable, and then Eric's departure would tear him asunder.

About two months later, while working in the library, Matt received an email from Parnell's outside lawyer, which attached an opinion from the Louisiana appellate court affirming Parnell's guilty verdict. The court ruled that Parnell's attorney had waived any argument that the attempted murder instruction was improper and, even if instructed differently, the jury would have convicted based on the overwhelming evidence of Parnell's guilt.

Ice washed through Matt's body as he fell into a fugue state, and disbelief created a sense of detachment barely containing his terror. Luther, noticing Matt's ashen face, asked if anything was wrong.

"The appellate court ruled against Parnell," Matt said.

"Shit. You need to get protection now," Luther said. "I'm calling Lieutenant Dietrich." After Luther had placed the call, he asked Matt, "Is there any hope for Parnell's case?"

"There's always hope. I never would have guessed the US Supreme Court would agree to hear my case. The Louisiana Supreme Court could still reverse Parnell's conviction, but it's not very likely."

Lieutenant Dietrich strode into the library accompanied by Ted. Matt wished he hadn't brought Ted.

"What's the problem?" Dietrich crossed his arms over his chest.

"Lieutenant, I've been working on an appeal for Parnell Jefferson in exchange for his protection," Matt said. "The appellate court just ruled against Parnell. Now I'm afraid for my life. Parnell's repeatedly threatened to have me beaten and raped if he lost."

"Ted, you hear anything about this?" Lieutenant Dietrich asked.

"Not a word," Ted said, shaking his head and with a barely concealed sneer.

"Parnell isn't stupid enough to make threats around the guards, but he's done it whenever they aren't around." It came out sharper than Matt had intended but was better than calling Ted crooked.

"Only verbal threats?" Lieutenant Dietrich asked. "You know we can't put everyone in protective custody who receives a verbal threat. We don't have the room."

Matt wondered whether Lieutenant Dietrich was being deliberately obtuse.

"Lieutenant Dietrich, I was arrested for killing a man outside a gay club. All the inmates think I'm gay. I think that puts me imminently at risk for sexual assault," Matt said. "The US Supreme Court has held that prison officials could violate a transsexual prisoner's Eighth Amendment rights by transferring that prisoner into a general prison population. I think that my sexual orientation is an additional and independent reason I should be eligible for protective custody."

"Have you been attacked since you've been here?" Lieutenant Dietrich asked.

"No. I told you. I cut a deal with Parnell for his protection," Matt said.

"If a homosexual is any man who has sex with another man, you know how many people I'd have to put into protective custody around here?"

"Lieutenant Dietrich," Luther said. "You know Parnell doesn't mess around. Parnell's going to kill Matt if he goes back to Building 2 tonight."

"All I know is verbal threats aren't enough to justify protective custody," Lieutenant Dietrich said. "But if you want me to take a closer look at the way things are going around here, maybe I should search the library."

"Yeah," Ted said. "Maybe you should check every seventh book." Lieutenant Dietrich scowled at Ted and a vein in his forehead started to throb.

"I have nothing more to say." Lieutenant Dietrich left the library and Ted scampered after him.

"Do you think he was paid off?" Matt asked Luther.

"He's been gettin' paid off for a long time," Luther said. "Ted just confirmed it."

"What do you mean?" Matt asked.

"Parnell's been using library books to smuggle dope from Angola to Wheaton for a coupla years now," Luther said. "Every seventh volume of a case reporter that goes to Building 2 has drugs hidden in it."

"And you knew about this?"

"Yeah," Luther said. "I've known about it for a while. But even us older folks can't get in the way of business. No one likes that."

"Why didn't you tell me?" Matt asked, hurt.

"I was trying to protect you," Luther said. "I figured if things went bad, then you could claim you didn't know and you'd be telling the truth."

"Shit," Matt said.

"If you want, we can go to the warden. Dietrich will try to blame me, but we'll just rat out Parnell at the same time. It'll give the warden another reason to help protect you from Parnell."

"Then what happens to you?"

"If I rat Parnell out, they're gonna have to protect me too."

"I hate to ask," Matt said.

"Don't ask," Luther said. "It's done." Luther went to the phone and called the warden's office. The warden's assistant informed Luther he was meeting with Lieutenant Dietrich and would call him back.

Matt emailed his current draft Supreme Court brief to Farrar and Lisa, along with a short note describing the potential threat from Parnell and Lieutenant Dietrich's refusal to place him in protective custody. Farrar emailed back saying he was "on it."

Matt watched the clock for the rest of the afternoon. He wrote a letter to his mother, telling her he loved her and thanking her. Fortunately, they communicated those thoughts so regularly he didn't need to give away the fact that he feared this letter could be his last.

Six o'clock arrived without any call from the warden or email from Farrar.

Ted appeared in the doorway. "Time to go back to Wheaton, Durant."

"Come on, Ted. Isn't there some way I can crash here tonight?" Matt asked.

"What? First time I picked you up to drive you here, you threatened to tell Parnell on me. How'd you go from there to begging me to keep you from him?" Ted asked.

"I was just kidding earlier," Matt said.

"You weren't and it doesn't matter," Ted said. "I'd be guaranteed to have an accident if I put you in protective custody. The lieutenant might have the juice to say no to Parnell, but I don't. Let's go."

Matt refused to rise from his chair. Even if Ted reported him to the Angola guards for refusing to move, their first reaction would be to stick him in solitary. But then Ted turned red and put his hand on his pepper spray.

"Don't make me do this, Durant," Ted said. "It's not the end of the world. They're just going to teach you a little lesson."

Matt looked at the pepper spray and realized that Ted would just spray him into submission and then take him back to Parnell. He considered whether he should take his chances and risk going back to Parnell wounded and even more vulnerable, but it wasn't a choice. Ted was a scumbag, but Matt wanted at least to get in a few shots at Parnell and his flunkies—he wouldn't go down without a fight. "Okay," Matt said. "I'm going."

"I'm so sorry," Luther said. Tears ran down his face.

"Don't be. You did the best you could. You're not the one who's going to beat me up," Matt said.

The drive back to Wheaton took forever. Matt regretted it was dark and there was nothing to see, unlike his drive from New Orleans to Wheaton—nothing to see and nothing to lose. He just needed to do as much damage as possible before they took him down.

The truck pulled to a stop, Ted deposited him outside Building 2, and then exited with truncheon in hand to make certain Matt went into the building.

He entered Building 2 and Parnell was waiting. "Bathroom. Now!" Parnell barked.

Once there, Parnell said, "I'm not gonna start fucking you up now because we gots to be at dinner in thirty minutes. But it's gonna be a long night for you." As he spoke, he ground his right fist into his left palm.

"I was disappointed and surprised by the appellate court's ruling," Matt said with an even tone, determined not to reveal his panic and to keep his focus locked into one of the more import-ant conversations of his life. "Their decision was wrong, and I'm sorry. But there's still hope. The Louisiana Supreme Court could still reverse your conviction."

"I've listened to too much of your bullshit for too long," Parnell said. "I've already got a lawyer outside. What do I need you for?"

"Did your outside lawyer offer an opinion on how I'd done?"

"Yeah. He said today that you'd done a helluva job and it wasn't your fault. But he's a fucking lawyer on the same losing side as you. He says you did a bad job, that means he did a bad job, too. His opinion don't mean shit." Parnell spat on the ground.

"What do you have to lose? Why don't you just wait until your appeal to the Louisiana State Supreme Court is resolved? If I lose that appeal, it's not like I'm going anywhere."

"Boy, you need be taught a lesson. You know how expensive my protection is for other folks? You've made me look like a fucking fool. And I don't stand for that. 'Sides, I figure someone like you starts by diddling dogs, kids, then dudes. And someone diddled my nephew. God, I hate faggots." Parnell said. "Why don't you enjoy dinner tonight? If'n you're lucky, your jaw ain't gonna be much good for eating for a real long time."

Matt went to dinner and sat, as usual, alone in a crowded row of inmates. The other prisoners watched him intently, but only Tyrone and a handful of others had any sympathy in their eyes. Matt didn't bother to eat; he didn't think he could keep it down, and one more meal wasn't going to make him any stronger. After dinner, he walked back to Building 2 with a leaden weight in his stomach.

Parnell was waiting for him with three large men. "I decided what I'm gonna do to you tonight. These guys're gonna beat the shit out of you and then run a train. But it's gonna be a clean train, if you know what I mean."

Matt knew what he meant. The prisoners' intravenous drug use and unprotected sex—both before and after arriving at Wheaton—meant many had HIV or AIDS. A clean train meant Parnell wouldn't include any prisoners he knew to be HIV-positive.

"You can go ahead and struggle if you want," Parnell said with an ugly grin. "Sometimes they like it better that way."

Matt allowed himself to be walked back into the bathroom, knowing none of the other prisoners would intervene. He focused on keeping distance between himself and his would-be assailants, remembering to think about striking, given that he was much smaller, and formulated a crippling opening combination followed by the moves most ingrained in his muscle memory—at least in theory.

As they passed through the threshold into the restroom, Matt lashed out. He stepped into a sidekick, stomping down on the knee of the inmate to his right. Matt heard a wet pop as the man collapsed. Before the inmate to his left could react, Matt threw two left jabs and then a left hook to the ribs to set up the real strike: a right palm to the middle of his face. His nose crumpled into a crimson stain.

Matt was clocked from behind at the base of his skull. He fell and looked up with bleary eyes to see Parnell holding a metal bed leg he'd somehow pried loose. Inevitability set in and he actually found himself less frightened than he'd been an hour before. At least he'd hurt two of the assholes.

That was his last coherent thought before the stomping began. He experienced the remainder of the attack in strobe-like flashes as he drifted in and out of consciousness—the inmates kicking his ribs into shards and splinters; Parnell smashing his face into a pulp; and, finally, Parnell kicking him in the balls with all his might.

Matt woke in the middle of the night on the concrete floor of the bathroom. He curled into a fetal position and sobbed until his body shook, which prompted a sharp pain in his ribs that broke his hysteria. He then drifted in and out of a twilight sleep for the rest of the night. No one in the building dared call for help, and Matt tried not to think about whether—if Parnell hadn't been around—anyone would have bothered.

Chapter 28

Parnell had been so enraged and had beaten Matt into such a subhuman state that—perhaps because of physical impossibility, some vague fear of legal consequences, because it was obviously unnecessary, or some combination—he hadn't been raped. The self-defense lessons had worked, just not the way he'd planned.

After days in an outside hospital, Matt was moved to the prison infirmary, but, for the next three weeks, his jaw remained wired shut. Matt received a letter from Farrar enclosing an angry and threatening missive he'd sent the warden before Parnell's ambush. Just as Lieutenant Dietrich had rejected Matt's pleas for protection, the warden had rejected Farrar's and—by the time Farrar had finished negotiating with the warden—it had been too late to go to a judge. Farrar had also been forced to file the briefs in the Supreme Court without Matt's additional input. At the time, he'd been incapable of speech.

Visitors weren't allowed in the infirmary, but his mother sent daily letters. Though she'd apparently learned of his hospitalization from Farrar, her letters contained few questions other than general inquiries about how the doctors thought he was coming along. Matt had been lucky for his first couple of years at Wheaton and she knew it. She couldn't bear to learn the details.

During his third week in the hospital, Matt began drafting a letter to Eric that he imagined he'd never send. He revised it over and over and over, obsessing over minor edits: rather than countenance a scratched-out word, whenever he improved on a word choice and struck its predecessor, he recopied the entire page. And then he'd cross out another and have to start again. He didn't explain the timing in the drafts, but he suspected if he ever sent it Eric would understand that it wasn't coincidental. He attempted to thank Eric—in between the lines—for his first meaningful sexual experience and his continued support, but he found it impossible to write in the necessary code.

During Matt's fourth week in the infirmary, he received a package he'd been awaiting anxiously: the transcript of Farrar's oral argument before the United States Supreme Court. Matt had read the final briefs, which he believed made a compelling argument, but the transcript provided the first opportunity to gauge the justices' reactions.

Matt tore the brown envelope open and flipped to the first page:

Chief Justice Roberts: We will hear argument next in No. 09–1359, *Durant v. Louisiana*. Mr Farrar.

Farrar: Mr Chief Justice, and may it please the Court. Matthew Durant was the criminal defendant in a murder trial where his sexual orientation was central to his defense. We believe the trial court erred in two ways: First, the trial court refused to excuse jurors for cause who expressed religious objections to being gay that admittedly influenced their perception of the witness's truthfulness. Second, the trial court permitted the prosecution to exercise a preemptory challenge based on the sexual orientation of a prospective juror. We believe each of those rulings violated the Equal Protection Clause of the Fourteenth Amendment, the Due Process Clause of the Fourteenth Amendment and the Sixth Amendment.

Justice Roberts:	Is your principal argument that those actions were without rational basis or that homosexuality should be a suspect class?
Farrar:	Justice Roberts, we're advancing both arguments, and I'm happy to address either one.
Justice Scalia:	Let's start with rational basis. Many state laws permit prosecutors' broad and mostly unfettered discretion to strike jurors. Are you saying that such laws are irrational?
Farrar:	No, Justice Scalia. I am saying the prosecution's use of that discretion to stack the jury against a gay defendant is irrational and not related to a legitimate government interest.
Justice Scalia:	That argument simply characterizes the purpose too narrowly. You're an experienced trial lawyer. Have you ever exercised a preemptory challenge to strike a juror based on a gut instinct?
Farrar:	Yes, Mr Justice. But we aren't dealing with a legitimate gut instinct in this case. And the purpose characterized as narrowly as you do would make it rational for a prosecutor to strike a potential juror based on race or gender.
Justice Scalia:	It might very well be rational to do so, right? I think that a prosecutor might

	legitimately think female jurors might have more sympathy for female defendants. It's only unconstitutional because it doesn't survive heightened scrutiny, correct?
Farrar:	Justice Scalia, I think it's unconstitutional both because it's irrational and because it fails to satisfy the heightened scrutiny.
Justice Scalia:	But do you agree it's constitutional for a prosecutor to strike a juror based on gut instinct, or hair color, or shifty eyes or any basis other than sex or race?
Farrar:	I agree it would be constitutional for a prosecutor to strike a juror based on gut instinct or shifty eyes because there's not a history of discrimination against those groups. I obviously disagree about whether a prosecutor can strike a juror on any basis other than sex or race.
Justice Scalia:	And the reason sex and race are different is because they're suspect classifications, right? They're classifications that this Court has subjected to a higher level of scrutiny based on the history and the purpose of the Fourteenth Amendment?
Farrar:	That's one reason, Justice Scalia, but I think the history and the purpose of the Fourteenth Amendment also counsel against permitting prosecutors to strike jurors based on their sexual orientation. I

271

also think a jury-selection process can be so fundamentally biased it independently violates the Fourteenth Amendment's requirement of Due Process.

Justice Scalia: How on earth does the history of the Fourteenth Amendment's Equal Protection Clause support your position?

Farrar: The Fourteenth Amendment embodies an antidiscrimination principle that protects discrete and insular minorities from animus based upon a characteristic that's not morally relevant.

Justice Scalia: But the framers of the Fourteenth Amendment obviously didn't envision it protecting homosexuals, did they?

Farrar: I believe the framers of the Fourteenth Amendment intended for it to be flexible enough to later include women or, for example, an unpopular racial minority that later migrated to the United States. The text describes a principle, not a rule or standard. And the sponsors of the amendment discussed how it was intended to embody an anti-caste principle broader than just protecting those subject to discrimination at the time.

Justice Scalia: But homosexuals existed at the time of the framing of the Fourteenth Amendment and the framers didn't envision equal protection applying to them, did they?

Farrar:	I believe in *Lawrence v. Texas*, Justice Kennedy noted on behalf of the majority that some scholars believe that the concept of homosexuality didn't arise until the late nineteenth century. The Fourteenth Amendment is also capable of addressing new forms of discrimination. Discrimination against Hispanics may not have been specifically addressed by the framers of the Fourteenth Amendment, but the principle and purpose of the Fourteenth Amendment answers the question of whether Hispanics are entitled to its protection.
Justice Scalia:	But those are all arguments as to why homosexuality should be treated as a suspect class, correct?
Farrar:	Justice Scalia, I think that you've recognized the essence of *Romer* and *Lawrence* is that government actions motivated by animus toward homosexuals have no rational basis. You may have disagreed with the reasoning of those opinions, but you didn't disagree with the logical consequences of those rulings.
Justice Scalia:	Does that mean that the prosecution would be constitutionally prohibited from striking a juror who'd engaged in bestiality, incest, bigamy, prostitution, masturbation, adultery, fornication or obscenity?

Farrar: To the extent that those activities are constitutionally criminalized in the jurisdiction, I believe the prosecution could exercise its discretion to strike jurors on those bases.

Justice Scalia: But the prosecution isn't limited to striking jurors based solely on their prior illegal acts, is it?

Farrar: No, Justice Scalia, but I respectfully submit that the prosecution cannot strike jurors based solely on their sexual orientation.

Justice Scalia: How is this any different from the question of whether the prosecution can strike a juror with a fifteen-year-old criminal conviction? Why isn't it a question of state law for state courts?

Farrar: Justice Scalia, it's different because the prosecution was attempting to insulate the jury from the view of a representative member of the community so the jury would be more likely to consider the defendant's sexual orientation as reflecting negatively on his truthfulness.

Justice Scalia: The prosecution is excluding a representative member of the community whenever it exercises a preemptory strike, isn't it? And what do you mean by "representative"? Does the jury need mirror the demographics of the local population?

Farrar:	Yes, every strike does exclude a potential juror, but not based on the defendant's sexual orientation.
Justice Roberts:	Mr Farrar, did the trial court undertake the sort of inquiry that we've mandated in the *Batson* line of cases to determine whether the prosecution has correctly excused a minority juror?
Farrar:	No, Justice Roberts, the trial court did not reach that question.
Justice Roberts:	Even if we ruled in your favor, why wouldn't we remand to the trial court to make that determination based upon whatever factual findings it makes after following the sort of inquiry we've mandated in the race and gender cases?
Farrar:	Your Honor, two points. First, any advantage that the trial court had at the time of jury selection in this case has diminished with the passage of time. Judge Masterson evaluated the demeanor of these lawyers and jurors years ago.
Justice Roberts:	But on remand couldn't Judge Masterson ask the prosecutor why he or she exercised the preemptory strike?
Farrar:	That's correct, Justice Roberts, but so can you. Mr Thibedeaux was the prosecutor in the trial court. And I would suggest that the evidence is overwhelming in this case that the prosecution struck the

juror because of his sexual orientation. First, the prosecution readily approved other jurors who indicated they would be less likely to believe a gay witness. Second, as we spell out in our brief, the prosecution engaged in one-sided and slanted questioning about minimum penalties and the death penalty that this Court has previously found suggest a bias based on the race or sex of jurors. Finally, the sexual orientation of the defendant and the likelihood he would be victimized based on that sexual orientation were the central issues in this case. It would be as if the prosecution had struck every black juror in the murder trial of an African-American defendant accused of killing a Klansman.

Justice Roberts: But in the race and sex cases, we also look at how the prosecution handled other black or female prospective jurors. Can you present any evidence that the prosecution exercised preemptory challenges against multiple gay jurors?

Farrar: No, Your Honor, but we suggest that's simply because gays are only about four percent of the population. I submit it would be a perverse result to rule that because there are fewer members of a minority, it should be more difficult to prove discrimination against that minority. I'd like to reserve some time for rebuttal.

Justice Roberts: Very well, Mr Farrar. Mr Thibedeaux, we'll hear from you now.

Thibedeaux: In every state and the federal system, the prosecution and defense have the power to strike jurors for any reason whatsoever. The principal check in the process is that each side receives the same number of preemptory challenges. And the prosecution and defense traditionally maneuver to choose jurors that may be to their relative advantage based upon intangibles ranging from demeanor, to tone of voice, to facial expression, to posture. Race and gender are narrow exceptions that, not surprisingly, are subject to stricter scrutiny under all of this Court's constitutional jurisprudence.

Justice Ginsburg: Mr Thibedeaux, Mr Farrar and Mr Durant suggest that the trial court erroneously refused to excuse for cause several jurors who expressed the opinion gay witnesses were less likely to be truthful. What do you make of that argument?

Thibedeaux: I dispute both its accuracy and relevance. Mr Farrar neglected to mention those jurors also testified they could follow an instruction to disregard the witness's sexual orientation in determining his truthfulness. And Judge Masterson gave such an instruction.

Justice Ginsburg: Mr Durant did mention it in his brief.

Thibedeaux: He mentioned it in passing without explaining how the instruction was insufficient. There's a strong presumption jurors follow instructions in both state and federal courts. I also believe the issue of whether a juror should be excused for cause is a question of Louisiana state law to be decided by Louisiana courts, just as if a juror expressed an opinion about prosecutors generally, criminal defense attorneys generally or police officers generally. The federal Constitution shouldn't arbitrate those disputes.

Justice Ginsburg: Can you agree that a refusal to excuse a juror for cause would violate due process if the juror said he or she would convict the defendant regardless of the evidence or law?

Thibedeaux: In the most egregious case, it could violate due process. But that's not what happened here. This case is the precise opposite of your hypothetical. The jurors who expressed doubts about the truthfulness of homosexuals also said they could follow an instruction not to consider the witness's sexual orientation. And those close questions about whether a juror should be excluded for cause should be decided by state trial courts applying state law.

Justice Kennedy: What reason was there for excusing the prospective juror who was gay other than his sexual orientation?

Thibedeaux: Justice Kennedy, I didn't believe he could follow the instructions regarding the minimum sentence in the case or necessarily divorce the application of the death penalty from his political views.

Justice Kennedy: But that was based on the sort of one-sided questioning about potential sentences that we've condemned in our race and gender cases, correct?

Thibedeaux: It was based on my perception that the witness was unwilling to apply the minimum sentence or the maximum sentence. In this case, that sentence was death.

Justice Kennedy: Did the gay potential juror testify about whether or not he could follow instructions regarding the maximum and minimum sentences?

Thibedeaux: I don't recall, Your Honor.

Chief Justice Roberts: Your time has expired, Mr Thibedeaux. Mr Farrar, you have two minutes for rebuttal.

Farrar: Mr Chief Justice, and may it please the Court. The name of the juror Mr Thibedeaux excluded was Mr Whitley. At page P459, Mr Whitley testified, quote, "If the judge instructed me if we reached certain factual conclusions, the defendant should be executed under the laws of the state of Louisiana, then I would make the necessary findings without regard to my opinions on the death penalty." End quote. At page P450, Mr Whitley testified that he was not aware of the minimum penalty for first-degree murder and that if the judge instructed him that the minimum penalty was life imprisonment, then it would not affect his determination of guilt. So much for Mr Thibedeaux's strongly held belief that jurors follow instructions.

Mr Thibedeaux, who was personally unwilling to rely on instructions to guide Mr Whitley's decision-making on this jury, just told this Court such instructions should have been enough to protect Matt Durant from jurors who'd expressed doubt and hostility about Mr Durant's sexual orientation. Mr Thibedeaux can't have it both ways. If he believes jurors always follow instructions, he had no legitimate reason to strike Mr Whitley. If he believes jurors don't always follow instructions, then seating jurors who expressed a bias against gays was wrong.

Unless there are any additional questions, I have nothing further.

The concluding exchange made Matt gasp and he didn't mind the resulting twinge in his ribs. Farrar had exploited the synergy between the trial court's two errors to the maximum and—even better—had shown that Thibedeaux's reasons for excusing Whitley were disingenuous.

Chapter 29

A week later, Matt lay in his infirmary bed trying to read, when he heard shoes tapping across the linoleum and glanced up to see Lieutenant Dietrich looming. Matt closed the book and placed it in his lap.

"Is this a good time?" Lieutenant Dietrich asked.

Matt nodded. He thought it odd Dietrich would bother to ask.

"The doctor tells me you're healing well, all things considered. Are you in pain?" The feigned sympathy grated, but Matt kept his facial expression neutral.

"My ribs ache, but they're getting better." He gave himself wriggle-room to exaggerate or downplay the pain, depending on whether he wanted or needed to stay in the infirmary.

"The doctor seems to think that you can be released in the next few days. We need to talk about where you're going next."

"Am I going to be safe from Parnell anywhere?" Matt asked.

"We control this prison, not Parnell." Dietrich crossed his arms over his chest. "And I think he's taken his revenge. You can probably just return to Building 2."

"You've got to be kidding me." Matt squeezed the book and his knuckles whitened. "Parnell and his goons almost killed me."

"No one else has said Parnell was responsible for the attack."

Matt flushed. "Well, you damned well know that anything that happens in Building 2 has to be approved by Parnell." His pitch rose as he teetered on panic's edge.

"But Parnell can't be held responsible for failing to prevent your beating. What are you gonna do—sue him? I don't think he has any money." Dietrich sneered.

Matt collected himself, forcing himself to remember that if he won this argument on debaters' points but angered Lieutenant Dietrich, he would lose everything. "What are my alternatives to Building 2?"

"We should discuss that." Dietrich uncrossed his arms. "I want to make sure you're not going to file any nuisance lawsuits against the prison or any of the guards first."

"Putting aside that the threat itself is probably illegal, you must have talked to someone about the Eighth Amendment case that I told you about," Matt said.

"We just want to avoid a frivolous lawsuit. You don't have a right to file a nuisance lawsuit."

"And if I hypothetically agree not to sue, what are the options?"

"We have an opening in Building 3."

"Building 3 is Bill's building. Bill might not hate me personally as much as Parnell, but he hates me enough to put me back in here." Matt shook his head, the book fell to his lap and his hands shifted to gripping the sheet. "And you know damned well the White Brotherhood hates gays."

"If you said wouldn't file a lawsuit and requested it, we could transfer you to one of the solitary confinement cells at Angola." Dietrich cocked his head to the side.

"Those cells contain the most violent criminals from both prisons." Matt began kneading the sheet and stared at the wall opposite his bed.

"The only time you'd see other prisoners is when you're escorted down the hallways. The other inmates won't have a chance to do anything without being seen by the guards."

"Guards like Ted?" Matt asked, glanced up at Dietrich, brows raised.

"Ted had an accident," Lieutenant Dietrich said. "He went to the library and somebody hit him from behind with a table leg. Luther and Reggie were the only ones there. First neither would admit to doing it, then I'll be damned if they didn't both admit doing it. We've thrown them in solitary, but I doubt that'll get us an answer." He paused. "The courts won't let us keep them there forever anymore as punishment." Matt wondered if he could ever be safe outside of solitary. Maybe he'd trade the risk of having his mind broken instead of his body, but he also knew in any contest between the two, he'd always choose to preserve his mind.

"What about when Ted returns?" Matt asked.

"He probably won't. He applied for a job at the Orleans Parish Prison months ago because he wants to move to a bigger city. Word is they're going to hire him."

"But will the other guards bother to act quickly enough if something happens? Most of Parnell's flunkies are here for life, so they might kill me anyway." Matt looked Dietrich in the eyes, thinking perhaps this conversation was headed toward keeping him safe from at least one threat.

"I have to say that the guards will be more watchful if you don't do anything to threaten this institution."

"In other words, you have an insurance policy against my filing a lawsuit based on the beating that you allowed Parnell and his thugs to give me."

"I didn't say that; you did."

Matt sensed that Ted's transfer was Dietrich's attempt to offer him a reward for not suing and pressed: "If I refrained from filing a frivolous lawsuit, could you get Luther and Reggie out of solitary? Could I get my job in the library back?"

"Maybe. George has taken over Luther's responsibilities for now, but we might be able to use three of you there. Let's both sleep on it and talk again tomorrow. I hope you feel better."

The insincerity of the parting courtesy chafed. And Matt suspected his only choice—at least from Dietrich's perspective—was solitary confinement, but he hated the idea of being trapped alone in a room all day to stew in his regrets.

Then another possibility occurred to him. Luther had mentioned Parnell had been sent to Wheaton to separate him from the Angola prisoners and that the white population at Angola was much smaller—Parnell and Bill should have far less influence there. What if he asked for a transfer to the general population in Angola? It was counterintuitive, but it just might work.

The following day, Lieutenant Dietrich returned. "So, have you thought any more about where you want to live after this?" he asked.

"I care more about Reggie and Luther right now," Matt said. "Have they been released from solitary?" He didn't want his failed attempts to protect himself to cost others.

"Yeah, they're out in Angola's general population, but you need to consider your own...predicament. I won't have time to see you before you're released tomorrow."

Matt doubted it and suspected Dietrich just wanted to ratchet up the pressure. It had the opposite effect. "I'd like to be transferred to the general population at Angola," Matt said.

"What?" Dietrich asked, eyes widening. "You know, no matter how bad things get in Wheaton or Angola, they can always be made worse." He narrowed them again.

Matt didn't care about the threat. The same emptiness that had overtaken him in the rodeo ring overtook him again; whatever happened would happen; he couldn't spend the rest of his days locked up in isolation with himself.

"Well, it's your choice," Dietrich said. "You can hardly sue for that."

The next morning, two guards arrived to escort Matt to Angola. They loaded him into the back of an ancient Jeep, which took off, stirring the top layer of the dirt road into a cloud of dust. He began to panic, terrified that he was committing suicide by transfer.

Unnerved and second-guessing his choice, he began whispering the words his mother had taught him as a child, kneeling by his bed at night, which had kept worries and nightmares at bay: "Our Father who art in heaven, hallowed be thy name. Thy kingdom come, thy will be done, on earth as it is in heaven. Give us this day our daily bread. And forgive us our trespasses, as we forgive those who trespass against us. And lead us not into temptation, but deliver us from evil: For thine is the kingdom, and the power and the glory, forever. Amen."

Matt still didn't know whether being gay was a sin, but the Lord's Prayer at least took no position. And if it was a sin it seemed a trivial one, especially here. In a world where no one has complete control, perhaps he needed to cede it—if only for a moment—not to those eager to define God for him but to God.

The Jeep stopped. He was escorted to a barracks building identical to those at Wheaton and the guards showed him the door and gestured toward it—Matt wondered if they feared entering. He grasped the rusty iron handle and wrenched it open, stepping into the gloom.

Silence greeted him as he stood backlit in the doorway and then, as his eyes adjusted, he heard claps multiplying to applause. A large man sidled up and threw an arm around his shoulder, gripping it in—comfort. What?

"Welcome home," said the man. It was Reggie. "Parnell warn't welcome in Angola when he came back, but you sure are, partly 'cause I'd love to kill that sunovabitch. Anyone he hates so much cain't be too bad."

Another man came up to him. "I ain't seen nothin' like what you did durin' convict poker. You didn't jes' outlast the rest of 'em. You beat the bull." Matt exhaled, holding back tears as he realized he had at last—at least—found temporary safety.

Chapter 30

Weeks later, Matt sat in Butler Park with other Angola inmates waiting for Eric. For the first time since his imprisonment, he felt at ease. Reggie had far more influence than he'd let on before and he seemed to trust Matt based on his respect for Reggie's determination to learn. It didn't hurt that he hated Parnell and the other inmates loved the story of convict poker. He'd found himself doing legal work for others again, but now found it engaging and diverting, as he had in private practice.

The bright sun cast a shadow on the picnic table that interrupted Matt's thoughts; he looked up to see Eric, who sat.

"So, the good news is that I haven't lost my hearing," Eric began, his expression grave.

"I didn't know I should be worrying about your hearing," Matt responded.

"Yeah, well, I've always felt I don't hear as well as other people." Eric said, then shook his head.

"And for how long have you had that feeling?" Matt asked.

"Maybe ten or fifteen years."

"And, over those ten or fifteen years, did you ever consider going to—I don't know—one of those people with white coats and stethoscopes." A smile tugged at the corners of Matt's mouth.

"Well, I never got around to it," Eric said.

"Too busy shopping for workout clothes and picking Lisa up from the gym?" A smile had now broken out on Matt's face.

"Something like that."

"So, what's the realization about your hearing now?" Matt asked, cocking his head to the side.

"About two months ago I bought premium Chinese earbuds for my iPhone online. They were really highly rated, and cheap, but not so cheap I didn't believe the ratings. Over the last few weeks, I've found it harder to hear out of my left ear. I thought maybe it was wax, and, well, I won't go into detail about how I ruled that out. But it finally occurred to me last week that maybe it was the headphones. I tried an old pair and—sure enough—it was the headphones." Eric said, with his hands outstretched and palm raised.

"So are you going to demand your money back? Rumor has it that some people trust you with multimillion-dollar negotiations."

"Hell no," Eric said. "I don't want to spend my free time doing that. I stopped negotiating for fifty bucks years ago. I'm just thrilled my hearing's fine."

Matt barked out a laugh and a snort escaped. Looking around, he saw friendly faces and he reached out to hold Eric's hand under the table.

Eric's eyes widened. "Is this safe?"

"Yeah," Matt said. "Live a little." With the sun directly above, baking those in the park, it began to sprinkle. "You know," Matt said, "whenever it used to rain while the sun was shining, my Mom used to say it was so beautiful the devil must be so mad he's beating his wife."

"Yeah, that's an old country expression," Eric said.

"Oh really? Did you learn it on Martha's Vineyard or in the uptown part of New Orleans?" Matt smiled.

Eric squeezed his hand. "Shut up and just enjoy it in case it really starts to rain." Matt nodded.

A couple of months later, Matt sat in the prison library as Reggie plodded through a reader when Luther burst around the corner, stuttering to a stop. He waved stapled papers and said, "Mr Farrar just emailed this to me and told me to get it to you fast." He placed the papers in front of Matt on the table.

It was a slip opinion from the United States Supreme Court entitled *Durant v. Louisiana*. Matt felt his stomach drop to the table; he couldn't believe how quickly the Court had decided.

Lightheaded, he lifted it with shaky hands and flipped past the preliminary pages to scan the opening paragraph:

> Our Fourteenth Amendment Due Process jurisprudence protects criminal defendants from being tried by jurors who have prejudged them as morally blameworthy. We need not and do not reach the issue of whether homosexuality is a protected class under the Equal Protection Clause to decide this case. Just as it would violate due process for a trial court to permit an African-American defendant to be tried by a jury including an admitted racist, a female defendant to be tried by a jury including an admitted sexist, or a Caucasian American to be tried by a jury including a black nationalist who hates whites, it is unconstitutional for a trial court to permit a gay defendant to be tried by a jury including an admitted heterosexist. Such a trial violates the Fourteenth Amendment's guarantee of due process of law.

Emboldened by that paragraph, Matt turned to the final page and read: "The judgment of the Supreme Court of Louisiana is reversed and the case is remanded for a new trial not inconsistent with this opinion."

On reading it, he realized he would have another chance to prove his innocence.

Matt wept.

Questions

I hope that *Defense of an Other* entertains as a legal thriller, but I also intend for it to be more. In reading books on writing fiction, John Gardner's *The Art of Fiction: Notes on Craft for Young Writers* (Vintage Ed. 1991) resonated with me most. Gardner writes of moral fiction and how the writer's subconscious influences the text, and as I wrote successive drafts, I interpreted and understood this novel in different ways. I'd be interested in others' interpretations and thoughts on some questions and issues that I've focused on in writing and rewriting the book:

1. Who are the heroes and why?

2. Who are the villains and why?

3. Do you think Matt self-handicaps? When? Why?

4. Is Matt self-loathing? When? Why?

5. How do the two scenes involving LSU football compare to the scene involving the convict rodeo?

6. Politicians often describe judges like Justice Antonin Scalia as strict constructionists, while lawyers tend to describe them as originalists, meaning that they look to the constitutional text first and then how a Constitutional provision was understood and applied immediately after it was drafted and ratified. Article I, § 2 on the eligibility requirements for

serving as president provides that "neither shall any person be eligible to that Office who shall not have attained to the Age of thirty five Years." What would it mean to strictly construe that language?

7. The Fourteenth Amendment makes it unlawful for any state to "deny any person within its jurisdiction the equal protection of the laws." What would it mean to strictly construe that language?

8. Why wouldn't the framers of the Fourteenth Amendment lay down specific rules in the Fourteenth Amendment rather than requiring "equal protection of the laws"? For example, why didn't the framers just forbid the states from discriminating against African-Americans in employment decisions, in setting qualifications for public office, in jury selection and in other specific situations?

9. Why would the framers of the Fourteenth Amendment draft it to protect "persons" rather than just former slaves or African-Americans?

10. Given that women did not even have the right to vote at the time the Fourteenth Amendment was drafted and ratified, does it guarantee them "equal protection"?

11. Given that public school segregation was widely practiced and at least some supporters of the Fourteenth Amendment also supported segregation when the amendment was ratified in 1868, is school segregation constitutional?

12. Does it change your view that, after the Fourteenth Amendment's ratification, many of the congressmen and Senators supporting it argued it also required passing separate legislation forbidding public school segregation and partially did so in the Civil Rights Act of 1875?

13. Does the fact that many ratifiers believed separate legislation was necessary to forbid school segregation tell you anything about whether the courts then had the power to forbid school segregation or whether it was the responsibility of Congress?

14. Does your answer change when you consider that Section 5 of the Fourteenth Amendment provides: "The Congress shall have the power to enforce, by appropriate legislation, the provisions of this article"?

15. Does it change your view that, by the time the Fourteenth Amendment was drafted and ratified, Supreme Court precedent had established for sixty-five years that the Court had the right, power and obligation to strike down unconstitutional laws because, as Justice Marshall explained: it "[i]s emphatically the province and duty of the [courts] to say what the law is," *Marbury v. Madison*, 5 U.S. 137 (1803)?

16. In the debates over whether the Fourteenth Amendment should be ratified, some sponsors argued that the Equal Protection Clause embodied an anti-caste principle. Senator Howard said it was designed to "abolish[...] all class legislation in the States and do away with the injustice of subjecting one caste of persons to a code not applicable to another." Does that change your opinion of whether the Fourteenth Amendment forbids racial segregation in schools? Does it change your opinion of whether the Fourteenth Amendment forbids discrimination against women because of their sex or gender? Does it change your opinion of whether the Fourteenth Amendment forbids discrimination against queers?

17. Should judicial nominees, particularly for the Supreme Court, refuse to answer whether critical United Sates Supreme Court cases, such as *Brown v. The Board of Education*, 373 U.S. 483 (1954), or decisions extending the Fourteenth Amendment's

Equal Protection Clause to gays or women, were correctly decided during their confirmation hearings?

18. Should judicial nominees, particularly for the Supreme Court, refuse to answer whether critical United Sates Supreme Court cases, such as *Brown v. Board of Education*, 373 U.S. 483 (1954), were correctly decided during their confirmation hearings based on the theory that they would risk prejudging cases that could come before them as justices?

19. If so, should judicial nominees be required to describe any opinion they've previously expressed to others—even if only verbally—about whether critical United Sates Supreme Court cases, such as *Brown v. Board of Education*, 373 U.S. 483 (1954), were correctly decided to determine whether they have expressed an opinion that could be interpreted as prejudging a dispute that might come before them?

20. Is someone who has never expressed a view—orally or in writing—about whether *Brown v. Board of Education*, 373 U.S. 483 (1954) was correctly decided qualified to serve on the United States Supreme Court?

21. Is there a difference between respecting many different views of religion and saying that some cannot be a legitimate basis for taking government action, like jury decision-making that results in imprisonment?

22. The Bible has been invoked in the past to argue that women and African-Americans were inferior and the law should continue to treat them as such. Assuming such arguments were wrong, were they erroneous interpretations of the Bible? Were such arguments inappropriate reasons for making government decisions because they were religious?

23. Martin Luther King, Jr. made religious appeals as part of his argument for the civil rights of African-Americans. Were those an appropriate basis for members of Congress to vote on the Civil Rights Act or the Voting Rights Act?

24. Mary prays, and Matt recites the Lord's Prayer. Are their prayers answered?

25. Imagine all the principal and secondary characters in this novel other than Matt as different facets of or possibilities for himself that compete in his mind—the story is told from his point of view. What is the significance of his killing in defense of another? What is the significance of doubling up as the instrument of death? The crowd at the LSU football game? His burgeoning relationship with Eric? The jury and its verdict? Imprisonment? The crowd at the convict rodeo? Gaining a chance at freedom by appealing to a higher court? An order granting, not acquittal, but a new trial? The two words describing Matt's reaction?

26. Many novels use the personal as an allegory for the political, such as Albert Camus' *The Plague* or George Orwell's *Animal Farm*. Could the plot here, including its primary and secondary characters, be interpreted as an allegory for Matt's personal experience of being closeted, outed and then coming out?

Afterword

I wrote the first draft *Defense of an Other* in 2007 and self-published the first edition under the pen name Paul Verity and with the title *Doubling Up* in 2011, all while struggling with a body and hormones that did not match my gender identity. I completed the book over a decade later after rewriting it, changing the title and changing the Matt's lot in prison but without ever changing the outcome of his appeal. I now publish it again almost four years after I started presenting authentically full-time under my chosen name, Grace Mead.

I wrote about a gay protagonist rather than a trans protagonist largely because for most of those eleven years I couldn't fathom sympathy or acceptance from most straight readers for a trans protagonist. The central legal argument here—that the Equal Protection Clause should offer heightened protections to gay men because they are a discrete, insular minority subject to virulent discrimination—applies with at least as much force to all other LGBTQIA individuals, including lesbians, trans individuals, and those questioning their orientation or identity.

The novel opens in 2007 and unfolds in a world where Matt Durant's trial and appeals are conducted without the benefit of the Supreme Court's recent decisions establishing marriage equality in *United States v. Windsor*, 133 S. Ct. 2675 (2013) and *Obergefell v. Hodges*, 135 S. Ct. 2584 (2015). The questions attributed to the Supreme Court Justices at oral argument in the novel are fictional but plausible before the marriage-equality decisions. For example, in dissenting from the Supreme Court decision striking down a state law making sodomy a crime, Justice Scalia warned the ruling would jeopardize the constitutionality of "[s]tate laws against bigamy, same-sex marriage, adult incest, prostitution, masturbation, adultery, fornication, [and] bestiality." *Lawrence v. Texas*, 539 U.S. 558, 590 (2003) (Scalia, J., dissenting).

Since I conceived of this novel in 2007, the issue of the use of sexual orientation during jury selection has arisen more frequently because, before 2013, Supreme Court precedent did not as obviously support such a challenge and fewer potential jurors were openly gay. As late as 2018, in reviewing a conviction from a 2004 murder trial, for example, a Massachusetts federal district court found the defense lawyer failed to preserve that objection based on the following excerpt from the transcript where the issue arose in a murder trial.

Defense Counsel:	Your Honor, I'd like to put on the record that I'm beginning to see a pattern on the basis of the Commonwealth with the exclusion of a homosexual white male. So I want to put that on the record as well.
The Judge:	Okay. You've put it on the record.
Defense Counsel:	For the Court's consideration. Thank you.
The Prosecutor:	Just so I may be crystal clear, there's absolutely no pattern. I don't even know of any even homosexuals that have been before us. This particular gentleman was dressed, in my opinion, like a female and he has breasts and so forth. And, frankly, I was just looking at this from a common sense point of view. This guy has a lot of identification issues, and I don't—"
The Judge:	Well, first of all, you have a right to present a challenge. You can challenge a person for

> any reason, as long as it's not illegal. It's
> very simply put.

Smith v. MacEachern, 2018 WL 1316202, at *3 (D. Mass. 2018).

But in 2014, after *Windsor* but before *Obergefell*, the United States Court of Appeals for the Ninth Circuit relied on *Windsor* to rule it unconstitutional for a lawyer representing a manufacturer of HIV medication to strike a gay juror because of his sexual orientation in a civil case, reasoning that heightened scrutiny was required because the decision was based on the juror's sexual orientation. *SmithKline Beecham Corp. v. Abbott Laboratories*, 740 F.3d 471, 480 (9th Cir. 2014).

Other courts have also recognized the interrelationships between the constitutional issues of jury selection and same-sex marriage. In 2014, the United States Court of Appeals for the Seventh Circuit cited *SmithKline* favorably when striking down an Indiana statute banning same-sex marriage. *Baskin v. Bogan*, 766 F.3d 648, 671 (7th Cir. 2014). But in that same year, a federal trial court in Louisiana found a ban on same-sex marriage constitutional, rejecting the Ninth Circuit's reasoning in *SmithKline*. *Robicheaux v. Caldwell*, 2 F. Supp. 3d 910, 918 & n. 8 (E.D. La. 2014).

In 2018, the issues raised by this novel remain pressing. Many disagree with those Supreme Court decisions. The topic of marriage equality remains emotionally laden for many voters and Justice Kennedy's majority opinion in *Obergefell* focused more heavily on the institution of marriage than the equal-protection issues. To what would have been my utter astonishment in 2007, lower federal courts have also ruled that trans people are entitled to heighted protection under the Equal Protection Clause, though the United States Supreme Court has not yet addressed the issue.

Despite this legal progress toward equality, from 2013 to 2015, in the years in which the Supreme Court was considering the same-sex marriage issue, according to data voluntarily reported to the FBI's Hate crime statistics project, there were over 3900 victims of hate crimes based on sexual orientation, including those who were murdered.

I hope this novel shows readers that they can and should understand the basic legal principles and arguments underlying these issues, no matter their profession or their conclusions. And these issues are deeply intertwined with other principles of equality that should be considered—by now—to be settled law.

At the very least, nominated judges, by that point in their careers, should be able to persuasively explain why *Brown v. The Board of Education*, 373 U.S. 483 (1954), requiring school desegregation over sixty years ago, was rightly decided. Robert Bork was rightly 'borked' because he couldn't do that; decades later, nominees, particularly for the United States Court of Appeals and the Supreme Court, should be able to do so. Many do not, and I believe that those who rigidly interpret the Constitution according to its original, applied meaning, like Justice Scalia and Judge Bork, cannot do so persuasively. The public should judge political candidates' and judicial nominees' explanations on those constitutional issues, including equal protection issues—or their silence on them—in deciding which politicians to elect. Constitutional law is too important to leave to lawyers.

A Note on Louisiana and the Characters

My first acknowledgment is to the state and people of Louisiana. The novel is set there because—despite now having lived longer in other states—I still have a strong affinity for Louisiana. Every character in this novel, ranging from whomever you think a villain to whomever you think a hero, lives in Louisiana.

The characters in this novel are fictional and composite, with most containing nods toward those I love. All but a few collect what I've admired or inferred or speculated about those I've been fortunate to know throughout my life; the rest are drawn from my fears and nightmares. I've worked through my own self-loathing through a series of approximations: thinking of racism, sexism, anti-Semitism, biases against those with mental health issues, biases against those from rural areas, biases against those of humbler means, biases against those with certain political beliefs, heterosexism, homophobia, and then, finally, transphobia as I met people of all sorts who were considerate and kind. In the end, having encountered so many different types of caring people, including trans individuals, I was left no choice but to stop hating myself.

Select References and Recommended Reading

Writing a novel has been a welcome respite from my day job, where I can't and don't make up facts. In *Defense of an Other*, I have striven for realism—rather than depicting reality— everywhere other than the discussion of the state of the Supreme Court's law in the late 2000s on equal protection.

I hope the trial scenes realistic, but they are inspired by trials I've participated in and read about in many different states, mostly outside of Louisiana. Every trial raises dozens to hundreds of legal issues, and I've elided many to advance the plot and focus the themes. In that sense, this book is analogous to casebooks given to law students, which include copies of judicial opinions edited to focus on the discrete issues being taught in that course. But I wanted to describe the trial at some length. Cases evolve from the underlying facts to a trial of those facts to an appeal over years, and I wanted to capture the humanity and complexity underlying what can ultimately seem narrow, antiseptic legal issues.

Although they don't lie at the core of my practice, I've been reflecting on equal protection issues for over fifteen years and I'm certain I've failed to include many important materials that I've read.

Nor have I tried to include the results of every internet search I conducted while writing this novel or a complete set of factual references. Wheaton is fictional, and I've taken liberties with the history of Angola; indeed, the description of Angola has at least one deliberate anachronism. Again, writing a novel should have some perks.

But for select references and recommended reading on the issues most central to this novel see the following:

Adarand Constructors v. Pena, 515 U.S. 200 (1995)

Balkin, Jack M., *Living Originalism* (Belknap Press of Harvard University, Kindle ed. 2011)

Bergner, Daniel, *God of the Rodeo: The Quest for Redemption in Louisiana's Angola Prison* (Random House, Kindle ed. 2016)

Bowers v. Hardwick, 478 U.S. 186 (1986)

Brown v. Bd. of Education of Topeka, Kansas, 347 U.S. 483 (1954)

Howard, Sen. Jacob H., Remarks Introducing the Fourteenth Amendment to the Senate, Cong. Globe, 39th Cong., 1st Sess. 2766 (1866)

Howe, Sen. Timothy, Cong. Globe, 39th Cong., 1st Sess. S. app. 219 (1866)

Lawrence v. Texas, 539 U.S. 558 (2003)

Obergefell v. Hodges, 135 S. Ct. 2584 (2015)

Romer v. Evans, 517 U.S. 620 (1996)

Scalia, Antonin, *A Matter of Interpretation: Federal Courts and the Law* (Princeton University Press 1997)

United States v. Windsor, 133 S. Ct. 2675 (2013)

Acknowledgements

Thanks to those at Clink Street and Authoright, including Peter Salmon, who offered keen insights and notes on how to improve the rewritten novel. Gareth Howard and Hayley Radford ushered me through the editing and publishing process. We all built on the draft developed over years, with the editorial support of Erin McKnight and William Kowalski. Jimmy Fusaro, at X-Fit in New York City, edited the passages concerning boxing and fighting and inspired those scenes; he's a tremendous personal trainer. Thanks also go to those at Universal Acting in Miami, where I took classes in 2017 for insights into how to strengthen the novel.

Too many individuals to mention have taught me how to be a better lawyer and indirectly improved the discussion of every legal issue addressed. All views and any errors are mine.

About the Author

Grace Mead grew up in Shreveport, Louisiana, and then went to Dartmouth College. After college, she went to the University of Chicago Law School, where she was Editor-in-Chief of *The University of Chicago Law Review.*

She then clerked for the Honorable Jerry E. Smith of the United States Court of Appeals for the Fifth Circuit, which has jurisdiction over the federal trial courts in Louisiana, Mississippi and Texas. After clerking, she worked for five years as an associate at Wachtell, Lipton, Rosen & Katz in New York. Since then, she has worked at Stearns Weaver Miller Weissler Alhadeff & Sitterson, P.A. in Miami, where, since 2008, she has been a shareholder. Again, all views and any errors are hers.

CPSIA information can be obtained
at www.ICGtesting.com
Printed in the USA
FFHW021045081218
49790885-54294FF